AGENT OF INFLUENCE

ANDREW WATTS

DALE M. NELSON

SEVERN RIVER PUBLISHING

Severn River Publishing
www.SevernRiverBooks.com

ISBN: 978-1-64875-195-0 (Paperback)
ISBN: 978-1-64875-196-7 (Hardback)

ALSO BY THE AUTHORS

The Firewall Spies

Firewall

Agent of Influence

A Future Spy

Tournament of Shadows

BY ANDREW WATTS

The War Planners Series

The War Planners

The War Stage

Pawns of the Pacific

The Elephant Game

Overwhelming Force

Global Strike

Max Fend Series

Glidepath

The Oshkosh Connection

Air Race

BY DALE M. NELSON

The Gentleman Jack Burdette Series

A Legitimate Businessman

The School of Turin

Once a Thief

Proper Villains

The Bad Shepherd

To join the reader list and find out more, visit

severnriverbooks.com/series/the-firewall-spies

1

The single-prop Cessna Supervan 900 shuddered in the humid air above the Caribbean. With the engine humming and the noise reduction from their Bose A20 aviation headsets, the pilots could not hear the thunder outside the cockpit, but in the night sky they could sure see the lightning. Bright white branches of plasma reaching out for miles, illuminating anvil-shaped thunderclouds.

"*Hijueputa*, that one was close," said the pilot. Marco saw him wipe beads of sweat from his forehead.

"We're almost at the last checkpoint," Marco said. "Just a little longer."

"It was stupid to push it tonight. Weather like this...stupid..."

"No work, no pay, man. Besides, you know how the boss is." Marco looked at the GPS map on the center console. The distance to their next drop was under one mile. "Okay, man, slow down. I'm crawling back there. Let me know when it's time."

The pilot didn't say anything. He was leaning forward, peering up at the nearest line of storm cells through his night vision goggles. The NVGs were American military issue, the latest version.

Marco removed his aviation headset and NVGs, unstrapped from his seat, and headed to the back of the aircraft. He used a red-light flashlight to see, holding it in his mouth while he muscled the rear side-cabin door aft, sliding it all the way open.

The outside air whipped past at over one hundred knots. Another flash of lightning and he could make out the ocean waves several hundred feet below. A shiver went up Marco's spine. He didn't like being this close to the edge. Marco had heard stories about his current employers flinging a DEA informant out this very door.

The cartels were great at messaging.

Keeping one hand on a metal safety bar welded into the cabin, Marco used his free hand to reach down and hurl a plastic-wrapped bale of cocaine through the open doorway. He reached down again and jettisoned two more bales. The watertight containers had small parachutes streaming behind them, slowing their entry into the ocean. Once there, the bales of cocaine would float, dark-blue beacon buoys attached. A retrieval crew was already on its way, a fishing boat moored at the nearby US Virgin Islands. Each kilo of cocaine cost about 2,000 US dollars to make but could fetch nearly 30 times that upon reaching the tourist-rich islands. After subtracting the costs of the flight, boat retrieval, and local island distribution fees, his employer would still make over five million in profit for the delivery.

Marco almost lost his balance as the plane went through a rough patch of turbulence. He slid the door shut, locked it, and then hobbled back up to the cockpit.

The pilot was waving his hand, trying to get Marco's attention.

Marco put his headset back on as he sat down.

"What is it?" he asked.

"Engine oil pressure." The pilot tapped on the master caution panel, where a single light was illuminated. The corresponding engine oil pressure reading was indeed low.

The pilot cursed. "We should have taken the twin." His employers had a Twin Otter aircraft with two engines. On a long, over-water flight like this, it would have been much safer. Their Cessna only had one engine. Low oil pressure in the plane's only engine was not good.

Marco said, "I've got a can of engine oil in the back. If we can set down for a few minutes, I can pour it in and that would probably be enough to get us home, even if there's a leak."

The pilot tapped his GPS screen a few times until he found the nearest airport. "Closest airfields are north. The Virgin Islands."

"You crazy, man? They're probably already tracking us on radar. DEA or the Coast Guard would probably be waiting for us..." Marco tapped on the touchscreen map. "What about this island over here? Says it's got a private air strip. Small, but we could go there."

The pilot squinted down at the GPS chart. "I know that one. Some rich guy owns it, I think. He'll probably have security guards."

Marco tapped the map again, changing the layering to show the satellite image. "The buildings are all on the northwest side of the island. It would take people time to get to the runway, even if they knew we were there. It's been storming hard so they won't be outside. We can land on goggles, keep the lights off. We'll cut the engine as soon as we touch down. We only need ten, fifteen minutes at the most. I'll check the oil and top us off, then we'll take off before anyone has time to reach us."

The aircraft jolted as they flew through more turbulence. More lightning in the distance.

"Fine," said the pilot.

Marco tapped on the GPS display screen. "There. Your waypoint is in."

The aircraft banked slowly left as the pilot turned them toward the private island.

A few minutes later they were making their approach for landing. As they flew in and out of rainsqualls, Marco could see the island's outline through his night vision goggles. It was about ten kilometers across and twice that in length. The runway elevation said thirty feet above sea level. Lights from buildings on the northwest side of the island glowed green on his goggles.

"You see the runway?" Marco asked.

"Yes, I think so. I look lined up to you?"

"Yeah, you look good."

Marco began calling out their altitude and airspeed to help the pilot with his approach. The windshield wipers were on, and rain was suddenly coming down in sheets, making it very difficult to see. The pilot was swearing. Marco could see him gripping the yoke. Both men were sweating profusely.

"Two hundred feet."

The rain stopped and the runway was in front of them. A few hangar lights were on, giving the NVGs more than enough ambient light for them to see. The pilot whistled. "You see all of those trucks?"

Marco glanced outside. Rows of what looked like military vehicles lined the runway.

"One hundred feet. Fifty feet," Marco said.

He heard the engine wind down as the pilot pulled back power, bringing the nose back and beginning his gradual pitch up just prior to touchdown. Then a jolt as they landed, the nose sliding side to side as the pilot stepped on the brake pedals.

"Cutting the engine," the pilot said as they continued rolling down the wet runway.

It happened fast.

Through his night vision goggles, Marco saw the silhouette of a man sprinting across the runway, waving his arms.

"Watch out!" Marco yelled.

The pilot cursed and Marco felt the aircraft jerk to the right. They swerved into the grass, the aircraft bumping along for a few seconds before slamming to a halt.

The pilot killed the engine and the cockpit was now deathly silent. Neither man spoke. Their chests heaving, the only sound between them was the anxious pull of breaths and the first droplets from another round of rain that was soon crashing in heavy sheets on the windscreen again.

"What the hell just happened?" asked the pilot.

"Come on, we need to hurry." Marco removed the headset and night vision goggles, opened his door, and stepped down into wet grass. The rain soaked through his clothes before he even cleared the aircraft. Loud thunder rumbled in the distance, and Marco could see the approaching storm just offshore. It was about to get much worse.

The pilot inspected the nose wheel with a red flashlight. "I think we can pull it out," he said in a voice that did not inspire much confidence. "There's a towbar in the cargo…"

"Shh," Marco hissed, his finger over his mouth. "Put out the flashlight."

The pilot did as commanded, then followed Marco's gaze.

Bright floodlights were coming on one at a time, illuminating the far end of the runway. Then a buzzing noise. Small, high horsepower engines. Like motorcycles or…

A convoy of all-terrain vehicles appeared on the runway, seemingly out of nowhere.

"Did they just come out of a tunnel?" the pilot asked incredulously.

Marco didn't respond. Their side of the runway was still dark, except for a few yellowish hangar lights about fifty meters away. Marco looked around, taking in their surroundings through the darkness and downpour. "You saw that guy, right? The man who was running?"

"Marco, who cares? What are you doing? Come on, help me get this unstuck." The pilot had retrieved the towbar and attached it to the front wheel. He was rocking and pulling in slow, forceful motions.

Marco said, "Those ATVs look like they're staying put."

The pilot stopped what he was doing and took a look. "They're pretty far down there. Come on, man. Help me get this out of the mud and ready to take off before they spot us. We still need to fill up the engine oil..."

They both heard a whistle. Marco saw movement in the shadows of the nearest hangar. A man in a white button-down shirt and khaki pants stood there, fear in his eyes.

Marco was about to speak to him when another man's yell echoed in the distance. All three pairs of eyes darted toward the convoy on the lit end of the runway.

The ATVs began moving, heading toward the plane.

Marco heard a buzzing overhead and saw a pair of blue dots hovering near the trees. He squinted, holding his hand above his forehead to keep the rain out. What were those lights...a drone?

"I don't like this, man," said the pilot. "Let's get back in the plane."

Marco didn't reply. He was still looking at the man standing near the hangar. He looked frightened, shaking his head as he scanned the aircraft stuck in the muddy grass.

The pilot had hopped up into the aircraft cabin. "There's a gun in the back."

Marco could feel his heart racing as the ATV headlights grew closer. A feeling of dread filled his chest.

And then the man near the hangar began sprinting toward the ATVs.

The ATVs came to a stop, gathered in a half-circle beneath the drone's blue dots about one hundred meters away.

"Marco, get in here," the pilot called from the plane. Marco shrugged. It felt futile, but he entered the cockpit and shut the door.

Through the rainy windscreen, he could just barely make out a group of armed men illuminated by the ATV headlights. They had apprehended the man in the white shirt and were forcing him to walk toward the vehicles.

"That's a lot of guns," the pilot said.

"Shh," Marco whispered. "Do you hear that?"

More buzzing.

Marco gingerly opened his cockpit door and peered into the night sky. The two blue LED lights hovered directly overhead. Marco could just barely make out the silhouette of the quadcopter rotors surrounding the lights.

Commotion in the distance. Some of the armed men were running to their vehicles. The others were already driving toward their plane...

"Shit. Shit..." the pilot said.

Marco said a silent prayer as the ATVs surrounded them. The gunmen moved in unison. They were incredibly fast. Some of the men trained black rifles on Marco and the pilot as others opened the cockpit doors, gripped them by the collar, and flung them outside.

Soon they were both kneeling on the runway, hands over their heads. Marco squinted in the headlights' glare as they folded his arms behind his back and zip-tied his wrists.

He recognized military precision.

The armed men were like trained security dogs as they watched over their three prisoners. Their task accomplished, they waited quietly, their expressions calm and intense behind the sights of their weapons. One of them had a beard and was talking into an earpiece. Based on how the other men were fanned out around him, he looked to be the leader.

Next to Marco, the pilot attempted to talk. He got out precisely two words before a rifle butt crunched into his cheekbone. Then he was on the ground, writhing in pain.

The rain and wind were dying down. Marco could see the man who had been running now bound and gagged and sitting in the back of an ATV.

Marco heard an automobile accelerating toward them from the far end of the runway. A sleek luxury SUV approached and parked behind the circle of ATVs.

The driver's side door opened, and Marco watched as a blond man of about forty got out and began walking toward them. He wore running shoes, athletic shorts, and a fitted polo shirt over hardened muscle. The bearded man joined the blond man as he walked, whispering something into his ear.

Marco winced and straightened as one of the guards pressed a rifle muzzle against the small of his back. The blond man approached them and hunched over, placing his face a few feet from each of the prisoners.

"Do you know who I am?" His voice was deep and strong.

"No," Marco's pilot managed to whisper.

"Were you sent here to spy on me?" the blond man asked.

The pilot glanced up at him, confusion on his swollen face. "No."

The blond man walked a few paces and faced Marco. His eyes were an intense blue, and a slight scar garnished his forehead.

"Do *you* know who I am?"

"No," Marco replied.

"Were you sent here to spy on me?"

Marco shook his head quickly. "No."

The blond man stood up, folding his arms across his chest and nodding slowly. "One of you is lying. Let us find out who."

_____

2

Guy Hawkinson spun two fingers in a circular motion, and his security detail sprang into action. Kirby, his bearded head of security, barked orders. The guards nearest the prisoners jerked them up by the arms and shoved them into separate ATVs. Soon the convoy was racing over dirt paths, through the island's tropical forest.

They reached their destination, half a mile from the runway. The concrete building was almost empty of furniture and sat beside a gun range. Guy's security team originally built it for close combat training, but today it would be used as a place to conduct interrogations.

Each of the three prisoners was placed in a separate room with black cloths over their heads.

Guy's men questioned the Israeli scientist first.

Hawkinson's team had been watching the scientist for weeks now, ever since their cyber defense experts discovered that he had installed malware in one of the company systems. The malware was removed, but they didn't confront him; instead, they tried to monitor his communications. They must have missed something. Guy's men were all surprised by the airplane landing.

Guy and some of the others observed Kirby while he conducted the interrogation. For the first thirty minutes, the conversation was frustratingly unproductive.

"You want me to use the software?" Kirby asked when he came out for a break.

Guy nodded. Kirby and the tech went back in, this time with the computer and cameras. An hour later, they were out again.

Kirby was a physically imposing man who'd spent more than a decade in US Army special operations, where he and Guy had met. Kirby then spent another decade working private security for Hawk Security Group in some of the world's most hostile environments, doing the types of jobs that militaries didn't want to do themselves. Or rather...the types of jobs that the politicians didn't want their militaries being liable for.

Guy knew Kirby had seen a lot during those two decades. So the concerned look in his eyes was meaningful.

"You watch the whole thing?" Kirby asked.

Guy sighed. "Yes."

"There any way he's lying?"

Both men looked at their technician, who had been running the computer. "I could give you a percent chance, but it would be really small. He was telling the truth."

Kirby turned to his boss. "What now?"

"Let's keep going with our aviators. Find out if they know more."

Kirby nodded. Guy's security men brought one of the pilots into the interrogation room. This conversation went quick. The pilot was scared shitless and told them everything he knew, which wasn't much. They used the software to check that he wasn't lying. The pilot and his copilot worked for one of the cartels and were flying a route given to them about an hour before takeoff. Their job was to drop bales of narcotics at specific points over the ocean. Laughably, the pilot thought if he came clean about the drugs, he might get out of whatever shitstorm he was in.

Guy pondered his story. He had trouble with the flight route. When Kirby came out for a break, Guy said, "Ask the pilot who programmed the flight route into the aircraft's navigation system, him or the other guy? And ask him how long he's known the other guy. His copilot."

Guy's instincts were correct. The copilot had programmed the flight route, and had also signed off on the maintenance that morning. And he'd only been working with the smugglers for about six months.

Six months. Had the Israelis been onto them that long?

Time for the final interrogation. Guy decided he would lead the questions.

Strong hands pushed Marco into a seat, then removed his blindfold. The room was barren: concrete walls, a couple of portable LED lamps, a table in the middle. The bearded man stood in the corner. The blond man—the leader— sat directly across the table from Marco.

Marco's wrists were still bound behind his back, with his arms positioned behind the chair so that he couldn't move without falling over.

The blond man faced an open laptop and was tapping the keyboard, scrolling over the trackpad with his pointer finger. A third man was setting up a mobile phone on a tripod so that its multiple camera lenses faced Marco. When he was finished, he took over the computer and began tapping commands on the keyboard, occasionally stopping to adjust the tripod angle.

Marco watched the camera lenses. Computerized black eyes, staring at him as he tried to remain calm. The third man stood, picked up the tripod-mounted phone, and began walking around the room, holding it so the lenses faced Marco.

"Apologies for the wait," the blond man said. "This will only take a moment. I'm curious, do you know what we are doing?"

Marco shook his head.

"Right now, we're scanning your facial features. With our network of security companies and government agencies, we have access to the most extensive bank of facial recognition archives in the world."

Marco shifted in his seat.

"Suffice it to say, we will know who you are very soon."

The laptop chimed, and the two men at the table looked over the results. The bearded man in the corner of the room walked over so he could see as well. He and the blond man exchanged looks, and then all eyes were back on Marco.

The blond man spoke in a calm, determined tone. "Well, I'm afraid the mystery is over. As you must know, my name is Guy Hawkinson. And it appears that you, my friend, are working for Israeli intelligence."

Marco let out a snort. "Your program isn't working right. Do I look like I'm Israeli? I'm Colombian. We landed here because we had engine trouble."

Guy shook his head, looking confident. "I don't think so." His chair creaked as he leaned forward, his eyes focused on Marco. "Let me tell you what we now know. We know that your aircraft departed from an uncontrolled airfield in

Venezuela approximately ninety minutes ago. Your flight path took you within ten nautical miles of several Caribbean islands. From the conversation we had with your pilot, we know that you were smuggling cocaine. You dropped packages into the water, where they would later be picked up by fishing boats and brought to the distributors on each island. Is that accurate?"

Marco frowned. "Are you DEA?"

Guy shook his head. "No. And you know that."

Marco shrugged. "Whatever, man. What are you going to do with us? There are no drugs on that plane..."

The bearded man said, "What were you doing flying in this area? We're thirty miles from the nearest major island..."

Guy held up a hand. "Kirby," he said. His name uttered, the bearded man went silent. Guy looked back at Marco. "Let's not pretend that I care about the drugs."

Marco looked confused.

He turned the laptop around so Marco could see the screen. An image of Marco's own face filled the left side, with a graph of blue lines connecting different points on his chin, forehead, nose, and other locations. On the right-hand side of the screen was his name, along with a summary of information.

Some of the text was in Hebrew, along with thumbnail-sized images of him from a life long ago. The days before Mossad had sent him to work in Central and South America.

Guy's tone shifted. Now he sounded sympathetic. "I've worked with Mossad before, you know. I have the utmost respect for you guys. In another world, I think you and I would be fighting for the same cause."

Marco remained motionless.

Guy turned the laptop around and slid it over to his assistant, nodding. The bearded man and his assistant began moving. One opened a suitcase and began taking out equipment while the other attached a series of patches and wires to Marco, including a clip over his fingers, probably to measure his pulse. Marco thought of resisting them when they attached the equipment, but the way he was restrained, and the bearded man's muscles, made him think any fight he gave them would be short-lived.

"These instruments will measure your biological response to our stimuli," Guy said.

"Stimuli?" Marco said.

The assistant began typing in the laptop again. Guy turned back to Marco. "As much as I respect Mossad, in this instance, you are trespassing on my personal property. And more importantly, you are involved in an operation meant to harm me."

Marco began to object, but Guy quickly shook his head and spoke in a much more dangerous tone of voice. "*Don't.*"

Marco's face flushed, but he didn't speak.

"It's ready." The assistant nodded toward the computer.

Guy slid the laptop across the table and turned it so Marco could once again see.

Marco couldn't believe what was on the screen.

The computer display cycled through color images of various people. Men. Women. Children. Most of them smiling or candid shots.

Almost all of them were people he knew.

Cousins. Friends. Family members back in Tel Aviv. A girlfriend from Bogota.

Guy continued to speak in a soft, confident tone. "Do you recognize any of the faces here?"

Marco forced himself to focus on his breathing. He needed to maintain control. He had been trained to beat lie detector machines. He needed to stick to his cover, not be thrown off by how much they had on him. But as the faces kept fading in and out on the screen, keeping his composure became harder and harder. *This was impossible. They couldn't have learned this much information about him. And so quickly...*

Guy said, "Are you familiar with the term micro expression? They are facial expressions—usually involuntary— that occur within a fraction of a second. These cues are hard to pick up with the human eye. Scientists think those who can read micro expressions better have higher levels of emotional intelligence, which is interesting when you break it down. Is emotional intelligence—one's ability to read and understand the emotions of another person—simply just the human eye and brain working together to evaluate a pattern in facial muscle movement? And taking that thought further, if we know that micro expressions are excellent indicators of one's emotional reaction to stimuli, could we then combine these indicators with other metrics such as your change in pulse, blood pressure, pupil dilation..."

Marco was watching the computer screen, still rotating through hundreds of images of people he knew. Then he noticed something. He began to see certain images repeat more frequently...images of people he had been especially close with...

Guy said, "...essentially to create a machine learning program that could read the emotions of a person magnitudes better than any lie detector. What would you need to achieve this? Well, you would need lots of data. Check. We have that. We're scaling these sessions across the globe with our defense and security partners. We house the data and use it to train our deep learning algorithms. But we also need stimuli for each subject. Again, we can tap into our partner resources. Public and private archives. This is where we find pictures and social media accounts of the subjects that your face and biological metrics are reacting to the most right now..."

The images on the screen began flipping between just two people. One was an ex-girlfriend. The other was a girl of about six. Their daughter.

Guy craned his neck to see the images on the screen. The other two men saw it as well. They had found what mattered most to Marco.

Guy said, "Listen carefully. You came here at the direction of Mossad. That means you know who I am. You know the kind of people I work with around the world. These images you are looking at were taken from social media and mobile phone cloud accounts. From geo-tagging their mobile devices, we are at this moment identifying their exact locations."

Marco felt sweat building on his palms.

Kirby and the assistant were huddled over the computer. The assistant looked up at Guy. "We're good. Same house. San Salvador. We have a team in Panama City. They can be there in a few hours."

Marco couldn't help but look down, feeling more defeated than any point in his life.

Guy said, "Sorry, my friend. You can't beat the machine. And if these women are important to you, then I need you to answer a few questions."

Marco's gaze was still on the floor. "What do you want to know?"

"Let's start with this. What does Mossad think we are doing here on this island?"

Two hours later, Guy stood outside the building, looking up at the night sky. The stars were so much brighter here, away from the light pollution of civilization. The door opened, briefly casting a yellow glow outside. Kirby stood in the doorway. Behind him, Guy's men were power-washing blood stains from the concrete floor.

"The engineers finished with the plane. It'll take off in a moment."

Guy nodded. "Just make sure it's far from here when it goes down."

"They know."

Guy said, "You think the Mossad guy told us everything?"

Kirby said, "Everything he knew, anyway. Over 99 percent chance of that, if you believe the AI."

"We're lucky they don't know more."

"US agencies might follow the rules, boss, but Mossad won't stop. Especially now that two of their agents are missing."

Guy said, "I know. I'm working on a mitigation strategy."

———

Tel Aviv, Israel

"The aircraft systems are back online. They're taking off, sir," a young woman from Israeli Naval Intelligence said from her console. She sat in the first of three short rows of computer stations, the glow of the monitor backlighting her profile.

The operations manager could see the green air track representing Agent Gorian's plane begin to move. He didn't know how their agent did it, but he seemed to be in the process of evacuating their AI scientist from the island. With no comms for the past few hours, everyone in the operations center had been fearing the worst.

Mossad's technology department had placed an omnidirectional beacon inside one of the rear passenger seat cushions that relayed the aircraft's navigation and avionics data via a line-of-sight encrypted radio signal.

The signal was detected by a photonics mast protruding from the ocean's surface ten kilometers west of the island. The mast belonged to one of the Israeli navy's most closely guarded secrets: an autonomous underwater vehicle capable of high-quality ISR and electronic warfare.

Half a world away, in an unmarked building in Tel Aviv, members of the Israeli Naval Intelligence and Mossad leadership watched the information their drone submarine was picking up.

"The aircraft is descending, sir."

"What are you talking about?"

"They're descending."

"Are they landing?" Mossad's head of this operation frowned.

"Not according to the GPS. Puerto Rico is still more than twenty kilometers to their northwest."

"Five hundred feet above sea level, according to the barometric altimeter. The setting could be off."

"But why are they descending? That is still accurate, correct? Are we being spoofed?"

"Two hundred feet," the IDF woman monitoring the submarine's data stream announced.

"Unlikely, sir. Hold on. We're getting another data packet upload. This one is bigger. Could be the video."

The woman who had been calling out the altitude spoke in a worried tone. "Signal is lost with the beacon. Last reported altitude was fifty feet MSL."

Some people in the room cursed. Others remained quiet.

Their agent's aircraft had most likely just crashed into the Caribbean Sea.

"Sir...the packet finished uploading."

"On the screen, please."

The woman clicked her mouse a few times and the screen in the front of the room changed to display a black-and-white video image. A Mossad technician had installed a very small camera in the Cessna's cockpit ceiling. It provided a fixed video feed of the aircraft's nose, sending the data wirelessly to the beacon for transmission external to the aircraft.

The screen displayed an image of the plane's nose and propeller as it prepared to land on the island. Flashes of lightning whited out the image every few seconds. The aircraft touched down on the runway, then the silhouette of a man ran across the field of view and the aircraft veered into the grass. The angle changed but showed nothing else of interest. The woman rewound the video and froze it on the running man's image.

A moment later the face was enhanced and zoomed in, using the program to extrapolate features and add more detail. When finished, the screen showed the profile of an Israeli man, their computer scientist who had gone missing two months ago.

"It's him."

3
_____

London, England

Ava sat in the black cab as it sped through the wet streets of London. A steady mist fell from the dreary gray sky.

"Sorry, madam, but it looks like we're going to have a slight delay," the driver said over his shoulder.

Ava felt the car slow and looked ahead. On the street, protesters held up a variety of signs, including one that read TRINITY IS REAL.

Her driver honked his horn as he slowed the cab to a crawl and said, "The news said there would be protests today, but I didn't think it would be this big. All these blokes angry at the tech companies, I guess. I don't blame them, but I don't see how blocking the intersection will help their cause much. Looks like the Bobbies are clearing it out anyway. Shouldn't be too long."

Ava saw some London police officers clearing the streets ahead of them. Another sign caught her eye. THE CIA FRAMED JEFF KIM.

Ava shook her head. Two years had passed since she last

saw Jeff Kim. They had been sheltering in a concrete bunker in the California mountains while a forest fire eviscerated everything aboveground, including vital sections of Kim's Pax AI Mountain Research Facility.

The fire was started by Russian intelligence operatives as part of a covert mission to steal Kim's technology. At least, that was what Ava knew to be true. Depending on who you asked, the fire was part of a global conspiracy known as Trinity.

As Ava looked out the window at the protesters, she thought about how that forest fire was a perfect metaphor for the world today. People were furious at the big technology companies, their anger stemming from primal fear. Just like that fire, technology was changing the landscape at an unfathomable pace. An overwhelming force, moving faster than any human, transforming every bit of organic fuel in its path into hot gray ash.

A policeman was blowing a whistle as a few of the protesters began pushing back. More police ran over, but as Ava's car moved forward she lost sight of them. The scene made her nervous. If things kept going like this, violence would spill into the open. As of now, the conflict was still confined to the shadows. And that was where she roamed. An intelligence officer fighting in the new cold war. A fight for future supremacy.

The cab made its way beyond the crowd and picked up speed. They drove a few more blocks before pulling over at the curb. Ava thanked the driver as she got out. He waved and drove away. A decade ago, she would have handed him cash in the local currency. Now the transaction was seamless, conducted by apps on their phones using cloud-based servers and GPS. With that transaction, information moved. Trackable information. This necessitated Ava's employer, Mossad, to insert countersurveillance software onto all of her devices.

If a foreign intelligence service was able to access the ride-share company's computers, they would have a very hard time matching up the false identities the Mossad software created on her behalf. But in its own way, the use of these cybersecurity programs was evidence of her being a spy. So she only used them when she really had to hide her activities.

Like today's meeting.

Ava headed toward a tall, modern-looking building with glass sides. Using her peripheral vision to scan for surveillance, she walked through the revolving door and took the elevator to the top floor. There she arrived at the front desk of one of London's most exclusive private membership clubs.

The man behind the desk recognized Ava on sight. He greeted her with a nod and guided her down a dark hallway and into one of the club's most exclusive private rooms. Expensive leather chairs were scattered throughout the room, and high-end artwork adorned the walls.

Ava's Aunt Samantha sat at a table near the window. A man in a suit was walking around the room, waving a black wand along chairs and bookshelves. Countersurveillance. Ava embraced her aunt, kissing her on each cheek.

Samantha gestured to the man scanning the room. "Sorry about this. He's almost finished. Have a seat. I had them bring us a selection of teas and treats."

Ava looked at the spread on the table and smiled. The women sat down and didn't speak until the man finished his work. Then he nodded to Samantha and departed the room, closing the door on his way out.

"Still taking precautions?" Ava asked.

"Old habits die hard."

Ava poured herself a cup of tea and let it brew, then took a sandwich from a plate. "They're sending me to D.C."

"Really?" Her aunt tilted her head. "You're concerned. I can see it in your eyes."

Ava sighed. "After everything that happened..."

"You are worried about your cover."

Ava stirred sugar into her teacup and poured in some cream. "I didn't think they would ask me to do this again, considering the way things ended with Pax AI."

Samantha sipped her tea. "Who will you be reporting to in Washington?"

"The new head of the D.C. station. A man by the name of Katz."

A flicker of distaste appeared on Samantha's face.

"You know him?"

"Only by reputation."

"And?"

Samantha said, "Katz is a careerist. A man like him sees the D.C. post as a way to build his political network. A way to improve his standing. What's the saying? If he's patting you on the back, it's because he's looking for a spot to stick the knife."

Ava removed her tea bag and set it down on the saucer edge. "Good to know."

Samantha shook her head. "You know how things are done. When we place people in certain assignments, it is for a reason. I would assume that Katz already has friends in high places."

Ava noticed that Samantha used *we*. She obviously missed her old job. Samantha, Ava's own handler for more than a decade, was forced to retire from Israel's Institute for Intelligence and Special Operations after the debacle with Pax AI two years ago. Samantha had been running Israel's largest operation on US soil in the history of Mossad, spying on Pax AI, America's most advanced AI company. A company with

US defense and intelligence contracts. Then everything fell apart.

Samantha had been cast as Mossad's fall guy. The ostensible "rogue officer." Not since the days of Jonathan Pollard had such a breach of trust between Israel and the US been made public.

Neither side's intelligence service truly believed the claim that the operation was led by a single person. But if both nations *pretended* to believe, each government could save face and maintain good relations, which was strategically important. Ava's punishment was unexpectedly light. She was assigned to Mossad headquarters, where she taught classes to trainees, and recently began working on active operations again. The US government had generously left her name off the persona non grata list. Only Samantha received that treatment.

Ava's aunt was understandably angry about the way things ended. But what really upset her, Ava knew, was being shut out of the game. Ava's guilt over how everything had unfolded morphed into a desire to make her aunt feel needed. And if she was honest with herself, it was half the reason that Ava occasionally still sought her aunt's counsel, the other reason being that after decades working for Mossad, Samantha was an excellent mentor.

"So why are they suddenly sending you to D.C.?" Samantha asked.

Ava paused. This was the awkward part. Knowing what to say and what to hold back. In all likelihood, she would get a slap on the wrist from Mossad's counterintelligence division if they found out what was going on here. Samantha had served her country for over three decades. She knew more secrets than the current prime minister. She still held a clearance and did contract work for Israeli intelligence. If Ava had put in the proper request to consult with her as a subject matter expert, it would probably get approved. But she didn't want Mossad to know that they were speaking regularly. As much as Ava didn't like to admit it, she didn't want her own career impacted any more than it already had been.

Samantha studied her niece's face. "I can see your hesitation. How about this? Let me see if I can guess why they are sending you to Washington, D.C.? An Israeli scientist, one of our top experts in the field of artificial intelligence, went missing a few months ago. And you are being asked to look into it."

"Why do you think that?" Ava's slight smile confirmed her aunt's guess was correct.

"I read the papers." Samantha smirked.

"I doubt that's all you read..."

"And I know your specialty." Her aunt shot her a dark look. "You know our AI scientist wasn't the only one to have gone missing in recent months."

"We know."

"My sources tell me that a certain American family may be involved. A family whose political clout is substantial."

Ava didn't respond. But her aunt still smiled, knowing she'd hit home. Ava wondered how her aunt still had such high-level information.

Ava steered the conversation to other topics. They spoke about the anti-technology protests in London and New York. The AI regulatory hearings scheduled for the US Senate. Ava was considered an expert on AI capabilities and policy, but keeping up was hard, even for her. The field was changing daily.

After a while, Ava checked her watch. "I need to head to Heathrow." She placed her napkin on the table and stood. Samantha did as well, and they embraced.

"Ava, one thing to be very aware of. If you are going back to America, it's not your cover that I would worry about. The CIA will be watching you from the moment you enter the country. You may not have been placed on their diplomatic expulsion list...but they know what type of work you do."

"I know this," Ava said, trying not to sound nervous.

Her aunt gave her a look. "Your new bosses know this, too. I would think very carefully about why they are still sending you there."

Ava smiled. "I have my theories."

"And?"

Ava put on her coat. "I can think of two reasons. One, I am to be a distraction."

"And the other?"

"I'm to be bait."

4

Langley, Virginia

Colt walked down the sixth-floor hallway of the CIA headquarters, sheepishly looking at the signs and numbered conference rooms to help him navigate the maze.

"You meeting with the DDO?" asked a slightly balding man of about fifty.

"Yeah, actually. You know where it is?"

"Sure." He held a Yeti coffee mug with a clear plastic cap in his left hand. The right hand shot out for a handshake. "Name's Fred. Fred Ford."

"Colt McShane." Strong grip. Thick, meaty hand. Ford had a wide frame that made him look like an ex-football player.

"I know your name. I'm headed to the same meeting; you can follow me. Right this way."

Colt began walking with Ford, who took several quick turns.

"I thought the title was Director of NCS now?"

Ford waved away the comment. "Ah, everyone here still

says DDO. Let the bureaucrats keep changing titles. It's the same job."

As they passed rows of cubicles, Ford greeted some of the workers, who smiled when they saw him.

Ford slowed to a stop at a blonde woman's cubicle. "Hey, Leslie, I saw your husband in that park again in Vienna. Kinda weird, though. He was taping some manila envelopes to the bottom of a park bench. It's probably nothing, I wouldn't worry about it."

The woman let out a laugh. "*Hey*, Fred."

"Hubby looked really relaxed, though, so tell him all those free Asian massages he's been getting are really paying off. Tit for tat, am I right?"

She shook her head. "You're terrible."

"Anyway, have a good one." Ford played it straight, tapping the top of her desk wall before walking way. Chuckles rang out from some of the surrounding cubicles.

Colt smiled. "You're the entertainment around here?"

"It's a tough job but somebody's got to do it," Ford said. They walked a bit longer before stopping in front of a closed door. Ford took a breath. "Well, here we are." He opened the door and held it for Colt. "After you."

Colt walked into a half-full conference room. He counted six people, two in military uniforms. Wilcox, Colt's former handler, was standing at the head of the long table. He had recently been promoted to the CIA's newest Director of National Clandestine Service. It was an unusual pick considering that he had been the Vancouver station chief. Lower on the totem pole than normal, but the CIA's rank and file were thrilled.

"Colt, good to see you. Thanks for flying in," Wilcox said. All eyes shifted to Colt.

"Thank you for the invite. Congratulations again, sir."

Wilcox nodded humbly and waved thanks. "All right, folks, let's take a seat and get started. Mr. Thorpe, if you would." He gestured to a tall, wiry man standing to the right of the room's main display screen. The man typed on a laptop connected to the screen. Both devices were adorned with purple TOP SECRET stickers.

"Director Wilcox, ladies and gentlemen, good morning. My name is Special Agent Will Thorpe, and for those of you who don't already know"—his eyes met Colt's— "I've been assigned by the FBI and DNI to be the new supervisor at the NTCU."

"So many acronyms," said Ford, shaking his head. Thorpe frowned.

The National Technology Counterintelligence Unit was a relatively new joint program that combined several federal agencies and the department of defense. Its mission was to monitor and respond to the rapidly accelerating national security threats posed by new technologies. The NTCU's focus was on artificial intelligence and quantum computing programs.

A series of images appeared on the screen. Thorpe said, "The island you see here is located about forty miles from the US Virgin Islands and privately owned by Hawk Security Group. HSG is owned and operated by CEO Guy Hawkinson, brother to venture capitalist Sheryl Hawkinson, and nephew to the distinguished Senator Hawkinson of Wyoming—"

"Who is on the Senate Select Committee on Intelligence," Ford interrupted.

Thorpe shot him a look before continuing. "Correct. The DOD, State Department, and CIA have each used Hawkinson Security Group extensively over the past fifteen years. This private island is something else. It has its own combat range, a runway large enough for a Gulfstream to land on, and my understanding is that prior to the family purchasing the island, it was used as a five-star resort."

A woman in a business suit at the far end of the table nodded. She was Gretchen Harlowe, Thorpe's number two. "That's right. The Hawkinsons have used the location to wine and dine prospective clients while demonstrating company capabilities. The family also uses it for personal retreats."

The image on the screen changed from pools and beach huts to a modern-looking office building built near the shoreline. Angular stone construction jutted out from the ground, forming multiple floors of panoramic tinted-glass windows.

Thorpe said, "But recently, we believe Hawk Security Group has been using the island for another purpose. And whatever they're doing there, it was deemed of the highest priority by Israeli intelligence."

Thorpe turned to a woman in a Navy uniform. A lieutenant commander, Colt saw. She also wore a gold pin on her chest signifying she was an Information Warfare Officer. The image on the screen changed to a submarine, and she said, "This is the most recent picture we have of Israel's new Unmanned Underwater Vehicle."

"A drone submarine?" Ford whistled.

"That's right," the naval officer replied. "Our underwater sonar arrays in the Caribbean picked up its acoustic signature over the past week. We've been passively tracking it ever since. The NSA then matched ELINT in the vicinity of this island to the same type of model of underwater vehicle."

Colt said, "The Israelis are spying on Guy Hawkinson's private island?"

"That's what we think." Thorpe turned to a man across the table. "The CIA's Israeli Division representative has joined us. Could you weigh in, please?"

The man said, "We know that an encrypted burst transmission was picked up by an Israeli satellite at approximately 2300 hours local time the day before yesterday. Within two hours of that transmission, the Israeli prime minister received a call from the head of Mossad. Within three hours of *that* phone call, an Israeli intelligence officer had orders to Washington, D.C. She made a stop in London and is currently on a plane to the US."

Thorpe said, "Would you mind telling us the name of the Mossad officer?"

The CIA Israeli desk representative said, "Her name is Ava Klein. We almost PNG'd her after the Pax AI incident. We were pretty sure that she was an Israeli intelligence officer operating without diplomatic cover."

Colt felt his face heat up as Wilcox glanced in his direction. Wilcox said, "You said *almost* PNG'd her. What happened?"

The Israeli expert said, "My understanding is that it was a State Department agreement. Both the US and Israel wanted as little fallout as possible, so her involvement got classified and... well, swept under the rug."

Wilcox said, "Mr. Thorpe, what does all of this mean?"

"We have several hypotheses. We think Miss Klein may be advising Mossad on an operation involving AI. It looks like they may have their own version of STONEBRIDGE, sir."

Colt shot a confused look at Wilcox. *What was STONEBRIDGE?*

Wilcox said, "It seems the Israelis have one hell of an operation going. Sending some of their most secret naval technology halfway around the world to get intelligence is quite a big deal for them, correct?"

Both the Naval intelligence officer and the Israeli expert were nodding. "That's right, sir."

The Navy officer said, "Absolutely. They never send

anything across the Atlantic. It must have been a massive undertaking."

The CIA Israeli expert said, "Which would imply this is of the highest priority to Mossad."

Wilcox turned to Colt. "What do you think?"

Colt said, "The last time Mossad was involved in an AI-related operation in this part of the world, their primary concern was that dangerous technology might fall into the wrong hands. Israel is known for taking preemptive action. Israeli intelligence seeks out and eliminates what it considers existential threats. If they are taking this much interest in the Hawkinsons' island, I would suggest we look closely at why that is."

Wilcox nodded. "I agree."

Thorpe said, "Another notable event occurred on the same evening. An unidentified aircraft was detected by radar, flying in the vicinity of the island in question. It did not have an active transponder, which is unusual. No flight plan was filed. Also unusual. Radar records show that the aircraft flew near the US Virgin Islands and then detoured to the Hawkinsons' island. Radar contact was then lost at about midnight local time. An emergency locator transmitter began emitting at about zero-four hundred local early the next morning. US Coast Guard commenced a search for survivors shortly thereafter. None were found. No sign of plane wreckage other than the floating beacon. There were heavy storms in the area so the aircraft may have gone down in a microburst. But the weird thing is that the ELT beacon didn't go off until several hours after radar contact was lost."

Wilcox shook his head. "What are you getting at?"

The Naval intelligence officer said, "A small aircraft flying around the Caribbean at night with no transponder and no flight plan is typical of drug-smuggling activity. They drop bales of cocaine into the sea, which are later picked up by local distributors."

Colt said, "But if the aircraft went down in a storm, one would expect the emergency beacon to begin chirping immediately."

Thorpe pointed at Ford. "Exactly."

Ford said, "You think the aircraft landed on Guy Hawkinson's island."

Thorpe held his palms open. "We need to consider that as a possibility."

Wilcox said, "And then the aircraft crashed *after* it landed on the island?"

"Or they dumped the beacon in the water to make it look that way," Thorpe said.

"Why would they do that?" Wilcox asked.

Thorpe shrugged. "A fake crash. Maybe the aircraft was part of a Mossad operation. Maybe it was successful, and the downed aircraft was a ruse. Or maybe it was not a successful op, and Hawk Enterprises didn't want any evidence."

The room was quiet for a moment.

Wilcox looked at Thorpe. "Has the intel we're getting from STONEBRIDGE gotten any better?"

Thorpe glanced around the room. "It's improving. But we'll need to discuss that in a smaller group. For opsec."

Wilcox turned to the others in the room. "McShane, Ford, and Thorpe, please stay. Everyone else, thank you for your time."

Half the group stood and departed.

When the door closed, Thorpe narrowed his eyes. "Director Wilcox, respectfully, these two can't be here if we're going to discuss..."

Wilcox raised his chin. "They're being read into *STONEBRIDGE*."

Thorpe let out a huff of disapproval. "I see. I would like to speak with the DNI about this..."

"I already did."

Thorpe's face turned a shade redder.

Wilcox said, "Mr. Thorpe, if you wouldn't mind, please give them the background."

Thorpe composed himself and began. "Gentlemen, the National Technology Counterintelligence Unit is running an operation code-named STONEBRIDGE. In all my years at the Bureau, this is the most sensitive, high-stakes counterintelligence operation I have been a part of. Our target is the very well-connected private business, Hawk Security Group, and their newly founded computer research firm, Hawk Technologies. The businesses are owned and operated by members of the Hawkinson family."

Colt said, "Please excuse the question, but I thought the Hawkinsons were cleared of wrongdoing after the Pax AI investigations."

"Not having enough information to prosecute is different than declaring them innocent," Thorpe said.

Colt narrowed his eyes. "Sure, but why didn't the FBI keep going? This STONEBRIDGE is a Tech Counterintelligence unit operation, right? Why did the NTCU get this?"

Thorpe shot an annoyed look at Wilcox, who nodded back patiently. Thorpe said, "A few things to think about. Let's say that the DOJ was reasonably sure the Hawkinsons had been involved in wrongdoing but weren't sure they could prove anything in the court of law. They could bring it to trial and try to prove it. But that would have two very undesirable results."

"The senator uncle?" Ford said.

"Yes, for one, the senator uncle," replied Thorpe. "Going after his dead brother's niece and nephew—from what we can tell, two people he is very close with—would create a political firestorm from Senator Hawkinson's allies. Things don't work the way they used to. People aren't held accountable by members of their own team anymore. Not unless it's child molestation or something..."

"Treason seems pretty bad," replied Colt.

"Yes, that would qualify. But the point is, the DOJ would have to *prove* it. They can't miss. And if it's not proven, then it's not treason in the public eye. It becomes a partisan attack. DOJ doesn't want to be seen as partisan. And the DOJ's political bosses don't want them to miss." Thorpe took a breath, clearly annoyed that he had to explain himself to Colt and Ford. "Furthermore, if we think the Hawkinsons were working with the SVR and we go public with what we know, it would expose a Russian intelligence apparatus operating inside the US, which is not something the CIA wants us to do."

Wilcox smiled. "Thank you, Mr. Thorpe. That is correct. The CIA would much rather identify agents and use that knowledge to their advantage. Flipping the agents to get higher in the food chain, or providing the agents with misinformation. Influencing their decisions."

"Hence, STONEBRIDGE," said Colt.

Wilcox nodded. "Correct. If the NTCU can get STONE-BRIDGE inside the Hawkinsons' inner circle, then we have an agent who can not only report on the Hawkinsons' actions, but also could potentially expose Russian intelligence operations to infiltrate our technology sector."

Colt said, "That assumes the Hawkinsons are still involved with the Russians. I can't see that being the case. Even if they were working with them two years ago, they must have cut ties after Pax AI."

Wilcox motioned to Thorpe, who said, "For the past year, we have been monitoring Hawk Technologies' expansion into the AI sector. Various intel reports have them covertly recruiting world-class machine learning scientists to help with this expansion. Because of their past ties to questionable foreign entities—especially those involved in the Pax AI espionage incident—we began checking the details of this technology-focused expansion. From information gathered during this investigation, we now believe that two members of the Hawkinson family, Guy and Sheryl Hawkinson, were both involved in a conspiracy to commit industrial espionage against the US company, Pax AI. We know that the SVR penetrated our own ranks when they recruited Special Agent Rinaldi, and that Rinaldi was involved with the SVR's multiple violent attempts to steal from Pax AI. If the Hawkinsons did indeed steal Pax AI technology, that means they likely aided the SVR in the Pax AI incident. I can think of few crimes more reprehensible than colluding with an adversarial foreign government. Rinaldi was a colleague. Now he is a national embarrassment. A source of shame for the Bureau and for the NTCU, which he was a part of."

Colt saw Wilcox shift in his seat.

Thorpe said, "Rinaldi was killed before he could be apprehended, so we can only guess at his motives, but what is clear is that he was on Russia's payroll." Thorpe paused a moment to study the room.

Colt tensed at Rinaldi's mention. He'd known the man too, and Rinaldi was supposedly there during the murder of one of Colt's CIA friends. Colt had spoken to him in the last minutes of his life, before a raging forest fire burned him to ashes.

Thorpe continued, "As I stated, STONEBRIDGE is an exceptionally sensitive operation. The Hawkinsons run an elite private security firm that the Defense Department, the State Department, the Intelligence Community—as well as many foreign entities—have relied on for world-class training, diplomatic security, intelligence and surveillance support, and direct action. They know their craft well, and they are a formidable opponent. Senator Preston Hawkinson of Wyoming sits on the Senate Select Committee on Intelligence. We do not know if the senator was complicit in, or had knowledge of, any crime. But our reports on Guy and Sheryl Hawkinson suggest that the family is very close, and that family loyalty comes above everything else. We must assume that Senator Hawkinson might be aware of his niece and nephew's possible illicit activities. So not only do the Hawkinsons have a deep understanding of the space they are playing in—national security, countersurveillance, and counterintelligence—but they also have potential cover from very high above. We need to be very careful with whom these intelligence reports get shared. This is as hard a target as they come."

Wilcox said, "Thank you for the background, Will. Please provide Mr. McShane and Mr. Ford with the required reading materials so they can catch up with the details of the operation."

Thorpe said, "Respectfully, may I ask why you think this is necessary?"

Wilcox considered the question for a moment. "Mr. McShane, you served with the CIA under a nonofficial cover for over ten years. Much of your work involved technology and defense companies in foreign nations. Hypothetically speaking, if you were going to handle an agent inside Hawk Technologies, how would you do it?"

Colt looked around the table for a moment, then straightened in his seat. "Hawk Security Group has classified government contracts all over the world. Some of them are black bag jobs with us, and other three-letter agencies. That means we've ensured they are held to the highest standard of counterespionage measures. Anyone who worked there would have to be squeaky clean—"

"But that wouldn't be enough," Wilcox said.

"No, sir, I don't think so. If the goal is to monitor and report on Hawk's technology development programs, I would want to recruit an agent who is an expert in a niche field of AI. Someone with a unique talent Hawk needs to hire."

"Why?" Wilcox asked. "Why not just a finance or marketing guy?"

Colt gave a sheepish smile. "Speaking from experience, these cutting-edge technology companies keep their dev programs close to the vest. Only the people working on the tech get read in."

Wilcox nodded. "Mr. Thorpe, what is your agent's corporate function? Do they have a background in artificial intelligence? Or quantum computing?"

Thorpe cocked his head. "Sir, our agent is quite capable of gaining access to hard—"

"That's a no," Ford said to Colt.

"Go to hell, Ford. I've already seen you wreck one operation and I'm not about to—"

"That's enough. Both of you," Wilcox said in an ice-cutter tone. "This operation is too important for your personal history to come in the way of performance. Sort it out. Find a way to work together or I'll have both of you reassigned."

Both Ford and Thorpe nodded begrudgingly.

Wilcox said, "Now my best analysis of the situation is that Mossad is about to accelerate what must already be a priority operation for them. This is a race, gentlemen. Make no mistake, Mossad is going after Hawk Technologies. And if they get there first, there may not be anything left for us to investigate. No espionage case for the FBI to prosecute. No Russian spy ring for the CIA to take advantage of. Not to mention that we'll look pretty bad if Israel acquires the most powerful AI technology on the planet because we couldn't do our jobs. So we need to improve our intel collection efforts, and fast." Wilcox again turned to Colt. "Two agents, Colt. What are your thoughts?"

Colt raised his eyebrows and blew a breath out of thinly parted lips. "If they already have an agent in place, but that agent doesn't have expertise in AI, I do think you'll need to add another. If you have two agents, you will obviously need to compartmentalize information flows. A second handler. Neither agent should know about the other's existence. Neither handler contacts the other's agent. This reduces the threat of capture and interrogation. Any legend trails would need to lead to different sources. Both agents would have to blend into the company and handle intense security sweeps. There's a risk that they'll bump into each other, but..."

Wilcox said, "But..."

"The pros are that you'll get multiple independent intelligence streams. The AI expert will give you access to the developmental programs that you really need. Two agents will get us a full picture that we can use to put together not only what Hawk Technologies is doing now but what they intend to do in the future. The other benefit is redundancy. If our security procedures and compartmentalization efforts are good, if one gets caught, we don't lose the other. Eggs in separate baskets."

Thorpe's expression was one of intense frustration. But he held his tongue.

Wilcox said, "All right, I want McShane and Ford to identify and train a second agent. Thorpe, they'll check in with you once per week. Your team will provide support. You will keep each other updated. McShane and Ford will ensure their agent's intelligence stream is protected and clean. Despite what you may think of Mr. Ford, he's very good at his job. And

McShane has a lot of experience as a NOC in the tech industry. This op is much too delicate to risk anything but the utmost level of perfection. Understood?"

Thorpe reluctantly nodded. "Understood. Just as long as Ford knows the chain of command."

Wilcox looked at Ford. "He does. Right?"

Ford nodded.

"We need to move fast," Wilcox said. "I'm going to give you two 90 days to identify and train your NOC. The clock is ticking."

Wilcox stood. He and Thorpe departed the room.

Ford turned to Colt. "So I guess we need to find ourselves a spy."

5

Weems, Virginia

The Hawkinson clan was gathered at Senator Preston Hawkinson's mansion overlooking the Chesapeake Bay. The family met there every year for the 4th of July. Private fireworks display. Gourmet pig roast. Rare wine and bourbon selections. Every detail was attended to. No expense was spared.

Over 100 people were in attendance this year, but only three of them were true power players. The senator himself, of course. Guy, his nephew. And Guy's sister, Sheryl. The three were gathered in the senator's ornate library while the festivities went on outside. The doors were closed, and Guy and Sheryl were waiting for the senator to finish a phone call.

From Sheryl's vantage point at the window, she could just make out their youngest brother, Charles, handing sparklers to her two teenage daughters.

Charles, now thirty years old, seemed to have inherited their mother's demons. Addiction. Instability. Screaming highs and dark lows. But still fiercely loyal to the family.

Their mother had been that way as well. That intense love had probably driven her insane when she found out about the infidelity. The three of them had been away at boarding school when it happened. A knife through their father's heart while he slept. Then a bath full of warm water and blood from her two slit wrists. Longways, so it worked. The dark reason the fortune was now controlled by the three people in this room. No one knew why Charles was left off the will. Maybe their father saw the demons in his eyes and knew it was for the best. Whatever the reason, she, her brother, and uncle had been anointed rulers of the clan. A small part of her felt guilty that she loved it so much. But she never let guilt sit in her head long.

Sheryl looked over at Guy, who was scanning through company reports on his tablet. Kirby, his second-in-command, stood dutifully over his shoulder.

"We're going to lose the French contract." Guy let out a sigh and shook his head. "Fucking Charles."

Guy was attempting to bring their half-brother into Hawk Technologies. Business had been dicey after the controversy surrounding Pax AI, but Guy was still making room, and had allowed Charles to lead a small project in France. From Sheryl's understanding, Charles spent a few days per week squinting into spreadsheets and nights snorting lines of coke off the bare skin of French women. She looked out the window again. Her daughters were with their father now. Charles was back at the outdoor bar.

When she turned back to the room, Guy was looking at her. He whispered, "You sure this is what you want to do?"

She nodded. "It is time."

The senator's chief of staff stood next to the senator behind a serpentine mahogany desk, pointing at his notepad. Sheryl had funneled a variety of wealthy donors toward her uncle, and they decided to schedule the calls while she was in the room. Most were VC investors or heads of businesses in the tech industry. She chose the callers by looking for those with deep pockets, malleable moral principles, and the desire to have a diversified portfolio. That last trait was most important. The four men and one woman on the other end of the line this afternoon loved to reduce risk through diversification. This meant expanding financial investments and product line-ups. It also meant donating to a variety of future presidential contenders.

At this stage in the upcoming presidential cycle, the senator's chances looked bleak. But the mere potential that he might be president someday was a great motivator for the donor-class. There was one thing Sheryl's investors liked more than reducing risk: big J-shaped growth curves. Getting in on the senator's political stock now was buying at the ground floor.

The current voice on the phone belonged to Roger Cox, an investor who owned five percent of the second largest social media platform in North America. He said, "I very much appreciate the opportunity to speak with you today, Senator."

"Likewise, Mr. Cox. Likewise," replied Senator Hawkinson.

"Sheryl said that you can be quite a reasonable man. So let me be frank. I'm concerned about a few pieces of legislation on the horizon. You and I both know that these bills are being pushed by activists who don't have a clue about...well, anything, really." Cox let out a snort. "They don't understand the economics of the technology industry and how it affects their own well-being."

"Uh-huh," replied Senator Hawkinson in a noncommittal tone. Next to him, his chief of staff quietly scribbled a few more bullet points onto his yellow notepad, then pointed with his pen for emphasis. The senator nodded, then leaned toward the speakerphone. "You are referring to the Free and Fair Technology Bill. Now, that bill is mostly aimed at companies over $100B in annual revenue."

"Which is very unfair..." said Cox.

The senator's face transformed into a crooked smile as he looked at his chief of staff. "Well, you can understand where the voters' motivation is coming from. Big brother watching them all the time, users feeling like they are being squeezed to pay for more and more, people becoming addicted to their technology devices..."

Sheryl cringed at the term "technology devices." Language was important. The terms one used communicated understanding. If her investors thought that the subject matter was not being taken seriously, they were likely to take their money elsewhere.

And given the circumstances, the Hawkinson family needed money.

The senator continued, "People are upset, fearful of having their jobs replaced by software and robots. Technology is eradicating their way of life..."

"Are you becoming an *anti-technologist*, Senator?"

Her uncle looked up at her, frowning. Sheryl shook her head. *Don't bite.*

The phone went silent, the senator not dignifying the question with an answer. Anti-technologists were the latest iteration of cult-like conspiracy theorists. But unlike the Trinity movement, the anti-technologists were moving into politics. Dark money funding luddite candidates in pockets across the country. It wasn't the normal rural-urban divide that traditional politics followed in recent decades. But it was seen as a fringe movement, and the senator found the question insulting.

When Cox spoke again, his tone was conciliatory but

urgent. "Mr. Senator, these activists want to break up all of big tech without understanding the consequences of such a move. Do you know how many people we employ? Not just people on our payroll but all our contractors, business partners...to say nothing of the small businesses we help to sell products. Millions of people, Senator. Millions of voters. Tech companies like ours are the new engine driving the American economy. Whatever gets into this bill...if it hurts our bottom line, it hurts the American people."

The chief of staff was holding his notepad up again, pointing to another bullet point.

The senator said, "What about this *tracking* nonsense? Do you really need to track everyone with your codes?"

Sheryl made a face at her uncle's terminology. He was an intelligent man. She was beginning to suspect that he was intentionally speaking this way, disarming his opponent by acting uninformed.

Cox said, "Senator, between us, we can change how we monitor our interests if that will help alleviate some of these so-called privacy concerns. But to be quite honest, most of our money comes from advertising revenue. If we don't have the ability to track people, we don't have a business."

Senator Hawkinson said, "Mr. Cox, I completely understand your position." He paused. "Here is the way I feel. It is not in the best interest of the American people to pass a law that harms our economy. Our country was built on entrepreneurial men like yourself. And it would be unfathomable to live in a world where politicians catered to the whims of the ignorant masses. I can assure you that we will put forth a bill that strengthens the partnership between the American people and our technology sector. I will not support breaking up companies like yours. And as for that tracking stuff, I'm not an expert, but I would imagine little technical details like that will get trimmed from the final bill. Trust me, very few people read legislation when you put three-thousand pages of boiler plate in there."

Cox laughed. "Thank you very much, Senator. Your words are a breath of fresh air. And you can count on our future support." Sheryl gave a thumbs up, and her uncle smiled, gently nodding. *Cox would contribute millions to the Super PAC.*

"Mr. Cox, this is the senator's chief of staff, Brandon Ridge. We're going to have to cut this short as the senator has another urgent meeting he must attend."

"My apologies, Mr. Cox," the senator said, "but it was a pleasure speaking with you. And the next time you're out by Washington, please let's set up a time that we can sit down and have a drink."

They said their goodbyes and the call ended. Senator Hawkinson looked up at his niece and nephew. Sheryl gave a polite golf clap from her seat.

The chief of staff said, "Amending the bill to take out the interest targeting will be a political challenge."

"Well you're very good at politics, Brandon." The chief of staff didn't smile. Senator Hawkinson turned to his niece. "Sheryl?"

She said, "Craft the bill in a way that limits only certain types of targeting and tracking. The bill should include language that regulates obsolete technology. If the bill uses specific technical methodology in its language, you'll be fine. You can run ads that say how you fought big tech and fought for privacy. We can buy some influencers and use our own media properties to give you credibility. Cox and company will still have their capabilities intact, because they'll be using new technology. New tracking methods that aren't covered in the bill. Everyone's happy."

"Brandon, you get all that?"

"Yes, sir."

"Good. Make it happen. Work with Sheryl on the details."

Guy stood looking out the window at the Chesapeake. As always, his face was expressionless, his mind racing.

"Guy, what did you think of this last one?" asked the senator.

Guy didn't move his gaze from the water. "Another one bagged and tagged, Uncle."

Senator Hawkinson glanced at Sheryl. "What's wrong with him?"

Sheryl's eyes moved to the senator's chief of staff. Seeing this, Senator Hawkinson turned to him and said, "Brandon, would you mind giving me and my family a few moments alone?"

"Of course, Senator. I'll be on the lawn if you need me for anything," he said, disappearing to the party outside.

A pair of HSG security personnel appeared in the doorway. Guy motioned for them to enter. They began shuffling around the room, scanning for electronic eavesdropping equipment and any signals that would indicate someone was listening in.

Senator Hawkinson said, "Is this really necessary?"

Guy didn't answer. He sat back down in the leather chair and began swiping through corporate reports on his tablet.

One of the security men set up a box that Sheryl knew to be a jamming device. The other man collected everyone's electronic devices and placed them in a Faraday pouch, where they would remain until the meeting was over.

When they were finished, Matt Kirby and the security men departed the room and shut the door. Sheryl walked to the room's wet bar, pouring each of them a drink from a crystal decanter. "Drinks?" she asked, and both men said yes.

Soon the three of them were alone and seated, each with a glass in hand.

"You have successfully piqued my interest," Senator Hawkinson said, taking a sip of his drink.

Sheryl began, "We need to discuss our advanced development project."

The senator winced. "Our agreement was that I would be kept in the dark unless it became—"

Guy huffed. "Well, it's become absolutely necessary, Uncle Preston."

The senator glanced between brother and sister. "Go on."

Sheryl said, "As you know, a little over a year ago, we came into ownership of some very advanced IP."

She left the juicy part unsaid. The intellectual property in question was taken from the Pax AI Mountain Research Facility. At the time, Jeff Kim's Pax AI was the most advanced AI company in the world. And his Mountain Research Facility was where they did their most sensitive research. Sheryl had secretly collaborated with a Russian intelligence officer named Petrov to make it happen. Their deal was for both the SVR and Sheryl's VC firm to acquire Jeff Kim's goldmine of AI and quantum computing technology.

Sheryl helped Petrov gain access to the facility through one of Guy Hawkinson's subsidiaries, which had been hired to provide Pax AI's security. When the security firm turned out to be dirty, Petrov took all the blame, eliminating any hard evidence the Hawkinsons were involved. There were still rumors and unfavorable news coverage, of course. Even a closed congressional hearing...the work of the senator's political enemies. But no criminal charges.

Guy said, "The fallout from the Pax AI incident had a negative impact on my business. Contracts with US agencies suddenly dried up. We couldn't win a bid."

Senator Hawkinson said, "You can't blame them. You were toxic, no matter which side of the aisle controlled the purse."

Sheryl said, "But in truth, our global security practice had already been in decline."

Guy nodded. "Ever since the wars in Iraq and Afghanistan began winding down, our contracts had been decreasing in size and number."

Senator Hawkinson said, "These things ebb and flow."

"No. This is more than that. For millennia, a soldier's job has been relatively the same. The tools have improved, sure. HSG has always adapted. We could perform more cost-effectively than almost any military on the planet. But over the past few years, the entire game has changed. Security buyers don't even want soldiers anymore. They want automated systems. Cameras and drones and robots. AI-based defense platforms are disrupting the industry with ever-increasing speed. Mercenaries are becoming obsolete. We can provide private security for VIPs, but we'll never hit a billion dollars in revenue again doing just that."

Sheryl leaned forward in her seat. "As you know, I evaluate new and growing companies as part of my job. I see where industries are being disrupted, and I place bets."

Senator Hawkinson frowned. "Those are all tech companies you specialize in, correct? What's that got to do with HSG?"

Sheryl said, "Every company is a tech company now. Whether they know it or not." She turned to her brother. They had reached the part of the conversation where they must cross a line with their uncle. A point of no return that would propel them forward on an unknown path. "After the incident at Pax AI," she continued, "we were supposed to share information. But through a series of unexpected events, the fire destroyed the entire facility before the technology could be fully transferred."

"I read the reports."

Sheryl looked at her brother and then back at her uncle. She spoke softly. "That was what external parties were led to believe, anyway." External parties meaning the Russians.

Senator Hawkinson raised his eyebrows.

Guy said, "I had my own team in the mountains that day. Electronic signals experts. We were able to covertly intercept the data transfer and limit any leakage."

"What are you saying?" Senator Hawkinson asked. "That you have had Pax AI's tech this whole time?"

Guy nodded. "For the past year, Sheryl and I have been recruiting some of the world's best AI and quantum computing experts to join us. A small team, but one dense with talent. The original intent was to transform Hawk Security Group into a modern defense contractor behemoth. One that could give our clients exactly what they were looking for: autonomous systems and deep learning algorithms that were lightyears ahead of the competition."

"But..." Senator Hawkinson said, sensing something.

"But." Guy nodded. "After we brought in some experts and they got a look under the hood, we found out a few things."

Sheryl said, "They were shocked to find that Pax AI was much further ahead than anyone realized. The implications of this advanced technology are significant. In the VC world, this tech would allow us to *own* multiple industries. I mean dominate. Entire industries. I began to formulate a plan on how to maximize our returns."

Guy said, "And that's when we were approached."

Senator Hawkinson frowned at him. "Approached by whom?"

"An organization. One with some very well-connected

members. They prefer to remain anonymous. I'm sorry, but we can't say much more about them right now. Suffice it to say, they opened our eyes to what's possible."

"You're being too vague. What are you saying?" Senator Hawkinson said.

Guy said, "Uncle, yesterday you were at a briefing of the Senate Intelligence Committee."

The senator narrowed his eyes. "Yes..."

"Was there any interesting activity in the Caribbean?"

His face reddened. "Yes...Why?"

Fireworks popped and boomed outside. Their heads turned toward the window. Blossoms of white smoke and fiery colors under a dusk sky reflected on the light chop of the bay. The initial volley of the evening's show.

Senator Hawkinson turned to Guy. "Tell me what happened on the island."

Guy said, "A plane landed. Two men on board. The plane was supposedly being used for smuggling drugs to the Virgin Islands. The supposed reason for the landing was an in-flight emergency, but one of the smugglers was a Mossad agent."

Sheryl looked at her uncle. "What have you heard?"

Senator Hawkinson placed his glass down on his desk. "They told us at the intel briefing that an Israeli drone submarine was operating in the Caribbean, and they think it was eavesdropping on US assets in the area."

"A *submarine*?" Guy said. "A drone submarine."

The senator nodded slowly, his voice soft. "Yes."

Guy said, "The Israelis don't operate submarines over here, let alone an autonomous one."

"That's what the DIA told us in our briefing. Very unusual behavior, they said. I'll only ask this once. Is there any chance that anything undesirable about this incident goes public?"

Sheryl said, "Which part don't you want being made

public? That the Israelis were trying to spy on us? Or the bigger thing?"

"What is the bigger thing?" Her uncle sounded frustrated. "Shit." He turned to Guy. "What did the agent say to you?"

Guy looked like he was going over everything in his head. "The agent was trying to evacuate one of our AI scientists."

"You have *AI scientists* on an island in the Caribbean?"

Guy nodded. "A group of them. One of our scientists was an Israeli man. Turns out he wasn't someone we wanted to do business with."

"Can anything be traced back to you?" the senator asked.

Guy began pacing the room. "The aircraft crashed into the sea away from our island but...three personnel were aboard. No one that we don't want to be associated with is still on our island."

"All your ducks are in a row, then..."

Guy looked uncomfortable. "There was a burst transmission. Encrypted. Based on the power and frequency, our team assessed it as low-range."

Senator Hawkinson leaned back in his chair. "What does that mean?"

Guy continued, "Well, until now, worst-case scenario, we were thinking there might be a low-altitude satellite or something. We *thought* we were in the clear. But if the Israelis had a submarine nearby..."

Sheryl took a sip of her drink. "If the submarine was in the right place, could it have picked up the signal?"

Guy nodded. "I think so. I would need to check with a few people. But probably, yes."

Senator Hawkinson said, "Assume the worst. What would have been in that signal?"

"I don't know. Something that would confirm we killed their agent."

"They must suspect that already."

"Maybe they have evidence of what we're doing on the island?" Sheryl said.

"And what are you doing on that island?" Senator Hawkinson asked.

Sheryl leaned forward. "We're securing our future, Uncle."

They all went quiet. More bursts of fireworks outside.

"If the Israelis were interested in what you were doing there before, you can sure as hell bet their interests are piqued now."

Guy said, "We'll need to move up our timeline."

Sheryl shook her head. "The only way to do that would be to go public and recruit."

Senator Hawkinson said, "Please explain."

Sheryl clasped her hands together. "We're creating a world-class advanced technology company using Pax AI's IP. No one knows we have it, or how far ahead it has allowed us to leap. We have been trying to stay covert. Almost all of our operations have been on that island, but it makes progress much slower."

Guy said, "This is a race, Uncle. We're a year or two away from winning. And winning will change *everything*. But if the Israelis interfere..."

Sheryl said, "We need to be overt. Scale up rapidly through acquisitions. Create a headquarters in the continental US and get funding from our partners. We can gobble up smaller competitors and begin funneling the best and brightest to our island to do the real work."

"That would make things easier," Guy said. "But the Israelis will be all over us. And if they are, it could draw more attention from other agencies." They looked at their uncle.

The senator's face transformed with recognition. He was a sharp man, and while he might not have all the details, he could smell the trail to power better than anyone. "Do you still have your contact in Moscow?"

Guy frowned. "We are no longer on good terms. Not after the Pax AI thing."

Senator Hawkinson said, "I suggest you attempt to contact him. Open a backchannel. Make amends. Give him a golden ticket if you must."

Sheryl and Guy looked up at that.

Guy smirked. "He is catching on quickly."

Senator Hawkinson said, "We need someone to keep tabs on the Israelis. Build your venture in the D.C. area. The Russians will have a strong operation there. Your people can't get caught fighting with Mossad. That would attract attention. But if the Russians did it for you..."

Guy said, "The SVR will definitely be able to keep tabs on the Israelis. And we need a tripwire in place. I can reach out. I'll be delicate."

Sheryl said, "We only need another year or so. Then it won't matter who knows."

6

Ava would have preferred the direct flight from Tel Aviv to Dulles, but the Mossad logistics wanted her destination to be JFK. She was nervous reentering the United States. She hadn't been back here since the Pax AI operation blew up in her face and that psychotic Russian named Petrov tried to burn a forest down with her and Colt still in it.

Colt. She sighed at the thought of him.

They had been lovers once. She knew that was the root cause of why she had violated every ounce of Mossad training and common sense when she was with him in Italy by admitting to him that she was a Mossad officer. Ava had objected when her superiors in Tel Aviv gave her this assignment. "How can I possibly go back? The CIA knows who I am." But those confident, stoic faces just stared back and assured her that her cover was still intact.

"Your cover is as good as it needs to be," they said. "Such is the relationship between America and Israel."

Had Mossad truly smoothed things over with the CIA? Would the FBI's counterintelligence division—their so-called "spy hunters"—be following her now that she was on American soil? Maybe Mossad just wanted to calm her nerves so that when she handed the Customs and Border Protection officer her "civilian" passport, she could still manage to smile.

After all, Ava wasn't entering the US under the guise of diplomatic cover. If she was identified, the Americans could eject her from their country, or they could imprison her as a spy.

But as it turned out, the dour-faced CBP agent in the New York airport barely gave her a second look.

He spent *just* enough time asking her what her business was in the United States to compare her face with her passport photo and, presumably, look for indicators of a forgery. When he was finished, he closed her passport book and pushed it back through the small opening in the glass screen that separated them. With a jut of his chin, she was clear to move on.

She always marveled at how lightly the Americans took passport control. When someone attempted to enter Israel, they were assessed for the physical signs of deception and asked the same questions by multiple people at different stations to see if the answers matched. Some of those questions were asked aggressively, provocatively, just to rattle them, throw them off. And they were watched by cameras, armed guards, and plainclothes Shabak officers.

Ava had only a small suitcase. Inside were the bare necessities and a pair of business suits she had purchased in London when she met Samantha. Ava didn't know the exact duration of her assignment but would purchase clothes from American stores if needed.

Once she'd cleared Customs, Ava left the airport and took a cab to Penn Station in Manhattan, where she boarded the Acela, Amtrak's high-speed train that serviced the eastern seaboard. The first-class lounge was dingy, but Ava was at least able to view her fellow passengers and try to correlate faces to people who might have been on her plane. The train departed on time, the windows filling with a beautiful yellow-orange sunlight as the train pulled onto the aboveground tracks, the silhouette of Manhattan surrounded by the afternoon sun. Ava inserted her earphones, began streaming some classical music. She ordered a coffee from the attendant and settled in for the three-hour trip.

This was not the best time to be operating without diplomatic cover in America. While Israel and the US had always had a close if not familial relationship, there were moments of irritation. Officially neutral without formally recognized alliances that might restrict necessary but unpleasant actions for their survival, Israel at times acted contrary to American interests. And while the two had always shared intelligence, Israel also spied on the Americans. If Mossad required information that the US wasn't inclined to share, they got it by other means.

Israel's aggressiveness, particularly toward Iran and their puppets in Syria and Lebanon, also rankled the starched shirts and Ivy League sensibilities of the Washington foreign policy elite. Shielded by two oceans, a nuclear arsenal that defied even hyperbole, and the world's most powerful military, America had the luxury of "rules" and "sides." Israel did not. The relationship was particularly strained of late. Both countries had new administrations and were still feeling each other out. Jonathan Pollard, an Israeli spy convicted in 1987 for a sweeping espionage campaign, served twenty-three years in prison and immigrated to Israel upon his release. He was personally welcomed as a hero by Netanyahu in one of his last acts as prime minister. Ava believed that to be an unnecessary victory lap that had immediately frosted relationships between the two intelligence communities.

Then there was the Pax AI incident. Officially, one Israeli citizen was made persona non grata: Ava's Aunt Samantha. Unofficially, Israel was also told that Ava shouldn't be stationed in the US anytime soon. That was two years ago. As far as Ava knew, Mossad never confirmed that she had been working for them. She sipped her coffee and tried not to think about how fucked she might be.

A few hours later, the porter handed Ava her bags at Washington, D.C.'s Union Station and she merged with the throngs of other business travelers, invisible in the crowd. She stepped into a bathroom, not because she needed to use it but because she wanted to see if anyone was watching her when she exited. Inside a stall, Ava waited a few moments, texted Moshe that she'd arrived, and then gathered her things to leave. Exiting the restroom, Ava scanned the crowd for a person whose face was ostensibly buried in a newspaper, someone pretending to be looking at a phone, or any of the other subtle tells of covert surveillance. Seeing nothing, Ava left Union Station by a side entrance onto First Street, walking past the monolithic parking garage, again checking for signs of pursuit. She walked north a half block to G Street, checked behind her again, and quickly crossed the street, just another busy traveler too much in a hurry to wait for a light. It was seven-thirty and nearly dark. Before rounding the corner to G Street, Ava took one last look behind her. There was no one on the street.

Ava was black.

The spring night was damp and cold and G Street was a poorly lit strip of asphalt between two looming structures. Beneath the yellow haze of a dim streetlamp near the end of the block, an Audi A6 sat idling at the curb, facing away from the parking garage. There were few cars parked on the street. This wasn't a part of town that saw much action after business hours. She crossed to the Audi. The company's US headquarters was located just outside Washington, D.C. in Reston, Virginia, and the cars were ubiquitous in the metro area. *Smart*, she thought. The trunk popped as she approached the car. She put her bags in and closed the trunk, noticing the Virginia tags indicating it was a corporate car. Ava got in the back seat, and the car pulled away as she was closing her door.

Dark, intense eyes looked at her from the rear-view mirror. "How was the flight?"

She recognized the gruff voice immediately and smiled. "Hello, Moshe."

Moshe was the Mossad officer assigned to her aunt during Ava's previous mission in the States. At Mossad's direction, he had been reassigned to support Ava for the final infiltration of the Mountain Research Facility. He was at once a protector, liaison, logistician, and confidant. Moshe was also one of the few people in the Institute that she truly trusted. Ava put her life in his hands once. One of the conditions she set in accepting this assignment was that Moshe would again be her security detail.

Moshe turned the car and headed west into Virginia, crossing the George Mason Memorial Bridge, better known to the locals as simply the Fourteenth Street Bridge. They crawled over the Potomac in Washington's legendary evening commute. The Pentagon sat on the riverbank on the other side. Beyond it, up a hill, she saw the illuminated bomb burst of the US Air Force Memorial. Moshe took the cloverleaf as soon as they crossed into Virginia, heading south on the George Washington Parkway past Reagan National, picking up exiting airport traffic. Moshe drove several block circles when they entered Old Town Alexandria. It was night now, and Ava knew surveillance detection was much more difficult.

Sometimes it counted on memorizing the shapes of headlights.

Three block circles later, Moshe was again heading south, where he picked up the southmost ring of the Washington Beltway and drove east into southern Maryland. From there, it was another fifty minutes to their destination along dark country roads seemingly swallowed by the forest around them. Moshe pulled off the state highway onto a long drive and stopped at a small brick building. A thick iron gate barred their way. The small shack was dimly lit by the glow of a monitor.

The guard stepped out. He wore a dark suit and a suppressed Uzi submachine gun on a tactical sling around his body. After Moshe passed a code phrase to the guard and the gate opened, he drove forward slowly along the snaking driveway for another tenth of a mile. He stopped in a large carport and they both exited the car.

"You can leave your things in the trunk," he said.

Ava nodded.

She noted two additional cars in the driveway and the house to their right at the end of a concrete path. The exterior was yellow-orange brick with a gray roof, a modern rambler style. The grounds were brightly illuminated, and she suspected getting anywhere near the door without being observed was impossible. Moshe led her inside.

The residence was deceptively large. A security guard— also armed with an Uzi —stood just inside.

"They are waiting for you in the living room," the guard said in Hebrew.

Moshe nodded and lumbered forward with Ava in tow. The guard closed the door behind them.

The living room was a wide rectangle with a fireplace on one side and pass-through to the kitchen on the other. There were windows on the rear wall and another small sitting area that faced the back of the property. The shades on the outer room were drawn. Aside from her and Moshe, five other people were sitting in the room. Ava only recognized one of them.

Ariel Katz.

Katz was known as "the Professor" within the Institute. He possessed an encyclopedic knowledge of intelligence operations. Some said that he knew more about his adversaries than they knew about themselves.

But beyond his gift for knowledge, Katz *graded* everything. He ruthlessly evaluated people, operations, and information that he received, often sending his observations back to the originator with harsh commentary. Ava had seen this kind of brutally honest feedback when she worked in Silicon Valley. The trendy name tech culture used for it was "radical honesty" or "radical candor." She personally thought it was just an excuse to be an ass.

But with Katz it was more than that. He was not trying to prove his intellectual superiority or subject command, he wanted to improve the final product—whether that was an intelligence report or an operations officer. Katz was known to be deeply committed to both the craft of intelligence and the state of Israel.

Ava hadn't argued this point with Samantha when her aunt cautioned her against trusting Katz during their meeting in London. She knew that was futile. But Ava did note the contradiction and thought it strange, something she would have to keep note of. It took a special type of person to succeed in this business. Some played because they loved the game. Others felt a call of duty to protect the state. And still for others, it was about ego. Careerists, chasing rank and accomplishment and forgetting the point of it all. Her aunt had painted Katz as being part of this last category.

Katz stood as she arrived, looking every bit the embodiment of his professor moniker. He was short and thin, wispy-haired and balding with round, wire-rim glasses. He wore brown pants, a white shirt, and a tan cardigan. "Miss Klein, it's very nice to finally meet you." His tone was crisp and businesslike. "I've heard very much about you."

"Thank you, sir. I'm pleased to be here."

"Your trip was uneventful, I trust." Subtext: *Were you followed?*

"It was very smooth," she said. *I'm in the black, Professor.*

"Good. Then let's not waste time on formality. Ladies and gentlemen, this is Ava Klein. Ava was an undercover operative responsible for the Pax AI infiltration. You were all briefed on that mission and how it ended. It's noted in the official record, but I'll state it again here. Tactically, the Institute considers Operation Galleon to be a success. There were strategic failures and those have been remedied, but Ms. Klein's performance was exemplary and of the highest standards of our profession."

Ava noted he didn't blame Samantha by name. Maybe she was already dead to them, a name to be memorialized and toasted.

"Thank you, sir," Ava said. "One question before we begin."

"Of course."

"They briefed me on this project in Tel Aviv and I was assured that my cover was still intact, but..." She paused, considering him with a slightly lifted eyebrow. "The CIA knew of my involvement. I stated that in my report. I knew their undercover officer personally. He...identified me."

Katz waved a dismissive hand. "It's been accounted for," was all he said.

"Sir?"

"As I said, it's been handled." Katz peered at her over the rim of his glasses, the muscles in his jaw tensing. She'd pursue this further, but clearly not here. Whatever the arrangement made with their counterparts at CIA or FBI's counterintelligence unit, it was certainly above the heads of the people in this room.

Samantha's words echoed again in her mind: *watch out for Katz.*

Katz informed her that there was food, drinks, coffee, and tea in the kitchen and that she should grab something now because they would be briefing for quite a while. Ava tried to decline, but Katz wouldn't hear it and had someone prepare her a plate. He told her he wasn't sure if she was practicing or not, but everything was kosher. Ava ate quickly while introductions were made. The others in the room were Mossad officers, three from the Washington, D.C. Station and two from San Francisco.

"Shira, would you start us off?" Katz said. "We're going to begin with a primer on the Hawkinsons before we dive into the mission itself."

Shira stood, smoothing out her pants. She was small and slight, tan with olive-colored eyes. Her blonde hair was cut short and pulled back into a tight ponytail. "Good evening," she said, and walked over to the television, which Ava hadn't previously noted was on. Shira picked up a remote and advanced her slides.

"The Hawkinson Corporation is a parent company for numerous subsidiaries. They began in the 1800s as a mineral prospecting concern in the American West and found several lucrative gold and silver deposits in Colorado and Wyoming.

By early twentieth century, they were already extremely wealthy when they incorporated oil into the portfolio, primarily in Texas and Oklahoma. The company used that wealth to purchase several small defense firms in the years following the Second World War, but before the American defense boom of the 1950s."

Shira gave brief profiles on the titular heads of the Hawkinson family, noting that the company was largely patriarchal and remained privately held, passing leadership from one generation to the next. "By the 1980s, Peter Hawkinson became CEO of the corporation and chairman of the board of directors of both the family trust and the board that runs the subsidiary companies. Peter has four siblings." Shira paused a moment, showing their faces on the screen. "We have complete profiles on each of them if you wish to read them, but only his younger brother Preston is relevant. None of the Hawkinson siblings except Peter and Preston were involved in running the business, and at this point, they were slightly estranged from the other three, who were largely enjoying the family's financial excess. The Hawkinsons divested their mineral and oil business in the 1970s, before the energy crisis of the late seventies.

"In the early eighties, Peter founded a telecommunications company specializing in advanced computing and communications equipment for the military and started a venture capital fund. In 1989, Peter executed a maneuver to remove his siblings' voting rights from the board of directors, giving him sole control over the Hawkinson Corporation. Preston supported him in this, in exchange for the company bankrolling his campaign for the United States Congress. He was elected as the sole representative for Wyoming in the 1992 election cycle." She advanced the slides. "In 1994, Preston sold the family of defense companies they founded or acquired during the massive consolidation of the American defense industry in the nineties. But as part of this deal, the Hawkinson Corporation was still paid for the patents on the technology developed even though the companies had been sold. Peter Hawkinson and his wife Mary were killed in a tragic murder-suicide in the '90s. It was all over the tabloids. This is important because of his earlier maneuver, and sole control of the company and the majority of the family trust fell to his children, Sheryl and Guy, both of whom were at university at this point.

"Sheryl received her undergraduate degree in international finance from Stanford and an MBA from Harvard. Upon graduation from Harvard, Sheryl went to work for the family's venture capital fund, specializing in technology acquisitions. Guy studied business at Yale and originally intended to attend law school and join the family business but changed his trajectory after his father's death. Upon his graduation in 1999, Guy was selected for the United States Army's Officer Candidate School. He was commissioned as an infantry officer, qualified as a Ranger and airborne before being selected for the Special Forces. Guy served six years in the Special Forces including service in Afghanistan and Iraq. He left the Army in 2007 and founded the Hawk Security Group, also known as HSG. Preston Hawkinson ran for and was elected to the US Senate in the 2000 election cycle, a position he still holds today.

"Three months after Operation Galleon and the collapse of Pax AI, they acquired this." Shira advanced the slide to a satellite image of an island. Reference data and topographical information on the sidebar showed that it was little more than an atoll, roughly circular and only a few miles wide. It appeared mostly covered in vegetation, though several structures and an airfield were visible. "This is an unclaimed island just outside the US Virgin Islands territory. They purchased it from the US government."

"Do we know what those facilities are?" Ava asked. There was something eerily familiar with the placement and design of those buildings from the satellite imagery, but she couldn't put a finger on it.

Shira shook her head. "We don't, unfortunately. We haven't been able to find plans for its construction anywhere. It appears that they've done this entirely in-house."

Ava nodded, satisfied with the answer, and the briefing continued. Then, a crash of memory hit her like a wave. She knew where she'd seen those buildings before.

"That layout," Ava said, pointing at the screen, "is almost identical to Jeff Kim's Mountain Research Facility."

"Are you sure?" Katz asked.

"I am." She stood and walked over to the screen, pointing at the buildings on the right. "It took me a minute because these were hidden inside the actual mountain, but I had seen the blueprints at one point."

"So your supposition is that Hawkinson is rebuilding the Pax AI Mountain Research Facility?"

Ava shrugged. "It sure looks like it."

Katz nodded, once again the Professor. Then he took over the briefing. "Hawk Technologies is now headquartered close to here in Northern Virginia, along with the remnants of the Hawkinson Corporation. They have satellite offices in Austin, Texas, and Mountain View, California, but the bulk of the operation is here."

Ava knew from her time undercover in Pax AI that it was becoming increasingly difficult to lure young engineers to work in Silicon Valley. Startups couldn't afford to pay salaries that met the stratospheric cost of living requirements, and there were numerous other factors to contend with that made places like Austin and D.C. much more attractive.

Katz said, "They've been hiring the top minds in artificial intelligence and are paying well above market rate. They are also acquiring companies at a staggering rate. They'll absorb the capabilities and talent that they want and jettison the rest. Severed employees are generously compensated and locked up with strict nondisclosure agreements. To date, no one has spoken."

"Have we tried to get anyone to share information yet?" Ava asked.

"A few light attempts, but nothing has materialized. Hawk Security Group still maintains their Carolina Training Facility near Fort Bragg. They have their own airfield. We've tracked multiple recurring flights between that location and the island."

Shira advanced the slides. "We managed to get an asset inside the island. He was born in Israel but was educated at Cambridge and stayed in the UK. However, his family still lives in Israel and he's a patriotic Jew. He was recruited by the Hawkinsons, but some months after working for them he began to get concerned. He contacted the Institute via his family in Israel. I handled the recruitment. He was our first viable confirmation that Hawkinson stole R&D from Jeff Kim. He said there was no way Hawk Technologies could have made such advances this quickly. He also feared that the people he was working for had no moral compass. They showed no restraint in what they built. He said, 'Machines only have the ethics of their creators.' It was very challenging to get large data sets off the island because of their electronic warfare capability, but our agent had a covert communications kit that he used to message us. From his communications, we learned that they are installing *massive* computing power."

Katz said, "A few weeks ago, our agent sent us an alarming message. He believed he had been discovered. Per our operating procedures, we planned an exfiltration. We had an officer, David Gurion, inside the Mexican Gulf Cartel, which is one of the primary actors in the Mexican drug war."

"We have an agent embedded in a Mexican cartel?" Ava asked.

Katz said, "The cartels have been known to provide terrorist organizations with weapons in exchange for money laundering. We'd keep our eyes on that."

Shira looked uneasy. "We redirected Gurion to conduct the exfil. Our techs fitted an aircraft with some sensing equipment we arranged for him to land on the island during a cartel smuggling mission." A grainy night vision video played on the screen showing a rough landing in bad weather.

Katz folded his arms across his chest. "The aircraft landed and was on deck for a little over four hours. After that, the aircraft took off and flew approximately forty kilometers west, then descended into the ocean. No bodies were recovered in the plane crash."

"Any chance they are still on the island?"

Shira's face was grim. "Our analysis of the flight records shows almost no inputs to the flight controls from takeoff to crash. We think it was on autopilot. There were no comms during the flight, and there have been no transmissions via our agent's Covcom. What's more, we were able to intercept some communications from the island that suggest there was some cleanup." Shira breathed out her nose, taking a moment to collect herself. "They were discussing the disposal of bodies."

Ava almost asked how they were able to capture this communication but figured if they wanted to tell her, they would have.

"We have an idea of how Guy Hawkinson's personal security team operates. Our own special operations teams have experience working with them in northern Africa. Hawk Security Group is known for being aggressive with interrogations and *always* covers their tracks."

"Meaning?" Ava asked.

"We assume that our agents died poorly," Katz said. "Whether their bodies were destroyed on that island or in the plane crash is irrelevant." He picked up a glass of water and drank, then studied the room.

Ava furrowed her brow. "Have we discussed any of this with the Americans?"

Katz said, "A few years ago, we would have. However, given our relationship since the Pax AI incident, and with Hawkinson's prior work with the Russians and the fact that Preston Hawkinson sits on the Senate Select Committee on Intelligence, we can't assume that the Americans will handle this information appropriately."

Shira cleared her throat. "Which brings us to Operation Sirocco. We intend to place one of our own inside the Hawkinsons' technology company."

"Who?"

"You, Ms. Klein." Katz's face was unreadable.

Ava was ready for this. "Sir, I say this with all due respect. But given the circumstances surrounding my last time in the US, I don't think my cover will stand up to scrutiny. Hawk Security Group has access to good private sector counterintelligence resources. Even if it isn't in the public domain, they will be aware of my association with Mossad."

"We *know*, Ms. Klein," Katz said forcefully.

Ava narrowed her eyes. "Why would anyone at Hawk Technologies allow me near them?"

Shira said, "You will be acting as a tech industry lobbyist.

Your legend is that you were away from Pax AI headquarters during the attack and returned to Israel for a time because you didn't feel safe there. You returned to America a year ago and have been commuting between the US and Tel Aviv ever since, acting as a consultant. You liaise between the Israeli tech industry and the Americans, trying to open doors for our companies to sell their technology here. I have a friend at AIPAC who will vouch for you as well." AIPAC, the American-Israeli Political Action Committee, was an organization that represented Israel's interests, primarily in foreign policy and defense, to the United States government. They contributed heavily to political campaigns of both parties, ensuring favorable representation regardless of the direction of the prevailing political winds.

Ava said, "The Hawkinsons will see right through that."

Katz nodded. "We know." He handed Ava a thick packet. "There's a detailed accounting of the companies you represent and your activities for the last two years. And other details of your legend."

Ava took the folder and flipped through the pages. Two years ago, Russian operatives forced their way into Pax AI's San Francisco headquarters in a violent attempt to steal Jeff Kim's most sensitive research. Ava was warned by her Mossad contacts and escaped just in time. As a result, Colt later learned that she was Mossad, as did Jeff Kim. Officially, Mossad denied her status as an operative upon her return to Israel. But some people knew. And if she was to operate undercover, that was an unthinkable risk.

"You'll find in your legend, Ms. Klein, that, like your aunt, you have been terminated from the Institute due to your botched participation in our Pax AI operation, Galleon. For the past two years, you've been carrying quite a grudge against Mossad, Israel, and Western intelligence agencies. This grudge has influenced who you work with, and what type of work you take."

The picture was beginning to form now, and Ava understood.

"This is what's going to get me credibility with the Hawkinsons," she said.

"Exactly," said Shira.

Katz continued, "You will be a known entity to Sheryl, due to her past involvement with Pax AI. Sheryl Hawkinson will be our first big test."

"She wasn't a fan of me when I was in San Francisco."

Katz said, "She is, by our estimate, a pragmatic dealmaker. So if you've got something she wants, she may see you in a different light. You worked closely with the exact organization that is now hunting the Hawkinsons. They know this, and will be taking measures to prevent our operations. We need to use this to our advantage. Retaining your services could prove invaluable for them, if you were loyal."

Ava sighed, shaking her head. "I don't know. Why would they think I would be loyal?"

Katz tapped on the binder that held her legend. "You have something to prove. You are a former member of your nation's national security apparatus. You are now an outsider. This is much like Guy Hawkinson. While he was once in American special operations, and he's recruited heavily from the armed forces, many in the defense and intelligence establishment now treat him like a pariah."

"Really?"

"Indeed. If you strike the right chords, you will be kindred spirits."

Ava nodded. "So I get close to Guy. Then what?"

"We need to find out what they are developing on that island," Shira said.

Ava said, "You must have some idea."

The Mossad officers exchanged glances. "We do. But reports vary widely, and some of them are quite alarming. We need to know exactly what they got and who they are going to sell it to."

"Okay."

Katz rose from his seat. "I'm sure you're tired from your long trip, Ms. Klein. Allow Shira to brief you a bit more and then you can get some rest. We've arranged an apartment for you in D.C. so you look the part. In your briefing packet there are more details on events we believe Guy Hawkinson will be at, for you to get close to him, but use your best judgment on how to manage your approach. You'll report to me directly and you will not, under any circumstances, utilize Washington Station."

"Understood."

Katz went to the kitchen to get some food.

Shira explained how their communications would work. She'd be issued a new phone, heavily modified by Mossad's technical division so that it could communicate securely with Katz. She was to only use it for setting up their physical meetings. Those would take place throughout the metro area on a varied schedule.

After another thirty minutes of reviewing the details, the meeting concluded. Katz walked Ava out and bid her good luck.

Ava followed Moshe to the Audi and got in the back seat. Soon she was deep in thought, the car ride to the District seeming to pass in an instant.

Arriving at her new residence, she wondered about the Institute's budget for this operation. They set her up in a two-thousand-square-foot penthouse overlooking Sixteenth Street in the heart of downtown D.C. The place was around the corner from K Street, where the majority of Washington's lobbyists and consultants had their offices.

Moshe helped set her things inside the condo and asked if she needed anything else. Ava thanked him and said no, but she'd check in with him in the morning.

Ava strongly suspected that Katz wasn't telling her everything he knew about the Hawkinsons and their island operation, but she also understood an intelligence officer's need to compartmentalize information. Especially given the fact that Ava could be captured and interrogated. But was Katz keeping secrets due to operational security, or something else? Would the Hawkinsons really consider her past as an asset to their organization or would she be rejected on sight? Or worse...would they know she was a dangle? Would they get her in close and drop the hammer on her when she least expected it?

Ava fixed herself a drink and sat near her window, gazing out over the busy D.C. street. There was a lot on her mind.

7

Langley, Virginia

Each day for the past week began with Colt meeting Fred Ford for coffee in the CIA's cafeteria. "Coffee is one of the few things they can't screw up in this place," Ford had said on day one. "Don't ever order the breakfast sandwich." They would then chat a bit, making small talk and veering into the periphery of their work. Eventually Ford would lead them through the maze of lower-floor cubicles at the CIA headquarters toward the National Technical Counterintelligence Unit (NTCU) compartment.

It was on these everyday walks that Colt understood what made Ford such a good case officer. He was affable, disarming, and charismatic. Within five minutes of knowing him, he was the guy you'd known your entire life and would happily spill your guts to. Colt watched with admiration as he transformed stone-faced intel analysts—conditioned by Directorate of Intelligence culture to keep operators at arm's length—into old friends, leaving smiles and laughter in his wake.

Ford recalled the inconsequential details about someone's life that most people ejected from their memory seconds after hearing it. He would recognize a face he hadn't seen in years, recall the relevant details, and then engage. Ford would ask about their kids by name, comment about the details of their favorite sports teams, or bring up a humorous story from a past overseas assignment. He provided good-natured ribbing to those who appreciated it, often serving himself up as the punch line at just the right moment. Most recipients of Ford's attention seemed delighted to take a break from their stressful jobs and engage with a friend.

While Colt could tell that most of this banter was genuine, he also recognized it for what it was. Intelligence officers would classify Ford's activity as network curation. The CIA was an incredibly political organization, and Ford was a savvy case officer. He had cultivated his own network at the CIA— fellow ops officers, trainers, linguists, staff operations officers, targeters, logistics officers—any one of whom might be able to help him at a crucial moment. When every one of these people had countless high-priority tasks to complete, what would make Ford's request float to the top?

The way he made them feel. Social loyalty.

Colt wondered how many times Ford had cabled in from some forgotten corner of the world with a fast turnaround request. Hey, can you hook a brother up? Just this once? And from the looks on these faces, they absolutely would.

This morning, after a particularly energetic run through the gauntlet, Colt and Ford reached the last part of their journey: a long, empty hallway that led to one of the segmented highest-priority classified compartments.

Colt commented on this morning's banter. "Mr. Popularity strikes again."

Ford shrugged. "Like I used to tell all my girlfriends in

high school, I may not be much to look at, but I'll make you smile."

"Did that work?"

"Not on the pretty ones," Ford deadpanned. "But on the chubby ones? Absolutely."

Colt chuckled.

"Here we are. Brace for the bullshit." Ford used his keycard to open the door marked NTCU.

Technically, the unit reported to the National Counterintelligence Executive (NCIX), formerly known as the National Counterintelligence Center. That organization was formed in 1994 after the discovery and arrest of longtime CIA mole Aldrich Ames exposed that the nation's CI capabilities were disparate, unfocused, and woefully unprepared for the challenges facing an increasingly complex security environment. The NCIX was located on the Office of the Director of National Intelligence campus a few miles from CIA Headquarters in the Tysons Corner section of McLean, Virginia. Though cybersecurity and economic espionage fell under the purview of NCIX, the unit was formed after intense lobbying by CIA and FBI counterintelligence leaders.

Proponents of establishing the NTCU argued that the threats posed by technological advances were evolving too quickly for a large organization, mired in government bureaucracy, to respond effectively. ODNI authorized the unit's creation on a provisional status, and required that its members be selected from all parts of the intelligence community, not just the FBI and CIA. The NTCU would report progress against designated initiatives to ODNI quarterly.

Deputy Director Wilcox staged something of a coup d'état when he authorized a workspace for NTCU in the bowels of the CIA's Langley headquarters, and through an amendment to their charter, ensured the unit would provide "day-to-day" operational updates to him. Given the community's extensive workload, it was highly unlikely that ODNI or the NCIX would move against America's head spymaster. If he wanted to do the extra work, have at it.

Colt and Ford walked inside the NTCU door. A large, cavernous chamber surrounded a glass-walled conference room. As they walked through the dark outer chamber, security cameras and sensors monitored them from above.

Colt saw Thorpe speaking with a few others inside the glass-walled conference room but couldn't hear anything they were saying. The conference room was air-gapped soundproof. "This is where the double-secret probation stuff happens," Ford had told Colt during his first visit.

"What's with the blinds? They really need that in here?" Colt asked.

Black venetian blinds hung from the conference room windows.

Ford laughed. "The blinds are drawn during briefings so that even the security cameras covering the exterior chamber couldn't see in. I heard one of the finance managers complained of the cost of the blinds when they were rebuilding this section. A cybersecurity expert pointed out that however improbable it may be, hacking into the CIA's internal security cameras was a legitimate goal of US adversaries. Chinese and Russian AI programs can now read lips and translate everything into text, then sift through the data and spit out the juiciest details of American spy operations. So, the blinds were ordered and installed. Sometimes the old-fashioned ways still work best."

Both Colt and Ford used keycards to open the conference room door and entered.

"Morning, gentlemen," Thorpe said, his voice frosty. "Please have a seat."

Colt and Ford sat down and Thorpe began the meeting. "The best information STONEBRIDGE has uncovered is coming from our human intel source. The FBI has placed an undercover agent, codename SLALOM, inside Hawk Technologies. SLALOM is in their corporate finance division. We have good intel on their merger and acquisition activity. We know how much Hawkinson is paying for these top scientists, and we know that they are diverting a lot of funds to confidential research projects. What we don't know enough about are the details of those research projects. So, to improve our collection activities, Director Wilcox has asked us to insert a second HUMINT asset. Mr. McShane and Mr. Ford will handle the CIA officer we put inside the Hawkinson organization."

Thorpe returned to his seat and asked the young FBI agent next to him to advance the slide. The mouse clicked and the screen changed.

Thorpe said, "To save time, we've narrowed down the list of prospective agents for you to choose from." Five faces with names and short biographical summaries appeared. A caution statement at the top and bottom of the slide reminded viewers that each of these individuals was currently undercover and not to discuss their names outside of a cleared space. Colt scanned the profiles. They were CIA case officers, all of them. New recruits, fresh out of the National Clandestine Service Training program.

Thorpe pointed to the top profile on the display. "We know this is your decision, but we really like Edwards. Stanford grad, double major in computer science and economics. Worked at BCG before applying here. Top marks at CST."

Ford said, "Appreciate you putting this together, but if it's not too much trouble, I would like to see the rest of the list."

Thorpe frowned. "What are you talking about? This is the list."

Ford said, "Come on. This isn't everyone. We need to see..."

Thorpe interrupted. "Please move on. Take us through these five names."

The young FBI agent looked between Thorpe and Ford, then cleared his throat and started to continue.

Ford waved his hand and said, "We're good. We don't need to go over any of these names."

"You're not going to meet with them?" Thorpe's face went tomato red.

Ford squinted at the screen, pretending to study the list again, and then shook his head. "Nah."

Thorpe stood, leaning forward and placing his hands on the table. "Wilcox tasked you with picking an agent. As much as it pains me, you'll be the handler. I've selected five agents for you to choose from. All are excellent candidates. We've spent a lot of time profiling and interviewing the—"

Ford turned to Colt. "Colt, those folks on that screen look like machine learning specialists to you? Quantum computing experts? AI engineers? Those were the skill sets we identified as being relevant, right?"

Colt felt all eyes on him. He needed to tread carefully. Though he'd spent a decade undercover, he was a complete unknown at Langley. Ford was Colt's supervisor and mentor now. Wilcox had confidence that Ford could shepherd Colt back into "big" CIA. Thorpe was the NTCU director, a respected leader in the counterintelligence community, and very well connected himself. The talk was he was on a short list to head up the counterterrorism center after this assignment. It was not a good idea to make Thorpe an enemy.

Colt glanced between Ford and Thorpe. "They're all impressive candidates, I'm sure."

Ford raised his eyebrows.

"But no," Colt said. "They'd get sniffed out on day one. We're talking about some of the most specialized expertise in the world, here. The bleeding edge of computer science. We need someone who can pass as world-class talent." Colt shook his head. "I'm sure they are all excellent case officers, but we're talking about someone who's an expert in artificial intelligence. That isn't something we can fake."

Thorpe said, "Wilcox gave us ninety days. How are you going to be ready by then?"

"We'll handle it," Ford said.

Thorpe took a deep breath. "You want to do your own talent search? You got it. It's your funeral." He nodded to his two subordinates, and they packed up their things and left the room.

When they were alone, Colt said, "You sure you don't want to look closer at that list? I think one of the names was actually from the S&T." Agency speak for the Science and Technology Division.

Ford shrugged. "We can't pick from a short list that was handed to us by *that* guy."

"You don't trust him."

"I don't trust anyone," Ford said dismissively. "Well, except you, of course."

"Of course."

"Well, and librarians. Oh, and chubby girls. But after that, *no one*."

Colt half smiled, wondering if he had made a mistake in trusting Ford.

The room was quiet now that Thorpe and company had

left. Ford leaned back in his chair, lacing his hands behind his head. "Let's go over Hawk Technologies' plans again."

"You mean their expansion into AI?" Colt asked.

"Yeah."

Since he'd been assigned to this operation, much of Colt's time was spent researching everything about Hawk Technologies' recent foray into artificial intelligence. Tech was a strange pivot from their traditional global security business, though their marketing people were doing their best to make a connection.

"Their public announcement this week said that they were hiring everything from full stack software engineers and AI researchers to PR managers and account executives. They specifically call out AI engineers. But tech firms around the world are all fighting for the same people. Hawk Security Group is well known as a private security contractor and they're going to have a hard time recruiting the kind of talent that traditional tech companies can get. In my experience, most developers are freaked out by government in general and defense in particular. Hawk is going to have a hard time getting the same talent that the big players can get. Google's Deepmind, Chinese companies like Baidu, smaller AI-first firms like Open AI...they are going to attract talent with name recognition and the scope of work, not to mention some bonkers high compensation."

"Okay," said Ford. "Let's say you're an AI engineer. Very talented, but somewhat on the inexperienced side. Where are you right now?"

"How inexperienced?" asked Colt.

"Very. Either first year in your first job, or in the application process."

"US citizen?"

"That would be easier for us, yes."

Colt said, "I mean...a lot of these kids are in college. Undergrad or master's programs. Top institutions." Colt rattled off a list of schools.

Ford said, "All right, now let's say you're the people in charge of hiring at Hawk Technologies. You want to leapfrog the big players. Humor me and say that the technology isn't the issue. How do you recruit?"

Colt frowned. "The tech is always the issue..."

"I said humor me."

Colt shrugged. "Okay...so just personnel..." He sighed, thinking. "I would probably acqui-hire."

"Meaning?"

"When larger firms are looking to break into a new market, they typically do it by buying a startup that specializes in the area they want to grow in. So, if I'm, say, a global security contractor, I look for the top startups innovating in the global security capabilities I'm interested in, and I buy them."

"How do you stop the talent from leaving?"

"I mean, unless you drop employment contracts on them, you can't, really, but you can typically retain the leadership team through the acquisition. If the employees have equity in the acquirer, it's easier to manage. You can simply write language into the contract. For a tech firm, oftentimes investors or the board will insist on their own guy being the CEO—this usually happens at the B or C round of funding. Whatever tech genius founded the company becomes CTO or Chief Scientist, if they weren't already, and that's who you're looking to keep on the leash for as long as you can."

"Makes sense," Ford said.

"But everyone does this, so the competition is pretty fierce."

"Is Hawk Technologies doing this?"

"I'm sure they are."

"So if we could get someone hired by one of those companies prior to the acquisition..."

Colt said, "Then our agent would work for Hawk Technologies. And probably skip a lot of the scrutiny they would get through direct hiring." He saw where Ford was going now. "It could work. What are you thinking?"

"You said Cornell is one of the best US-based academic institutions for AI programs. I have a contact there. We've used him to recruit people before."

"Okay."

"Let me send him a message, see if he's got anyone that might fit our profile."

Colt was silent for a time, staring at the blank screen in the conference room.

"What is it?" Ford said.

"We only have ninety days. You're talking about recruiting someone from a college program and using them as an agent rather than using one of our own? It's going to be impossible..."

Ford's eyes narrowed slightly. "You hungry? You like gyros?"

Colt looked at his watch, dumbfounded that Ford avoided the question entirely. "It's ten-thirty."

"Good. We'll beat the lines."

They stopped in Ford's office long enough for him to send a message to his contact at Cornell. Then they left the George H.W. Bush Center for Intelligence in Ford's car, a silver Jeep Grand Cherokee decked out with lots of offroad gear, and turned left onto a road that took them past the southern edge of CIA's massive campus. Out the window Colt saw rolling, forested hills that seemed out of place this close to Washington, D.C. Soon they were on the beltway, passing Tysons Corner, and after a few more turns were back onto VA-123 heading toward Vienna.

It was a long drive for gyros. As Clandestine Service Officers, neither of them could publicly acknowledge—even to their families—that they worked for CIA. Following his ten-year assignment as a NOC, Colt told his parents that he left his job with the investment firm out of a desire to serve his country again and that he was taking a mid-level position with the Commerce Department. Ford's cover was that he worked for DoD, one of the masses shuffling into and out of the Pentagon every day. The cover was vital. It was their shield, their reserve chute, the thing that would save them in the field if they were ever compromised or captured. Even here in Northern Virginia, where it seemed like half the population had a top-secret clearance, maintaining cover was essential.

Because you had to assume someone was always watching.

To make sure they weren't, a fifteen-minute drive to lunch could turn into thirty every so often. Ford pulled into the strip mall parking lot in front of a restaurant called Skorpios. The late-morning air was crisp, the sun shining. Ford wore a quilted gray vest with the sleeves turned up on his shirt. Colt hadn't seen him wear a suit jacket yet. He wore a black wool mid-length topcoat over his own suit with the collar turned up. One of his instructors told him once to dress in a style that was different from his personal one, making it harder for an adversary to establish a pattern.

They entered the restaurant, a bell jingling as they opened the door. The smell of seasoned meats slow roasting over a fire immediately hit Colt's nose, reminding him of his Mediterranean port calls back when he was in the Navy. His mouth watering, he scanned the place quickly and saw that it was already filled to capacity. A good sign. He picked up a few bits of conversation in Greek, another indicator that Ford had struck restaurant gold.

They ordered and took their meal to-go. Both got the lamb gyro and fries, but Ford also grabbed a double order of chicken souvlaki and baklava. Colt gave him a look and Ford shrugged. "I'm a growing boy."

They took their meals back to Ford's Jeep and drove another half mile north to a small parking lot where the road intersected with the Washington and Old Dominion Trail, an old railroad that had been converted into a bike and pedestrian path. They found a quiet and secluded bench with good sight lines and dug into their lunches.

"Damn I love this place," Ford said.

Colt was still unwrapping his gyro and Ford was three bites deep, tzatziki sauce dribbling from his chin. "There's just something they do to the lamb. I don't know what it is," he said, mouth half full of food. "But it's delicious. Just like I remember it."

"You were stationed in Greece?"

"I was." Ford nodded. "I graduated fourth in my class at the Farm, high enough to get my pick. Chose Athens Station."

"Surprised you didn't pick Moscow."

"Naw, Greece was amazing. Crossroads for everything from an intelligence standpoint. You're on the Med so there's proximity to the Near East, lots of overland traffic smuggling: arms, drugs, and whatever the hell else was coming out of the Balkans then. Good jumping off point for Lebanon. It was a great first assignment. I went to Madrid after that, beautiful but boring, and from there to a small, unacknowledged post in Munich." Ford took a few bites. "That was something," he said. "It was kind of a gentlemen's game in the nineties. Clinton wasn't super involved in foreign policy, kind of left us to our own devices. For better or worse. Then the budget got cut because they thought they could do everything with satellites and drones. The thing is, turns out you can't. And then..."

"9/11 happened."

"Yup. Upended everything. They recalled a lot of us to headquarters pretty much immediately, once they got air travel sorted out. Work changed after that. Clandestine Service wasn't quite gutted in the nineties, but near enough. We pulled a lot of double duty. Year in Afghanistan, then we decide to go to Iraq for whatever the fuck that was about. Back to Afghanistan. Back to Iraq. Finally got a break and transferred to the Far East Division. Singapore, Beijing. I made some good friends there. Went back to Singapore where some of those friends could travel for business or vacation. We had a lot of success figuring out what the adversary was up to. Lot of that was because of this one friend I had."

Ford trailed off, lost in thought. Colt knew he was being circumspect because they were in public.

"Yeah, I like Greek food too," Colt said through a wry smile, poking at Ford's long-winded answer to his question. Ford laughed. Colt said, "You didn't spend much time stateside, did you."

"Tried to avoid it. That overseas stuff is fun, you know? I didn't want to just ride a desk at Langley. I was never interested in company politics either, hitching myself to this star or that one. I spent almost my entire career in the field. I knew that would cap my advancement, but I also didn't mind. I suppose, though, that's how I ended up having to negotiate with people like Thorpe rather than getting to dictate terms." They ate in silence for a time. Ford balled up the foil gyro wrapper and the small box the fries came in and dropped them in the bag.

"Hey, man, look," Colt began, "it's okay if you don't want to tell me...but what's between you and Thorpe anyway?"

Ford's eyes went to the paved bike trail. He could see the older officer tracking a cyclist pedaling down the path.

"That is not a story for this bench," Ford said without taking his eyes off the cyclist. He stood and Colt followed.

They dropped their bags in a trash can and walked back to Ford's Jeep. The drive back to Langley was filled mostly with small talk, Ford sharing that this assignment was the longest he'd spent stateside in his entire career. By the time they returned, many of their colleagues had left for lunch, and he was able to get a decent spot in the Agency's amusement park-sized lot. They walked through the rear entrance and rode the escalators up to the mezzanine level, badging through while an armed security guard looked on. From there, they made their way down to NTCU, where they shared an office.

Thorpe was scheduled to be in a three-hour briefing session with some members of the senior staff and they would have space to talk. Ford led the way to his office, stopping by the communal coffee pot first. Once they both had a cup, Ford entered his office, which was a small, glass-faced room that overlooked the unit's common area. Some members of the unit were in the common area, eating lunch or working.

Ford walked around to his desk, not bothering to power on his computer to check messages that may have come in while they were at lunch. Colt closed the door behind him and took one of the chairs in front of Ford's desk. Ford didn't have much in the way of office accoutrements, no pictures of family, just a few mementos from his various assignments. There was a long wooden name plate, however, with "FRED H. FORD, GLG-20" carved into the front.

"Okay, that's funny," Colt said. Ford gave a cursory laugh and they sat. The plaque was a reference to the 1985 comedy,

Spies Like Us, in which Chevy Chase and Dan Akroyd became spies classified as "GLG-20s."

Colt sipped his coffee and said, "Earlier you were asking me what type of person would make a good agent inside one of these top AI companies."

"You know that world better than anyone else on the team, Colt. None of the people on Thorpe's list would work." Ford was one of the few people who had been read in on Colt's nearly decade-long non-official cover assignment. "We need someone with the right talent and ability. It sucks that we won't have long to train them. But we need to find someone who could actually get hired by an artificial intelligence firm and do well enough to get high up in the organization. We need to pick the type of person we would want to recruit as an operator, too. Brains, street smarts, and ice cold under pressure."

Colt shrugged. "We could talk with HR, have them run every ops officer's resume and see who studied computer science in college. Another option would be to talk to S&T, see if someone might be up for an undercover assignment."

Colt knew that occasionally case officers leveraged other CIA personnel, intelligence analysts, scientists, staff officers, whatever the op called for, even placing them undercover. Usually, those were for very short assignments—a few hours or perhaps just a few meetings—because they weren't clandestine services officers and didn't have the training to know what to do if things went sideways. As far as Colt knew, no one had ever been used in a long-term cover assignment.

"That's what Thorpe did. I don't think it works in this situation." Ford shook his head. He paused for a moment, then said, "Will Thorpe and I used to be pretty good friends. We were assigned to Beijing Station together. This is about four years ago."

"Wait, what?"

"Yeah, he was the FBI's LEGAT in Beijing." LEGAT, or Legal Attaché, was an FBI agent assigned to a US Embassy overseas and was intended to be the senior US law enforcement officer in that country. They handled issues of Americans getting into trouble abroad and bilateral cooperation with the host nation law enforcement activities. Though, in a tacitly hostile environment like present-day China, the LEGAT's role was largely a counterintelligence one.

"Now, you spend enough time in operations and you can figure out who the climbers are, the politicians, the ambitious ones. That's not necessarily a bad thing; sometimes it can work out in your favor if you play it right. I knew Thorpe's type. Still liked him and I'll say this, he was a good G-Man. I had a guy who would slip American whiskey into the diplomatic pouches for us because Chinese booze is unregulated and terrifying. Thorpe and I got to be pretty good friends. We'd usually close down the work day with a bourbon and just shoot the shit. I was Deputy Chief of Station and mostly doing cables, supervising the case officers, stuff like that. Anyway, I'd been cultivating this asset I'd first met in Singapore at a trade expo. Chinese aerospace engineer who found himself in a little-known bureau called the Ministry of Technical Cooperation."

"Sounds benign," Colt quipped.

"Yeah, they're all frickin' spies." Ford sipped his coffee. "It doesn't exist anymore, but the intent of the 'Ministry of Technical Cooperation' was to plumb American industry for our secrets under the guise of figuring out how their companies could work with ours. Most of them thought that their job was to establish legitimate business contacts with the West. Though, I will say that the Chinese view espionage differently than we do. They teach their people that it's their patriotic duty to spy on...well, basically everyone."

"I'm familiar."

"It's crazy, right? It's like, a normal thing for them. Anyway, I'd been working on this asset, Xiao, for about three years. Whenever he traveled to Singapore, he would meet with his good friend Connor Burke, a lowly arms control officer with the State Department."

"Your cover."

Ford nodded. "So, he'd fly into Singapore—ever been there? Fun town. He'd fly in and we would get a beer. And he becomes this gold mine of information. He's probably been told that his job was to make connections with American businessmen and government officials like me, so he's only too happy to talk. Eventually, Xiao gets promoted into a mid-senior-level position in the Ministry."

"So what happened?"

Ford said, "By now we've figured out that MTC is effectively a front for State Security but not even the MTC's *employees* know that. Xiao's job is now to read the intelligence they were getting from the US aerospace industry and identify ways that the Chinese military and aerospace firms could exploit it. Essentially, he was performing technical analysis for Chinese espionage operations."

"How'd you find all of this out?"

"Xiao told me," Ford said flatly. "I'd transferred to Beijing Station and kept running Xiao as an asset. This guy was completely guileless. When he still thought I worked for the State Department, he was sharing all this stuff with me because that was the chip he had to trade. See Xiao, he wanted to move to the States, of all reasons, because he wanted to work for NASA. It had nothing to do with patriotism or spying for the motherland, he just honestly wanted to work for NASA and build experimental airplanes. 'For the benefit of all,'" Ford said, quoting the NASA motto. "By this time, China was on an unprecedented technological run, but there was still this view that they were playing catch-up with the West. Xiao just wanted to work for us and do cool engineering. But"—Ford rolled his hand—"because of his position now as part of the Chinese intelligence apparatus, the Chinese government denied his visa requests. Anyway, through Xiao we're able to learn that the Chinese have a source inside the F-35 program. Xiao's job was to translate that material and figure out what they could use. There are hundreds of Chinese engineers working on this problem, if not thousands, but Xiao's specific assignment was to lead the team to reverse-engineer the low observability." Ford waved his fingers. "All the sciencey shit that makes it practically invisible on radar. So, one night over drinks, I share with Thorpe that my source is telling me we might have a leak in the F-35 program."

"You shared that?" Colt asked.

"The FBI has the lead on counterintelligence, as you know, so it was the type of thing we would share, yes." Ford's face darkened. "But being the career-minded guy he is, Thorpe gets a hard-on for this Chinese source inside our F-35 program. And his superiors in Washington are *really* anxious. They want to move fast. I briefed the Chief of Station and he agreed to bring Thorpe in on the operation. The plan is for Xiao to identify the mole. See, we didn't know if they were an industry person or, God forbid, they were in one of the DoD's program offices. And yes, the CHICOMs probably had many sources inside the F-35 program, but whoever they had was getting really rich R&D shit and we wanted to close that down."

"And in exchange, Xiao gets to defect to the US and a job at NASA?"

"You got it," Ford said, nodding. "There was no chance in hell we were letting that guy within a hundred miles of JSC, but I had no problem letting him think it. So, yeah, that was the plan. But Xiao is also a fifty-year-old engineer with a wife and two kids in high school. He's a spy, but not a very good one."

"I don't follow." Colt raised his eyebrows.

"He was great at relaying what he was receiving but I had a lot of concerns about his ability to actively collect. And that's when Thorpe and I started having problems."

"Like what?"

"The plan called for Xiao to help us identify where the F-35 source was located. Based on the intel, we theorized it had to be Lockheed or the program office. We knew Xiao's boss at MTC was an officer with the Ministry of State Security's Third Bureau, the Political, Scientific and Economic Division. CIA surmised that he would have access to the raw collection material that was then scrubbed and parsed out to MTC engineers. So Xiao would put in the requests for information, and his MSS boss would act as the filter between the US-based mole and the Chinese engineers. This filter effect would prevent us from turning an engineer and using their questions to do exactly what we were trying to do—sniff out our F-35 mole."

Colt said, "So you needed Xiao to bypass his boss. To ask the questions directly."

Ford nodded. "Right. We needed to ask the right questions to narrow down what this Chinese agent had access to. So I told Xiao what we needed him to do. It involved gaining access to a highly secure section of his building at night using a fake credential we made, and then accessing an air-gapped government computer while we killed the security cameras. Xiao would install a special software program that the NSA created, giving us access to raw intel stream on the air-gapped computer. But this process would require him to do this multiple times for collection and updates to our information requests. The data on the computer would change depending on who logged in. If Xiao logged in with our credentials, the NSA program would let him see the unfiltered raw data. If anyone else logged in, it would create a filter so that our queries weren't mentioned."

"This sounds high risk."

"It was. High risk, high reward. Xiao was terrified. He didn't think he could do it without getting caught. The guy's hands shook uncontrollably when he talked about it. You've worked agents before, right?"

"Yes," Colt replied.

"You can ask different things of different people. Depending on their personality, skill level, occupation, etcetera. Right?"

"Sure."

"Well I could tell immediately that Xiao was not capable of doing what we were asking. So, I went to Thorpe. Told him we'd have to take a different approach. I offered to have Xiao tee up another asset for us. But Xiao wasn't going to be able to execute the mission as drawn up. I can't ask my agent to risk this much and try to do something he probably isn't capable of doing."

Ford's whole demeanor had changed. He obviously didn't like talking about this. "I still remember Thorpe's response. The guy looked me in the eyes and said, 'That's the *job*.'"

"He said that?"

"Yeah. Like he knows."

Ford drained his coffee cup and told the story of what happened next. Colt listened with the rapt attention of one who's watching a tragedy, already knows the ending, but can't take their eyes off the screen. Ford tried to make one more attempt to convince Thorpe that Xiao was not capable of what they were asking. But Thorpe couldn't be dissuaded and had the full force of FBI Washington at his back.

"A case officer's first duty is to their agent. It's our sacred charge," Ford said. "I went to my station chief. He commiserated with me, but he was feeling the pressure too and gave me some spiel about sometimes it's mission first. So I pressed ahead. I prepared Xiao as best as I could and dangled the carrot again. Told him that this was his ticket into the United States. Do this for a few weeks until we get what we need and his whole family would be on a plane to LAX and a new life. Told him that NASA might even be in the cards."

"MSS counterintelligence got him," Colt said evenly.

Ford nodded, looking at the floor. "What we didn't appreciate at the time was the extent to which Xiao's exceptionally poor tradecraft had put him on the MSS radar. He was too overt, and he got their attention. CI guys were all over him. Last time I saw him was on a bench at Houhai Park, looking at the lake. He was probably fucked at that point anyway, but I'd handed him the hack and he was done. In a top-tier denied area like China, the rule is that for every two assholes in black suits you see, there's forty surveillance assets you don't. I thought we were black, but you never really *know*. State Security picked Xiao up after our meeting that night. I didn't know it until he missed his next check-in. I was about to go to his house when the news broke. 'Ministry of Trade Cooperation employee arrested for espionage.'"

"I'm sorry, Fred. I've been there, and it sucks."

Ford looked up at that. "Yeah. Then you know. It's about probabilities. You play this game long enough against elite-level opponents, and chances are you're going to lose an asset. It's almost inevitable. Maybe they get a quick execution. Then you have a drink on the anniversary of their death, try to look out for their kids somehow. But a little closure at least. Or...maybe they're sentenced to life in Qincheng Prison. And nothing you do can clear your conscience."

Ford rubbed the bridge of his nose and fell silent.

Colt spent ten years under a nonofficial cover. He guessed that he had more time undercover than almost anyone operating in the clandestine service today. He had experience running agents and had even recruited an SVR officer. He'd watched that woman get gunned down in the street because Russian intelligence had found out she was working for the Americans.

Ford said, "Any time an agent gets caught, there is a shitstorm back stateside. The first thing Langley does is have a bunch of people that haven't been in the field in ten years start second-guessing everything you did. Thorpe sold me out to cover his own ass. His official statement in the after-action report was that he'd offered his professional advice during the planning stages and I'd ignored him. At this point, I knew I was fucked, so I stuck to my guns and said Thorpe pushed me into a collection attempt that wasn't there with an asset who wasn't capable of it. I didn't have a paper trail backing me up, there was no official record that I disagreed with him previously, so it looked like CYA musical chairs and I was the one standing when the music stopped. Objective lesson, Colt: when you disagree with your boss, write shit down. But the worst part was, my Chief of Station didn't back me. Didn't even put in a word. They said I 'exercised poor tradecraft.' I got a tour curtailment and was sent back here to work the China desk. Word was, they expected me to park myself somewhere and retire. I was about to, but Wilcox talked me out of it. We served in Afghanistan together in '02. I was on his team, buying off Northern Alliance fighters. He convinced me to stick around, said he had something planned and wanted me on it. Here we are."

Ford studied his empty mug for a time. "The coffee down here is shit."

They stayed silent for a moment, until Ford's computer chimed. Colt saw Ford's expression transform as he scanned the screen.

"What is it?"

"Looks like my contact at Cornell has a few names for us to check out." He re-scanned the email and then looked up at Colt. "Wanna take a trip to the Finger Lakes and find us an AI expert we can also train to be a covert agent and insert into one of the world's most capable private security firms in less than ninety days?"

Colt half turned his head. "Uh..."

"I'll take that as an enthusiastic yes."

8

Ithaca, New York

Colt followed Ford through the labyrinthine maze of the Cornell University spring College of Engineering job fair. They were in a massive field house filled with booths and banners identifying the myriad companies. Colt scanned the area as they walked, making note of the companies and faces present. Students stood in lines ten to twenty deep for the big-name firms like Google, Tesla, Apple, SpaceX, and Amazon.

"This is us," Ford said, walking to their table and hanging his coat over the metal folding chair behind it. Their corporate banner was draped over the table, a blue-and-white stylized logo with the words "Autonomous Systems" in a modern-looking font.

"'Take the next leap in artificial intelligence,'" Colt said, quoting the tagline underneath the banner. He had to hand it to the logistics guys. They were good at what they did. "Autonomous Systems" was a front, created specifically for this operation. They had an address in Cambridge, Massachusetts, a website, a vision statement, and fake bios for the fake founders. They even had a phone number that, if anyone called during business hours, would be answered by a receptionist named Janice. She would dutifully take down messages and could satisfactorily answer basic administrative questions. Her actual name was Cynthia Kim, a staff operations officer at Langley.

Ford and Colt were given briefings to backstop their legends as Autonomous Systems employees. Colt was pretending to be an HR manager, while Ford played a business development role.

Professor Jonathan Turner—Ford's contact—had given them a red-and-white folder with the Cornell seal emblazoned on the cover. The folder contained the names of twenty students he thought would be ideal candidates, given the requisite skill set Ford had described. Turner recruited for CIA on a periodic basis, identifying promising engineers he thought would make candidates for the Agency's Science and Technology Division. Turner had a security clearance and worked for S&T many years ago. He knew enough not to ask Ford too many questions about this current recruitment.

Ford thumbed through the folder, looking over the candidates. Colt continued to scan the crowd, a combination of training and habit. When he saw Ford pulling a handful of resumes from the folder, he asked, "Anyone look good?"

"There's a few here," Ford said in his usual clipped tone. "They all look like great engineers but I'm not sure they're what *we* want."

Ford handed him the stack and Colt started leafing through it, scanning the resumes. Like most jobs, you couldn't tell who would succeed in the Clandestine Service by simply looking at a resume. But there were patterns. The CIA looked for students who excelled in multiple disciplines. Did they make the honor roll and play a varsity sport in college?

Develop skills outside of academic studies? Was there a track record of independence? Evidence of critical thinking? Some of the candidates on this list had held internships with the top tech companies. They were attractive because many of those organizations were known for incorporating a variety of psychological and behavioral factors into their screening process on top of the technical aptitude. Techniques that were not unlike the Agency's own initial vetting process. He saw a few had internships or studies abroad—also valuable experience for a clandestine officer.

Turner arrived with coffees, handing them out to both men. "Good morning, gentlemen," he said cheerily.

He looked like a professor. Navy chinos, an off-white sweater, and a herringbone blazer. Turner had white hair and a thick but well-trimmed beard. He wore wireframe glasses and was just slightly overweight.

"I see you've already found some prospects," Turner said, looking down at the stack in Ford's hand.

"You certainly have some impressive students, Professor Turner." Colt handed the CV that he'd placed at the top of the stack to the professor. "Let's get started."

The next several hours were like speed dating with a bunch of ultra-smart overachievers. Some of them were able to hold a conversation. Others could barely hold eye contact. Ford and Colt had two semi-private sections behind their table, and they took turns doing rapid-fire interviews with each one, spending about twenty minutes with each candidate.

By four p.m. the lines were diminishing, the crowd dying down. No one had approached their table in the last fifteen minutes, and Colt had just interviewed the last candidate on Professor Turner's list. He sat down next to Ford behind their table.

Ford said, "So? Any keepers?"

Colt squirmed. "I don't know, man. If you made me pick one...maybe? They were all very impressive, don't get me wrong. Exceptional technologists, that's for sure. These guys have the right AI skill sets. One girl I met was a quantum computing prodigy, from the sound of it. They're almost all going to end up at a top tech company, I think."

"But that's not why you have that tone in your voice," Ford said, eyeing him.

Colt shook his head. He lowered his voice. "It's the X-factor that's missing. These weren't the types of people we would recruit to be case officers. And what we're asking this person to be able to do, in a short time..."

Ford nodded. "I know. I was thinking the same thing. Maybe what we're looking for doesn't exist."

Just then some commotion caught their attention near the door. A woman dressed like a job candidate was arguing with a person holding a clipboard. Colt saw that she wore a blue jacket over her business attire. The blue logo on her chest looked like an Air Force symbol.

"She doesn't look happy," Ford said.

Colt saw Professor Turner nearby and called him over. "Professor, who's that woman?"

Professor Turner looked over at the door where the woman was arguing with the administrator.

"Ahh yes, Nadia. Nadia Blackmon. I don't think she's supposed to be allowed in here today. Apologies that you have to see this..."

"Who is she?"

The professor said, "Nadia is a graduate student. But she has had some trouble adjusting to the academic lifestyle. I don't know if she'll make it through the program."

"Do you have a resume I could see?" Colt asked.

"For who, Nadia?" Professor Turner said. "I don't think she would be a good fit. Very different sort than the others I've sent your way in the past..."

Ford was looking at her now. The woman had her arms folded across her chest as she waited for the job fair administrator to finish speaking. He said, "If it's all the same, do you have her resume?"

Professor Turner made a face. "One moment." He walked over to Nadia and the man holding a clipboard. After he spoke to them, Nadia handed the professor a few pieces of paper, which he brought over to Colt and Ford's booth. Nadia watched with curiosity.

The two CIA officers scanned her resume. A graduate student specializing in machine learning, and a former US Air Force officer. Nadia graduated from the Air Force Academy with a degree in data science and had completed an internship on a DARPA program focusing on cyber warfare. She became a Cyber Operations Officer upon graduation and spent the next eight years attached to intelligence and special operations units.

"Professor, this candidate looks promising," Ford said, his voice clipped. "Why isn't she being let into the job fair?"

"She has a bit of an issue with authority. There was an incident with a professor in her program. Nothing was proven, but given her background she seemed the most likely culprit. She denied it, of course, as did her classmates."

Now Colt was getting impatient. "Professor, what happened?"

"Dr. Rathbun is a tenured professor with us here. He...he's an exceptional computer scientist, but a touch rough around the edges. Old-fashioned. And perhaps in today's parlance, a tad sexist. I don't know how it began, but as I understand it, Nadia challenged him."

"Challenged him?"

"There was some conversation about the GI bill and the professor feeling like those who came here using it diluted the talent pool. Then Nadia pointed out that she was attending by using the GI bill and the professor expressed surprise that she had access to the same benefits because...well, he said something to the effect of her military service not being on the same level as her male counterparts."

Colt said, "Oh shit. Them's fightin' words where I come from."

Ford smiled. "She didn't take that well."

"No. Nadia is quite a gifted student. From what I was told, she began challenging the professor on a point in a lecture on large data structures that he had gotten wrong...I suspect he was embarrassed at being corrected, then he said something to the effect of women being more courteous in his day." Professor Turner sighed. "And *that's* when the trouble began..."

Colt said, "What trouble?"

"Professor Rathbun claimed his phone had been hacked."

"Hacked," Colt said skeptically.

"Yes. Apparently, whenever Rathbun approached a woman, his phone made some, ah, embarrassing noises."

"What kind of noises?"

"Um. Flatulence, I believe," Turner said, clearly embarrassed.

Colt observed a glimmer of amusement in Ford's eyes, but both men kept a straight face.

Turner went on. "Rathbun said it was her, demanded she be expelled, but the ethics committee interviewed her and every member of her class and no one would admit to knowledge of the event. Rathbun, however, was responsible for selecting our job fair candidates today and Nadia, well, she wasn't placed."

"So, Rathbun assumed it was her even though it was never officially proven and blackballed her from an internship?" Colt asked.

"That's correct. I'm not sure she's the right fit for you people ..."

Colt shot a sidelong glance to Ford. "We'd like to speak with her anyway."

Professor Turner raised his eyebrows. "Well. It's your decision."

Professor Turner quietly ushered Nadia over to Colt and Ford's table.

Colt put her at about five foot eight, dark hair cut above the shoulders, dark eyes. She was very fit-looking. The look in her eye gave Colt the impression that she was an intense competitor. From her attire, Colt saw that she knew how to dress for an interview.

"I'm Peter Bishop," Ford said, using his Agency-assigned cover for this assignment, "and this is my colleague, Tom Reed."

Ford invited her to sit across the table from them and the questions began. They rapid-fired a list of questions meant to test her knowledge of artificial intelligence. The interview was being recorded. Colt would have experts check her answers later, but he knew enough about the subject, and saw from her confidence that she was providing satisfactory answers.

"So you were a division one athlete?"

"Yes, sir, that is correct. Soccer at Air Force."

"You still play?"

"I play on some adult leagues. But I have switched to mini-triathlons for my competitive fix."

"Impressive," said Colt. "I see you went into cyber after the Air Force Academy? Why did you choose that field?"

"At the Air Force Academy, if you are a senior and they find out you don't want to be a pilot, they make you sit down with this O-6—sorry, that's a colonel—and explain to him why you feel that way. Then you have to spend another twenty minutes letting him try to talk you into being a pilot. Maybe that's changing with all of the drones nowadays. But for me, it was a waste of time. I was a computer science major and I wanted to work in that area. That's the next battlefield, you know?"

Colt watched Ford suppress a grin.

Colt said, "And did you like cyber operations?"

Nadia shook her head. "Unfortunately, I found out that the services are way behind. The cyber ops career field used to be called 'communications officer' and it was just rebranding. Most of the time, you're just managing base comms. I wanted to play on offense, but that wasn't the real job. I did get selected for JSCE, though, and that was cool. Got to jump out of airplanes."

"What's JCSE?" Colt remembered from his time in the Navy that service members had so many acronyms to contend with that they rarely used the long form, even when speaking with the uninitiated. CIA was the same way.

"Joint Communication Support Element. It's a rapid deployment comm unit that sets up radio, telephone satcom, whatever, anywhere in the world on a moment's notice. Airborne. Reported directly into the Joint Chiefs. We did a lot of mission support for special ops and missions like that. It was really exciting."

"Why did you decide to get out?"

"It had been eight years at that point. And like I said, the military isn't exactly cutting-edge in tech. I think AI is fascinating and want to work in that area. We're only scratching the surface of what computers can do. The DoD has an 'AI working group.' But good luck with that."

Colt smiled. "I think it's hard for government to stay current, given all the rules around acquisition and the like. Our firm has some government funding so we're pretty familiar with the frustration that comes with it. Would you consider working with government again?"

"Oh yeah. Don't get me wrong, innovation is happening. I got to participate in a DARPA project when I was at the Academy and that was really cool. I know all about the government-funded think tanks, I just didn't think the military was keeping pace. I applied to some post-graduate fellowships and a few positions with government agencies." Nadia paused. "I didn't hear back, though."

They spoke for another fifteen minutes and Nadia's answers far exceeded their expectations. She was quick on her feet, and showed technical mastery of machine learning better than her peers in the prestigious graduate program.

Colt looked up and saw Professor Turner hovering over Nadia's shoulder, indicating that their time was up. He stood and extended a hand. "Thank you for speaking with us today, Nadia. It looks like our time is about up..." Colt and Ford exchanged a glance. Colt nodded.

Ford said, "Nadia, we would like to speak with you again and our position is an immediate need. Apologies for the short notice, but what are your plans tomorrow morning?"

Colt and Ford sat at a long conference table near a window overlooking Cayuga Lake. The sky was dark and brooding and spoke of a spring storm that was going to blanket Ithaca in wet snow. Colt was dressed casually in a sweater, jeans, and a blazer, while Ford was slightly more dressed with chinos and a sport coat. They were in an office space they'd rented out for the day. One of the logistics guys had set this up and swept the room for listening devices before Colt and Ford moved in. He was waiting out front, posing as the front desk guy.

At exactly eleven-thirty, he led Nadia in.

Colt and Ford stood as she entered. The logistics guy asked if she wanted anything to drink; when she declined, he said he'd be out front if they needed anything.

"Thanks for coming back to meet us," Ford said.

"How come this is off campus?" Nadia asked.

"We'll get to that. But first, I wanted to ask a little more about your military service. Can you tell me why you chose to join?"

"Sure," she said. Colt could see the curiosity in her eyes. It wasn't a line of questioning that she expected. "I wanted to serve. My dad was Air Force. He flew F 16s in the first Gulf War. He had to get out after the war because of the RIF and went to fly for the airlines, but stayed in the reserves. I guess it was in my blood. I picked cyber, though, because I really think that's where the next fight is going to be. My dad and I argue about this all the time. My internship at DARPA had an enormous impact on me. One of the guys there told me that the Chinese have a million hackers targeting US civilians. The Chinese government actually has a help desk that they can call." She pantomimed picking up a phone. When she spoke, her voice was equal parts comic and sarcastic. "Yes, I can't get into Bank of America, do you have an exploit I can use? Oh, thank you." Nadia shook her head. "That was ten years ago. Think about what they can do today. We're going to get our asses handed to us and we are so far behind." Nadia looked away then, ashamed at the outburst. "Sorry."

"No, that's good," Colt said reassuringly. "I can see that you're really passionate about this sort of thing. And you're right, we are going to get our asses handed to us if we don't do something about it. To your point, we have a near-term threat with ransomware and the like coming out of Eastern Europe and Russia. That works because most civilians don't understand tech and it's the current, proximate threat, but not the strategic one. People are worried about the carjacker in their neighborhood but they're ignoring the serial killer."

"That's a comforting thought."

"You mentioned that the next battle would be a digital one," Ford said. "Can you tell us a little more about what you mean by that?"

"Sure," Nadia said, drawing out the word.

Colt could read in her eyes that she was stalling to think of the answer. She also had no idea what she was doing in this room.

"The Russians have already shown that they can threaten our critical infrastructure by shutting down pipelines. The computer systems that run most of our electrical grids were designed in the nineties and haven't been markedly improved since. A military base is a hard target, right, but they get power from the public utilities. Overseas it's not much better, maybe worse. What if the Russians started targeting the power grids supporting our bases in Europe? They could be on the German border in no time, and no one could do anything about it. They shut down power on the eastern seaboard—how many bases do we have in Florida, the Carolinas, and Virginia? Now we don't have backup. Cyber is the ultimate force multiplier. The Russian conventional forces are garbage, but their asymmetric capabilities and trade craft are scary good. And—" Nadia caught herself. "You guys still haven't told me much about what your company does."

Colt smiled. "Well, let me just say that our company shares a lot of the same concerns you do. We think you are correct that the next conflict will be a digital one. In many ways, it's happening right now. And you are probably right in your conclusion that the US is behind the power curve. AI changes everything. But its effect isn't like what you see in the movies. We're not talking about building Terminators. Well, not yet. But modern organizations —both government and private— are now training machines to perform human tasks at machine speed. If the Chinese government had a million civilian hackers ten years ago, it could be billions today. But these hackers never sleep, eat, or slow down. They just relentlessly poke the virtual fences looking for holes. They scrape social media, break into our cellular networks, and now every American with a MAC address can be tracked. Air traffic control isn't safe. Neither are the power grids or the ports. And the rate of progress is getting steeper. Imagine a machine that could accurately parse and contextualize every piece of open-source intelligence in the world. Warfare is about creating the conditions that allow you to strike at the time and place of your choosing. We believe that is exactly what our adversaries intend to do."

"I'm sorry. What exactly does your company do?" Nadia asked.

"We don't call it 'the Company' much anymore," Ford said. "Although some of the older hats still do."

Nadia frowned, turning her head. Then her eyes lit up. "You guys are CIA? Are you recruiting for black hats? Offensive cyber ops? Like what we did to Iran's reactor?" Then she added, "I mean...allegedly."

"No," Colt said. "If that's where you want to be, we can

help make it happen. But we're here about something different in the short term. We are recruiting for an operational role within the Clandestine Service."

Nadia cocked her head, thinking. After a moment, she said, "Is it dangerous?"

"Hell yes," Ford said.

"I think what my colleague means to say," Colt told her, "is that all intelligence work, by definition, contains an element of danger. However, you will be trained. This is a special assignment. It's not like you'll be recruiting agents in Moscow, but..."

"Wait. You want me to be...like...an *agent*?"

"Agents are the foreign assets we recruit to betray their government," Colt deadpanned. "No, this is a different type of role. We would be placing you inside a commercial company as an officer of the CIA under a non-official cover. This is a program the CIA has run for decades that allows us to collect various types of information. Primarily economic intelligence. We will help you land the right job where you will periodically report on what you learn."

Ford added, "We will make sure it's a job where you get to continue your research into artificial intelligence. More importantly, you will provide an invaluable service to your country."

"Nadia, it's a lot to think about," Colt said. "This would be a major life change for you. You could not tell anyone that you worked for CIA, not even your parents. I see you aren't wearing a ring. Do you have a significant other?"

"No."

"Well, if you meet someone and get married during this assignment, we have ways of handling that."

"Cyanide pills for my dates?" she quipped.

"I'm starting to like her," Ford said.

Colt gave a thin smile. "Nadia, you are an independent,

critical thinker. You've served your country and care about its future. You possess a selfless dedication to duty. No doubt this was instilled in you during your military experience. And you have a high tolerance for operational pressure. You are the type of person we are looking for."

Nadia nodded. "Thank you."

Colt took a breath. "The question you need to answer for yourself is whether you have the ability and desire to manage that pressure daily during an assignment that could last years. It is mentally and psychologically challenging. You would be operating on your own, observing and reporting on things around you. Never letting yourself get attached to the people around you. It is very tough. Trust me."

"You've done this type of work?"

Colt said, "I can tell you that it is extremely rewarding to make this type of contribution. And you bring authenticity to the role. I can teach someone how to pretend to be a diplomat. I can't teach someone how to be an expert in artificial intelligence. We need someone with that type of expertise."

Nadia said, "I mean, it sounds fascinating. But it's a lot. Normally, this is the kind of thing I'd bounce off my dad, but I guess that's kind of out of the question."

Colt nodded knowingly. This was a conversation he'd had himself ten years ago. He knew exactly what was going through her mind right now. He also knew there was no way she could fully appreciate the gravity of the decision she was making. They didn't give her enough information to do that.

"How long do I have to decide?"

"Take the weekend to think about it," Ford said. "It's a big decision. One that we have both made, so we understand what might be going through your head right now. Take your time, be sure."

Ford stood, indicating that the meeting was over. He

handed her a blank business card. It had no agency seal or names. Just an 800 number written in blue pen. "If you decide you're interested, call this number within the next week."

"Who do I ask for?"

"We'll know it's you." Ford smiled.

"Thanks for your time, Nadia," Colt said.

The guy from logistics was waiting at the door to escort Nadia out.

"What do you think?" Ford asked.

"On paper, I think she's a lock." Colt watched the dark clouds over the lake and hoped they made their flight to Dulles before they opened up.

"But?"

"I think she's got the right building blocks, but it's impossible to tell if she can handle it."

Ford said, "You can never know. All you can do is see if they have the ingredients, and then we place our bet. Does she have the right ingredients?"

"Military experience. Leadership. Competitive spirit. She's a patriot. She's selfless. And she's got the AI expertise we're looking for. I'm not sure we'll find anyone better."

"Then that's the best we can do," Ford said.

Colt nodded. "Think she'll say yes?"

"Yup."

"How do you know?"

Ford shrugged. "She had that glimmer in her eye. Like she found a new game to play and wanted to see if she could win."

Ford was right. When they landed at Dulles a few hours later, he checked his voicemail. Nadia had called the number and left a message.

She was in.

9

Langley, Virginia

The next day, both Colt and Ford were back in the office, meeting with Thorpe and other members of the NTCU team.

"As I was saying," Colt sighed, "the reason it won't work is that engineering interviews are technical. They don't just bull shit their way past some HR stooge, they have demonstrated that they understand these concepts in a practical way. A live coding challenge isn't uncommon. They are going to be heavily scrutinized by other engineers and that's just to get in the door. We also need them to evaluate the level of technological advancement once they're in. That's something that an ops officer probably can't do. The tech advances too quickly now. Even if we had an operations officer with a computer science or engineering background, they'd probably be too far removed from current technology to be authentic or credible."

Thorpe closed his eyes and nodded. Colt could read in his body language that he was coming around.

"I get it," Thorpe said. "But I need you both to understand that there is a timetable. The intelligence community is incredibly concerned about how quickly the Hawkinsons are advancing this tech business of theirs. We assume they stole significant amounts of Pax AI research in that operation. The NSC has been briefed on STONEBRIDGE and agree that this operation cannot be pushed back. Now that the Israelis are involved, everyone is on high alert. We cannot let them beat us to the punch here."

"Wish we knew that in China," Ford said acidly.

Colt jumped in before Thorpe had the chance to argue back. "We feel strongly about the person we've identified and plan to train as much and as soon as possible."

"What if we changed the mission profile? Could we insert someone who wasn't an engineer and didn't have to pass for one?" This was Gretchen Harlowe, Thorpe's deputy from the FBI side of the unit. "Couldn't we insert an exploit into their systems or perhaps a covert transmitter once we're inside?"

Colt was baffled and had to draw on his best acting skills to retain his blank facial expression. This was the kind of day-one idea that would have been discussed and thrown out before STONEBRIDGE was even greenlit. Thorpe didn't correct her or say anything else, so Colt assumed he was being tested. His next thought was whether this was something Thorpe and Harlowe planned in advance.

"The Hawkinsons will have some of the best cybersecurity in the industry. Research data will be isolated offline and protected with multifactor authentication that most likely has a biometric component that can be immediately verified to authorized personnel. They will have post-intrusion detection software that can tell them not only that an exploit has been injected, but precisely what it's doing. I'll assume that a transmitter was ruled out in the planning stages because the target will have technical countermeasures that render it useless. Does that answer your question?"

"It does, thank you." Harlowe gave him a practiced smile that wasn't *quite* condescending.

Colt studied the room. Both Thorpe and Harlowe had blank, tired expressions. He saw nods from the other agency member, Stan Baker, who was from S&T and acting as a technical advisor on the operation. *Might speak up once in a while*, Colt thought.

Thorpe spoke next. "So, what do you propose?"

"Hawk Technologies' acquisition trends over the last four months suggest they are attempting to grow in facial recognition, deep learning, and social intelligence. They've made three attempts to buy companies specializing in the latter space and have been unsuccessful."

"What's social intelligence?"

"It's a subset of AI," Baker said, finally jumping in. "It focuses on simulating human emotion. The benign applications are those annoying virtual assistants companies use to replace call centers, but there are some scary implications like being able to predict and perhaps influence behaviors in people."

"So, what are you proposing exactly?" Thorpe said.

Colt studied the man for a moment. The National Technical Counterintelligence Unit was an interagency outfit primarily staffed by CIA and FBI personnel. The FBI had operational control because they were the lead agency for counterintelligence, but this phase of STONEBRIDGE was a clandestine operation and therefore fell entirely within CIA's purview. Could Thorpe overrule them? Possibly, but he would have to burn significant political capital to do it and would likely put himself at odds with Director Wilcox, who by-name-requested both Colt and Ford for this assignment. Colt already knew that Thorpe was going to object to his proposal, if for no other reason than because Fred Ford was a part of it, but he also knew that the objection might not go any further than this room.

"We have two viable ways to insert an operative into Hawk Technologies given the timelines we have to work with," Colt began. "The first is we plant someone in a company that Hawk Technologies is already trying to acquire. The due diligence on an M&A activity typically takes eight to twelve months, so we need to find someone they're already looking at. The second option is we plant our person directly in Hawk Technologies' hiring pipeline."

"How would we do that?" asked Harlowe.

"We'd need to manipulate their HR system so that candidate makes it all the way through. They'd still have to pass the interview process. I think the former has a higher degree of success and is easier to hide the asset."

Thorpe pushed back from the table, signaling that the meeting was over. The others around the table stood. "Gentlemen, you already know my thoughts on this. I don't think there's enough time to recruit and train someone for what we need."

He patted the air softly with his right hand. "I will grant you that you've convinced me that we can't make someone an expert in this stuff, but I just don't see how you'll be ready in time. We don't have any flexibility on the dates. The NSC Principles Committee is expecting results quickly. STONEBRIDGE goes as planned."

And with that, the meeting was over. The room started clearing.

"Colt, a word, please," Thorpe said.

"I'll catch up with you," Colt told Ford. The older officer's expression was inscrutable.

Thorpe waited until the door closed and they were alone.

"You seem like a sharp officer and I think you know your

stuff. Certainly better than I do. I know firsthand that Director Wilcox puts a lot of faith in you."

"Thank you," Colt said, noncommittal. "That's very generous."

"A word of advice. Be careful how closely you hitch your wagon to Fred Ford. He's going to push it too far. He can't help himself. When he implodes, and he will, you don't want to be caught in the blast radius. I'd hate to see him ruin your career too." Thorpe gave him a wan smile and clapped him on the shoulder. "Have a good night." And he left.

Colt stood in the empty conference room for a moment.

Was this just a petty bureaucrat dragging a rival through the mud, or was there something Ford hadn't told him yet?

When Colt emerged from the conference room, he saw Ford and Thorpe standing in the common area, both looking at him expectantly.

"What is it?" he asked.

"We needed to be in the director's conference room three minutes ago."

"What's going on?" Colt said, already moving.

"We'll find out when we get there," Ford said. "Whatever it is, they aren't talking about it over the phone."

Minutes later they were being ushered into the small, wood-paneled conference room on the seventh floor. Two people were already inside, seated near the head of the table and looking pensive. If Colt were meeting the deputy director for the first time instead of his old boss and handler, he'd probably feel the same. The woman was young—Colt placed her in her early thirties—blonde with a short ponytail, pert nose, and a slightly pouting expression that he chalked up to nerves.

She wore a light blue blouse and black skirt. The man was older, mid-forties, hawkish nose and salt-and-pepper hair.

Colt smiled and greeted them as he sat down beside Ford, while Thorpe took a seat farther down the table, at the opposite end of where Deputy Director Wilcox would likely be.

Ford asked the room, "Anybody know what this august forum is about?"

"Don Walters, Russia section."

"Heather Freely," the woman said.

"Russia section?" Ford repeated. "Well you guys always have good news."

The conference room's interior door opened and Deputy Director Wilcox walked in with the Deputy Director for Intelligence, Michael Webb. Webb led the Agency's analysts, taking the raw material collected by case officers or the Agency's numerous technical assets and turning that into finished intelligence. Prior to being named DDI, Webb led the president's daily briefer team. He was tall, slightly stooped, early fifties, and had black hair and was a little thick around the middle.

"Thanks for coming up here on such short notice," Wilcox said. "I know it's getting to be the end of day."

Colt smiled, but inwardly he thought sadly that Wilcox thanking people for attending a meeting they were summoned to meant his transformation into a seventh-floor bureaucrat was now complete.

"Let's get started." Wilcox went around the room and introduced everyone, pausing when he got to Thorpe. "Heather and Don, this is Will Thorpe with FBI. Will heads the National Technical Counterintelligence Unit, headquartered here. This is a typical Agency meeting, one side of the table isn't cleared to know anything about the other side." Sporadic chuckles broke out around the table.

"Understood, thank you, sir," Walters said, smiling. "Gentlemen, this is Heather's show, I'm just here for moral support. Before we begin, this is code word classified intelligence and we rate this source with high confidence. Heather?"

"Thank you." The woman stood and walked to the end of the table with a briefing book in her hand. She gave it to Wilcox and then returned to her place at the front of the room. As she was walking, Walters cued up the slideshow. "Sir, this information is coming from GT-CATALYST, which is our most highly placed source within Russian intelligence. An American HSG employee named Mathew Kirby is attempting to schedule a meeting with a Russian business development analyst. It looks highly suspicious. Date/time TBD, but CATALYST believes soon. We looked back at call records and can corroborate the report. A burner phone contacted the economic affairs section at the Russian embassy to inquire about doing business in Russia. NSA matched the voice signature to Kirby."

"The language they used was very specific," Walters said. "We believe that it was a code sequence."

"Kirby said he worked for an oil and gas company looking for a new play in the Black Sea region and asked to speak with an Anton Nikitin. The Agency has no record of an Anton Nikitin anywhere in the Russian government and subsequent analysis has also come up negative. We believe this was also a codeword to direct them to a specific individual. CATALYST was not privy to the code sequence and is speculating, but said it's consistent with Directorate S protocols. CATALYST also stated that an operations analyst was going to be dispatched from Moscow to meet with Mathew Kirby in person."

Walters chimed in again to add a few more details about how they verified this information with another source one of their case officers was running out of Moscow proper. He reiterated that they had high confidence in the material. Colt saw Webb nod in agreement.

Freely continued. "We can confirm that the 'analyst' being sent from Moscow is this man, Colonel Sergei Petrov."

She advanced a slide showing a man in an SVR uniform on the left side and grainy surveillance photos on the right. "Petrov was the *rezident* at the Russian consulate in Houston. One of the youngest *rezidents* in SVR history and a rising star within Directorate S. He was abruptly recalled two years ago, following the Pax AI incident. Petrov was sent to a posting in Kazakhstan and has been there for the last eighteen months."

Colt felt Wilcox's eyes on him.

Petrov. Holy shit.

He was the Russian intelligence officer responsible for their attempt to steal Pax AI's R&D. He also assassinated Colt's agent right in front of him in the middle of San Francisco.

"Colt, anything you want to add on Colonel Petrov?" Wilcox asked.

"What am I allowed to say?"

"It's relevant to STONEBRIDGE. You can speak candidly," Wilcox said.

Colt straightened in his seat. "Two years ago I recruited an SVR officer operating out of the Houston consulate. She reported to Petrov. From her, we learned that the Russians had a large-scale operation targeting US tech companies. They were specifically looking to make gains in artificial intelligence and had penetrated Pax AI."

"This was the Trinity thing, is that right?" Thorpe asked.

"That's correct," Colt said. "For those not familiar, Trinity is a domestic extremist organization that claimed responsibility for the killing of a Pax AI scientist. We believe that was actually an SVR assassination directed by Colonel Petrov. The SVR figured out there was a leak in the *rezidentura* and traced it to my agent. She was executed just before a scheduled meet. I was there. The Russians used a remotely operated, high-powered rifle fired from an autonomous vehicle."

"Jesus Christ," Ford gasped. "I read about that. That was him?"

"That's what we believe." Colt nodded. He'd replayed that day a hundred times in his head. Svetlana thought she was compromised and was ready to plan her exfil. She would only meet somewhere public, believing that in America there was safety in crowds. Instead, she was killed in broad daylight.

"Petrov is dangerous. He's a throwback, trained in the old KGB model but with a sense of post-Soviet breakup reckless abandon. We think he is, or was, connected with Guy Hawkinson."

"Take a look at this." Freely advanced the slide again. A black-and-white surveillance shot of a white male appeared. Close-cropped dark hair and lantern jaw. "This is Mathew Kirby, the man Petrov is scheduled to meet with." She pointed at the screen. The photo on the right filled in, showing a man in an Army dress uniform—Ranger and Special Forces tabs on the shoulder, Freefall Parachutist Badge, Combat Infantry Badge.

DDI Webb said, "He is employed by the Hawk Security Group. He's in their executive security practice and works directly for Guy Hawkinson. Supposed to be his right hand. They served together for about four years."

"Any idea why Hawkinson would try to meet with the SVR now?" Colt asked, though he believed he already knew the answer.

"We don't know for certain," Freely said.

"Is there any way CATALYST can find that out?" Wilcox asked.

"It's possible, sir, but from what we understand, the SVR

has gone dark on everything about the Mathew Kirby meeting. The last information CATALYST saw was that Petrov is being recalled from Kazakhstan."

"So Petrov will meet with Hawkinson's man?" Wilcox asked.

DDI Webb said, "Or they might just want to question Petrov about it as a former Hawkinson subject matter expert."

Colt's mind raced as he tried to understand the implications.

Wilcox said, "Colt, I see those wheels turning up there. Say what's on your mind, please."

Colt spoke up. "Sir, we think the Hawkinsons may have stolen some of Pax AI's technology, possibly working with Petrov and his SVR team to do it. We know that Petrov was banished to God knows where in Kazakhstan. Not exactly a good career progression after being the highest-ranking SVR officer stationed in the US. That tells me the Russians didn't get what they came for that day."

Ford was nodding. "You are wondering why Guy Hawkinson and his sister didn't end up drinking a Russian Polonium smoothie?"

"Yes. If the Russians knew that Guy Hawkinson had recovered the Pax AI technology and not shared it with them, they would be incredibly pissed."

Wilcox narrowed his eyes. "So, you are saying...the Russians *don't* know that?"

Colt was looking at the images on the screen. Petrov. Guy Hawkinson. His mind was a whirlwind of intel reports on artificial intelligence and double-agents working in Silicon Valley. "Sir, I always had a hard time believing that Guy Hawkinson —a veteran, and a businessman with such close ties to the US military and the Intelligence Community—would work with the Russians, let alone their foreign intelligence service."

Ford said, "People will rationalize a lot if the price is right..."

Colt shook his head. "I've studied the Hawkinsons a lot. If it's his sister, yes. I agree. But Guy Hawkinson, I don't know. I think he meant to screw over Petrov from the beginning. He used Petrov to get Pax AI's IP, and then made it look like it was destroyed in the fire."

DDI Webb said, "Hawkinson Security Group isn't exactly the model of global justice."

Hawk Security Group enjoyed a pretty awful reputation in general. They'd started off providing specialized training for the US military, and it wasn't uncommon to see operators with HSG-branded gear—a stylized hawk clutching crossed swords in its talons, a clear riff on the Special Forces insignia. HSG branched out into private security and executive protection when Iraq started to go south, and by the 2010s they were fielding mercenaries throughout Africa, augmenting America's unacknowledged low-intensive conflicts.

Colt said, "That may be true, but my money is on Guy Hawkinson screwing over the SVR. And if that's true..."

"Then we have an opportunity here," Ford announced to the room.

Colt nodded.

"Are you able to use CATALYST to plant information?" Colt asked.

Freely cast a sidelong glance to Walters. "We haven't tried it yet. I can't guarantee that they'll have contact with Petrov."

"What are you thinking, Colt?" Wilcox asked.

"We don't know why Hawkinson is reaching out to Petrov. Suffice it to say that he wants something, otherwise he wouldn't take the risk. We aren't one hundred percent certain that Guy Hawkinson worked with the SVR to steal Pax AI technology. STONEBRIDGE exists because we want to prove

Hawkinson is connected to the SVR. But what if we can get CATALYST to plant the information that supports our hypothesis? What if we give the Russians evidence that Guy Hawkinson has the Pax AI technology."

The room erupted in conversation. Wilcox fanned the volume down with his hands.

Ford was smiling. "He's right. Based on the way the Russians react, we'll be able to confirm the Hawkinson-Petrov connection. Plus, the disruption we create gives us time to get STONEBRIDGE in play. If Freely and her team can help drive a wedge between Hawkinson and the SVR, that helps STONEBRIDGE."

Wilcox said, "So you would leak evidence that Guy Hawkinson has had the tech this whole time. Any chance this comes back to bite us?"

Walters gave a terse laugh. "I would expect a Russian reprisal, possibly a violent one. But we can leak something in a way that we'll be in the clear."

Wilcox nodded. "Okay, let's run with it."

10

Moscow

Sergei Petrov believed his time had come.

The cable came in overnight, sent to the SVR station at the Russian embassy in Kazakhstan's capital city of Nur-Sultan. He'd been recalled to Moscow. Instructed to report to SVR headquarters immediately.

Never a good sign.

Petrov took a morning Aeroflot flight to Moscow's Domodedovo Airport, the only one of the day. At the Moscow airport, he was met by an SVR major who escorted Petrov to a black sedan idling outside.

The car pulled away from the airport and headed northwest to Yasenevo. Petrov looked out the window during the quiet drive. The sky was the color of wet cement. Wet slush, soaked brown with the road debris, gathered in ugly clumps along the curb.

Soon they drove onto the SVR's sprawling headquarters complex tucked behind walls of pine trees. As the car came to a halt, Petrov tried to make peace with his fate.

Until yesterday, he'd been reporting to the *rezident* in Nur-Sultan, working several operations to gradually degrade the "reforms" undertaken by the Kazakh government. There he was running disinformation campaigns, obstructing journalists, and framing local politicians. Ensuring that Moscow maintained its influence.

Petrov's work there was clearly beneath an officer of his rank. He was a colonel, reporting to another colonel. It was insulting to a man of his capability. But Petrov knew that it was penance. His Pax AI operation in America had caused Russia embarrassment and pain. Agents were exposed and killed. SVR officers and civilian diplomats were expelled. New economic sanctions were leveled against Russia by the US and her western allies.

Petrov had followed orders, attempting to execute a high-risk, high-reward operation that would have given his country a game-changing technology. But he had failed. For the past two years, Petrov thought that he had been lucky...his banishment to Kazakhstan was to be his punishment.

Moscow, whose operational paranoia was eclipsed only by their inferiority complex with the Americans, must have wanted to hide him away until the time was right. Now he would receive his true punishment. His superiors, or perhaps the president himself, had finally decided to make him pay the ultimate price for his failure. All that time he had thought himself spared from this fate...he had been delusional, Petrov now realized. Russian intelligence never forgets.

The major was joined by two armed guards as he escorted Petrov through sparsely decorated hallways of the SVR headquarters. How many officers had he known whose careers ended this way? A summons to a "conference room" or an "office" only to find themselves in an empty cellar room, a pistol barrel pointed to the back of their ear...

Petrov kept replaying the details of the Pax AI operation in his head. Thinking about what he could have done differently. Wondering what decision he could have made to change his fate.

The major continued leading him through a labyrinthine of corridors until they reached an elevator and got in. The major pressed the button. Up? That was strange, Petrov thought. His stomach fluttered as they rose to the top floor.

Here the walls and furniture became increasingly adorned with pictures of the heroes of the Russian Federation, which was, today, the USSR in nearly everything but name. Their walk, as wordless as the drive in from Domodedovo, ended at a huge set of double doors.

This was confusing. Petrov would have expected the basement.

The major turned to face him. "Good luck, Colonel." The young man spoke without emotion. He nodded once and departed down the hallway.

Petrov was alone.

He narrowed his eyes and set his chin, carrying his head high and proud, like a true Russian. He'd meet his fate like an officer, by God. Petrov pulled the handle and opened the door. He stepped through the threshold.

The room was large, with high ceilings and wood panels on three sides. Two-story windows comprised the wall to his left. A long wooden table in the center sat beneath a massive painting of Yuri Andropov. The room was a gilded nightmare of Soviet-era decoration. It was like stepping through time. Three men sat at the table. He knew all of them.

Out of instinct, Petrov's eyes went to the corners of the room, looking for the bearlike security men who would grapple him should he choose to resist.

But there were none.

"Thank you for coming to join us, Sergei," the man seated to the left of the head of the table said. Aleksei Gruzdev, head of Directorate S—Illegal Intelligence, the master of spies.

Next to him, a step removed both physically and organizationally from the seat of power, was Dmitriy Koskov, Director of the Americas Division and Petrov's old boss. Koskov was a salacious, balding gargoyle of a man, but he was damned effective.

Finally, a youngish man in his early fifties sat at the head of the table. He wore a black suit and red-and-gold patterned tie, and had a deceptively friendly expression on his face. He had thin eyebrows that pronounced his eyes and gave them a predatory cast. His brown hair was lightly dusted with gray. Valentin Ivanov, Director of the Foreign Intelligence Service.

"Good evening, Colonel Petrov. Please, take a seat."

Petrov quickly took his place in the chair indicated by Director Ivanov.

"Would you care for some tea, Colonel?" the director asked.

"Yes, thank you, sir."

Director Ivanov waved a hand and an aide prepared a cup of tea and set it in front of him. The director then dismissed the adjutant. "I met with the president yesterday," he said. "He has approved a bold new operation directed against the Americans. And we would like you to be a part of it." The director paused.

Petrov said, "I am honored to serve."

The three men stared back at him, unmoved.

Director Ivanov said, "There are two important goals within the president's plan. First, he wishes for Russia to become a global leader in artificial intelligence, believing it to be tantamount to our nation's success in the years to come.

Secondly, he wishes to stifle America's technological capability."

"These are ambitious and wise objectives," Petrov said.

"I am so glad you agree," the director responded, his voice flat. "There are major shifts since you were last in the US. American society is nearly at a tipping point. Seeds we have sewn over the last decade are beginning to come to fruition. A growing movement of anti-technologists, motivated by this Trinity organization, shows much potential. The planning of an active measures campaign is already underway, which will be led by Gruzdev."

Aleksei Gruzdev nodded. "It is good to see you out of Kazakhstan, Petrov. I look forward to working with you again." Petrov had met with Gruzdev many times over the years. As head of the illegals program, Gruzdev oversaw spies who were an invaluable part of the active measures programs Petrov supported.

Ivanov said, "Our new program will build on the ground-work of our previous disinformation campaigns. Our colleagues at the GRU have been praised by the president."

"Their Unit 29155 has gotten all of the credit," Koskov said, a stern look in his eyes.

Petrov got the message. The SVR was falling behind in the internal race to win the president's favor. Along with the FSB, the SVR and GRU were like jealous children in a dysfunctional family. An unending competition for their father's attention and respect. Things he rarely gave.

Director Ivanov continued, "Our plan is to use the rapid technological changes sweeping over society to drive deeper the wedge between the American people. We will fan the anti-technology flames, amplifying the right news articles and social media communication, and using deepfake videos. Technological achievement will become their enemy. It will pry jobs out of the hands of hard-working Americans. We will inspire a fear of progress. We will rebrand technology as a cancer upon their values. We will ensure that artificial intelligence is closely associated with any cultural and economic changes that are unpopular."

Gruzdev said, "Beyond setting Americans at each other's throats, we intend to influence American public policy. We want them to intensely regulate their technology firms. This would stifle innovation and may even push some of these companies to move their operations outside the US, where we can establish avenues of control."

Petrov said, "The anti-technology campaign coupled with American nationalism isolates them from the world. If our main enemy is isolated, he is easier to defeat."

Koskov said, "We plan to target the software development activities in Ukraine, Poland, Romania, Bulgaria, Hungary, and the like. Convince the Americans that their outsourcing is dangerous and unpatriotic. Convince them that a software company in Romania is just a cover for a ransomware factory. We will strike a similar tone with Western European nations."

Petrov nodded. He understood the strategy. It undermined the economies of former Warsaw Pact nations who edged too close to the West.

"Soon, they will see that it is cold and lonely outside the Russian hearth." Ivanov smiled, and it was a cold, vile thing. "Aleksei," the director said. "I think it's a little late in the day for tea. Perhaps something a little warmer."

"I have just the thing," the head of illegal intelligence said, and stood from the table. He walked over to the credenza where Ivanov's adjutant had prepared the tea and pulled the stopper on a crystal decanter. He poured two fingers into each glass and then cupped them in his long, dagger-like fingers. Ivanov was tall and lean, but still well-muscled. Petrov couldn't imagine on a practical level how a man of such proportions achieved such legendary status within the service. How could one so recognizable possibly ever be undercover? Gruzdev returned to the table and handed the tumbler of vodka to each man, in order of rank.

"To the success of our new operation," he declared, and savored a sip. "Beluga?" he asked, pleased at the drink's quality.

"The same," Gruzdev said. "So, should we tell the colonel why we recalled him from his position on the front lines? We don't want him to think it was just for holiday." He smiled at this, as did the other two, some private joke between them.

"If you would be so kind," Ivanov said.

"Sergei, the director has already discussed the president's initiative, which I will be leading. In time, you'll join this operation as well, but we have something else in mind for you first."

Petrov sipped the vodka. It was smooth with hints of pepper.

"Hawkinson," the goblin Koskov grumbled.

Each face in the room darkened as the men watched Petrov for his reaction.

"Hawkinson," Petrov repeated, narrowing his eyes.

"*Da*," Koskov said. "He has recently contacted us through a covert channel you established during your last operation in the United States. He asked for a meeting. *With you.*"

"Hawkinson promised us research material from the American company," Gruzdev said in his oil-on-water tone. "This would have accelerated our own development by a decade. But we received nothing but economic sanctions from the west. And now he reaches out to you. Why?"

Why indeed? Petrov thought to himself.

"The president also is very interested in another piece of

recently received intelligence, this one from our colleagues in Washington, D.C. Apparently, there is new evidence that Guy Hawkinson may have been responsible for the way the Pax AI operation ended."

Petrov frowned. "I don't understand."

"We were told that the fire consumed the Pax AI Mountain Research Facility before the technological blueprints and software could be transmitted."

"That is correct. I was there."

"Perhaps that is not exactly what happened." Director Ivanov's tone warned that Petrov was in dangerous territory. "Perhaps Guy Hawkinson made us into fools?"

Unsure of what to think, Petrov decided to play it safe. "I assume you already know how you would like to respond to Hawkinson. Please tell me how I may be of service."

"Before we do, you need to know one thing," Director Ivanov said. "And this comes directly from the president. Sergei, the gloves must come off."

11

Petrov was given a dimly lit office and a stack of files to review. His head was swimming. Earlier that day, Petrov was convinced that his time in the service was about to meet an abrupt and violent end. Now he would be working on one of the SVR's most important cases in years.

But first, Hawkinson.

His superiors intended to send him to the US under a false name. Inserting him as an illegal was dangerously stupid. He was known to the Americans. He would have to be extremely careful not to get caught.

Hawkinson requested him by name, so Petrov understood why he was being sent. But they wouldn't have chosen this path unless they felt he was expendable.

If the operation failed, if Petrov was captured meeting with Hawkinson, if Hawkinson didn't, as the Americans said, play ball, the Center and the Kremlin had deniability. Petrov was a rogue officer. He disappeared from his posting in Nur-Sultan and was attempting to turn this American businessman for who knows what purpose. We deeply regret this incident.

And what have you been up to, my old friend, Petrov mused, looking over the Service's files on Guy Hawkinson. For as bold as this operation was, he wondered (privately, of course) if the Service leadership and perhaps even the Kremlin had gone soft. For all their supposed love of the "old days," they seemed to have little of that operational vigor today. Petrov was amazed to learn that after Hawkinson's betrayal, he was still alive.

What kind of signal did that send to their enemies? But then, that is why Petrov was being sent, was it not? An agent of vengeance for the state? It was a role he was comfortable playing. But if revenge was all his president wanted, there were other ways. No. Petrov was being sent because he had the ability to decide whether revenge was the best course of action. Or was there profit to be made? A new source of income that could be acquired for the president and his loyalists, sliced up and stuffed away in unscrupulous banks.

Petrov reviewed Hawkinson's file.

Guy Hawkinson was a former American military officer, a capable and decorated Special Forces soldier. He chose not to make a career of the Army, opting instead to leave when he was still young. He chose to profit off America's endless appetite for military adventurism, taking the helm of his family's private security business, HSG. Over the next decade he made them into a private army, and an incredibly successful one. Hawkinson's sister—an investor and advisor to the visionary technologist Jeff Kim—suggested that her brother's firm would be an ideal candidate to provide the advanced security required for Kim's company, Pax AI. It was the kind of nepotism that was so rotten within the unrestrained American capitalism, Petrov knew.

But it provided Petrov with an opportunity.

Over the years, Petrov, often in San Francisco as part of SVR operations infiltrating and stealing secrets from American technology firms, had formed a working relationship with the morally flexible Sheryl Hawkinson.

With Sheryl's help, Petrov was introduced to Guy and made an arrangement for a Hawk Security Group subsidiary to provide security for the Pax AI Mountain Research Facility. The subsidiary in question had hired some of Petrov's men a few weeks earlier. They were Russian mercenaries who would follow orders and disappear. Whether they disappeared by choice or by shovel, Petrov didn't care. What he cared about was stealing the most advanced AI and quantum computing technology in the world.

He had orchestrated a brilliant plan. Using the already-stolen Pax AI weather prediction algorithm, the SVR started a small forest fire more than a day prior to the operation, knowing that it would develop into a monster aimed right for the Pax AI Mountain Research Facility. When the Pax AI researchers and government employees evacuated, the last line of defense would be the Russian mercenaries posing as Hawk Enterprises security personnel, who would provide unobstructed access to the facility.

But nothing happened as planned.

Petrov was forced to evacuate when the flames began to consume the area, and prior to retrieving the precious data.

Most thought that the Pax AI technology was lost in the flames that day.

But some suspected that it wasn't. The Russian president thought that perhaps the Hawkinsons had double-crossed them. But if so, why would Guy Hawkinson be contacting him now, almost two years later?

Petrov had occasionally followed Guy Hawkinson's movements from Kazakhstan. Petrov's intelligence access wasn't as good as it had been when he was the Houston *rezident*. But even with open-source searches, Petrov could make some inferred connections. Guy Hawkinson had created a business unit focused on analytics and information warfare. He had quietly begun recruiting new employees to help build it into...what, exactly? Was it to be a competitor to companies like Palantir? Or a private sector version of the GRU's own offensive cyber warriors? Some of the LinkedIn profiles of his new employees showed robotics backgrounds. Was this new section of Guy Hawkinson's company going to create military robots and drones? That would make sense.

But Petrov's instincts told him otherwise. A good amount of the new hires had backgrounds in AI and quantum physics. Hawk Technologies didn't have any valuable intellectual property in that realm. Unless...

Unless Guy Hawkinson did more than just leave the SVR out to dry when the Pax AI operation failed.

Unless Guy Hawkinson actually *did* get the technology that the SVR hadn't been able to acquire. Petrov tried to think back to that day. What had his subordinates from the technical division told him? There had been a lot of unexpected electronic interference that inhibited their ability to download the transmissions from Pax AI's research facility. His men had claimed it was bad "space weather" or electromagnetic interference caused by the large wildfire.

But what if that interference was man-made?

Guy Hawkinson surely had people on his payroll with the right experience and capabilities.

Petrov clenched and unclenched his jaw as he turned this thought over in his mind. He would keep this to himself for now. First things first. He needed to reach out to Hawkinson and respond to his message.

Before the final operation with Pax AI, Petrov established a backchannel for Guy Hawkinson to use. A covert way to establish contact with Petrov. The phone number was for an office belonging to the "TransUral Development Corporation." There was no such business. The phone number, after being bounced to a dozen switches around the world, was answered by an automated voice. If the caller used the correct passphrase, it would send the text transcription and recording to the appropriate SVR operations officer.

The Hawkinson message provided a callback number. It was daytime in America. Petrov went to the technical office and had one of the SVR's communications experts make the call. He stood over the woman's shoulder as she dialed.

"This is Ivana Semanov with the TransUral Development Corporation. I believe you inquired about development opportunities. Is this still your intention?"

"Yes, it is," a man answered. The computer monitor next to the SVR woman displayed the results of a voice analysis.

Name: Mathew Kirby

US Citizen

Current Employer: Hawkinson Security Group

Petrov frowned. He had looked up the alias Mathew Kirby before this call. There was no legend to backstop it, nothing beyond the name to convince a looker of its legitimacy. If the Americans were observing, they would do the same thing the Center would, which was to confirm it as a false identity...which would draw more scrutiny. It was sloppy, and unlike Guy Hawkinson.

"We will provide you details on where and when to meet in the next few days."

"Understood," Kirby replied.

The SVR woman hung up. Petrov thanked her and departed the communications room.

He continued working until midnight and then left the office. He walked across the snow that had fallen earlier that evening, crunching and cold beneath the soles of his shoes.

Petrov maneuvered his way through the dark campus, showing his identification twice to the armed patrols that stopped to question him. Finding the small block of apartments for visiting officers, he informed the clerk of his identity and was shown directly to the room. It was small and spartan, decorated in golds and blond wood. *Efficient*, the Service would say. A bottle of vodka and a glass waited on the small table that served as the dining area. Petrov flipped the glass over, unscrewed the bottle cap, and poured a modest amount. He walked over to the window and watched the snow fall in silence as he sipped the vodka. Finished, he replaced the glass next to the bottle and went to sleep.

The next morning Petrov showered and dressed in a freshly pressed uniform, then returned to work. Gruzdev had assigned him an aide who could help him access confidential files and ensure that his commands were carried out. Petrov also suspected that the aide was there to watch him. If Petrov was once again to be used as a scapegoat, they needed to gather evidence.

Petrov gave the young man his morning assignment, detailed intelligence assessments on the Hawkinsons' operations as well as Jeff Kim's activities since his company fell apart. That kept the aide busy for most of the day and allowed Petrov the solitude he needed to work. He pulled the office's yellow-orange curtains open, letting in the gray morning light, then called down to the commissary and ordered breakfast. Twenty minutes later, a pair of young stewards brought in a tray with fried eggs, *draniki* with a creamy sauce, and tea. Petrov ate while he devised a plan.

He wished to meet with Guy Hawkinson in person and take the measure of the man. To look into his eyes and question him. If Petrov did that, he was confident he could get a feel for whether he indeed had acquired the Pax AI technology once thought lost. Furthermore, Petrov could determine Hawkinson's future intentions and trustworthiness.

Director Ivanov hadn't directly stated it last night, but Petrov surmised that the Pax AI technology could play a central role in the Russian president's influence campaign against the Americans. Their previous measures had been akin to erosion, a gradual wearing down of systems and societal trust. But American technological counterintelligence was catching up with their efforts.

In short, the Service needed to leapfrog the technical and societal countermeasures the Americans had developed. When Russia possessed the technology to condition the Americans to doubt their own eyes and ears, the war would be won. Would Hawkinson provide the necessary weapon?

After a few days of perfecting his operations plan, Petrov ran his intentions past his superior, Koskov. They made a few minor adjustments and then Petrov had the communications woman send Hawkinson rendezvous instructions via their secure channel.

The support directorate prepared his passports and travel documents. Moscow to Istanbul, a change of identity, then an overnight in Madrid, followed by a high-speed train to Paris under yet another identity. Then a flight to Mexico City from Charles de Gaulle. He would remain in Mexico City for a few days, working out of the *rezidentura* before finally entering America.

There was one more thing he needed to do before leaving. Petrov picked up his phone and dialed the number of an old friend. Leonid Oborin was ten years Petrov's senior and had been a colonel in the *Spetznaz* before retiring and taking a position with The Vavakin Group, Russia's leading private military firm. Not unlike Guy Hawkinson's own outfit, The Vavakin Group provided highly trained mercenaries to a

variety of conflicts around the world. It specialized in operations where the Russian government did not want to become
directly involved, or where the Federation simply needed to
augment their forces. Vavakin operated in Syria alongside
Russian special forces and in Central Africa helping friendly
governments quell dissent and disorder. Or to nudge the less
friendly ones. The Group, as they were simply known, was
effectively an extension of the Russian state, just a more deni-
able one.

"It is good to hear your voice, my old friend," Oborin
boomed into the phone. Subtext, *I'm happy to see you return
from the land of the dead*. He wouldn't dare say that over the
phone, however. They had both played this game long enough
to know not just that someone was listening, but *who*.

"Yours as well, Leonid. I am back in Moscow for a few days
before my next assignment. Are you free for lunch?"

"Of course."

"Excellent. I'm at the Center. Can you make it today?"

Oborin confirmed their meeting and Petrov ended the call.
He had something specific in mind for this operation and did
not want to risk Service assets. His superiors may have
thought he was expendable, but he had no intention of getting
caught.

Petrov was met in Mexico City by an SVR illegal who took him
to a room at the Courtyard Mexico City Airport where the *rezident* was waiting. He knew the man by professional reputation
but had not worked with him previously. The *rezident*
informed Petrov that sweep teams had been through this
room already and deemed it safe. Petrov would have their full
support while in Mexico City, but any communication would

be through dead drop. To protect his cover, Petrov could not visit the embassy compound. The *rezident* was not briefed on Petrov's assignment, only that the Center directed him to provide whatever help he required.

Petrov traveled with a laptop that had an encryption card allowing him to communicate securely with the Center. He was issued a smartphone with a North American SIM card. The Service designed an encryption app using a front company based out of Ukraine called GhostPhone. The app allowed its users to make end-to-end encrypted phone calls and texts, providing them with "military-grade encryption." It also allowed the Center to listen in on every conversation and observe every text.

Petrov had the SVR send a final message to Hawkinson, informing him they would meet in Miami in three days to discuss the current state of their partnership.

12

Miami, Florida

Petrov entered the US through the busy border crossing near Matamoros. After a twenty-minute wait in traffic, US Customs inspected his paperwork. Two Caucasian women, both in their thirties, sat in the car with him, one behind the wheel. She answered the CBP agent's questions in flawless American-accented English. Impressive considering she had lived most of her life in Moscow. The Russian government language school certainly didn't give her that level of expertise. But this was the YouTube generation, Petrov thought to himself. They had unfair advantages.

After the crossing was complete, the two female SVR illegals drove Petrov another two and a half hours to the Corpus Christi International Airport. He had thought about using the Brownsville Airport, but decided against it after reading about the large amount of law enforcement located there. In Corpus Christi, he boarded a small turboprop aircraft that flew him to Miami. Now that he was inside the US, flying was the quickest way to travel without having to present his identity to anyone.

He entered Miami that afternoon. The *rezident* there was not aware of his presence; he was now on his own. Two of The Vavakin Group men met Petrov at the airport in a black Mercedes G-Class. He stepped into the thick air outside the arrivals lounge at Miami International and cut his way to the SUV. They departed immediately. There was no small talk, no perfunctory exchange of pleasantries. Oborin handpicked each of the men on this detail and they were all trained in countersurveillance. They left the airport and drove east several miles to Interstate 395 North.

"Is everything in position?" Petrov asked.

"Yes, sir," the driver responded.

"Excellent."

He checked his watch. Three hours until the meeting.

Petrov would not normally have scheduled a meeting with an asset within hours of his arrival, but he trusted Oborin's competence, and since he was operating without the Miami *rezident's* support, there was little reason to be here early and risk discovery by the Americans. The Mercedes exited the interstate and moved west before looping back south, a circuitous route intended to identify and confound any surveillance. They arrived at Petrov's hotel, the JW Marriott in Miami's Financial District. The hotel room was nicer than any of his apartments in Moscow and certainly more posh than any of the issued quarters on the embassy compounds where he'd been posted in his career. But it was suitable for his legend, a Lithuanian businessman traveling from Argentina.

Petrov checked in with his Lithuanian passport and was shown to his room. He changed clothes, then took his laptop bag and phone and returned to the Mercedes. Once he was in the car, Petrov opened the GhostPhone app on his phone and had the SVR send another message to Guy Hawkinson, this time with their meeting location.

Their destination in Little Havana was a mere three miles from the hotel, but The Vavakin Group men again took precautions on their route to foil any potential surveillance. When the driver was sure they were clear, they continued to their destination. The vehicle pulled to a stop in front of a busy sidewalk. Petrov and his security man in the passenger seat got out while the driver parked the car.

They'd passed a bank on their route and a digital sign informing Petrov that it was eighty-seven degrees. After spending the last two years in Kazakhstan, it felt like he might melt. Petrov approached a burnt-orange stucco building behind a crowded sidewalk. The storefronts here were all brightly painted and varied; many had artwork as well. He'd spent a lot of time in Cuba over the years on various assignments and felt this was a faithful representation. Two sets of chairs lay beneath large umbrellas in the shadow of a palm tree in front of the store. The storefront itself was covered with colorful advertisements for the items within and fliers for neighborhood events. A single sign over the door said "CUBANA CAFÉ" in blue letters over a white background.

The Cubana Café had once been a front for the Cuban *Dirección de Inteligencia*. The proprietor, a retired DI officer named Fausto Perez, operated this as a listening post and safe house for forty years. The cluster of antennas on the two-story roof, ostensibly to receive satellite signals for *futbol* broadcasts, could also send encrypted transmissions back to Havana. Petrov had cultivated a strong working relationship with the Cuban DI, unified around their common goal of undermining the Americans.

Perez knew only that his facility would be used for a quiet meeting today and that he would be compensated for his time.

The café was quiet but for the squeaky overhead fans that needed oil and the tinny Cuban music playing from a radio that clearly couldn't handle all of the brass. Petrov walked to a table at the back of the café and sat facing the door. Fausto appeared from behind the counter wearing a light green guayabera over white pants. His skin was the color of a cracked walnut, and he had a thick mustache and most of his hair, though it had since turned gray. Petrov ordered a Cuban sandwich and coffee.

Petrov's senses were on high alert. After all this time and planning, he would finally speak with Guy Hawkinson.

But Hawkinson didn't show.

Instead, a man Petrov recognized as Mathew Kirby walked in. Alone.

Petrov knew Kirby's face from the Service's extensive profile on Guy Hawkinson and his personnel. Kirby headed to the corner seat where Hawkinson had been instructed to sit. Next to Kirby, the two hulking monsters from The Vavakin Group watched.

Kirby wore a tropical tan suit, blue shirt, and no tie. He had black wraparound sunglasses and the ostentatious watch of a former operator. Petrov sighed. This man's tradecraft was terrible.

"Where's Hawkinson?" Petrov said with icy calm.

"Guy sent me instead. We think it's better this way. More secure."

Petrov thought this American looked arrogant. "Were you followed?"

Kirby shook his head. "No."

Petrov raised his voice just enough for it to be heard at the next table. "We'll take this conversation elsewhere."

At that signal, the two Group men at the other table pushed out of their chairs. Kirby frowned but followed Petrov into the dimly lit hallway, the Group men behind him. As soon as the door closed behind them, the first man put one of his serpentine arms around Kirby's shoulders and upper arms and his other around his elbow.

"Hey, what the hell?" Kirby was just starting to struggle when the second Group man shouldered his way through and plunged a syringe into Kirby's neck. He struggled for a few more seconds like a fish dangling on a line, mostly out of panic and instinct, but soon went slack.

Kirby wouldn't become completely unconscious; he would retain motor functions, but for the next several hours, he would be about as pliable as bread dough. They guided him out of the hallway to a white panel van waiting in the alley behind the café.

Inside the Cubano Café, Fausto Perez was quietly cleaning the two tables, chairs, and door handle. Soon, there was no trace that Petrov and his men had ever been there.

Kirby came to in a sweltering warehouse after they'd hit him with a bucket of salt water. He was naked and bound in a chair underneath a single light.

Two of The Vavakin Group men stood on either side of him, and several more lurked in the shadows.

Petrov kept his temper in check. Kirby's attendance was unexpected, but Petrov had this location as a contingency in case Hawkinson chose not to cooperate. He calculated that they had about two days to work on Mathew Kirby until they would need to escalate to more expedient measures of eliciting information. After that, it would negatively impact their operational schedule. The Center expected results quickly and wanted to know why Hawkinson chose this time to resurface.

"You know who I am, yes?" Petrov said.

"Yeah." Kirby's words already sounded more lucid as the drug they had given him to bring him out of the incapacitated state took effect.

"Why did Hawkinson contact me?"

Kirby paused, and Petrov could see that he was searching for an answer. "He wanted to discuss a business proposal."

"What are the details?"

Kirby said, "My boss is having trouble with Israeli intelligence. They are running operations against his new business venture."

"The technology business?"

Kirby nodded, looking a little surprised that Petrov knew about it.

"Why are the Israelis interested?"

Kirby shrugged. "I don't know. But it's a problem for my boss."

Petrov paused, thinking. It was the Israelis that had an agent embedded in Pax AI. She had been instrumental in their disruption of Petrov's operation to steal their AI technology. It made his blood boil to think about it. But something else bothered Petrov about this...

"I must ask you something." He leaned in close to Kirby's face. "Tell me the truth. Did Guy Hawkinson gain access to the Pax AI technology two years ago? Or was it destroyed in the fire like I was told?"

Kirby's eyes twinkled. "It burned, bro. Everyone knows that." He had a smug self-assuredness about him. Common for men in his line of work. Less common for men who were tied up and under interrogation. Realizing that Kirby didn't believe he was in danger, Petrov walked out of earshot, beckoning Pavel Lukyanenko, the leader of his security team, to come close. Lukyanenko spent fifteen years in the Russian Special Operations Forces prior to joining the Group.

"Pavel, have your men conduct a perimeter sweep of this location. We know we weren't followed, but it's possible Kirby has a tracking device on him." Lukyanenko nodded and departed immediately.

Before securing Kirby to the chair, they'd taken his phone and watch. The phone was off, but it could still be tracked. Petrov removed Kirby's watch from his pocket and examined the Rolex Submariner, then handed the watch and phone to one of the Group men. The soldier dropped both on the concrete floor and smashed them with a hammer. Petrov moved some of the debris aside with the tip of his shoe, as though inspecting it.

To his credit, Kirby didn't react.

Petrov then instructed the soldier to examine Kirby's clothes. The soldier produced a tactical knife from a pocket, opened it, and proceeded to shred Kirby's suit and shirt, looking for a transmitter that might have been sewn into the lining. When that was done, they pried the heels off his shoes.

"If you want to check and see if I swallowed one, you're going to have to wait a few hours. I had a light lunch," Kirby said.

Petrov made a simple motion with his right hand, and the soldier to Kirby's left punched the back of his head, hitting him with such force that the chair slid forward.

Petrov stood over Kirby, then turned and pointed to a rolling door about fifty feet behind him. "Do you see that door?"

"Yes," Kirby said.

"On the other side of that door is a fishing boat. Not terribly glamorous, but it will take me anywhere in the Caribbean I wish to go. Or anywhere I wish *you* to go." Petrov could see the grim light of recognition enter Kirby's eyes. "Now, approximately two hundred and twenty miles to the east is a prison on the outskirts of Havana. It is an...*unpleasant* place." Petrov took a few steps back from Kirby. "You know, the Cuban *Dirección de Inteligencia* hasn't had the opportunity to interrogate an American in some time, and certainly not a former Green Beret. I'm sure they would welcome the chance to prove themselves."

Petrov paused and studied his subject. Interrogation wasn't his specialty. When they had time, the Service relied upon the devils in Line KR for that in the dungeons beneath Moscow. But they had neither time nor the dungeons, so Petrov would have to rely on more expedient measures. He hoped Kirby would not force him to go to Cuba. That would be incredibly time-consuming. But he also could not allow this smug American to call his bluff.

Who are we if we don't honor our words? Petrov mused.

Then he frowned. "If you do not answer my questions, you are going into a hole and will be swallowed up. You see, there are rules in this game. If I catch an American spy in *my* country, we put him in prison until such time as we can exchange him for one of our own. But there aren't rules for people like you. You will simply disappear. Guy will not go to the authorities for assistance because it will expose him as a traitor. He will not risk your government finding out that he is working with the SVR. So you, my friend, will be abandoned."

Petrov walked halfway around the chair to stand at Kirby's side. Kirby, still dazed by the blow to his head, warily looked back at him.

Petrov said, "The thing about my friends in Havana is that they don't believe this is a game between gentlemen. They have no decorum. But they are frighteningly effective. They just are not very efficient. It does tend to take them a while to get there. So, I ask again: did Guy Hawkinson get the Pax AI technology and then lie to me about it, saying it was destroyed?"

Kirby's bravado seemed to dissipate.

He gave a stammering, rambling explanation that Guy was genuinely concerned about meeting with Petrov after the Pax AI operation failed. He talked about "operations security" and some other nonsense. Petrov knew he was holding back. The question now became, was he holding back out of loyalty, or did he simply not know the answer?

Petrov made a few more polite attempts to tease out the information, but Kirby continued to be evasive. Petrov then informed him that he would leave Kirby in the care of these fine Russian men until he decided to become more cooperative. Then Kirby was blindfolded and gagged while the Group men worked on him for the next several hours.

Petrov knew that while judicious and selective violence could be effectively applied during an interrogation, there were limits. Eventually, a pain threshold was reached and the person would simply say whatever the interrogator wanted to hear to make it stop. The key was to wear the person down, to break their training. They could employ isolation, sensory or sleep deprivation, extreme discomfort, and wildly varied temperatures—many of the same measures used against *him* in the Lubyanka by the Line KR devils.

No one resisted interrogation indefinitely.

As his men worked on Kirby throughout the night, Petrov took several photos and sent them to Guy Hawkinson using the GhostPhone app. The message contained images of a naked and bloody Kirby that would automatically delete from Hawkinson's phone once he looked at them, though the Center would retain copies.

Once the app confirmed that Hawkinson had seen the pictures, Petrov sent another message.

Your employee informed us that you were not honest two years ago. His condition is your repayment for that mistake.

We understand the problem you are trying to solve with the Israelis. We are open to doing business once again, for the right price. We would like to see what you took two years ago. Meet in person this time. Instructions to follow.

Hawkinson's reply came within seconds.

We will discuss further soon. Bring my man. I'll bring your payment.

Petrov read Hawkinson's message in surprise. He waited a moment for Guy to write more, but no further messages were sent.

Petrov walked back into the warehouse. "We're done here," he said in Russian.

13

Palo Alto, California

Guy watched his older sister sip from her martini glass, lost in thought as she stared into the blazing red skyline as the sun plunged below the horizon. She was quiet tonight, the way she always got when she was worried about something. Their brother Charles was there too, but he looked more angry than worried.

They were on the upper deck of Sheryl's private residence, a three-story wood and glass marvel that had made its rounds in all the architectural magazines. The home was situated in the Westridge area of Portola Valley on almost four acres of forested land.

Guy helped himself to two fingers of 25-year Macallan from the wet bar. He took a sip of his scotch and said, "I'll need to respond quickly."

"When does he want to meet?" Charles asked.

"The day after tomorrow," Guy replied in a soft tone. He'd had one of his sweep teams from the security practice check the house for listening devices when Sheryl bought it, and they had returned once a month since then. The place always came back clean, but Guy found himself lowering his voice regardless.

Sheryl said, "We shouldn't have gone to them. Something like this was bound to happen."

Charles said, "You need to counter." The look in his eye told Guy what type of response his brother meant.

Guy knew this period of conflict would come eventually. It was inevitable. There was so much chaos after the Pax AI incident: murders, a fire, theft, espionage. For a while, Guy thought that Petrov would betray him after he didn't receive the Pax AI technology. There were loose connections between Guy and Petrov. Surely the Russians could have sunk him if they really wanted to.

There were hearings where Guy was called to testify. Not even Uncle Preston could shield them from *that*. But eventually the heat faded. Petrov was expelled. Guy and his associates were cleared of wrongdoing. All the blame was left on the Russians, and their connections to Guy were said to be coincidental.

For a while, Guy began to think that he and Sheryl had gotten away with stealing the Pax AI technology and making the SVR think it had been destroyed. But now that they were growing their technology business, the Russians would begin to suspect the truth. Perhaps his sister was right. Petrov had been a reckless choice for helping with their Mossad problem.

And now one of his men was captured.

"You're not meeting with him," she said flatly.

Charles said, "He has to."

Sheryl scoffed in disgust. "Charles, you don't know anything. Stay out of this."

"I'm afraid he's right," Guy said. "I must meet with him."

"They obviously don't want to help us." Sheryl came out of

the womb issuing orders. She'd never met a challenge that couldn't be bested either by her sheer force of will or her family's considerable resources. But she'd never played the game against the Russian intelligence service.

Guy drained his scotch and set the tumbler on the counter. "We still need Petrov's help. Now that we're in the open with our AI business, the Israelis will be all over us. We need support. Counterintel. Countersurveillance. Muscle. Things we can't do ourselves without drawing suspicion."

"He tortured one of your men. We went to Petrov with our proposition, and he attacked us."

Guy sighed. "My employee is hurt because I sent him there. I regret putting him in that position. But it is a sunk cost. We must keep our priorities in front of us. That means putting aside our emotions and communicating with Petrov. If he can be reasonable, we can still make a deal. If not, I'll make sure he gets the message that he can't push us."

Sheryl was incredulous. "You don't think he made up his mind already about whether he wants to work with us? Don't you think what Petrov has done to your man is enough of an answer?"

Guy shook his head. "No. I know the type. What Petrov did to Kirby was a message, not an answer."

Charles looked skeptical. "So Petrov and the Russians were expressing their displeasure?"

Guy bowed his head. "This is the way things are done. Communication between these types of people takes into account reputation and pride. The Russians let us know that our reputation, and their pride, was hurt. We made a deal with them two years ago, and the Russians must have confirmed that they got shafted. The secret is out. Our people have been tearing that Pax AI technology apart and studying it since the day we got it."

Charles said, "And the Russians got nothing."

Sheryl looked back out over the sunset. "Guy, did you know your man would be harmed?"

"I suspected it."

"And you sent him anyway?" She turned to face her brother.

Guy said, "Do you love your daughters?"

"More than anything."

He turned to Charles. "And you? Do you love your family?"

"Of course."

Guy looked at Sheryl. "You would sacrifice anyone or anything to protect your girls, would you not?"

Sheryl nodded.

Guy shrugged. "This is the way business is done. Sometimes we must communicate through crude means. But aside from family, our relationships are transactional in nature. We betrayed Petrov, and Petrov has now returned the favor. If he did not kill Kirby, there is a reason."

"What?" Sheryl asked.

Guy looked back at his sister. "Because the Russians want what we have."

14

Guy was wheels up from San Jose on the HSG Gulfstream G800 by eight o'clock that night. He enjoyed a steak and a glass of wine before asking the flight attendant to convert one of the G's couches to a bed. He changed into a T-shirt and men's yoga pants, popped an Ambien, and slept the rest of the way to Florida.

The Gulfstream landed at Peter O. Knight, a general aviation airport on the Davis Islands just a few miles from downtown Tampa, the HSG headquarters and MacDill Air Force Base. The flight attendant woke him thirty minutes before landing. He changed into a suit and refreshed himself in the aircraft's lavatory while the flight attendant prepared a light breakfast and coffee.

He met Wade Dyer on the tarmac.

Dyer was a hair under six feet tall, early fifties, and bald. He had a hooked, hawk's-bill nose, craggy face, and the kind of piercing eyes most normal people found frightening. Dyer wore a navy tropical-weight suit, robin's egg blue shirt, and sunglasses. He'd spent thirty years in the Army, mostly in special operations and much of that in black ops, either with a CIA covert action team or JSOC. They shook hands and Dyer led Guy to one of the black Audi A8Ls HSG used for their executive transport service. The doors had Kevlar plates in them, run flat, puncture-resistant tires, and impact glass. Guy put his gear in the trunk and sat in the passenger seat. Hot coffee in an HSG-branded travel mug sat in his cup holder.

"Car is clean," Dyer said.

"We're going to MacDill. We've got a meeting, then we'll be back at HQ for the rest of the morning. I need to be airborne by noon."

They left the airport and took the low, arcing bridge from Davis Islands to Tampa proper, merging with the sludgy flow of morning commuter traffic on Bayshore Boulevard, Tampa's own Miracle Mile. The morning sun was bright and the Hillsborough Bay to their left glittered. To their right were a seemingly unbroken string of palm trees and mansions. MacDill occupied the end of a small peninsula reaching out into Tampa Bay. Morning traffic around the base was brutal.

After a few minutes, Dyer asked, "So what's this all about?"

"The Russians."

"I mean I figured that, given what you sent me to look into."

"I sent Matt Kirby to talk to them about something. They took him. Roughed him up bad," Guy said in a dry, emotionless voice.

"Why?"

"I'm trying to negotiate a new deal. The Russians are trying to send a message about the last one."

"How is he? Kirby."

"He's in bad shape." Guy took a deep breath. "I'm going to make it up to him."

Dyer shot a glance in Guy's direction. "We going to do anything else about it?"

He looked at Guy silently for a moment. His men were operators. They knew that in war, alliances were often transitory and transactional. But Guy's men were also part of the brotherhood. The majority of them were veterans, and the instinct to avenge a fallen brother was strong.

"Did you get the information I asked for?" Guy asked.

Dyer changed lanes. "I identified several locations, but I think Mali is our best bet."

Guy nodded. "Sounds like a good choice."

Moscow had been making inroads into Africa over the last several years, attempting to reestablish themselves as a global power and compete with China and America for Africa's incredible resource wealth. Though for Moscow, it was as much about the prestige of once again having client states as it was about rights to bauxite mines, diamonds, or rare earth elements. That some of these countries, such as Mali, still had ties to their former colonial parents made undermining that relationship all the sweeter for the Kremlin.

Mali was a landlocked West African nation that, like so many of its neighbors, struggled with postcolonial government. They revolted and shrugged off French rule in 1991 and were largely stable until the Tuareg rebellion in 2012, which began the Mali War. French military forces intervened in an attempt to stabilize the country, but as the war dragged on, the conflict was joined by external forces such as al Qaeda who were looking for an opportunity to take root in the chaos. A brief and fleeting peace was reached in 2018 only to be followed by two subsequent coup d'états in 2020 and 2021. The Kremlin sought to exploit the latter of these two.

Late in 2021, the Mali government, a military junta answerable only to themselves, made an arrangement with The

Vavakin Group to provide an independent "stabilization force" to help them fight the jihadists who hijacked the rebellion and turned it into an Islamic insurgency. The junta claimed it was no longer appropriate for a colonial power to provide that security. The move set Mali at odds with neighboring Niger and Chad, both of whom were partnered in the fight against Islamic militants and feared Russian expansion in the region. The government of Chad took it a step further, claiming that the militants who murdered former president Idriss Déby that year were trained by Vavakin Group forces. The proposed security agreement was already causing instability among Mali's neighbors and it hadn't been signed yet.

"I did a workup last night of everywhere the Russians are engaged in Africa as well as where they're using proxies. Hard copies are in a tablet under your seat." Guy reached under and pulled out the tablet. It scanned his face and requested his personal code, which he typed in. Then he read the information while Dyer ran down the intelligence sources he'd used to compile it.

"Just give me The Vavakin Group deployments. I think those are the contractors the Russians are using."

"What makes you say that?"

"I don't think the SVR would chance getting their hands this dirty on US soil. This guy Petrov used mercenaries to do all of his wet work in San Francisco."

"He was there?"

"Yes, he was."

"Which is why the Russians sent him to Siberia..."

"Kazakhstan."

Guy saw that Dyer was gripping the wheel. "So is today going to be our response for Kirby?"

"First things first. I need Petrov to deal. Today's about that."

Dyer shook his head and sighed. "Fuck."

Guy turned to face Dyer but didn't say anything. Dyer glanced back at him, then faced forward to focus on driving. He knew better than to keep asking. Guy wanted payback just as much as he did, but he had to be unemotional about his business decisions. Guy reached for his coffee and took a sip as his mind calculated the multiple steps ahead, considering the best way to extract vengeance and value from his adversary.

When they reached MacDill's Bayshore Gate, Guy handed Dyer his DoD contractor ID card. Dyer showed that and his own US Army retiree card to the security forces airman who waved them through the gate. Five minutes later they pulled into the parking lot of the squat, concrete monolith that was US Special Operations Command headquarters. Dyer took the tablet from Guy and put it in a messenger bag, then removed a lanyard with a series of badges that would gain them access to the building.

Marine Lieutenant Colonel Ray Carter met them at the door and guided them through security. Carter spent his entire career in Force Recon, most recently as the commander of a Marine Raider Battalion. He turned down his promotion once to stay in command longer, but after the second time he was informed that it was "up or out." Grudgingly, Carter accepted the silver oak leaf and a staff position at USSOCOM headquarters. He was already chaffing at staff duty and was anxious to get back into the field with his Marines, where he belonged. Carter had worked alongside HSG's direct action teams in the past and Guy knew him well. Carter was six-three, Black, and built like an NFL safety.

"Thanks for seeing us on short notice, Ray. I really appreciate your time," Guy said when they'd reached his office.

"Anything I can do to help. What's on your mind?"

"Wanted to get your advice on something. We're picking up a new European client for some ops in Africa and they're concerned about the Russians, especially the use of private armies." Guy flashed his trademark smile. "Ironic, I know. Anyway, we wanted to pick your brain about The Vavakin Group and how active they are."

The Marine scoffed. "Yeah, those guys are assholes. If you really want to know the straight shit, you need to talk to Jorge Villareal. He's a master sergeant, Army-type, out of SOCAF. He's been coordinating ops in Mauritania and before that was assisting the French with their mission before the junta kicked them out of Mali. But I'll tell you what I know."

Carter explained that the Russian mercenaries were operating in Mali on a provisional basis while the government finalized the deal. The military junta that took over in the most recent coup was supposed to hold a constitutional referendum in February and they hadn't finalized the contract with The Vavakin Group. In the meantime, Vavakin was deployed in limited numbers but wasn't yet authorized to take direct action. In preparation for Vavakin's eventual green light, several neighboring countries requested US support, and SOCOM was coordinating several Special Forces deployments in addition to the conventional forces that AFRICOM was preparing.

"You want my advice, I'd tell your client to hold off. That place is a shit show now and it's only going to get worse." Carter grinned. "But I don't want to tell you how to run your business."

"Not at all, man," Guy said. "We appreciate it. And it's probably good advice. Thanks for your insight. We've put a couple new toys up at our training center. Next time you're up at JSOC, let me know and we'll make sure you get a tour. The road course is killer."

They spent a few more minutes shooting the shit, but Carter informed them that he had to brief the general at ten hundred and needed to get moving. He didn't indicate *which* general, exactly, but Guy had been on this base enough to know that if you took a big enough step, the odds were good you'd trip over one of them. He had what he'd come for. They thanked Carter for his time and made their way to the car, then drove to the HSG headquarters in the historic Rivergate Building in downtown Tampa.

HSG was originally chartered in North Carolina to be close to Fort Bragg and the Joint Special Operations Command, and their premier operations training facility was still located there. But he'd moved the company headquarters closer to the decisionmakers at US Central Command and Special Operations Command, both headquartered at MacDill. Guy checked his watch when they hit the elevator. He had exactly ninety minutes to pull together a covert operation before he needed to be on an airplane to his meeting with an illegal Russian intelligence officer.

All in a day's work.

The flight to Naples lasted forty minutes.

Guy used the encrypted communication app to text Petrov when they arrived. Rendezvous instructions promptly followed.

His team had vehicles waiting outside the terminal upon arrival. Guy and two men from the detail rode in the black Cadillac Escalade while the other two took the BMW 5 Series sedan.

Petrov instructed him to meet at five o'clock at Anthony Park, just across a thin river from the airport that eventually connected with Naples Bay. The drivers conducted an extensive surveillance detection route, with the BMW acting as a chase car, hanging back behind the SUV to see if they were being followed. Certain they were black, they drove south back to Naples and their destination.

As they entered Anthony Park, Guy understood why Petrov chose to meet there. It looked to be a manufactured peninsula jutting out into the brackish river. There was a single access road from the community, making it easy to see someone coming. Guy's instructions were to meet at a dock in the northeast corner of the park. He'd looked at overhead photos before arriving and saw that while the dock itself looked to be concealed by trees and had poor sight lines from any direction, approaching it required walking up one of two tree-lined paths or across an open field. No way could he sneak up or get his security team in place without Petrov knowing.

Guy exited the car and his security detail formed up around him. He wore a small black messenger bag made of ballistic nylon. Inside were several portable, encrypted hard drives that contained terabytes of Pax AI research material. This was a fraction of what the Hawkinsons managed to get from the company, but it would hopefully mollify Petrov and his masters until they could arrange a more effective means of transport.

Guy chose to walk along the easternmost path that formed the park's perimeter. He instructed his security detail to keep him in sight. One man would stay with the vehicles, one would orbit the field, and the last would be on the western path approaching the dock to ensure that no one ambushed them. A punishing Florida sun, harsh even in the early evening, radiated down on him as he stepped through the shadows beneath the trees and onto the weather-beaten wooden dock. Buzzing insects and bird calls filled the air. Guy could hear the river gently lapping at the posts that held up the dock. He walked to a small observation area at the end and texted Petrov to say that he was in position.

As he waited, he tried not to second-guess this meeting. Ten years ago, he would have thought himself a traitor to his nation. Making a deal with Russian intelligence was against everything he had once identified with.

A lot had changed.

Guy thought about his nieces. His sister. His brother and the rest of their family. He thought about the company and the life he had built.

And he thought about the discovery his scientists had made on the island. The Trinity people he had met. The things they had shown him.

The implications were vast.

The world was changing and sides would no longer be defined by geography or political ideology. Old loyalties couldn't matter as much. He needed the Russians today; whether he needed them tomorrow was up to them.

Family was all that mattered.

Up until this point, Guy had used the Russians and their massive intelligence apparatus to further his company and his family's goals. It had been a one-sided transaction, with circumstance and clever misdirection helping the Hawkinsons avoid paying their side of the debt. That would end now.

Guy was about to commit espionage.

He'd long ago become jaded, losing the patriotic idealism he'd clung to as a boy after multiple deployments. He loved his country. But he saw America for what it was: a deeply flawed place, led by inept and power-hungry politicians. Brainwashed by geriatric media moguls who didn't give a shit what their opinion shows did as long as they increased profits. None of them were in the warrior class.

His men bore the scars of war. As did the innocent souls whose country was torn apart by people they didn't know for reasons they couldn't possibly fathom. But it was Afghanistan and America's utter abandonment of its allies and civilians there that really hit home. After twenty years of bloodshed and unfulfilled promises, that debacle finally convinced Guy that the US had been fighting for nothing at all. Guy knew he profited off America's need for defensive capability, but he'd always thought that his company served a noble purpose. Now he felt like one of the pawns in a geopolitical game played by men who had no real stake in it. Leaving the Afghanis who risked everything to fight with the US was the ultimate betrayal by a government that knew no concept of accountability.

His loyalty had faded. The country he knew and loved was a shadow of itself.

And besides...everything was about to change.

Everything.

Sheryl had explained the implications of this new AI technology a little over a year ago. She had convinced Guy that they were on the verge of a new age, an epoch ushered in by technological advancement that would render antiquated concepts of government irrelevant.

He and Sheryl would be ready for the shift. Their family would be among the new ruling class.

"We will be kings and queens," Sheryl had whispered to him. "But we must be first..."

Sheryl didn't want to rule the world. She wanted to rule the people who ruled the world. After decades of fighting, Guy simply wanted to build a world where flawed bureaucrats couldn't order better men to their death. If he had to be a king to achieve that, so be it.

Guy's phone vibrated in his pocket.

He drew it out and opened the GhostPhone app.

"Good afternoon," Petrov said. "I see you have a bag with you. Does that contain my research?"

"It does."

"Excellent. Stay right where you are. And don't signal any of your friends." The line went dead before Guy could ask if they had Kirby.

Guy heard an outboard motor and looked out over the brackish river. Thick trees cast long shadows on the brown water as a small motorboat approached the dock. There were four men, including Petrov. Two looked very much like soldiers. The fourth was slumped over, leaning on the man next to him like a drunk. Kirby.

The engines reversed, slowing the boat's approach to the dock. Petrov extended his hand for the bag, looking smug and expectant. Guy handed it to him. The two Russian soldiers hefted Kirby's lifeless body onto the dock.

Rage welled up from the pit of Guy's stomach. It took all he could muster to control it.

"He's alive," Petrov said. "He didn't have to be. Neither do you."

Guy said, "I'm going to have two of my men come get him."

Petrov nodded. Guy waved to Dyer, who jogged over with another HSG man. They picked up Kirby and helped him back to their vehicle.

Petrov said, "I understand that you would like to resume our partnership. Please understand the terms of our arrangement. If you renege on any deal we make now or in the future, members of your family will look as Mr. Kirby does now. Is that clear?"

Guy flexed his jaw. "Yes."

"I understand that Mossad is a problem for you."

"That's correct. We're opening an office in Northern Virginia. Much of the work we do will be related to this AI technology. Based on some recent events, we strongly believe that Mossad will conduct operations to monitor and disrupt our work."

Petrov eyed him, remaining quiet while he digested the information. He seemed to be trying to determine what to believe. Finally, he said, "I still believe that a partnership would be to our mutual benefit. We have much to offer each other. I will speak to my leadership. I expect they will want to invest in your efforts—discreetly, of course."

Guy said, "Of course."

"They will need assurances. My leadership will want to be a part of any successes that you have. We will need to work out the details. In exchange, we will make your Mossad problem disappear. And we will receive regular updates on your progress." Petrov flashed a crocodile smile.

"This is acceptable," Guy said.

"It better be. I will be in touch," Petrov said. Then one of the soldiers shoved their watercraft off the dock.

The engine kicked up and the boat glided away, heading back upriver.

Guy went to check on Kirby. He was breathing, but his eyes were closed. Guy lifted the lids and saw them wide and unfocused, telltale signs of heavy sedation. They needed to get him to a hospital immediately.

Guy watched the boat disappear around a bend to the right, then nodded for Dyer to come over.

"You do what you came to do?" Dyer asked when they were out of earshot of the other men.

Guy nodded. "Yeah. Petrov will provide help with Mossad.

But we still have a problem. The Russians don't respect us. There's only one way to gain the respect of men like that: a show of strength."

"Mali is a go?"

"Affirm."

15

Langley, Virginia

Colt said, "All indications from the Farm are that Nadia is progressing well. She's in the middle to upper third of her class."

He was wrapping up his weekly briefing to Thorpe in the NTCU conference room. Through an opening in the venetian blinds, he saw Ford orbiting outside.

Colt's briefings to Thorpe on Nadia's status were bare-bones. Neither he nor Ford wanted to give more than was needed. Nadia's actual training with the National Clandestine Service was one of CIA's most closely guarded secrets. The training center didn't even want to share progress with *him,* reminding Colt on several occasions that she was in the training pipeline and not yet on her follow-on assignment. Colt gently reminded his contact at the training center that Nadia was, for all purposes, special.

"Any questions?" he asked Thorpe.

"No, Colt. Thanks for the update." Thorpe gave him a wan smile and was already moving on to the next task. As Colt stood to leave, Ford blew through the door holding a zippered pouch.

"Our friends at the Russia desk called me while you two were talking. There's fresh intel from CATALYST."

The team running CATALYST didn't share a location, not wanting to give away any details that could lead to their agent's identification. But based on the type of information they were passing along, Colt guessed that the agent was either at the SVR headquarters in Yasenevo or the Russian Embassy here in Washington.

"Let's have it," Thorpe said.

Ford unzipped the pouch and handed over the contents. As Thorpe began reading, Colt could see the header's bold-face, block letters. Some of the words had already been blacked out and redacted.

"It says that Petrov and Hawkinson met. There was an exchange. Petrov confirmed receipt of data storage devices. SVR technical experts are confirming that the storage devices contain Pax AI technology," Thorpe said, reading aloud. Without looking up, he added, "So this means that Hawkinson gave the Russians trade secrets from an American company."

"May I see the report?" Colt extended a hand and quickly scanned the document. "Petrov assesses there will be no repercussions from the initial meeting results? What does that mean?"

Thorpe looked at him. "You didn't hear? Surveillance said Kirby never came back from the first meeting. His hotel room in Miami contained some of his valuables and personal belongings."

"They killed him?" Colt asked.

"We don't know," Thorpe said. "There's no record of Kirby anywhere."

Ford said, "And Hawkinson still gave Petrov what he

wanted? That's not the type of guy I thought he was...no pun intended."

Colt shot Ford a look.

Thorpe said, "We can now confirm that Guy Hawkinson is working with the SVR. We need to up the surveillance on him immediately."

Ford said, "And if Petrov really did have Kirby tortured, that sounds a lot like payback for the Hawkinsons screwing the Russians out of Pax AI technology two years ago..."

Colt nodded. "Agreed. But why the hell give them anything now?"

"You were there," Thorpe said. "What was Kim working on?"

"A lot of different things. Jeff Kim was using a combination of advanced AI and quantum computing to create prediction programs. That was some of the scary stuff. For example, he developed an algorithm that could predict speech patterns really far in advance. Like minutes in advance. You can YouTube a demonstration."

"Oh, I think I've seen that. In Canada, right?" Thorpe asked. "Help me understand why that should scare me."

Colt said, "Okay, imagine a deep learning system analyzing everything available that the person has ever said or written. I mean everything. And then combine that with the same data from countless other people's life communication history. Add in a powerful quantum computer that can use the deep learning prediction with quantum computing to test out infinite variations of if-then statements."

Both Thorpe and Ford stared back at Colt with blank faces.

Ford said, "I certainly get it, but my friend here doesn't. Could you dumb it down...for *him*, I mean."

Colt sighed. "Okay, this might sound crazy, but remember,

Jeff Kim was five to ten years ahead of *everyone* on this stuff. He's a once-in-a-generation mind. Two immediate applications come to mind. First, with this technology one could effectively predict the future."

The room went quiet. Ford blinked.

"For a moment, I thought you were going to say something crazy," he replied.

Colt continued, "Seriously. We're doing it already when you think about it. Tech companies are already predicting speech. Now if you improve that capability over time with deep learning, a capable AI program could predict how a person will think or react to a given stimulus. The more information and the better the tech, the more accurate we become at predicting the future."

"So if you had that AI capability, you could go into a negotiation and pretty much guess what the other side was going to ask for? Or how they'd react to a counteroffer?" Ford said.

"Exactly. You could prep instant responses based on the possible permutations of how someone might react to different stimuli. And like a chess match, you could improve your chances of achieving your goal by *introducing* certain stimuli. This technology gives an edge to equity traders trying to predict the market, political ad makers trying to shift opinions, and battlefield commanders trying to stay two steps ahead of their enemy. Pax AI was creating a machine that could authoritatively predict what someone would think, long before it happened."

"I don't know, guys. That sounds like sci-fi stuff to me." Thorpe had his arms folded across his chest.

"Landing on the moon was sci-fi stuff...until we did it," Colt said. "For what it's worth, I think we're at least another decade away from being able to do most of what I just said. But whoever gets there first..."

"It would be very powerful." Ford nodded.

"And now the Russians might have it."

Colt nodded. "That's not all. I mentioned increasing your chances of success by introducing certain stimuli. That was the other crazy thing I saw at the Pax AI facility. They were working on an IARPA project. Developing an AI that could reliably manipulate people's opinions. If you can take people's communication history and create an intensely accurate psychographic map of their personality and way of thinking, and you can control the stimuli they see, you can get very good results on shifting their opinion. What we're talking about here is basically mind control. It's propaganda on steroids. With a powerful AI system, you can create the world's most powerful propaganda machine. You can control people...or rather, you can convince them to want you to."

Ford shook his head. "Man, I miss the good old days where you just had to worry about caterpillar drives and Mig-31 Fire-foxes and shit."

Thorpe stood and handed the paper back to Ford. "I don't know that I believe all of this AI apocalypse stuff. But I do agree with you that Guy Hawkinson passing the most advanced research in artificial intelligence to the Russians is a grave threat. They will find a way to put that to use." He crossed his arms and his tie bunched slightly beneath his arms. "Gents, I don't want to re-litigate old arguments, but there's a certain amount of damage done here. Colt, would you say this is years' worth of research?"

"Yes. It would take the Russians billions to replicate this on their own, and that's if they could ever get there."

Thorpe said, "Right, that's my point. We don't know if this is everything that Hawkinson stole from Pax. So, what's the hit we take? How much further along do the Russians get because of this?"

"I don't need a computer to predict what you're going to say next," Ford said. "And the answer is no."

"Damnit, Fred," Thorpe boomed. "It isn't a game. Time is not on our side here. How much more damage are we going to allow Hawkinson to do?"

"We're not putting someone in the field before they're ready."

"And how long does that take?"

Ford said, "We need a few more months."

Thorpe was shaking his head. "No way. I have the NSC Principles Committee breathing down my neck for progress." His voice was steadily rising in pitch and anger. "And they don't even know about *this* yet. Either your asset is ready to insert into Hawkinson's company or we need to find someone who can go now."

"You put someone who isn't ready, isn't convincing, in that company and they're going to get sniffed out immediately, and that's if you can get them there in the first place. I am not putting an asset at risk—"

"Well you'd know all about that, wouldn't you." Thorpe pushed past both of them, pausing at the door. "Listen, fellas, you have weeks, not months. Understand? Get your agent ready."

16

The next two weeks had Colt scrambling to build out Ford's plan, while Ford maneuvered through the Agency's bureaucracy to get the top cover they needed. That meant convincing the DDO they needed to pull their operative out of the clandestine service school well before she graduated.

Colt and Ford decided to use some of Nadia's Cornell research work as the basis for a fake startup tech company. They even began recruiting, using headhunters to hire real engineers and data scientists. With her new resume, Nadia was made to look like the ideal candidate for Hawk Technologies' talent poaching. CIA had already determined that while Hawk Technologies' cybersecurity was excellent, they'd outsourced their talent acquisition to a boutique firm specializing in the tech hires, and Agency cyber operators were already inside that company's network.

The question was how to make this fake company and Nadia enticing enough to flag on the Hawkinsons' radar.

The company, called Cognitive LLC, operated in what the industry termed "stealth mode." That meant they didn't advertise or hire publicly, and avoided the press. This was common when working on an experimental, proprietary product and the firm didn't want to expose themselves to competition or talent poaching. Colt got CIA permission for the company to temporarily use In-Q-Tel as a funder, giving them some additional bonafides. In-Q-Tel was an intelligence community-backed non-profit venture fund that invested in companies that had technologies relevant to the IC. The "Q" in the name was a nod to Ian Fleming's "Q Branch." That would add some vital social proof that this company was legitimate and a worthy acquisition target.

Colt was working on a big PR push. From his previous cover assignment, he had connections with many of the leading technology writers and bloggers. He contacted several of them, saying that he'd moved on from his previous role and was not advising companies. This was another common industry practice and it didn't raise any flags. Many VCs hung up their own shingle for a time before being asked to join a startup as a board member or executive. Colt described the company as an emerging leader in the study of embodied cognition, which promised to advance the way machines acquired knowledge and reasoned over it. Cognitive promised technologies that improved the quality of visual recognition of objects and language processing by machines, and could even help humans understand how memory worked. Very enticing stuff for the media cognoscenti to devour. Colt also made sure to get a piece championing a recent Cornell master's degree graduate and former Cognitive intern, Nadia Blackmon, who was joining as a lead researcher but was expected to rise quickly. He said it was a great "women-in-tech" story, and he also made sure to get profiles done on some of the leading hiring sites. With Professor Turner's guidance, Nadia's academic record, extracurricular activities, and master's thesis were modified to better backstop the legend and make her more attractive to the Hawkinsons.

CIA's logistics team rented Cognitive an office in Arlington's Ballston neighborhood, which was home to numerous technology companies, In-Q-Tel, and the Defense Advanced Research Projects Agency (DARPA). They created a slick web presence, complete with digital marketing material and a blog, and even recruited someone from the Science and Technology Division to manage the Cognitive Twitter account, dropping content on their future products.

While Colt put the company operation in motion, Ford convinced Wilcox to pull Nadia out of the Farm and insert her into Cognitive. Wilcox then had the unenviable task of explaining that maneuver to the National Security Council. Inserting a CIA operative into an American company as originally outlined in STONEBRIDGE was not a popular decision or an easy sell, but choosing to move forward with an untrained and unqualified asset was a nearly impossible one. But Wilcox went for it, agreeing with their reasoning. The Hawkinsons' tradecraft was exceptional and their hiring practices showed a rigorous, multistep process that ensured only the best applicants made it through. An intelligence officer, no matter how good, wouldn't be able to bluff their way through the technical interview, which included supervised coding exercises, meaning that a candidate was given a problem and had to program their way out of it under the evaluator's watchful eye.

Nadia was given a codename, YELLOWCARD. She was pulled out of clandestine service training under the auspices that she'd washed out. Not an uncommon occurrence. Altogether, Nadia had a mere six weeks of training.

The Agency set her up in an apartment in Clarendon, just a few Metro stops down from Ballston and the Cognitive office. She and Colt first met in a park in Manassas, Virginia, about an hour outside D.C. It was late spring and the temperature was in the upper sixties. She explained that she followed all of the practices they taught her to ensure she was black before they met.

"Is this how you fire people?" Nadia asked once they sat down on a bench.

"You're not being fired, Nadia," Colt said. "We had to pull you out early because the mission timeline moved up."

"But I was having so much fun," she said in a flat voice. "Two nights ago I was mucking about in knee-deep swamp water looking for a dead drop."

"None of this can be helped, unfortunately. You're still going to be trained, but this time by Ford and me."

She gave him a look. "Really?"

"Yes. As part of your cover, you'll be joining Cognitive, a small AI-focused company based in Arlington. In-Q-Tel is a backer and they're in line for some DARPA contracts. They're doing some interesting work with image recognition."

"Deep learning, nice," Nadia said. "That's one of the toughest nuts to crack, interestingly. It's fun. What's In-Q-Tel?"

"It's a non-profit VC firm the intelligence community uses to fund technologies that we might find useful," Colt said. "You will train with Ford or me at night after work and on weekends. Sometimes you'll have to leave work during the day for a training block. You'll need to come up with convincing reasons for being out of the office so as not to arouse suspicion. I've got someone on our team who did a tour instructing at the Farm as well. You're going to be as well prepared as you can be, but it will still be risky." Colt twisted to face her. "This is going to be dangerous, Nadia, and I need you to know that you can back out at any time. Just say the word."

"You haven't even told me what I'm doing yet."

Colt took a deep breath. "Are you familiar with a man named Guy Hawkinson?"

"Yeah, I know of him. The special ops dudes I worked with in the Air Force trained at his company's place outside Fort Bragg. They had all this HSG swag."

"We believe he is colluding with the Russian foreign intelligence service—"

"The SVR," Nadia interjected, and then tapped the side of her forehead, smirking. Colt couldn't tell if she wasn't taking this seriously yet or if this was just her way of deflecting stress.

"Right. The SVR. Anyway, two years ago, we believe the Hawkinsons worked with the SVR to steal a massive amount of R&D from Jeff Kim."

"Jeff Kim? *The* Jeff Kim?"

"That's right. Some of his most advanced work from Pax AI. Until recently, the US government believed the SVR was involved, but they only had loose connections between Guy Hawkinson and the incident."

"I remember that. It was all over the news. It was the fire, right? It destroyed one of Jeff Kim's facilities," Nadia said.

"That's correct. But you know what wasn't in the news? We think the Russians set that wildfire in the first place. They used an advanced AI weather prediction program to set the fire in just the right way that it would burn down the Pax AI facility. They knew down to the minute when it would strike. And they used that knowledge to cover up their attempted theft. The SVR thought that the technology was destroyed in the fire and the mission was a failure. The Hawkinsons were never charged. But the counterintelligence team I work with has been watching them since then. We think the Hawkinsons actually did steal the Pax AI technology before the fire destroyed it. They hid that from their SVR collaborators, and then decided to lie low for the last eighteen months to make sure they got away clean. Guy Hawkinson had to testify at a Congressional inquiry, but his uncle, a senator from Wyoming, made sure the questions they asked him were softballs."

"Holy shit," Nadia said, listening raptly. She was taking this seriously now, Colt thought.

He said, "Then a few weeks ago, seemingly out of the blue, Guy Hawkinson covertly reached out to his old SVR contact. They met. And we think Guy Hawkinson gave him data that included the Pax AI technology."

Nadia was shaking her head. "What kind of traitorous asshole does that? Wasn't that guy in the military? What the…"

"I know. We think there is a lot more to the Hawkinsons than meets the eye. They have been transforming Guy Hawkinson's security company into more of a defense-related AI technology company."

"What does that mean?"

Colt smiled. "We don't really know…that's why you're here, and why we recruited you out of Cornell. The Hawkinsons formed an advanced technology company two years ago, but only made it public in the last twelve months. Since then, they've been buying up other technology firms and poaching the best talent they can get their hands on. We don't know exactly what their goals are. You know as well as I do that AI can be weaponized in ways that we don't have countermeasures for. But building a weapon just to sell it to someone else doesn't seem to fit their profile. They're already rich and have the kind of political power you can't buy. We need to get someone inside that organization to find out what they're up to, someone who can convincingly make their way through a technical screening. Once inside, someone who has reason to access their sensitive research material."

"Someone like an AI specialist from an Ivy League computer science program?"

Colt grinned. "Know anyone?"

He described the plan in detail. The Agency had set her up in an apartment and swept it for listening devices, and would continue to do so under the auspices of a weekly cleaning crew, who could also be used to supply her with equipment that she would need. She'd "work" at Cognitive, an Agency front company. Everyone there was either a CIA employee or a contractor, though none of them were read in on STONE-BRIDGE. They only knew that their job was to make people believe that Cognitive was an emerging leader in artificial intelligence.

"So, now that you know what you're being asked to do, are you willing to move forward?" Colt asked. "Ready to spy for your country, Nadia?"

"I'll do it," she said, a serious look in her eyes.

Two weeks after their meeting, Colt messaged her on the Agency-issued phone to give her a time and place to meet that night.

Nadia arrived at a parking garage in downtown Bethesda, Maryland, that served several streets of outdoor shopping and dining, a good place to blend into a crowd. Colt instructed her to purchase a coffee from the Quartermaine shop in Bethesda Row and then walk south to a small plaza between the two main streets, where she'd find shops, restaurants, and several benches. Colt watched her approach from behind a newspaper at the far end of the plaza. He waited ten minutes and then strolled over to the bench, sat down, and pretended to read on his phone.

"Where was I standing when you arrived and how long was I there?" Colt asked.

"I spotted you when I walked in, but I didn't know it was you until you lowered the newspaper." Nadia took a sip of her coffee. "I assume you got there before me."

"Good. Without looking, tell me what you remember about the couple to our right."

"They're having an argument about something. It's not going well for the man."

"What are they wearing?"

"She's in a sundress and he's in a black University of Maryland polo."

"Excellent. Now, how long did it take you to get here?"

"Like, an hour. I left right away, but traffic around here is atrocious."

"Did you come straight here?"

"Of course."

Colt placed his phone in his pocket and stood. He turned toward the bench, pretending to tie his shoe. "Don't ever do that again. Ever. You need to run surveillance detection routes each and every time we meet. Assume you're being watched and act like it. Don't meet with me or Ford ever again unless you know for certain you are black. You just put all of us in danger, and risked the mission."

"What about tonight's lesson?"

Colt was already walking away. Hopefully, she'd learned it.

The next evening, he met her on the Potomac River Walk in Georgetown. It was a short distance from Ballston as the crow flew, and walkable if one used the pedestrian section of the

Francis Scott Key Bridge to cross from Virginia into the District.

This was another test. Would Nadia choose the easy route?

She did not. She took an Uber from the office to a Metro station servicing Arlington National Cemetery. From there, she took the Metro into the District by way of the Blue Line to Chinatown, then hopped in a cab to the National Mall, where she could not only blend into the crowd but also easily check her surroundings for possible tails.

She called a Lyft this time for pickup outside the Washington Monument, and from there they drove north to Dupont Circle. While in the car, she pulled a lightweight black hoodie out of her backpack and put it on. Once they arrived at Dupont, Nadia descended into the Metro Station, taking the Red Line to Cleveland Park and then using a rental bike to head to Glover Park, the neighborhood between Georgetown and Cleveland Park along Wisconsin Avenue. Ironically, this was also home to the sprawling Russian Embassy complex. There was no Metro access to Georgetown, so Nadia walked downhill to the riverfront on a zigzagging path that took her through residential neighborhoods, then doubled back to join the heavy pedestrian traffic on Wisconsin Avenue.

Her journey took ninety minutes.

"Did you notice my countersurveillance team?" Colt asked when they were finally together, the Potomac reflecting the street lights next to them as they walked.

"No..." Nadia looked at him sideways, her voice apprehensive.

Colt tried to disarm her. "Good. That means they're doing their job. But you'll need to get better at spotting them. Your life depends on it."

She made no reply and they kept walking, soon arriving at the Georgetown Waterfront Park.

He motioned for them to stop and sit on a bench overlooking the water. Above, cars drove on the elevated Whitehurst Freeway. No one was in immediate earshot, but it was a warm evening, and the lawn was full of people on blankets enjoying the weather. Bikers and runners moved by on the paved path that ran along the water.

"That was the first lesson of the night," Colt said.

"What, not being able to spot a tail?"

"No. That everything is a test." Colt looked out over the water. "Assume that you are always being evaluated. By me. By Ford." He turned to look at her. "And most importantly, by our adversaries. You need to understand, there are people in the D.C. area and around the world who are working their ass off every day, trying to find out *your* identity. The Russians, the Chinese. Hell, even some of our allies would love to know your identity. Because you know what you are? You know what your identity is, to an intelligence service?"

Nadia's expression was one of intensity and sorrow. "What?"

"Your identity is currency to them. Information is the currency of all intelligence officers. If a counterintelligence team learns who you are and what you are doing, they'll pass that up the chain. And that information is used. Maybe it gets traded among our adversaries. Maybe our adversaries use your name to negotiate with the US. But at some point, when the wrong people learn your name, bad things will happen. Someone will get killed or captured. Missions will be exposed and fail. You must understand that."

Colt thought he saw Nadia shiver, but her face remained steady. "I get it." She nodded.

"Remember the other night, when you failed to run a

surveillance detection route before meeting me? As a precaution, I conducted a three-hour SDR to make certain I was black before going home. It was a late night."

Nadia looked down at the grass.

Colt said, "You can't make this mistake again. We don't have time, and the stakes are way too high. Not running an effective SDR each and every time you meet with an agent is one of the fastest ways to get them killed."

Colt could read on her face that she was finally understanding what she'd become a part of, the seriousness of the choice she'd made. Being a case officer was a twenty-four-seven job. There was no off switch, no clock to punch. Every hour of every day, a clandestine service officer had to assume that someone was watching.

Colt took a breath. "Okay, shake it off. The next lesson tonight is one you'll hear me say over and over. Ready? *Your cover will save you*. When all else fails, fall back on that. At some point in your career, you are going to be tired, hungry, wet, in pain, scared, and a hundred other things that make someone break. When you're all those things, remember your cover. Repeat your legend like a mantra."

"Will it be enough to make up for my lack of training?" Nadia asked hastily.

Colt felt a twinge of guilt. "We're going to get you trained up, Nadia."

"All right." She sounded doubtful. "Well, know this." She looked back at Colt. "I'm a hard-ass worker. And I'll be smart. If there's a problem, it won't be for lack of effort or brains."

Colt smiled. "Good. Glad to hear it." Then he added, "You know, I mean that about the importance of your cover. It matters more than the training in a way. When I was at the Farm, one of my instructors told us, 'We're going to fill your heads with the collected wisdom of generations of professional intelligence officers. Everything the Central Intelligence Agency has ever learned about spying and running spies, we're going to teach to all of you. And you know what you're going to remember when you're in some basement underneath Moscow or Beijing or Tripoli? Not a goddamn thing. So you remember this instead: *your cover will save you.*"

Nadia's clandestine training continued in the weeks that followed. Sometimes she would meet with Colt or Ford for hours of lectures or scenarios. Murder boards where Ford and Colt would tag team, firing off different "what if" situations and seeing how she would react. Sometimes they would actually role play and train her to give the appropriate response. Other training sessions were short, practical exercises like running her own surveillance or managing a dead drop.

One night Colt sent her into a bar to elicit information from someone: name, phone number, birthday, and astrological sign because he was feeling snarky. Then he sent her into a different bar to find someone who hated their job and uncover information about them that she could use for a recruitment. They wouldn't actually be recruited, of course. But she needed the reps.

Colt taught her how to use the CIA's cell phone security procedures to make sure she wasn't tracked via GPS or passive cell-tower pings. "Keep a social media account but participate in a way that doesn't give away any information and fits with your legend," he said.

Nadia was finally feeling like she had the hang of this street work. Tonight's training had her in Tysons Corner mall, recovering a message from a dead drop and placing it at another mall in Reston Town Center, twenty minutes away by car.

While in her Uber en route to Tysons, Nadia had spotted two G-men in a Toyota sedan tailing her. She was beginning to recognize them. These guys were FBI counterintelligence, one of the crews that specialized in catching spies in the D.C. area. A fishing pond of foreign intelligence officers that was constantly being restocked.

FBI counterintelligence teams were occasionally detailed to the CIA to help train new officers. Ford had told her weeks earlier that these guys knew Nadia's description but not her actual identity or what she was training for. They didn't need to know the fish's future plans to make a catch.

"I need to change my destination," Nadia said to the driver.

"Okay, just put it in the app," the man said.

She took out her phone, wondering if they would be able to track it. She was using all of the proper phone security procedures that Colt had trained her in. Nadia made the proper input and then announced, "It's in."

The driver nodded. "Just across the street."

He dropped her off at Tysons Galleria, the ritzy mall about half a mile from Tysons Corner. Locals referred to them as Tysons One and Two. Nadia had been getting more and more familiar with both locations during her training.

Inside Tysons Galleria, Nadia wore a black N95 facemask and a maroon leather jacket that reached mid-thigh. She used her phone's camera to check behind her as she entered the mall, pinching to zoom in on the FBI surveillance car parked on the curb behind her. One of the agents was getting out when she took the picture. He was about fifty yards behind her, so she didn't have much time. If they were cheating, which they loved to do, more agents would be waiting for her in Tysons Corner. But those agents would rely on updates from her current tail.

Nadia turned a corner and walked into one of the busier clothing stores. She headed to a changing room she had identified a few weeks earlier and, once inside, raced to remove her jacket and facemask, setting them aside on the bench. From her shoulder pack, Nadia wrapped herself in a purple scarf, then put on a black wig and fake prescription glasses. She stuffed her old clothes into her bag and hurried out of the store, around another corner, and into one of the large department stores. Again, she took a snapshot with her phone and checked her six.

She saw one of the agents in the photo. He was about fifty feet back but hadn't been looking her way. Nadia walked fast through the department store, taking the escalator down one level and then heading back out into the mall. She scanned her surroundings, checking for bystanders who might be looking her way or for anyone who had a phone pointed at her.

She walked out of the mall and marched through the new pedestrian bridge connecting Tysons Galleria to Tysons Corner. This narrow channel would make it impossible for surveillance to remain hidden. On the other side of the bridge, she waited five full minutes, heart pounding.

Nothing.

She had lost them.

Nadia headed to the dead drop, a family bathroom on the first floor. She locked the door, headed to the sink, and squatted down to look underneath. A small SD card was taped to the bottom of the sink. Not exactly NASA-level engineering, but fine for training.

Nadia again changed her appearance. She removed her

wig, exchanged her reading glasses for sunglasses, and fixed a baseball cap over her head. To better hide her face, she wore a colorful Athleta-branded facemask. Spies loved facemasks, she mused.

Twenty minutes later she was on the Silver Line Metro, heading to Reston. She looked outside at the cars on the road. Nadia felt good. Accomplished. She was really getting better at this...

One of the FBI agents sat down across from her.

Nadia turned her head and saw his partner holding down the rail on the other side of her Metro car.

How the hell?

The Metro slowed to a stop.

"Doors opening," the FBI agent said. "Better luck next time, kid."

Nadia's face reddened as the other agent winked at her and departed the train. She got up and left as well.

Colt was waiting for her on a bench outside the station.

"What happened?" Nadia asked. "I did everything right."

Colt placed his hand on her bag. "May I?" She handed it over. He fumbled through her bag until he found what he was looking for. Removing a brown leather keychain with a silver circle in the center, he said, "This yours?"

Nadia made a face. "No. What the? How did that...what is it?"

"An Apple AirTag. One of the best tracking devices on the planet, now widely available to consumers."

Nadia blew out a breath. "Where did they get me?"

Colt said, "We tucked it in your bag when you were waiting for the Uber."

"You were tracking me the entire time."

He nodded and held up the tracking device. "Technology is making this game harder. You'll need to be more aware of your surroundings. Keep far enough away from people that something like this can't happen. And if you get close enough for someone to do this, make sure you check yourself for ticks afterward. Always assume the worst."

Fuming, Nadia took the tracking device and turned it over in her fingers. "I can beat this."

"Greetings, fellow traveler," Ford said to Colt, who was sitting at a table in the unit's communal area. "Got a minute? Step into my office."

Colt followed. It was late and he was surprised to see Ford still there. Colt had just returned from another late training session with Nadia, followed by his own ninety-minute SDR to return to Langley to finish up paperwork.

"This training stuff is crushing me. I'm exhausted."

Ford sat behind his desk, and Colt took the chair across from him.

"Yes, well, I have good news and bad news on that front..."

Ford had two glass tumblers between his thumb and forefinger and a bottle of Four Roses Small Batch Bourbon in the other. He poured two fingers into each and pushed one over to Colt, clinking it with his own glass before Colt could object to the drink. "How's our girl YELLOWCARD?"

"She's coming along," Colt said, eyeing him cautiously.

Ford nodded and took a sip.

"What is it?" Colt asked. "Why do you have that guilty look on your face?"

"And thus spoke the angels from on high, up in the seventh floor. They hath commanded that thy timeline was officially fucked."

Colt stared back blankly. Then he took a big swallow of bourbon. "Mind translating? It's been a long day..."

"I talked to Wilcox about an hour ago."

"And?"

"Straight from the horse's mouth. We have been given all the extra time we are going to get."

Colt tilted his head down. "You're kidding me."

Ford shook his head. "Afraid not. We've got reports from the Israel desk that Mossad might be using a commercial cover to get closer to Hawkinson."

"That seems especially provocative for our allies," Colt said.

"There are no friendly intelligence services..." Ford recited the old CIA adage. "Bottom line is—and I hate saying this—we need to get Nadia inserted into Hawk Technologies as soon as possible. Like, now."

"Fred, I gotta be honest. I don't know that she's ready...you know we tracked her with a 50-dollar commercial device today?"

Ford frowned. He didn't want to lose an agent any more than Colt did. "Would you have been able to follow her without it?"

"No, probably not. She's doing all the right things. Learning fast. Honestly, she's a great pickup for the clandestine service. But the game's getting harder."

"Well, we have a couple of weeks at best," Ford said, sympathetic. "The National Security Council is spooked about something, and they want us to go now." He looked over his shoulder. "I think Thorpe is pissed we outmaneuvered him with Nadia. He might have gone to the FBI director, who probably went to the attorney general, who took it to the NSC."

"You think he really did that?"

"That's what I heard. Regardless of how it happened, we

no longer have time for Plan A. We can't wait for the Hawkinsons to find Nadia's fake little startup."

"Well what are we going to do, have her apply directly to Hawk Tech? That's very risky."

"We might have another option," Ford said.

"What option?"

"You heard how Hawkinson is considering buying a company called EverPresence?"

"Where did that information come from?"

Ford said, "It's new, from Thorpe's agent in Hawk's corporate finance section. SLALOM is involved in all of Hawk's work prior to any acquisition. He's doing his due diligence on EverPresence right now. But SLALOM says Hawk is 50/50 on whether to pull the trigger. They aren't sure if the IP is valuable enough."

Colt shook his head. "How does this help us?"

Ford said, "Look, if we absolutely must insert Nadia now, perhaps the best way would be for her to be hired by EverPresence, where she would then join Hawk Technologies as part of their acquisition. EverPresence is bigger. Several hundred employees. Easier to slip in if you're surrounded by a crowd."

Colt frowned. "But how are we going to get her hired by EverPresence so fast?"

Ford held up his hand. "Relax, I can handle that part. But we'd have to be sure. We can't get Nadia hired and then change course. That would look suspicious. We would only want to go this route if we're sure that Hawk is going to acquire the company. Like I said, they're 50/50 on that decision right now."

Colt stood and began pacing the room, holding his glass.

"I see that little hamster wheel turning," Ford said, smiling. "Good things happen when you feed that fucker."

"I have an idea," Colt said.

"Well, the hamster does. Come on, give the little guy some credit, Colt."

Colt said, "You said before that we needed to dip our agent in honey to attract the bees. Right?"

"We're certainly deep in our biology metaphors now, but yes..."

Colt stopped pacing. "Same philosophy, but for company acquisitions. If you're Guy Hawkinson, and you're thinking of buying EverPresence, what's the sweetest honey around? What would make EverPresence look amazing?"

"I give up," Ford said, taking a drink.

"Interest from the genius himself. Jeff Kim."

17

Mali

Wade Dyer flew to Guinea's capital, Conakry, where he met the executive officer for the HSG unit operating on the border. The company had a large presence in Guinea: forty "security advisors" and another twenty providing logistics and support. Their efforts were part of a contract with the DoD's US Africa Command to provide security assistance and training for the Guinean military in hopes of delivering much-needed stability for the country's upcoming election after years of military coups. They flew by helicopter, a demilitarized UH-60M that Hawk Security Group purchased, retrofitted and modified for their overseas missions.

Dyer briefed the team on their mission before he departed, and they'd been drilling for the last two days. Their contract in Guinea was broadly and loosely defined, and they were largely left on their own. As such, when they were conducting practice raids in the jungle, none of their Guinean advisors thought anything of it. Dyer arrived in the late after-noon, joined the team leads for the final briefing, and got dressed in his tactical gear. The men sanitized—no Hawk Security Group or United States insignia, no morale patches.

They crossed the border after dark.

Their target was sixty miles to the north, a village that ISIS had taken over six months ago. They rode in General Motors' new Infantry Squad Vehicle, built on the Chevrolet Colorado frame. The vehicle was designed on the principle that a high-speed, mobile all-terrain vehicle that could get an infantry squad into position was much more effective than the slower, hardened Mine Resistant Ambush Protected (MRAP) vehicles that had more in common with an armored car than an infantry vehicle. They had sixteen soldiers and a spare vehicle, which also contained the additional fuel they'd need for the return trip. GM donated the prototype ISV to Hawk Security Group for field testing while it was still in the initial testing with the Army. They wanted real-world test and evaluation, and HSG was only too happy to oblige.

Hawk Security Group wouldn't share the results of this particular operation; of course, no one would know that.

Dyer took command of the operation, as he'd promised Hawkinson.

Each ISV held up to nine soldiers, and two of them were typically equipped with M2 fifty-caliber machine guns, which they had just replaced with a pair of Russian-made DShKs. The soldiers were armed with the A-545 assault rifles recently adopted by Spetsnaz and, more importantly, The Vavakin Group. HSG made a point of having current versions of their adversaries' weapons to conduct realistic training. Getting them to Africa on such short notice had taken some effort, but Wade Dyer's career was making problems disintegrate, and this was nothing new. It also wasn't the first time he'd smuggled rifles into Africa.

They thought about trying to secure some UAZ-45 all-terrain squad vehicles, the Russian copy of an HMMWV, but ultimately decided against it. They didn't need the notoriously unreliable trucks to sell the ruse; the weapons would do that.

The geography of southwestern Mali was not unlike the southwestern United States, with a yellow-brown rocky surface broken by squat scrub trees and occasional rock formations. The area was particularly green now that they were in the rainy season and the Senegal River had swelled. The village was a jumbled collection of low, square adobe buildings and thatch huts woven from local trees. The source of water made the village an ideal target for ISIS. HSG's intelligence reports suggested that ISIS had taken over the small fishing village and was using it to stage attacks closer to the capital of Bamako. As far as they knew, ISIS fighters slaughtered the villagers to a man.

Dyer had little respect for ISIS as an opponent. As terrorists, they were shockingly brutal and effective, but as combatants he found them undisciplined and disorganized. That the organization existed at all was mostly a testament to the shifting sands of America's political landscape and lack of effective foreign policy.

Dyer gave the "go" order at 0200.

Snipers dispatched the sole pair of sentries at the village's southern end. They were going to conduct the raid at standoff distance rather than going in close, the way they typically would. As much as they might like to, the intent was not to completely obliterate the enemy.

Dyer gave the order to "wake them up," and two of his men fired a pair of old RPG-29s into the center of the village, blowing up two of the buildings. The ISVs with the machine gun mounts were positioned at the southern and eastern quadrants and coordinated fire with the fifty-caliber DShK machine guns, primarily aiming for the buildings and laying covering fire for the HSG soldiers. The intent was to simply cause chaos and confusion among the ISIS fighters, hitting them in the dead of night and using tactics dissimilar to those of American special operations forces. Four of the HSG troopers spoke Russian, communicating with each other on a separate radio channel. ISIS wouldn't be able to listen in on the frequency, but this provided cover if any national signals intelligence organization was able to intercept the chatter.

They had almost five minutes without any kind of coordinated resistance, let alone a dedicated counterattack. The machine guns shredded the buildings on the outer edges of the village, forcing the ISIS fighters to move inward for cover, and as they ran, HSG troopers cut them down with small arms fire. One small group of fighters crept out of the village's north side and attempted to ambush HSG's eastern firing position, but they were picked up on night vision and quickly dispatched.

The firefight lasted less than ten minutes.

Dyer gave the pullback order in Russian, a command they'd all memorized earlier that day. One of the gun trucks remained to cover the unit's escape, laying down an almost continuous stream of fire. The men left behind the two RPG-29s and empty magazines, and were long gone before these fighters could communicate with the other ISIS groups in the area.

The group met at a resupply depot to refuel and take water before completing the journey back to their camp in Guinea, crossing the border before sunrise.

Dyer was on a helicopter for Conakry by 0900. While he was waiting on the flight to Lisbon, he called a BBC reporter he often fed information to. She was undoubtedly aware that

Hawk Security Group had a contract to provide security assistance and training in northern Guinea—through the US government, he was quick to point out. They were getting unconfirmed reports that the Russian Vavakin Group mercenaries had just struck an ISIS camp in the southern region of Mali, not far from the capital.

18

San Francisco

Jeff Kim rose from his meditation and stretched. This was a longer session and his legs ached from the position he'd held. The meditation studio he had built on his property was just steps across the perfectly manicured back lawn. The convenient location gave Kim ample time throughout the day to focus.

The meditation studio was a square, modernist design with skylight windows that could be dimmed upon command. Kim's bare feet felt cool on the clean bamboo floors. The building was a soundproofed cube, and his staff knew not to enter when he was in a session. Above all else, Kim cherished his privacy.

He rolled up the yoga mat and placed it in a rectangular holder, then retrieved his water bottle from the counter and returned to the main building to resume his workday. Most of his time was spent at home, working in isolation. Jeff had come to believe that security and privacy went hand in hand. The only person he could really trust was himself.

"Good afternoon, Mr. Kim. How was your meditation?" The voice was soft, neutral, and ubiquitous. Kim had come to think of the voice as more of a "presence" and not simply an aural input. That would be reductive. Saturn, his self-designed AI assistant, was so much more than that.

"Centering," he replied.

"You had four calls during your meditation session. You also had six text messages and forty-three emails."

"Anything I need to know about?"

"You would only consider two of the messages worth listening to," Saturn replied.

"Please respond to the others."

"Yes, Mr. Kim. Would you like to see drafts before I send the responses?"

"That won't be necessary."

"Yes, Mr. Kim. Shall I read you the two messages deemed important now?"

"Yes."

Saturn was magnitudes more advanced than commercially available AI assistants. After years of training, it was able to accurately predict what Jeff Kim needed to know, and how he would respond to various communication stimuli. Instead of predicting a few words of text, Saturn wrote full-page email responses to Jeff Kim's employees without him even knowing the contents. Building this level of trust in his AI had taken time, but Kim knew that Saturn wasn't just a bot. It was an extension of himself. Saturn saved him hours per day, allowing him to do more and focus on the highest-priority tasks.

Saturn began reading the two messages in a tone and speech pattern that sounded almost identical to the actual sender. It wasn't a perfect representation yet, but Kim was getting closer. And Saturn was improving these skills without Jeff's direct involvement.

He was on shaky ground, legally. California's privacy laws prohibited recording conversations without prior consent, and there were, without question, broader implications of being able to accurately replicate a voice. That was one of the many reasons the underlying technology Saturn used only existed on Jeff's private server at his residence and was physically and virtually walled off from the outside world. Additionally, the owners of any voices that Saturn attempted to replicate signed both nondisclosure agreements and research authorizations. Kim didn't like liability.

Saturn was one of many private R&D initiatives that Jeff worked on in the isolation of his home lab. And Saturn was his sole research assistant. A lifelong *Star Trek* fan, Kim had originally named his AI assistant "Computer." But as Saturn grew more advanced, Kim eventually chose the name of the Roman god of wealth, renewal, and generation. It was Saturn who ushered in Rome's Golden Age, according to mythology. Jeff thought that an appropriate moniker. In addition to serving as the test bed for Jeff's more advanced experiments in artificial intelligence, Saturn ran everything in his home that could possibly be automated.

There were a few tasks that robots couldn't yet perform well, deep cleaning and cooking being notable examples. So Kim employed humans for those purposes. His human assistants were expected to enter and exit on a precise schedule, and Saturn monitored each of their activities in the house via surveillance video camera, alerting Kim to any deviation from their expected track.

For the sake of efficiency, a nutritionist curated Jeff's weekly meal plan in advance, and a world-class chef prepared all dinners in Jeff's kitchen. The remaining daily meals with their specific macronutrient content, optimized for performance, were submitted via email to Jeff. The emails were, like all communications, filtered by Saturn, who notified Jeff when and what to eat.

A lesser mind would worry that this system gave a dangerous amount of control to a machine. What if it was hacked? What if it got something *wrong?*

But Jeff Kim knew that Saturn was giving him the most valuable resource available: his time. Kim had the ability to reinvest that time like a business could reinvest its profits. Growing his own capability. Compounding his own growth rate.

Kim had great ambitions, and he needed all the time he could get.

He needed to make up for past errors. Kim had trusted the wrong people. As a young technologist, he had once believed most people shared his utopian ideal of what the world could become. Using technology to unite, to solve problems like climate change, hunger, and disease. Kim still believed that people would pursue these noble goals if they were guided by the same values.

And values programming was everything.

Values programming was one of the key obstacles to creating a safe artificial general intelligence. Values were what guided all intelligent systems, whether they be human or machine. And with today's internet, society was being shaped by a superintelligence with poor values programming.

Mankind, connected by an increasingly faster and more capable global internet, was arguably the world's first superintelligence. All of the planetary knowledge was now connected into one giant neural net that circled the globe. Humanity's choices were incentivized by the values that guided this human superintelligence. And those values were often divergent from Jeff Kim's utopian ideas.

In authoritarian regimes, leaders made policies that benefited themselves, not Kim's utopian values. In democratic governments, leaders created rules that were guided by the opinions of their voters. That might sound better. But how were those opinions shaped? By the media they consumed. And who chose what media was displayed as stimuli? Corporations. Some of these corporations were led by authoritarian founders, and others by shareholders. But almost all of them were driven by a single value: maximizing profit.

As Kim grew older, he began running his own corporation, attempting to maximize profit and program values into artificial intelligence systems. He learned some important lessons. While profit-maximizing markets had served mankind well for millennia, evolution had finally passed a threshold. Like democracy, market-based economics was the best choice in a sea of worse options. And like democracy, markets weren't perfect. As machines accelerated technological development, global society was now suffering from this imperfect values programming.

And in Kim's well-educated opinion, only so much time was left until it all came crashing down.

When he came to this realization, he made a decision. He needed to extricate himself from the bad actors who wanted to leech off his creations. If Kim was going to change the world, governments and corporate raiders alike needed to be cut out of his life's work.

So while he wasn't the one who lit the match in the forest, Jeff Kim was the one who burned it all down.

A lot had changed as a result of his actions. Pax AI's government contracts were canceled immediately and he was barred from doing business with the federal government again. Kim's top-secret security clearance and his company's clearance were revoked. Wall Street's reaction to that news was understandably swift and severe. While his company wasn't public yet, private investors decreased their value estimates overnight. The headline in the *Wall Street Journal* was "Crash AI." Pax AI was toxic. They lost many of their commercial clients. Kim's public relations team did their job, blaming most of the downfall on a Russian espionage operation and some on those Trinity crazies.

Lawsuits were ongoing. To outsiders, the damage had been done.

But this had all been part of Kim's plan. If everyone thought he was valuable, the leeches would still be clinging on to him. He needed the world to think—for a time, anyway—that he had lost all of his valuable technology, and therefore, his capability.

But no one knew about his covert operation. For beneath his meditation studio lay a massive supercomputer system, one with discreet access to outside computing power. Enough capability to continue his AI research with Saturn.

Soon Kim had rebuilt Pax AI into a commercially viable business. The march of progress moved ever forward. He and Saturn were developing concepts Jeff believed could change the world for the better. Investors were again interested. The first major release was an initiative they called ACTioN, or Autonomous Cargo Transport Network. They teamed with an electric vehicle manufacturer that was attempting to fill the void of utility and transport vehicles to create a fleet of safe, reliable, self-driving cargo transports. ACTioN already had one hundred vehicles on the road and had landed a development contract with a major ecommerce company.

"You have a visitor," Saturn announced.

A wall-mounted screen lit up, showing a blue Chevrolet Bolt pulling onto his main driveway.

Saturn said, "The vehicle is registered to a car rental company. Traffic cameras indicate this car departed from SFO sixty minutes ago. Of note, the cell phone in the vehicle is unregistered."

Normally Saturn would use the data signature from the driver's cell phone as it communicated with the local cellular network to identify the owner, then do a public records search and share any relevant information.

While no one was allowed to arrive unannounced, there was a safe list of trusted individuals who didn't have to go through the background check. Anyone deemed a threat was flagged to the private security guard at the station outside Jeff's compound, another unfortunate necessity.

"I believe I have identified the driver," Jeff said, looking at the ultra-high-definition flatscreen monitor. "Search Colt McShane. A former Pax AI business associate."

Instantly a picture-in-picture image appeared next to the vehicle showing an old Pax AI security photo with the name "Colt McShane." Saturn said, "Mr. McShane is now employed by the Commerce Department as an Industry Analyst III in the Bureau of Economic Affairs. Previously, he worked for the venture capital firm—"

"I know who he is," Jeff said. "He doesn't work for the Commerce Department."

"Are you sure, Mr. Kim? I have his department personnel file here."

"Colt works for the Central Intelligence Agency. He was undercover when he was a consultant for us." Kim's voice trailed off as he studied the screen.

What in all hell was Colt McShane doing here?

Colt thanked the security guard and drove through the gate, the massive wrought iron bars rolling shut behind him. He guided his rental up the drive to the circular car park in front of the house, then pulled his sport coat from the backseat and approached the front door. It opened before he had an opportunity to knock.

Jeff Kim stood at the entrance, looking like he'd aged quite a bit since the last time Colt saw him.

"I'd say it was nice to see you again, Colt, but I'm afraid I don't have any context for our meeting so it's difficult for me to say whether that's true yet." Jeff flashed an awkward smile.

Colt liked Jeff a lot and certainly respected his incredible intellect. He believed then, and still did, that Kim was a once-in-a-generation mind. He was awkward around people and incapable of small talk, but when discussing subjects that he was passionate about, he was engaging and dynamic.

"Well, it is nice to see you, Jeff. You look good."

Jeff stood on the threshold for a moment before stepping back to allow Colt to enter the house. "Please, come in," he said.

No sooner had Colt stepped into the house than a voice spoke from the ceiling. "Mr. McShane does not appear to have any recording devices and is not transmitting a signal, apart from his cell phone. He is also unarmed."

"That's Saturn," Jeff said. "Something of a virtual assistant, or at least a more modern take on the concept."

Colt nodded, impressed. There were half a dozen ways that the bot could communicate with Jeff and inform him that Colt wasn't transmitting a signal. Interesting that he wanted Colt to know that he'd been scanned. Wanting to prompt the conversation, Colt turned and scanned the doorframe. He found two small black spheres in the upper corners.

"I have to be a little more cautious these days, I'm afraid," Jeff said. "May I offer you anything?"

"No, I'm fine. Thank you."

"So, what would you like to talk to me about?"

If Jeff had the ability to scan him for weapons and recording devices upon entering the house, he would certainly be able to record the conversation.

"Can we talk outside? Also, please promise that there will be no monitoring or recording of this conversation."

The words sounded awkward to his ears and Colt felt strange saying them. But if Jeff wouldn't respect his wishes, he had flown a very long way for nothing.

Coming here had required Wilcox's approval, with Thorpe attempting to block them from making what he termed a "potentially catastrophic security risk and an unparalleled lack of operational discipline."

Wilcox, who Colt could tell was beginning to tire of running interference between his people and the FBI, agreed with Colt that if Thorpe wanted to advance the STONE-BRIDGE timeline, this was the most obvious course of action. Colt, however, had to agree to a lengthy and exhaustive series of counterintelligence briefings with both FBI and CIA counterintelligence personnel to discuss the risks of what they were attempting.

Jeff agreed to the terms and led Colt outside. As they stepped into the backyard, Jeff said, "Saturn, don't follow," and guided them to a small patio next to the pool.

They sat and Jeff said nothing, instead staring at Colt intently.

Colt had pitched potential agents many times before. But usually, the initial recruitment attempt followed weeks, if not months, of careful cultivation by the case officer. Before making the attempt, the case officer reviewed their plan with the chief of station, and in some cases Langley. The offer was based on a deep and thorough study of the individual by the case officer, using the levers they believed would turn that recruit into a spy. Money was most common, especially in poorer countries, but the opportunity to defect to the United States was a powerful motivator for many. Some did it on ideological grounds, becoming disillusioned with their mother country once they caught a glimpse of its darker center.

This was different.

He wasn't proposing that Jeff Kim become a spy, necessarily. But he would be asking Jeff to become a participant, if an unwitting one, in an espionage operation against an American citizen. This was dangerous ground. If Jeff reacted poorly, he could go to the authorities, or worse, the press. While everything Colt was asking him to do was legal, as was their operation, public exposure would end STONEBRIDGE immediately. To say nothing of what Senator Preston Hawkinson would do if he found out.

"Jeff, I want to start by saying how much I admire you and everything you've built. Your contributions to the tech industry, the scientific community, and our society are impressive. For whatever it may be worth, I'm sorry for the way things ended."

"Thank you," Jeff said without smiling.

"That's part of what I wanted to talk to you about. I know how much damage was done to your company. I can only imagine the personal strain." Colt paused. "I'd like to give you the opportunity to do something about that, if you're interested."

"Continue."

"You are familiar with Guy Hawkinson."

"They accused him of collaborating with Russian intelligence to steal my life's work. Never proven in courts, government, or public opinion..." Kim's eyes revealed hostility at the mention of Guy's name.

Colt raised his chin. "What if I told you that we could prove that he was working with the Russian government when your facility was destroyed?"

"What do you have in mind?"

"Are you familiar with a company called EverPresence?" Colt asked.

"I am. They're building a fully immersive VR environment. Them and everyone else. But they're further ahead than most. It's good technology."

Colt said, "Guy Hawkinson is interested in it too. Maybe interested enough to acquire them."

Kim's face darkened. After a beat, he said, "Why would a defense and security contractor want to buy a company like that? It's not their core business." He tapped his fingers on the table. "So that means his firm developed other capabilities unrelated to their core business. I can think of one way they might have done that."

Colt could see Kim's nostrils flaring. "It would be in our best interests if Guy Hawkinson did acquire EverPresence. The surest way I can think of to make that happen is for someone reputable such as yourself to show interest in the same thing."

Kim smirked. "Careful, Colt, you're going to get in trouble with the SEC."

"This conversation never happened."

Kim rubbed his chin.

Colt prompted, "If you cooperate with us, the Justice Department is prepared to lift your prohibition against doing business with the federal government. Furthermore, you and your company will be able to hold facility clearances again."

"I'll do it," Jeff said quickly. "As soon as I have a letter from a US attorney confirming the arrangement in writing, I'll do whatever I can to help."

He stood and extended his hand.

"Thank you, Jeff," Colt said as they shook. "We really appreciate this. More than you know. Hawkinson is dangerous and you're helping us take him down."

Jeff smiled. "I look forward to doing my part."

19

Washington, D.C.

Since she'd arrived in Washington three months ago, Ava had immersed herself in the life of a top-tier consultant. She'd been hired by the Hyperion Strategy Consulting Group, a firm that helped to rebrand businesses, organizations, and even countries that suffered from negative perceptions. They were the people called in when an oil spill turned into an environmental disaster, when a defense contractor was revealed to sell vehicles to an oppressive regime, or when a country was accused of those pesky human rights violations.

The swanky 16th Street penthouse Mossad set her up in was perfect for entertaining, and Ava arrived at the tail end of the spring social season. She'd already held several exclusive cocktail parties to court power brokers and potential clients alike. Ava had a curated list of prospects that the firm wanted her to target and was given a few minor accounts from her peers. She did her best to make it clear to Michelle Reynard, Hyperion's Chief Operating Officer and head of the consulting practice, that she was ambitious, driven, and uninterested in waiting in line.

Mossad wanted her with Hyperion—rather than any of the other K Street Bandits—because the firm was courting the Hawkinsons. Reynard had recently approached a close contact named Lev Denowitz, Vice President of Business Development for the North American Division of Israeli Aerospace Industries, to get some feelers on the Hawkinsons. Though Israeli Aerospace Industries hadn't worked with the Hawkinsons, both the Israeli defense industry and Ministry of Defense had, and Reynard wondered if they could give Hyperion a recommendation.

The Hawkinsons were in trouble. The only way their public image could get any worse would be if their family patriarch had secretly been a Nazi collaborator. But Michelle Reynard knew this was an opportunity, and told her staff as much. Word on the street was that the Hawkinsons were building a technology firm and attempting to rebrand themselves to grow beyond their reputation as mercenaries, and worse.

While Ava thought her work at Pax AI might give her an edge, the assignment was given to Hyperion's rockstar lead associate, Derrick Dodds. Derrick's resume was almost too good to be true. He had attended Duke on a basketball scholarship, where he graduated with honors and was a member of the 2010 NCAA National Championship team. Ava looked him up and learned that he barely played the entire season, but no one would ever know it from speaking with him. Dodds also had a year with USAID, a Harvard MBA, and ten years in increasingly impressive consulting firms. He'd been with Hyperion for the last three.

Dodds was Black, six-two, lean, and athletic, with a tight fade haircut that was just retro enough to be currently fashionable. He dressed well, in Tom Ford and Boglioli, and drove a sleek-looking, top-of-the-line Porsche SUV.

Ava had attempted to charm him, informing Dodds that she'd worked with the Hawkinsons in the past, flashing her dark eyes and suggesting maybe they could strategize over drinks after work one night.

Dodds declined.

Ava knew poaching was common in the consulting indus-try. As cutthroat and underhanded as the competition was between firms, the internecine warfare between individual consultants within a given company was even fiercer. Hype-rion encouraged aggressiveness in their employees, holding fast to the belief that only the strong survived. Ava would have to refine her approach.

She spent her evenings preparing for her ultimate mission. Working through Moshe, Ava read everything Mossad's Wash-ington Station could provide her on Guy Hawkinson, including a detailed psychological profile. The profile described Guy's personal habits and interests, even detailing his taste in women—tall and well-endowed. The reports also contained comprehensive analyses on the Hawkinson busi-ness enterprise and their overall fundraising efforts. She vora-ciously consumed these files each night, looking for a way in. Ava thought she had developed a plan, but she still needed to figure out how to sidestep the firm's top consultant.

She decided to meet with Michelle Reynard. Perhaps the women's network was the answer?

Reynard met with Ava after close of business in her office, which boasted an impressive twelfth-floor view of K Street. It also had a wet bar that could be used for entertaining high-profile clients and lubricating late-night strategy sessions with top performers.

Reynard was in her early fifties, though she looked much

younger: tall and lithe with blonde hair pulled into a precise ponytail, brown eyes, and naturally tanned skin. Like Ava, she was a Columbia MBA, though Reynard's was in international development. She'd worked in London for ten years, Berlin for three, and had been lured to D.C. by Hyperion's board, who felt they needed a bold new hire to run their consulting practice. She was divorced and didn't speak of her ex-husband, saying only that he couldn't keep up and letting the other person infer what details they wished. Reynard worked fifteen-hour days and, at this point in her life, didn't take shit from anyone.

"I hope you like martinis," she said, when Ava arrived at her office at the appointed time. Reynard was dressed in red, the year's current power color. "James Bond ruined this drink for a generation. Anyone who tells you to shake a martini is a damned Visigoth."

Reynard made martinis in a shaker and poured equal amounts into the two glasses she'd set aside. She placed a lemon peel in each glass, handed one to Ava, then sat in a black leather couch that ran along her window.

"Cheers," Reynard said. "Now, before we begin, I just want to tell you how impressed I've been with your performance so far. You've made a big impact in a short period of time and everyone has noticed. Your approach on that BAE pivot probably saved the account."

"I'm glad I could be helpful," Ava said, taking a small sip.

"Good. Good. Listen, between us girls, you should know that I may be cleaning some dead weight around here soon. You're completely safe. But I would like you to be prepared to pick up Tony's book."

Ava gave her a half-surprised, half-appreciative smile. "Oh. Well, thanks. I'll keep my mouth shut on that."

"Of course. Anyway, what did you want to talk to me about?"

Ava set her glass down on the coffee table. "I hope I'm not being too forward, but I feel like I can be open with you. I want in on the Hawkinson pitch. This isn't about dead weight. Derrick is very, very good, but...after studying Guy Hawkinson, and with my experience in tech, I think the pitch might land better coming from me."

Reynard eyed Ava over the top of her martini glass. "Derrick is one of our best. We need to have our best on this account. Why do you think you should get it?"

Ava said, "I know the Hawkinsons from my time at Pax AI. And I managed one of the programs HSG worked on when I was with the Israeli Ministry of Defense." Ava gave Reynard a small, knowing smile. "And I know what makes Guy Hawkinson tick..."

Reynard smirked.

Ava knew that now was the time to work in some of the information the Mossad profilers gave her. "For instance, I know that every major decision Guy Hawkinson has ever made in business has only come after seeking his sister Sheryl's guidance. Though he has a close group of advisors, mostly people he's served with, Guy doesn't make big decisions without first talking to her. I also know that he has a slight hero worship of Jeff Kim, someone I worked side by side with for years. Many of Jeff Kim's decisions were my recommendations first."

"Wasn't the way Hawkinson's relationship with Jeff Kim ended part of why he needs PR help now? You don't think that puts you at a disadvantage?"

"On the contrary, it's quite an asset. I know how they think. Derrick's pitch is about a *rebranding*." Ava shrugged. "Damage control? No. Hawkinson doesn't think he did anything *wrong*.

And we can't imply that. If we do, they're going to walk right out of the room."

"So how would you handle it?"

Ava said, "Simple. Tell them that our job is to bring their vision of the future to the world. We understand how important this new technology-focused business is to them. We craft a strategy that shifts Wall Street's opinion about Hawk Security Group as much as it does the general public's opinion. Everyone loves a winner. If investors buy in, their image will improve as a result. If we come out of the gate suggesting a way to minimize damage...it will be the same as accusing them of a crime. We might as well invite Bain to the meeting and just do a handoff."

Reynard gave a terse laugh and they both sipped their drinks.

"You make a compelling argument and I think you definitely know your subject matter. Guy taking pointers from his sister isn't lost on me. I do think having a woman on the team lends us some agency." Reynard took another sip, then set her glass down. "I'm not going to take Derrick off the account. He's earned this, but I do think your approach is sound. I'm going to invite you to join the strategy team and give you a seat at the table for the pitch. Fair?" Reynard stood and smoothed out her skirt. The meeting was over.

Hawk Technologies occupied the top three floors of a brand-new, mirrored-glass building in Tysons Corner, just a few miles from CIA headquarters. Hyperion brought a small team —Reynard, Ava, Dobbs, and three others—and the meeting opened with the usual small talk.

Ava did her best to get close to Guy during the reception. If he knew of Ava's past history with Pax AI and his sister Sheryl, he hid it well, giving no indication that he recognized her face or name when she was first introduced. Inside, Ava felt relief. Eventually, it would come out. But if she had gotten this far, that was a good sign.

He wore a black suit with a subtle black pinstripe pattern, crisp white shirt, and blue tie. He was medium height, still in excellent shape, and had sandy blond hair parted on the right side. He asked her about Israel, and Ava laughed at a joke he made. She had purposely chosen a tight dress that accentuated her best features, and she could tell that Guy had noticed her.

"You know I've met your sister a few times," Ava said, touching him gently on the arm.

Guy cocked his head. "Oh, I wasn't aware."

"When I worked with Jeff Kim out in San Francisco."

He stiffened at the mention of Kim's name and appraised Ava with renewed interest. "I see. Interesting…"

Just then Michelle Reynard opened the pitch by thanking Hawkinson for the opportunity to meet with them. She introduced her team and then Dobbs took over. He told Hyperion's story and provided two quick but impactful case studies of other companies that trusted their reputation to Hyperion. Dobbs softened his part considerably thanks to Ava's advice and Reynard's coaching, but the subtext was the same—Hyperion could remake their image into whatever they wanted it to be.

When it was Ava's turn, she spoke directly to Guy and drew on Mossad's profile of him to craft her presentation. They believed Guy was attracted to and influenced by powerful, assertive women. The Mossad psychologists said that he ultimately desired to have power over them. It was about the hunt.

Ava praised Guy's technology-first vision, a bold pivot toward a business future that took advantage of the power of artificial intelligence. She emphasized that future winners needed to take risks now, and implied that Guy Hawkinson was just such a person. With *his* vision and guidance, Hyperion could craft a strategy that would put Hawk Technologies on the edge of the future.

Guy was eating it up. Hanging on every word. Ava was radiant...mastering her presentation.

And that was when Sheryl Hawkinson walked in.

***

An intelligence officer's worst nightmare was being unmasked.

Her pulse quickened as Sheryl studied her face, but she kept speaking, wrapping up her talk, forcing herself to remain calm. Ava had trained for this exact scenario many times in the past—running into someone who could break your cover.

Though Ava's legend said that she was a former Ministry of Defense employee, disgruntled and ousted because of loyalty to the previous PM, Sheryl Hawkinson *knew* her. Sheryl had been both an investor and advisor to Jeff Kim. They'd interacted socially at Pax AI functions. Ava couldn't be certain if Sheryl knew whether she was Mossad or not, though in that eventuality, Katz advised her to say that the MoD job was a cover for her fictitious firing from Mossad. It would sound plausible, establish Ava as a potential axe-grinder, and tracked with Mossad's public perception of not claiming former officers.

Sheryl took a seat at the table, set down her phone and tablet, and locked eyes with Ava. She wore the slightest hint of a smile and gave Ava a barely perceptible nod as she completed her presentation, concluding with the bold statement that Hyperion was the only firm capable of bringing Hawkinson's vision to life and they looked forward to a fruitful partnership.

The meeting wrapped.

Reynard thanked everyone for their time, and as they stood, she made her way over to Sheryl to shake hands, introduce herself, and suggest they meet for drinks. As the Hyperion team filed into the hallway, Sheryl caught up with Ava. "It's nice to see you again, Ava," she said. Her voice always sounded dry and brittle to Ava, like leaves at the end of autumn.

"You as well."

"Landed on your feet, I see."

Ava started to reply but decided against it and left the room. She had not expected Sheryl's presence here. According to the San Francisco Station, Sheryl was supposed to be back home this week. Was Sheryl wondering about the coincidence of Ava Klein, former Pax AI senior staff, ending up at Hyperion just as they were about to pitch Hawk Technologies? A good intel analyst would flag it. Ava swore to herself softly.

Reynard stayed back in the conference room to speak privately with the Hawkinsons. Ava saw Sheryl look in her direction at least once, her expression unreadable. Reynard looked over as well, but did not acknowledge Ava and closed the conversation with a smile and a short laugh.

The Hyperion team met for lunch at the Capitol Grille on Route 7, just around the corner from the Hawk Tech offices. They had a private room in the back and were just about to order drinks when Reynard got a phone call. The conversation was short and Reynard gave nothing away. When it was finished, she thanked the caller for their time and lowered the phone.

Before she addressed her team, Michelle Reynard turned

to the server and said in a deadpan voice, "We'll take three bottles of the Opus One." She looked at her team. "We got the Hawkinson account!"

The room erupted into cheers. She praised everyone for their dedicated preparation and excellent pitch, truly one of the best she'd seen. The server reappeared with the restaurant's sommelier, who began reviewing the wines available. Reynard walked over to Ava and asked her for a word, leading her to the edge of the room beneath a dramatic painting of a ship at sea.

Ava, whose nerves had been balancing on a razor's edge since she saw Sheryl, knew what Reynard was about to say. *Sorry, dear, while you've helped Hyperion win the account, they asked you not to be on the team.*

"Ava, there's something I want to talk to you about before the celebration gets too out of hand," Reynard said.

Here it was.

"Of course," Ava said.

"You were magnificent today. Truly. I was very impressed that you were able to ramp up on this thing so quickly." The server appeared and handed each of them a glass of wine, then disappeared. "Just really, really impressive. This is still Derrick's account. It wouldn't be right for me to give it to someone else, even though I'd agree that you saved the pitch."

"I understand."

"But how would you feel about being Hyperion's liaison to Hawk Technologies? Guy, in particular, was very impressed with you. Sheryl also spoke highly of you and remembered you from your time with Pax AI. Apparently, you made an impression. Normally, this is something we'd give a more junior associate, but for something as high profile as this...I think it's best that we put one of *our* best on it. Wouldn't you agree?"

Finally, Reynard smiled.

"So, I'd be working at Hawk Technologies?" Ava asked.

"That's right. We'd need to finalize the arrangement. Ostensibly, you'll be reporting to Derrick, but I'm going to take a personal interest in this one. You'll be at the client site most days and, I suspect, taking your cues directly from Guy."

Ava was surprised. "Um, yes. Wonderful. When do I get started?"

"Right away. The formal contract is going to take some time to iron out, but we have a limited consulting agreement that we can get in place this week. They are eager to get started and so are we."

Ava took a shallow sip of her wine, savoring it as much as her victory, then allowed herself a smile. She was in.

20

Arlington, Virginia

"Okay, tell me. How the hell did you do it?" Colt said.

Nadia stared back at him triumphantly. "Must have been all your great training."

They were in her Clarendon apartment for one of their final meetings, if all went according to plan. The noise from Wilson Avenue could be heard outside. Happy hour and dinner gatherings. People enjoying the warm summer night.

"We placed one of those tracking devices on your person again. Yet the FBI lost you. You had surveillance following someone else around for almost two hours. How'd you do it?"

Nadia held up her phone and shrugged. "I used a program."

Colt raised his eyebrows. "You used an anti-tracking program."

She winked. "Got it off the dark web from someone I trust. He didn't ask questions. I checked the code for anything malicious using a program I wrote. I'm actually kind of surprised that something like this isn't standard operating procedure."

Colt said, "Maybe it should be. How does your program work?"

"Each one of those tracking devices has a distinct ID. There are a lot of them in use. They use Bluetooth and ultra-wideband technology. The anti-tracking program uses my own phone to see if any others are in close proximity to me for a long time. If I go into a populated area like, say, a Metro station, there is almost certainly going to be someone else with a cell phone in range. The program uses a bug in their security to swap one ID for another. That bug might not be around for much longer. But I should be able to reliably use my program to issue an alert if one of these things is latched on to me. It can also be used to disrupt Bluetooth trans-missions."

Colt was starting to realize that Nadia had a scary blend of talents. "Um, I think the Science and Technology team is probably going to want to discuss this with you further. But that's amazing. Good job. And you really pissed off those FBI guys."

"Payback's a bitch." Nadia's eyes twinkled.

Colt laughed.

Nadia's apartment was effectively a safe house, and one of the few places they could debrief in relative security. An agency sweep team went through here once a week disguised as housekeepers to check for surveillance devices, and Colt timed his meetings to coincide with those. The apartment building had two street-level entrances and an underground garage, affording him multiple ingress and egress points so he could visit undetected.

Nadia's final weeks of training focused on collection. Spot-ting potential intelligence targets. Gaining access to the data. Sifting the valuable wheat from the chaff, and surreptitiously collecting it. Her assignment today had been to find selected bits of Cognitive's "trade secrets" and smuggle them out of the building.

Nadia didn't know Cognitive was a CIA front. Colt briefed her that the startup was connected with the Agency, a legitimate firm. When she expressed concern about spying on a real company, Ford just told her "you'd only be stealing the secrets we already gave them." In reality, Cognitive's "employees" were either Agency personnel, cleared contractors, or retired operations officers. They were not read in on STONE-BRIDGE, but did know that a critical effort was underway that required them to create a convincing fiction.

Cognitive's CEO was read in. He helped Colt and Ford craft some potential trade secrets and hide them within the company's virtual and physical files. The support divisions at Langley worked tirelessly to paint the picture that Cognitive was a working, breathing company. This would help Nadia when she was finally in the field, serving the dual purposes of authentic training and a solid legend. It wouldn't stand up to the scrutiny of a dedicated and months-long due diligence investigation that would precede any acquisition effort, but the company would certainly feel real to a visitor.

Once Nadia was inserted into Hawk Technologies, she would be expected to collect anything of intelligence value as well as to actively but cautiously solicit information on the Hawkinsons' objectives. These lessons were designed to train her specifically on how to conduct industrial espionage. Nadia had uploaded the results of her efforts this week to Colt's computer, both the files she appropriated and the photos she took with her camera. As a modern technology company, Cognitive kept very little in terms of physical files, but Nadia thought to bluff her way into the HR office—called "people ops"—and got a few moments alone with the personnel records. She was able to get a current employee roster as well as their hiring applications. These were all fakes, created by CIA's logistics division to preserve covers. Colt was impressed. That was an ingenious move and something he hadn't asked for.

"How did the button cam work?"

"Let's find out." Nadia picked up a small box and set it on the coffee table. She opened it and removed the button inside, dropping it into the palm of his hand. Colt set it inside a small cradle attached to a USB dongle and inserted that into his laptop. The upload commenced immediately. They believed that Hawk Technologies would have a secure area built to the same standards as an intelligence Secure Compartmented Information Facility (SCIF). They would store the most sensitive R&D here, physically isolated and completely inaccessible from the internet. Phones, tablets, and laptops wouldn't be allowed in that space, so they needed a way to get information out. The tech team devised a camera concealed inside a button sewn onto a light black sweater. It was remote-controlled, activated by tapping a different button on the sleeve of her sweater.

Colt studied the photos, zooming in on the files. "Not bad. We need to work on your aim." He looked over at her. "I'd like you to practice with some objects in your apartment, just to get a feel for it, but this isn't bad for a first go."

The apartment's front door opened and Ford blew in with gale force. He carried two bags and the aroma of Mexican food quickly filled the small apartment. "I'll say this for Arlington. It's a little hipster for me, but their taco game is strong."

He set the bags on the counter and began pulling out their contents. This had become their routine on debriefings and training missions conducted in the apartment. Ford busied himself in the kitchen while Colt reviewed the results of the collection effort.

After a few moments, he closed the laptop and leaned back in his chair. "This is all really good, Nadia. Great work."

"Thank you," she said.

Colt told Ford about Nadia's own method of throwing off the FBI tracking devices. He whistled, impressed.

"How'd the mock interrogation go today?" Ford asked.

Nadia made a face. "Eh, not as good. I need to work on that stuff. They're tripping me up on details."

Ford said, "Just be glad you're getting the nice-guy version."

"What do you mean?" Nadia asked.

"I was waterboarded once." Colt gave her a grim smile. "They don't teach it anymore, but it was in the curriculum when I did my resistance training. Everyone breaks when they start doing that stuff. That was the point of the exercise. You hold out as long as you can and try to give the least damaging information. That wasn't always the policy, right? People thought Gary Powers was a traitor for not taking a cyanide pill. Now, the Agency would much rather get you back and find out what the inside of the adversary's counterintelligence apparatus looks like. I read the report today. You did fail the exercise, but don't let it get in your head."

While Nadia wasn't looking, Colt saw Ford cast him a concerned look.

"Failure is the best teacher," Ford said, bringing over plates of partially unwrapped tacos, chips, and guacamole. "We fail in practice so we don't fuck it up for real."

The exercise had been a mock interrogation that Colt set up with a couple case officers currently assigned to the CI division at headquarters. They had Nadia report to a nondescript office at the Agency in Herndon, one of several clandestine CIA locations in the D.C. metro area. The two case officers proceeded to interrogate her, both pretending to be FBI agents complete with badges.

Even knowing that it was an exercise, Nadia gave them more information than she should have. Making mistakes wasn't hard when she was being questioned by professionals trying to trip her up on being inconsistent with fake information.

"Don't dwell on it," Colt said. "But also remember that your cover will save you and everything is a test."

While they ate, Ford turned on the television to the nightly news. The lead story was the rising tide of anti-technology protests erupting throughout the country. They had the reach and intensity of racial justice protests and associated riots from previous years. Video showed protestors in Austin smashing the glass on an Apple Store downtown. There were similar acts of vandalism in San Francisco, San Diego, Atlanta, Seattle, and Tampa. Most of these rioters were radicalized and communicated with each other almost exclusively online, an irony that appeared to be lost on them.

But the news story also mentioned that the anti-tech movement was starting to gain momentum among a wider segment of the population who didn't take to the streets. The newscaster recited facts and figures, providing anecdotal stories. Every day there seemed to be more problems related to rapidly changing technology. Car accidents involving autonomous vehicles. Cloud computing outages that halted online businesses and everyday delivery applications. Erroneous credit card and banking transactions. Disruption to e-commerce.

The story then shifted to the counterpoint, which was an interview with Jeff Kim. He had avoided the public eye almost entirely in the last two years, communicating primarily through spokespeople, and even then sporadically. This was his first public interview since the loss of his Mountain Research Facility. The current segment was cut from a longer interview, scheduled to air on the network's Friday night magazine show, which they were heavily promoting. The interviewer was asking Jeff about the ACTioN partnership and its implications.

"We're already seeing these vehicles operate with a higher level of safety and efficiency than their human counterparts," Kim said. "Think about it from the emissions standpoint alone. If America relies on line haul trucking for the majority of its cargo delivery, how many tens of millions of pounds of noxious gas does that provide each year? To say nothing of the inherent dangers of driver fatigue. Our autonomous trucking initiative is showing that machines can do this job better, safer, and infinitely cleaner than the way it's being done today."

"But what about the jobs you'd be eliminating?" the interviewer asked. "We're not just talking about the drivers. There are vehicle mechanics, gas station attendants, fuel truck drivers."

"In a perfect world, I'd automate those too," Kim said, and they both laughed. "But you bring up a good point. Technological advancement is inherently disruptive. People chastised Henry Ford for creating an assembly line, then the unions fought the robotization of those same assembly lines seventy years later. Why? Because it was taking a menial job from a person and they couldn't see their way past it. Aren't we better served, as a society, if that person is freed up to do meaningful work? I don't know about you, but I don't want to spend eight hours a day drilling holes. I'll make a robot do that and I'm going to solve bigger problems. With the resources we're saving with our autonomous delivery initiative, we could easily reinvest the profits to create higher-paying technology jobs. For example, as part of this program, we're offering every truck driver we take off the road retraining in a coding academy to learn how to write computer code."

"Jeff, as I'm sure you're aware, there have been numerous tragic accidents involving autonomous vehicles recently. The spike in the last six weeks more than doubles the crashes in the previous year. Certainly that's cause for concern?"

"Of course, but let's remember that an airline crash used to be a common occurrence and the loss of human life is far, far greater there. People still flew and flew safely. The accidents pushed the government to increase regulation, the manufacturers to build better planes, and the airlines to train better pilots. I'll also add that as we've increased cockpit automation —along with improvements in aircraft design and safety systems—we've seen a tremendous increase in airline safety."

The anchor teased their interview with Kim again and cut to commercial. When they returned from the break, they featured Senator Preston Hawkinson thundering on the evils of big tech. "Our citizens are rioting in the streets because of the so-called tech elites, people like Jeff Kim who are trying to take jobs away from hard-working Americans. These patriots, who are exercising their First Amendment rights, are expressing their displeasure at big tech and at those across the aisle from me who are refusing to act."

"You know what gets me about him?" Ford asked, and then took a massive bite of the small taco in his hand. "He's the biggest anti-tech firebrand we have in government. Every year or so, he introduces or co-authors legislation to break up 'big tech,' as he calls it, wants to 'hold people accountable.' All of the usual bullshit. And here his niece and nephew are, founding an advanced technology company, hiring up the biggest and brightest AI researchers they can find. The case officer in me—pay attention, Nadia— can't help but wonder if he's some sort of false flag."

"For who?" Nadia asked.

"Sheryl and Guy. Look, the majority of our tech companies

and research institutions are in our most populated states. California, Texas, Florida, New York, Georgia. This legislation never makes it to House floor; there are too many Congressional districts in both parties at play. None of them are going to go after their donors. Besides, he's a senator from Wyoming. He doesn't have a dog in this fight."

"But, like you say, he raises a bunch of stink every so often, grandstands for the cameras, and gets people to look at him. Nothing happens in Congress, and whenever he does this, there's always the regular run of stories focusing on the big tech companies. And no one is looking at—"

"What his niece and nephew are doing," Ford finished for her. "You're getting it, kid."

"All right, let's turn the TV off. Where are we on the new job hire process?" Colt asked.

"My resume is out there online," Nadia said. "I've applied to the EverPresence job posting. About ten recruiters have reached out to me on LinkedIn, but no one from EverPresence yet. But you wouldn't believe the salaries the other companies are offering..."

Ford snorted. "Can't be as good as a GS-12."

Nadia laughed.

Colt wasn't in the joking mood. "Fred, is your contact going to be able to deliver?"

Ford nodded. "The cyber guys tell me we're good. We just need confirmation that Hawk Tech is actually going to purchase EverPresence before we pull the trigger."

Ford had worked it all out with a CIA retiree from his network. EverPresence used a headhunter firm to do its recruiting, and the CIA retiree was now in charge of that firm's security. As any good CIA officer did, this retiree had made friends at his new job, and was going to pull some strings and insert Nadia into EverPresence's candidate pool, making sure that her name would never be identified. The moves would push Nadia to the top of EverPresence's hiring recommendations. "They hire more than 50 percent of those top recommendations. So Nadia will have to do her part in the interviews."

Colt didn't like it. There was still a lot of risk. And if it didn't work, they would still need to find another way to get Nadia into Hawk.

"Holy shit, you hear about this?" Ford said, holding up his phone. "My buddy on the Russia desk told me about this earlier. Apparently, the Mali government hired Vavakin Group to beef up their military forces last fall. They just up and wiped out an ISIS camp a few nights ago, which prompted all of the *other* terrorist groups in the region to retaliate. It's a total shit show. Firefights all over the southern part of the country. Mali's president ordered the Vavakin mercs to get out by the end of the week." He picked up another taco. "I hope this doesn't boil over. I don't want to go back to Africa."

After dinner, they continued the lesson. Colt reviewed measures Nadia would use to gain access to cleared areas, and they discussed the techniques for unlocking restricted material. Poor information security practices were pervasive even at the best companies. They went over all the places people tended to store passwords. It was a big problem in high-security facilities because employees couldn't bring their phones—and password-keeping apps—inside.

"Big problem for them," Nadia said. "Opportunity for us."

"Exactly," Ford said.

"In our next block," Colt said as they were winding down, "we're going to focus on how to spot a foreign intelligence officer. In general, other nations—even friends of ours—spy on our industrial base relentlessly. But since we also know that Hawkinson colluded with the Russians in the past, it's possible the SVR has people inside his company now. He might not be aware of it."

"I hadn't considered that." Nadia looked like a college student studying for exams. Stressed, overwhelmed, and nervous.

"Barbarians at the gate, wolf at your door, pick your metaphor," Fred quipped.

"You did good today," Colt said to Nadia. He needed to build her up.

It was nearly midnight, and they were all spent. Nadia said goodbye and the two men departed. They stopped to talk at Ford's Jeep, parked a few blocks away on a dark neighborhood street.

"Do you think she's ready?" Ford asked.

"We'll see," Colt said.

21

Falls Church, Virginia

At Yasenova's direction, Petrov moved his operation to Washington, D.C. The SVR wanted him to personally oversee all operations related to the Hawkinson project. While his continued presence inside the US was risky, so were electronic communications, which could be intercepted and monitored.

The Center authorized Petrov to receive clandestine support from the Washington *rezident*, but maintained that he should still report to Koskov directly. Under no circumstances was he to approach the Russian Embassy.

Petrov's communication with the Center was handled via secure messaging that used an end-to-end encryption card, similar to technology the Spetznaz used to encrypt their satellite radios. He had a degaussing device, made to look like a small safe, in his rented Falls Church safe house. If he had to, he could quickly destroy both the air-gapped laptop he used to read secure communications, the encryption card, and his phone. The computer was stored in his safe when Petrov wasn't at home, and the SVR could remotely destroy it in the event of his capture.

He closed the laptop and poured himself a glass of bourbon, one of his favorite American vices. Drink in hand, Petrov went to sip it in solitude on his back porch. He needed some time to think about the Hawkinson operation.

Koskov and the Center were quite pleased with the trove of AI research Guy provided. It almost made up for being two years late.

The earliest analysis suggested that it would advance Russian artificial intelligence research significantly, getting them closer to parity with the West.

The GRU, Russia's military intelligence agency, would quickly weaponize the new technology. They would use it to further their cyber-attacks on the American financial sector and data and cloud computing centers, and cause considerable trouble to several autonomous vehicle systems. With these attacks, Russia could covertly pour fuel on the fire of the anti-technology movement.

Petrov thought the GRU, as usual, was acting too quickly. In their haste, they made mistakes. He worried that the Americans would eventually discover the vulnerabilities and counter them.

But Petrov didn't need to worry about this yet. He thought about the next part of his mission: identifying and disrupting Mossad's operations against Hawkinson. On his travel to D.C., Petrov had studied Hawk Technologies, the new AI-focused arm of the Hawkinson business empire. He understood their business and growth plans. He knew their physical location, and SVR researchers had conducted a thorough analysis of everyone who was publicly working for the company.

As Petrov sipped bourbon in solitude, he thought through how he would design a surveillance operation against such a company. He would have information warfare specialists probing every inch of their finances and human resources materials. He would set up physical surveillance on key personnel. He would have a team of analysts monitoring all of the company's plans and operations.

And he would recruit or insert agents on the inside.

Just like Mossad did with Pax AI.

Yes, that's what he would do. And that's what Mossad must be doing. Petrov took out his air-gapped computer and read over the SVR report on Mossad's Washington, D.C. operations. The head of Israel's Washington team was a man by the name of Katz. Petrov made a note to have all surveillance on Katz increased to the maximum level and forwarded to his team daily. They had illegals, sleeper agents, in the area who could be active for this, guaranteeing Katz wouldn't recognize his surveillance. Mossad likely had files on the SVR officers in Washington.

Petrov needed to contact Koskov to go over his intentions. He wanted to begin searching for any potential agents who might be inside Hawk Tech or trying to gain employment at the firm.

Koskov, however, was quite busy tonight. The Center was embroiled in this Vavakin Group disaster in Mali.

Koskov himself was pressing his *rezidents* to comb their agents and see if this was somehow the work of American special operations forces. Vavakin's leadership swore they had not launched an unsanctioned, unprovoked attack on enemy forces.

The president was furious. He was not a man who took embarrassment well. The day Vavakin was kicked out, the United States made a public statement that they would be happy to resume security cooperation with the people of Mali. It was a slap in Russia's face.

So with the SVR in crisis mode, Petrov decided to wait an extra day to discuss any Mossad plans.

The doorbell rang, and the hairs on the back of Petrov's neck stood up. He set his glass down and walked to the front door. If it was the FBI, they would have already been inside the house.

He looked through the peephole.

Nothing.

He opened the door and saw a food delivery man holding a white plastic bag. Petrov thought of telling the man he didn't order anything, but his instincts told him to take the bag. The man disappeared and Petrov closed the door, hurrying to the kitchen and opening the bag.

Inside was a white container of steaming hot food from a local Ethiopian restaurant. A phone rang inside the bag. Petrov felt his face growing hot. He peered inside and saw a prepaid phone.

He pressed the answer button and held the phone to his ear.

"You see the news?" Guy Hawkinson asked.

Petrov narrowed his eyes. "Ethiopian food."

"It was as close as I could get without being too obvious."

Petrov blinked. Then, understanding hit him. *The Mali operation...*

"I'm told this restaurant is excellent," Guy continued. "So please don't let the food go to waste. I promise it is free of polonium."

Petrov's mind raced. Of course, this made sense. US special forces didn't have any troops near Mali but Hawkinson's private army did. They had a company-sized unit deployed only a few hours away by air in Guinea. A cadre of former special forces, armed, equipped, and supported not far from the Mali border. It would only be a few hundred kilometers to the village where The Vavakin Group allegedly attacked the ISIS fighters. *The Mali operation was Hawkinson.*

...and my superiors have no idea.

Guy said, "I know you are thinking through whether I could have done it, and why I would have..."

Petrov gave a short laugh and Guy stopped speaking, probably wondering if his Russian friend had gone mad. But Petrov was admiring the sheer brashness of the move, the blatant disregard for consequence. He had newfound appreciation for his asset. Guy Hawkinson was a man to be respected.

Petrov could tell the Center none of this, and Guy Hawkinson had known and counted on that.

Petrov finally spoke. "If my president ever learned that someone—anyone—was responsible for his humiliation, he would dispatch someone to deal with it immediately. Anyone involved would face a painful end."

"I understand," Guy said.

"We both do," replied Petrov.

They were in this together. If the true story of HSG's participation in the Mali attack got out, the Russian president would go after them both. Guy Hawkinson had made his show of strength and bonded them in one swift move. He was Petrov's ticket to career resuscitation. Without Hawkinson, Petrov's value to the Kremlin plummeted.

"See you at our next meeting. Enjoy the food." Guy ended the call.

Petrov fell into a seat at the kitchen table, shaking his head.

He liked this American, he decided. He would begin hunting for agents immediately.

22

Nadia's capstone training exercise was convincing the Cognitive CEO that she should join him on a business development meeting at the National Reconnaissance Office (NRO) in Chantilly.

The NRO was the government agency that operated many of the country's spy satellites. Cognitive was pitching their image recognition tech to the satellite jockeys in hopes that they'd bite. As a new employee not directly working on that project, Nadia's attendance was a tough sell.

She spent two days working on her approach before finally pitching him. The CEO, Jack Newton, gave a company "all hands" to talk about the NRO deal's importance and what it would mean for them. After that, she followed him to the break room while he refilled his coffee and pitched him. Nadia said it would be great for her development to see him in action, and she knew that she needed to bolster her business skills if she was to grow as a leader in the company. She said even though she wasn't on the image rec project, which they called iNSIGHT, she knew the technology and could speak to the challenges of predictable image recognition. He agreed.

When she arrived at the NRO, they cleared security and were ushered into a secure conference room, where she found Colt and Ford waiting. That's when Nadia knew this had been a test. She looked at Cognitive's CEO, who just smiled. Colt and Ford stood and gave her genuine applause.

"Congratulations," Colt said.

"You did good, kid," said Ford.

Realization dawned on her. Newton smiled when he saw the recognition in her eyes. "Sorry, I'm part of it too."

"I suppose you're going to tell me your name is not really Jack Newton?" Nadia asked.

"Afraid not."

Colt explained that Cognitive was part of the test. They needed to make sure that she could not only operate under-cover for a sustained period of time but also be able to collect intelligence. Colt said that every staff member was either a retired case officer or cleared contractor employed by the CIA, but none of them except "Jack Newton" were read in on STONEBRIDGE.

"For what it's worth," Jack said, "I thought your tradecraft was very good. I knew that you'd be snooping around, but I didn't know when or where. That was part of the test. Our security people didn't pick up on anything you did. Colt showed me what you collected. Pretty impressive."

Nadia beamed.

The last few months had been a whirlwind and the most intense time of her life, but she'd loved every minute of it.

This was what she was meant to do.

"Take the rest of the afternoon off," Ford said. "We're going to take you out to celebrate tonight."

"What's going to happen to Cognitive?" Nadia asked.

"We need to keep it running for a little while longer and then we'll shut it down," Colt said. "It needs to be closed down believably because it'll be on your resume. It still needs to look and feel like a real company, but we don't need to keep running it anymore."

"What's next, then?"

Colt and Ford exchanged glances.

"We're arranging for you to be hired by a company called EverPresence," Ford said. "They're doing some virtual reality internet shit."

"It's an immersive VR, but realistically rendered," Colt added. "They think they can accurately create a real-world image inside their headset that the human brain won't be able to differentiate."

Ford shot him an annoyed look. "That's what I said. Anyway, we know the Hawkinsons are already attempting to buy that company. We're going to insert you there so that when they do, you get swept in with everybody else without it raising any flags."

"Like a Trojan Horse."

"Exactly like that," Colt said. They congratulated her again, and Nadia left with Newton so she wouldn't be seen departing with Colt and Ford.

That night, they took her out for a celebratory dinner at one of Ford's favorite places, an Italian restaurant called Lupo Verde. It was in a quiet, upper-northwest D.C. neighborhood called the Palisades, nestled between Georgetown and Bethesda along MacArthur Boulevard beside the bluffs overlooking the Potomac River. Nadia arrived at eight for their reservation. She'd taken an Uber from her apartment because there wasn't a Metro stop nearby, and Ford told her this would be the one night she was off duty for a long time. Nadia found the Palisades to be quaint and idyllic, with tall maple trees shading the streets and lined with hundred-year-old town-homes. Lupo Verde was at the end of a block of small shops and restaurants, each occupying a historic townhome. She was told the reservation would be under the name "Hamilton," and when she arrived, she was guided to a table on the third floor where she found Ford and Colt, both with bottles of Italian beer. She joined them, a cocktail quickly appeared, and they set to celebrating.

Nadia enjoyed an incredible meal, truly some of the best Italian food she'd had in this country, and told her companions about an Air Force deployment she had where their aircraft mysteriously "broke" at Naval Air Station Sigonella and she was forced, *forced*, to explore Sicily for the weekend while the aircrew attempted to figure out why their plane wouldn't fly. Miraculously, the problem was resolved the following Monday morning, but Nadia spent two days on a gastronomical bacchanal and developed a lifetime love of authentic Italian food and wine.

Ford was as gregarious as ever and Colt was his usual dour, reserved self. She got the impression that he was the kind of person who was always working. Even when he was off duty, he wasn't really. There was a problem to solve, a mystery to unravel, a conspiracy to unmask. She knew that he loved the job, and he did it as much for that as out of patriotic obligation.

Colt told her once, "The thing that made you join the Air Force is the thing that makes you want to do this job. When you're tired, when you're cold, you're lonely, or you're hurt. When you haven't seen your family in two years. You do it because someone *has* to. Truly. But also"—and then he flashed one of his rare smiles—"you do it because you *get to*."

"But mostly for the money," Ford had added, straight-faced.

It was a Wednesday night and the restaurant wasn't busy. There was no one within three tables of them, but dinner conversation still kept to prosaic topics and stayed well away from work. There was the inevitable discussion on world affairs, though to the casual observer it would sound like fifty percent of the conversations happening in Washington, D.C. at that exact moment. They talked about the situation in Africa they'd seen on the news, a Russian defense contractor being kicked out of Mali for picking an unauthorized fight with ISIS.

"I hear about cybercrime constantly," Nadia said, and swirled her wine like she'd seen Ford do. "I'm just wondering how much of a threat the Russians really are at this point. My entire time in the Air Force, all we talked about was counter-terrorism. The fighter guys talked about China, but that was mostly blowing smoke about how the F-22s had eight-to-one superiority over everyone."

"I'm not worried about the Russian military," Colt said flatly. "They're disorganized and poorly equipped. Everything we learned about them after the Cold War appears to still be true, which is that they have good front line units but no depth."

"They've got a first string and a scout team and nothing in between," Ford said. "But their special forces are scary." Colt nodded in agreement. "Russian tradecraft is very good and they are sneaky bastards. Their technical capabilities are also very good. It was their special forces that allowed them to take Crimea in 2014, and they just wrecked the Ukrainian resistance."

"How so?"

"There's a story about a Ukrainian special forces major who was running this whole guerrilla war against them. The Russians knew his name but couldn't figure out where he was. It was driving them nuts." Ford took a drink of wine. "So they had the SVR do some digging and learned his mother's name and phone number. They called her and impersonated his unit commander, said, 'Your son is hurt and we can't find him. Could you call him?' So she did. They used his cell phone signal to zero in a smart bomb and took him out."

"Jesus Christ."

"Don't go to sleep on Ivan. He's as dangerous as he ever was. Maybe more, because I think they're getting desperate."

"Like Ford said, their technical capabilities are good. They seem to have a particular aptitude at cyber."

Colt steered the conversation to happier subjects after that.

They had a wonderful dinner and it lasted far too short for Nadia. These two had become her big brothers, in a sense. She barely knew them as people, really. Not about their pasts or what they did in the Agency before STONEBRIDGE, except for what little they shared that was part of the lessons, but she knew their character. But they were the only two people in the world who understood what she had been through in the last few months and what she was preparing to do. That made them close.

It was nearing ten-thirty and they were some of the last to leave the restaurant. Colt and Ford both had espressos; Nadia abstained. Ford picked up the check, and they said their good-byes beneath the yellow streetlight and a moonlit night. Nadia was slightly buzzed, but she'd backed off the wine in the last hour and felt pretty good. Colt and Ford said they were parked on the street. She called an Uber and waited, watching her big brothers fade into the night.

Nadia received a text saying that the compact car she'd requested wasn't available and she was instead getting a black Suburban. She received a text a few moments later indicating that it was arriving. She saw the lumbering beast of a vehicle roll down the otherwise empty MacArthur and flagged it down with her hand. The large SUV pulled up to the curb and she opened the door. The tint on the windows was so dark, she was amazed it was legal.

"For Nadia?" she asked.

The driver, whom she couldn't really see, said yes and she got in, climbing into the middle row of seats, which were a pair of captain's chairs with a middle console.

Nadia pulled her door closed.

She heard the locks engage, and the vehicle started moving.

No sooner had they started forward than a pair of rough hands grabbed her from the row behind. Thick hands with a rock-hard grip. A gag was quickly tied around her mouth.

And then everything went black.

23

Somewhere

The heavy cloth bag over her head made everything completely black.

They—whoever _they_ were—had secured her to the seat despite her attempts to resist them. She tried to jump out of the chair but was restrained by a set of huge hands with a vise grip. She was pulled hard into her seat while a different set of hands secured her with a heavy band that felt like a cargo strap. Finally, they put something over her ears, blocking out all sound.

Nadia fought against the restraints, riding a wave of panic.

She pushed, pulled, and threw herself against them, a caged animal trying to claw its way out.

The headphones were yanked off her head and a thick voice with stale breath said, "If you don't stop struggling, it will be worse for you." The man had a heavy accent. Nadia wasn't a linguist, so any of the Slavic languages sounded the same to her and she just assumed it was Russian. He jammed the headphones back on her roughly, and Nadia was again in the silent dark.

The dinner conversation came crashing back over her: the Russians' ability to crack cell phones, tracking their targets by them. She knew they had a sizable operation in Washington, but to grab an American off the streets was unheard of.

Hands dug into her pants pockets and ripped out her cellphone. Not that she could've seen to dial anyway, but any hope of Colt using that to track her died. The first thing they'd do would be to turn it off. They must have been watching the restaurant. Saw her standing alone after Colt and Ford left.

Did they know about Colt and Ford?

Did they know about STONEBRIDGE?

Nadia remembered the techniques they'd taught her at the Farm: how to remain calm in stressful situations, what to do if she was captured. She tried to force calmness into her mind. They could make things feel very real at the Farm, but you knew it was still a simulation. It was hard to remember everything they taught you when it was really happening.

Colt told her once that he was trained to tell time without a watch. Unfortunately, she hadn't stayed long enough for that block, and without senses to draw on, she had no idea how long she was in the vehicle.

It felt like an eternity.

Eventually, the vehicle stopped and she was dragged out. Her legs didn't cooperate, though, and Nadia found herself on a hard patch of dirt with a rock pressing into her thigh. She was hauled up to her feet, the headphones were ripped off, and she was frog-marched along what seemed like a winding path. Or maybe they were just walking her in circles to throw her off.

A few minutes later, Nadia was pushed into a wooden chair. Her ankles and wrists were strapped to it, and then the hood was ripped off. She expected a bright light to be shining in her face, but there was none. Instead, someone threw a bucket of ice water on her.

She heard a fan whirring and was blasted by a wave of frigid air. Nadia didn't know if she was alone or not; it was hard to hear over the sound of the air conditioner. It was impossible to tell time without the sensory input to gauge its passage. Her world was utter blackness.

On top of that, Nadia could not remember ever being so cold in her life. Her clothes were soaked through, the cold seeping into her bones.

The air conditioner stopped abruptly and a bright light blasted into her face. Nadia winced her eyelids shut and turned away. Just then, a piercing siren went off right behind her. It was a blaring klaxon, like a fire alarm.

Then the alarm stopped. Her ears were still ringing. The light still shining brightly in her eyes.

"You are American?" a voice said.

She saw hands appear at the side of her face. The palms were calloused, and whoever it was smelled of motor oil. The hands pulled the gag violently from her mouth without untying it. She dry-heaved until an open fist hit her head from behind. She actually saw stars swimming in her blurred vision.

"If something is in your mouth, keep it there," the voice said.

She couldn't make out his dimensions. The man was a formless black silhouette surrounded by intense bright light.

"You are American?" another man asked. This one sounded Russian too.

"Yes," Nadia said in a small voice. She felt pure terror in every part of her body; even her *cells* were afraid. She wondered if help would ever come. Did anyone know she was missing?

"You are spy?" the Russian asked.

"No. I'm an engineer," Nadia said.

"Engineer? You make weapons, then? Engineer?"

"No, I don't make weapons. I'm a computer scientist."

"You make cyber weapons. Cyber weapons for the Americans."

"I don't do anyth—"

Another bucket of ice water hit her in the face.

"I didn't ask you a question!" the Russian thundered.

The air conditioning unit came on again and she immediately began shivering. Then the lights went out and she was alone again.

Nadia began shaking from the cold with such force that her muscles ached. After a while—she didn't know how long —they threw another bucket of ice water over her.

More shivering in the dark. She tried to remember her training. Colt said it again and again: *your legend will save you.* She knew she had to stick to her legend. But as she shivered, she kept thinking about the stories she'd heard of the interrogation techniques some foreign services used. Why would they take her? How did they know about her?

What would they do to her?

A horn blasted in her ears and then the bright lights came back on. After a moment, she once again saw the outline of a man standing next to the lamps in front of her.

"I see you worked for the Special Operations Command," he said, his voice a soft purr behind the Russian accent. This was a different voice than the first man who had barked at her earlier.

Nadia said nothing in response.

"You were a cyber operations officer in the United States

Air Force, yes? And a special operator. A woman special operator. Very impressive. Why did you attack my country?"

"What are you talking about?"

"I ask the questions." He leaned forward past the invisible barrier between light and dark. "And you *answer* the questions. Are we clear, Ms. Blackmon?"

Blackmon. He has my name.

"Yes."

"Excellent. Why did you attack my country with cyber weapons?"

"I didn't."

"I'm told otherwise. What did you do for the Special Operations Command?"

"I ran a communications network. Radios, phones, emails. I didn't handle the classified stuff. I just made sure they could talk to each other."

The interrogator scoffed. "Sure."

He continued asking her questions about her service and her time in Special Operations Command, pressing her for minute details on everything from her time at the Air Force Academy to her military service to her graduate studies. He even seemed to know about vacations she took, and asked if a backpacking trip to Croatia was an attempt to spy on Russia. When he asked questions, he never phrased them as "did you ever?" It was always "why did you" or "when did you." He led with the presumption of guilt.

The Russian grilled her for about an hour and then the lights went out again. She was unsecured from the chair, the sack was put back over her head, and she was pulled to her feet and pushed, stumbling, through a door.

Nadia was exhausted and had a bad headache. She also needed to go to the bathroom but didn't want to ask.

The Russian kept hold of the hood as he shoved her

forward, ripping it off with the force. He pushed her into a small concrete cell with no windows or vents. There was only a bucket, which she gratefully used to relieve herself.

The room was the size of a closet—big enough to sit but not to lie down, which she suspected was the point. She couldn't stretch out her aching legs unless she stood. Nadia sat and pulled her knees to her chest, hugging them to force warmth back into her body. She thought about throwing the bucket's contents on the Russian when he opened the door. That would not end well for her, but the little spark of defiance kept her going.

Truly alone and with a modicum of safety—at least she could *feel* the walls and their proximity to her and know that no one was sneaking up behind her—Nadia didn't relax, but the extraordinary tension that had been building in her body began to loosen. Still wet, she continued to shiver and felt her muscles ache from the exertion. Nadia had no idea how long she'd been at this, but suspected it must have been hours.

She struggled to remember her training. The lessons were there, but without the drill, without the practical application of them in a multitude of scenarios, they were just abstract concepts in her mind. About as useful to her current situation as differential equations or the ethics of machine learning.

They pulled her out of training too soon, she realized. This was why Ford and Colt were always giving each other concerned looks when they thought she wasn't watching. Nadia would break, just like she had during Colt's mock interrogation.

She couldn't keep this up for long. She was a grad student, not an intelligence officer. Who was she kidding? Goddamn Colt and Ford for removing her from training before she was ready. If they hadn't pulled her from the schoolhouse, she wouldn't be here.

She remained in the dark, still grasping her knees and shivering.

The door rattled and Nadia's eyes shot open.

How long had she been sleeping? An hour? Two?

The door jolted open and a group of them stood behind flashlights.

"Strip," one of them said.

Oh shit.

Her heart began pounding. She didn't move.

"Strip. To your underwear. Strip now."

She still didn't move. One of them came in and shook her violently, slamming her up against the wall. "Do as you are told."

Humiliated and frightened, Nadia removed her damp clothes, letting them fall in a pile on the already wet floor. She left her bra and underwear on. A second man reached through the doorway and hauled her out of the cell.

Soon she was thrown onto a flat table. It was large, like a doctor's table, with a slightly cushioned surface. A fresh wave of panic rolled over her as they tied down her bare wrists and ankles using thick nylon straps.

Then the questioning resumed.

The Russian interrogator said, "What is your interest with Guy Hawkinson?"

"What are you talking about?" she said, trying not to let them hear her fatigue.

He slapped her hard across the face. She tasted blood. Then another bucket of ice water, and she began shivering more.

"What is your interest in Guy Hawkinson?"

"I don't even know who that is."

"Why do you lie to me, Nadia? We know you are a CIA spy. We know they recruited you at Cornell."

How the hell do they know that?

The man barked something in Russian, and one of the others laughed.

"You were recruited by the CIA. The sooner you admit that, the better it will be for you."

Nadia felt incredibly vulnerable, lying practically naked, tied down on the table. This ogre seemed to know everything. She tried to remember what she was supposed to say.

"I wasn't recruited by the CIA at Cornell. I was recruited by a company called Cognitive," she muttered.

"Cognitive is a front for the CIA," the ogre spat. "Admit that to us now, or you go in the box."

What box?

"I'm just an engineer, man."

"You are a spy."

He turned to his associates and yelled something in Russian. Two of them approached the table, unstrapped her, and carried her to the corner of the room. They stuffed her into what looked like a wooden trunk barely large enough to fit a body. She tried to fight, squirming as they shoved her inside. But they were very strong, and her efforts were fruitless. She screamed into the darkness as they closed the lid and tried to bang on the walls of the trunk, but there was barely enough room.

Then the noises came.

"Now the insects," one of them called out.

She heard a weird buzzing near her feet. Growing louder. Soon the trunk was bombarded with creepy noises. The sounds of bees near her ears. She panicked and instinctively tried to turn away from it but then realized it was a charade.

They weren't really hurting her.

They were just trying to make her afraid.

The noises stopped and one of them called out, "Tell us you are CIA and we will stop."

Nadia suddenly felt angry. As loud as she could, she yelled, "Go fuck yourselves."

The Russians went silent. For a moment she worried that she was going to regret it. But then she decided it didn't matter. She would give them hell. They could do whatever they wanted, but she wouldn't let them win. This was a competition. A challenge, just like many others she'd taken on in her life. They had no idea who they were—

The trunk opened and the strong hands grabbed her. One of them pulled her head back as another covered her mouth with a cloth. Then they began dumping salt water down her throat.

———

She guessed that it was the morning of day three when they came for the last time.

It was hard to tell. The Russians randomly filled her prison cell with strobe lights and blaring noise whenever they left her there for a long time.

The questions grew increasingly detailed. They had a lot of information about her. They must have been following her for days or weeks. They knew the days she walked to the Whole Foods on Wilson Boulevard for groceries. They knew that she occasionally went to the Liberty Tavern for a beer after work, by herself. They knew she kept odd hours and asked her where she went when she returned home late at night. Nadia stuck to her story: she was a newly hired software engineer, an AI researcher for Cognitive. No, she didn't know that it was a CIA front company. She didn't know what that even meant. The questioning went on for days.

They started using salt water when they drenched her. Her skin became scratchy, sticky, and uncomfortable. She was starving and tired, and starting to hallucinate when left in her cell.

No one knew she was here.

No one was coming for her.

Through the fog of fear and cold and nerves and hunger, she kept repeating to herself what Colt had told her. *Your cover will save you.*

She looked up at the Russian, no longer sure if he was real or a hallucination. He had something for her to sign, and a plate of food ready for when she was finished.

Her eyes bloodshot, her chin still high, she recited, "No, I am not CIA. I am an engineer."

They dragged her back to her cell, starving.

Inside the cell, her thoughts drifted to a dark place. Her life, as she knew it, was over.

All for trying to do the right thing. All for serving her country.

At the Academy, they had to listen to lecture after lecture from the American POWs in Vietnam, how they worked to subvert their captors at every turn. But they had each other, at least. She had only herself.

Your cover will save you.

Nadia hugged her knees and repeated Colt's words over and over in her mind. They became her mantra.

She remembered the other thing he told her, the second piece that she was not to forget.

"Get up!" a voice shouted.

Had she been asleep? She wasn't sure. It hadn't seemed like she had been in there long this time. They were marching her back to the interrogation room. She could see her stomach muscles as she walked. She must have lost five pounds over the last couple of days. She felt weak.

Nadia could see the glow coming through the blackout curtains or boarded windows, whatever the hell they'd done to the place. Today they strapped her to the chair. She got the lights, the siren blast...but this time, no water. No box. Nadia was looking at the sores that had developed on her skin from the salt. They itched like hell.

They asked her the usual questions about the CIA, about Guy Hawkinson, about being a special operator, about launching cyber weapons against the Air Force and what they were called, what her targets were. They asked her to describe the Defense Department's offensive cyber capabilities. Nadia said she didn't know, she managed communications programs. She wasn't a hacker. She didn't know anything about Guy Hawkinson. She was an AI researcher for a tech company.

She found herself wondering how much longer she could keep this up.

The lights came on. Bright daylight from the overhead LEDs. Not in her face this time.

Nadia blinked, looking around. She was alone in the room. A Black woman she didn't recognize walked toward her, holding up an ID card and saying something Nadia couldn't understand, even though she was speaking English. The woman placed a white bathrobe around Nadia's body and a straw in her mouth, and Nadia gulped a sweet, satisfying drink of some type of flavored water from a bottle.

"We'll get you some food soon." Another woman came in, this one wrapping something around her wrist. Nadia thought it was another strap to tie her down, but then she heard a whooshing noise and the strap filled with air. They were taking her blood pressure. Looking in her eyes with a medical flashlight. Checking her vitals.

"You're all done, Nadia. It's over now," the Black woman said. "Are you okay? You did great. You'll get a few days of leave and we'll monitor you to make sure you are taken care of."

The woman taking her vitals handed Nadia a few crackers, which she quickly accepted and ate. It was the most delicious food she'd ever tasted.

Just then the door opened and Colt and Ford were there, looking simultaneously proud and sorry.

Colt placed his hand on her shoulder. "You okay?"

Nadia looked up at them. "It was all fake?"

"Training. It's over," Colt said softly.

"You did good, kid," Ford said. "Are you all right?"

Nadia was clenching and unclenching her jaw, looking past them both, into space. Then she looked up at Colt. "I understand now."

Colt nodded. "It's tough training. But we all must go through it before going into the field."

"Gentlemen, you can speak with her later," the medical attendant said. "We're going to take her to debrief with the instructors and then get some rest."

Colt said, "All right. Thank you."

"Instructors?" Nadia said.

Ford snorted. "The interrogators. The fake Russians. They're instructors from the Farm. They'll tell you what you did well and what you need to improve."

Nadia was ushered out, and soon Colt and Ford were alone.

Ford said, "Last time I'll ask. She ready?"

Colt nodded. "Yeah. I think she is."

24

Langley, Virginia

"Colt," Ford bellowed from across the NTCU's common area. "You need to get in here."

In the span of their short relationship, Colt had seen Ford navigate a complex series of minefields, each potentially devastating to their operation. And each time, Ford kept his jocular, hail-fellow-well-met persona with a wry smile on his lips and a witty rejoinder at the ready.

Something must really be wrong.

A TV on one of the walls was set to a global news channel. Ford was positioned in front of it, arms folded tightly across his chest.

Colt looked up at the screen.

"Oh no," he said.

"Get your helmet, sailor, cuz it's about to start raining shit."

The headline on the news feed read:

PAX AI CEO JEFF KIM TO ACQUIRE VR STARTUP 'EVERPRESENCE'

"What the hell," Colt whispered. "I thought Kim and I had a deal..."

Ford wheeled on him. "You better call your boy, Colt."

"I've got a feeling he's not going to take my call right now. Look." Colt pointed at the screen, and the feed cut to Jeff Kim standing outside the blue-green glass walls of Pax AI behind a perfectly xeriscaped terrain, an equally perfect California sun shining down on him. A small group of people stood just slightly behind him.

Kim had been a key part of Colt's plan. The Hawkinsons were still in the M&A process, evaluating EverPresence for acquisition. According to SLALOM, the FBI informant, the Hawkinsons didn't have the cash on hand for the purchase because of other acquisitions they'd made recently, and wanted to be sure EverPresence was worth it. Jeff Kim's interest in EverPresence was to be communicated via a few carefully orchestrated "leaks" in the press, and some quiet words passed to Sheryl Hawkinson through people Colt knew could get her ear. If Jeff Kim was interested, the Hawkinsons would be motivated to finalize the purchase. And with Nadia already in their hiring pipeline, she'd be onboarded by the time the deal closed and shepherded in with the rest of the EverPresence employees.

Ford and Colt had still not managed to insert Nadia into EverPresence, but she had managed to get an interview with them this week.

That would no longer be necessary.

"Thank you for joining me on this historic day," Jeff said on the TV screen, a rare smile on his face. "I've been on quite a journey, personally, professionally, and spiritually since the unfortunate events of two years ago. I chose to stay out of public life while I thought deeply about the contributions Pax AI could make to innovation and to our society. When I founded the company, I did so because I believed technology could be a powerful force for good, a catalyst for change, and a necessary disruptor to free us from the shackles of the past. It is with that in mind that I happily announce today that I have made an offer to acquire EverPresence. The EverPresence team has assembled some of the brightest minds in our field, and their work bringing together virtual reality and artificial intelligence has been truly inspired. Together, we can forge a bold new path that reframes how humans interact with technology and how we benefit from it. We've already had great discussions on how we might advance neuroscience, medicine, the way we learn, and, certainly, entertainment."

Ford muted the TV when EverPresence's CEO stepped forward to speak.

"Hell hath no fury like Will Thorpe embarrassed," Ford said.

And he was right.

"What in the actual fuck!" Thorpe thundered, his voice so loud it almost shook the walls. They'd all been summoned to Wilcox's office to explain what happened and talk about their next steps.

Thorpe said, "I can't believe we even *entertained* this cockamamie idea, let alone actually went through with it. Do you have any idea what kind of a security breach this is? Jeff Kim now *knows* we're targeting the Hawkinsons."

"Well, that'll about cover the fly-bys," Ford deadpanned.

"You still have the nerve to think this is funny, Fred? It's amazing you still have a job. You're off STONEBRIDGE, effective immediately."

Wilcox calmly said, "Gentlemen. First of all, no one is off

STONEBRIDGE. Will, you don't have the authority to manage the assignments of Agency personnel." Wilcox spoke in his usual measured tone. "And I'm not firing anyone." Colt felt better until Wilcox added, "*Yet*. We need to understand what happened. I would also remind you, Will, that you authorized this."

While Colt appreciated the top cover from his former boss and mentor, it was cold comfort in the face of failing in front of him.

Wilcox asked Colt to review his interaction with Kim and give his best interpretation of what happened. Though he'd been required to get Wilcox's authorization before pitching Kim, given the sensitivity and potential for a leak, Colt described their meeting exactly as it unfolded. Since Kim already knew Colt was a CIA officer, there was no need to bring that up; Colt simply told him the government was concerned with the moves the Hawkinsons were making in light of their suspected industrial espionage at Pax AI. Jeff was in a position to help; all he had to do was show interest in EverPresence.

"This is what you call showing interest?" Thorpe said.

Colt's face was hot, but he ignored the jab.

"I had no idea Jeff would do this," Colt said. "He seemed very motivated to get his clearances reinstated and I think he was also looking to get back at Hawkinson."

"How did EverPresence fit into Hawkinson's strategy?"

"SLALOM says they wanted to incorporate the VR training simulation into their existing offerings to the military and security community. They think that's a billion-dollar industry," Thorpe said. "They'd probably do a carve-out of the entertainment-focused tech and sell that off for rapid capitalization."

Wilcox was silent for a time, fingers tented and eyes closed.

The room was deathly quiet. The rest of them didn't even breathe. Finally, he said, "I'm not going to punish people for taking risks because that's how we train them not to take any. Frankly, the Agency has become too risk-averse in the last few years. But this was a mistake and we now have a genuine problem on our hands. First, we need to assess the risk to STONEBRIDGE. What does this do to our getting an operative inside Hawk Technologies. Second, we need to assess the potential for disclosure and understand what that potential damage is."

"It's catastrophic."

"I know you're frustrated, Will, so I appreciate that you haven't fully considered the impacts before rendering your opinion. Please do so in the future."

Thorpe looked at the floor, holding his tongue.

Wilcox turned to Colt. "You need to meet with counterintelligence and security. I'll tell them you're coming. We need to know how big the blast radius is on this thing."

"Yes, sir."

"STONEBRIDGE's priority has not changed. We still need to uncover what Hawk Tech is developing down on that island. We need to get there before the Israelis do. And we need to do it quietly, so the Hawkinsons don't take action counter to our objective. Is that understood?"

A round of "yes, sirs" throughout the room.

Wilcox said, "Good. Now I want to see a new plan by close of business today for how you guys are going to get YELLOWCARD operational inside Hawk Tech."

Colt and Ford looked at each other.

Thorpe nodded. "No problem, sir."

Wilcox stood up from the couch. "Now, if you'll excuse me, I have to make an uncomfortable phone call to the attorney general."

Colt's mouth moved to speak, but the words never got out. Wilcox and Thorpe left.

Ford said, "Well, this is going to be interesting."

"We need to call Nadia," Colt said. "She's going to see that news and wonder what in the hell is going on." He looked at the ceiling. "I'm going to have to tell her not to take that interview with EverPresence."

Ford collapsed back in the chair. "This is a shit show."

Colt said, "We're going to have to get her hired directly."

Ford breathed out through his nose. "There's a reason we didn't do that in the first place...because it puts her under the microscope."

"I know," Colt said. "But we're running out of options."

25

Great Falls, Virginia

"I thought Kim couldn't make any acquisitions," Sheryl said. She paced the rug inside Guy's new Virginia home. Outside, their younger brother Charles cooked Sheryl's daughters lunch on a $20,000 Kalamazoo grill. The girls were reading on lawn chairs under a large umbrella.

Guy Hawkinson's mansion was three levels of stone, stucco, and blue glass. He sat on a long, cream-colored couch facing the massive two-story window that overlooked the rear of the property. There was a bourbon, untouched, on the table in front of him.

Sheryl was seething. "I distinctly remember the Justice Department saying that was part of his plea agreement. He couldn't acquire another company for five years."

"They lifted the restriction a year ago. Kim's lawyers got it overturned on appeal," Guy said.

"Well, we can goddamn sue EverPresence for breach."

"No, we can't," Guy responded. He knew she wasn't really this upset about the acquisition falling through. Guy looked outside at his brother and nieces. "Are your girls all right? After New York, I mean."

"They're fine," Sheryl said.

"I should have assigned more security to you." Guy shook his head. "It won't happen again."

"Charles was there. He was helpful. His failure at your company was a blessing in disguise."

Sheryl had been in New York City to do an interview on CNBC two days ago. She and her daughters were accosted by violent anti-technology protesters in the streets outside the building. Charles fought them off as the women fled to their limousine. After Guy's French account was shut down, Charles had been spending more time in Sheryl's entourage. He was very protective of her girls.

Uncle Preston, wearing seersucker, stood at the window, looking out over the backyard. "The tide is shifting." He sounded forlorn. "People are having a hard time with all of the changes."

"Which is why we need to speed up." Sheryl looked at Guy. "Jeff Kim is doing this to spite *you*. He doesn't even know *why* you wanted it. We needed EverPresence. Hawk Technologies doesn't have a product that we can take to market. We need cash flow. Hawk Security Group's contracts have been drying up. We could have used debt to purchase EverPresence. Then it would have generated a lot of cash, quickly. But without that company....Guy, if we do not have legitimate revenue, how will we finance Hawk Tech R&D? The banks won't lend unless they know what we're doing. And we can't divulge..."

"You know there are other ways to get the money," Guy said.

"I mean *legitimate* revenue streams. There will be a lot of unwanted attention on our island if we—"

"Enough, both of you." The senator glared at them.

"Sheryl is correct. This is a problem. We don't have allies in the Justice Department to block Kim's purchase. And I obviously can't intervene in the Senate, it would be too obvious. But you need cash. So, where do we go from here?"

Hawk Technologies branded itself as an advanced technology company, focused on developing security solutions for the defense, intelligence, and cybersecurity sectors. Their primary offering, an AI analytics program called Prometheus, augmented human intelligence analysts. When ready, it would be able to parse billions of records from all available intelligence sources, developing insightful conclusions. Prometheus would draw patterns and linkages better than any human being could.

Hawk Tech had a contract with DARPA to develop a prototype of Prometheus. Unsaid was the fact that Prometheus gave the Hawkinsons access to a treasure trove of US government intelligence data. But it was still in development, and Prometheus wouldn't be available for another year.

Guy rose and walked to the window, holding his glass. He joined his sister and uncle as they looked out at Charles and the girls. He glanced down at the engraved Hawk Security Group insignia on his glass and sighed. "I know what we can do."

"What?" Sheryl said.

"I'll sell HSG," Guy said in a flat tone. Saying it felt like a knife to the gut.

Senator Hawkinson looked at his nephew. "Would it be enough?"

Guy nodded. "The company is worth a little over one billion today. Even if I sell quickly, I can get seven hundred and fifty million. Based on our latest projections, that gives us two years of runway for the island."

"Are you sure?" Sheryl asked.

Guy shrugged. "It's time. The tide is shifting. This week you were harassed by some protesters. Next week they could be storming our house. Seizing our property. People are afraid of change. The world can't go on like this."

Sheryl grasped her brother's shoulder. "This is smart, Guy."

"How quickly can you move?" Preston asked.

Guy said, "After I sold off one of my divisions a while ago, I was approached with some bigger offers. Competitors, mostly. But I kept one of them warm just in case there was a situation like this. It'll take a few months to close the deal, but I can have this started within a few weeks."

"Are you sure you want to do this?" Preston said.

Guy raised his glass. "To our future."

26

Three months later
Tysons Corner, Virginia

The deal closed in record time.

The terms of the sale allowed Guy to keep control of HSG's elite executive protection service, transferring a few dozen personnel into the corporate security section of Hawk Technologies. He would keep his inner circle, and best operators, with him.

Colt and team learned from SLALOM that the money from the sale—eight hundred and twenty-five million USD—was pipelined directly into what was being termed internally as the "Island Research Initiative." NTCU leadership still did not know the details of how the money was being spent.

SLALOM attempted to find out, but was told to wave off after they were nearly exposed.

Nadia's insertion into Hawk Tech was high risk.

The process involved a CIA cyber expert accessing Hawk Tech's talent acquisition system, inserting Nadia's resume into their talent pipeline, and adjusting the resume ranking algorithm in a way that Nadia's resume rose to the top. She was selected for an interview at the end of July and after several technical rounds, hired onto the Prometheus team.

After she was in place at Hawk Technologies for a few weeks, the CIA shut down Cognitive. Colt orchestrated some press releases stating that the company decided to close its doors and "rethink its solution and product/market fit" using the usual industry buzzwords. There was little mention of it in the trades, as early-stage tech companies folded frequently.

Nadia began reporting on the Prometheus team right away, typing up reports nightly from her apartment, always ready to delete the files in case someone unexpectedly knocked on the door—or worse. She was still on edge after her days-long mock interrogation training. Normally Colt or Ford would pick up her reports via covert communications procedures, encrypted apps the CIA felt were secure.

Occasionally, on nights like tonight, Nadia would conduct her absolute best SDR and then meet Colt at a safe house. This allowed Colt to see her in person to take her temperature and ask any extra questions the NTCU needed answered. But mostly, it was to let her know that she wasn't alone.

"Analysts in the NTCU praised your detailed reports," Colt said.

"Glad to hear it."

"But remember, we think the island research is where they're doing the real R&D. That's where we believe the Pax AI tech went. And we have reason to believe that they're spending a shit ton of money there. So the island is your true objective, if you get an opportunity."

"Understood, I'll keep digging."

Her personality had changed a bit, Colt noticed. She was still intense, competitive. But more serious. She didn't see this as a game anymore.

"My manager at Hawk Tech is pleased with how I'm doing," she said. "I've been given my own team of junior developers and data scientists."

"How many?"

"Two developers and two data nerds."

"Anyone of interest?"

"Not really. One has some family in Pakistan. I'll write up reports on them and send it to you by the end of the week."

"How's security?"

"Well, this being my first time doing this, I think it's exceptionally good. They've got former Hawk Security Group guys working both physical and cyber security. And they hired some top cyber defense guys from outside. They have the development servers isolated from the public internet and there was a fairly intensive review process to request access to open-source code.

"It's a common practice in most software development firms. Requests were rarely granted at the place where I interned. Engineers learned eventually that they might have to rebuild a component that may well exist in the public domain, but they were paid enough above market salary not to grouse too much."

Colt said, "Okay. Well, keep grinding. Stay alert. And when the opportunity presents itself, take it."

A week later, Nadia closed down her workstation and stood. She removed her ID card from the computer, placing its lanyard around her neck, then checked her watch. It was time.

She joined the throng of employees moving through the glass hallways and into the terraced auditorium. Ten rows of seats wrapped around a circular stage with two large screens behind it. Both screens showed the Hawk Technologies logo, a bird of prey clutching lightning bolts in one talon and a scroll in the other. Nadia selected a seat in the middle.

The lights dimmed shortly thereafter as did the self-tinting glass surrounding the conference room, rendering it black and opaque.

Guy Hawkinson appeared on stage. He wore jeans and a black polo with the Hawk Technologies logo.

"Ladies and gentlemen, welcome to the October Leadership Forum." He paused for applause, then began his presentation with a discussion of financials before asking every member of the Prometheus team to stand for recognition of the great work they were doing. Hawkinson shared more of the financial data, and then something unexpected.

The image on the screen transformed into a satellite view of a small island surrounded by emerald waters.

"My friends, many of you have no doubt heard of the Island Research Initiative," Guy said on the stage.

A palpable hush fell over the crowd.

"We launched the IRI eighteen months ago, shortly after Hawk Technologies was founded. It's part high-tech research center, part leadership retreat, all amazing."

More applause. Nadia scanned the facial expressions of others in the auditorium. They were starry-eyed, reverent, excited.

Guy continued. "Our goal with the IRI is to have a place where the top scientific minds of our time can gather, to explore, to collaborate, and to innovate"—he tented his fingers dramatically—"together." More applause. "Technology allows us to solve the greatest problems humanity faces today. Our Caribbean Island Research Center will serve as this company's spearhead into our pursuit of artificial general intelligence, and create a bold new future for the world." Guy waved a hand across the crowd, encompassing many of the audience members. "We have outfitted our research center with the latest in quantum computing technology. It is a futurist's playground. And I am going to invite some of you...to join me there."

An electric shock went through Nadia's body. *This* was something. Hawkinson just confirmed his company was pursuing AGI. It helped explain their massive capitalization effort. But why would they need a quantum computing facility on an island in the Caribbean? Why not just build it here?

Hawkinson explained that the selection process to work on the island was highly competitive.

"Only the top one percent of talent at the company will be considered. From that, a smaller group will be chosen."

Some employees were already working there, Nadia learned. Hawk Technologies would be choosing the next "class" of candidates over the next few weeks. Interested candidates should notify their division vice president directly.

Nadia needed to get into that group. And she needed to let Colt know what she had just learned.

As soon as the meeting ended, Nadia pushed through the crowd and made her way to the nearest restroom, the only place she could think of where she could discreetly communicate with Colt. She stepped into a stall, closed the door behind her, and pulled out her phone. The whiz kids at the Office of Technical Services created a novel way for her to covertly send short messages to Colt, by way of a word matching game they devised. Opening the app, Nadia found a grid with randomly generated letters and three open fields. She entered the two or three words of her message, in this case "meeting" and "hurry." The app would then scramble them. To someone looking over her shoulder, it would appear that she was playing a word guessing puzzle with a friend. She and Colt had prearranged meeting places. Nadia would tell her team she was heading out for lunch and to run some errands, and no one would be the wiser.

She stepped out of the stall and saw a dark-haired woman standing at the sink, reapplying lipstick.

The woman smiled. She was pretty. And oddly familiar-looking. "Hello," the woman said with an accent Nadia couldn't place.

"Hi." Nadia washed her hands, trying not to stare. She knew the woman's face, and it was really bothering her...

A bone-chilling sensation ran up Nadia's spine.

The woman was Ava Klein.

A Mossad officer. Someone who knew Colt by sight. And according to the NTCU, someone who had been sent to the US to penetrate Hawkinson's circle.

"Were you in the leadership forum just now?" Ava asked.

Nadia was drying off her hands, deliberately trying not to make eye contact. "I was, yes."

"What did you think?" Ava was studying Nadia's face, holding her lipstick tube.

"About the island?"

"Yes," the woman said.

"It's very exciting. I mean...AGI is the holy grail...it's what a lot of us got into this field to do, you know?"

Ava gave Nadia a funny look. "Yes. Right. Although I'm not a scientist. Just a consultant. Guy brought my firm in to work on communications and strategy." She flashed Nadia a million-dollar smile, then held out her hand. "I'm Ava, by the way."

"Nadia," she said. "I work on the Prometheus team."

"Oh, yes, I saw you earlier when they recognized your team. How long have you been with the company?"

"Not long. I was with a startup called Cognitive before that, but it just folded."

Ava nodded her head knowingly. "Mmm. Yes. That is not uncommon in this business, I'm afraid. But you landed on your feet at least."

"It was really nice meeting you," Nadia said, sliding toward the door.

"You too. We should have lunch sometime. I'd love to find out more about your work."

Colt slowed his Agency-issued car as he neared the entry to Pimmit Run Park in McLean. The red and gold of autumn was on full display. It was a crisp morning but warm in the bright sunshine.

The suburban park gave them the concealment of two professionals taking a stroll at lunchtime while making it easy to see people approaching from behind. Nadia had signaled him that she needed to speak.

Just before Colt turned into the park entrance, he passed a black sedan with its hood up. The man in the driver's seat was looking at his phone like he was searching for a number.

"Shit."

Colt accelerated past the park entrance and turned onto a side street. He then took an indirect route away from the area, heading back for the Beltway.

There was a problem.

The man by the sedan was an FBI special agent. A member of their highly trained Foreign Counterintelligence Surveillance team. The raised hood had been a signal. Someone on his countersurveillance team had detected a tail on Colt, right when he was supposed to meet with Nadia.

Not good.

Colt took an exit and pulled over to send a message to Ford. He typed a coded text, telling Ford what had happened.

Ford, pro that he was, would immediately send a coded communication to Nadia with further instructions.

Step one for Nadia was to make sure she was still black. She would travel on a pre-planned route, allowing FBI countersurveillance to check her for ticks as she moved. If declared clean, she would then continue to a new meeting location.

Colt headed to an underground garage just off the Route 7/Route 123 interchange. He drove to the second parking level, where Ford and two FBI cruisers were waiting. Ford was talking with Special Agent Chris Connell, the squad leader. He was young for a team lead, but a fast riser and Colt liked him a lot. Connell was a good cop and an exceptional spy hunter. He was holding a tablet.

"What happened?" Colt asked when he got out of his car. The garage air was damp, cold, and smelled of trash.

"We picked up a three-car team following you, a loose ABC pattern." Connell opened the tablet and showed Colt the images —his car and three others that were leapfrogging their coverage of him. "We gave YELLOWCARD the wave-off signal too."

"So she never made it to the park?"

"No."

"Good. Any idea who it is?"

"Not yet. They're white, non-Hispanic males, that's about all we can tell. One of the cars stopped at the Pimmit Hills trailhead. We think they were following you and not YELLOWCARD. As far as we can tell, she is still clean."

"There's more," Ford said.

"We also took these." Connell swiped to a new set of photos, surveillance shots taken with a long-range telephoto lens. The photos were of the Hawk Tech office. Colt recognized several members from Hawkinson's senior staff.

"What am I looking at here?" he asked.

"Wait for it..." Ford said.

Ava Klein was walking with Guy Hawkinson outside of the Hawk Tech building.

"Shit. When was this?"

"This morning," Connell said.

Ford said, "Would YELLOWCARD recognize Ava?"

Colt thought about that. "Yeah. Probably. Might have been what spooked her. Although she also just gave us a snapshot of what they're doing on the island. I had assumed that's what she wanted to meet about..."

"If Mossad has penetrated Hawk Technologies, it might explain why there's a surveillance detail on you," Ford said. "They might have seen you in the area, known the kind of work you've done in the past."

Colt looked away, swearing softly to himself.

He had told Ford about Ava Klein's role in the Pax AI operation two years ago, highlighting the fact that Ava probably saved his life. But Colt decided to leave out the part about their romantic history.

Assuming Ava was still working for Mossad, she was once again operating illegally within the United States without diplomatic cover. Mossad was taking a huge risk inserting her back in the US. Whatever their interest was, it was worth putting a serious strain on their relationship with America to do it, if disclosed. Ava could be looking at lifetime in a US prison.

Colt read the reports.

Officially, Mossad burned her and kicked her out of the service. She'd gotten some job with the Ministry of Defense.

That also seemed like an exceptional cover to Colt. He gave a short summary of Ava Klein for Connell's benefit.

"I agree that's a great way to sneak someone back in and take the heat off," Connell said. "If she's here illegally, we can have her booted."

"Not yet," Colt said. "If Mossad is inside Hawk Technologies, they likely know something we don't. They wouldn't have risked exposing Ava if it weren't for something big."

Ford said, "We need to meet with Nadia as soon as she gets black. She's gonna be jittery after all of this."

"Can you handle that," Colt asked.

Ford said, "Of course."

"Okay, good. Next, we need to figure out what Mossad knows about Hawk Technologies."

"How are you going to do that?" Connell asked.

"I'm going to ask Ava."

27

Bethesda, Maryland

Ava met with Katz in a safe house in Bethesda, a suburb on the District's northwestern border. It was Metro accessible and just eleven miles from Hawk Technologies' headquarters, though in terms of Washington traffic that could well be an hour's journey. Still, Ava found it much easier to manage than the previous location in southern Maryland. She found Katz in the living room watching US national news on a big-screen TV. Jeff Kim was on the news again.

Ava was glad to see that Kim had finally emerged from under his shell. She had befriended the reclusive genius as part of her infiltration of Pax AI and genuinely liked him. His was a mind like Einstein, with the disruptive, unflappable drive of Jobs. Jeff Kim was the man all those other Silicon Valley tech bro founders wished they could be.

Ava wanted to reach out to him after the attack, but that was impossible. The mission was over, she was recalled to Tel Aviv, and that was that. Ava noted with some sadness that in his recent interviews, Jeff seemed hardened, almost fierce in his defenses of technology. Certainly, it must be hard to see so many blindly rioting against the notion of technological advancement. The underlying claims were laughable—that technology companies were controlling what people saw, manipulated what they thought, all served up by malevolent machines programmed to subvert humanity. It would be comical if people weren't believing it.

Equally disparaging were the hammering attacks of Senator Preston Hawkinson, who took every opportunity to rail against the likes of Kim. He'd taken a particular ire to Jeff's autonomous delivery system, claiming that it was not only stealing jobs from well-qualified Americans but that they were also giving control of part of their critical infrastructure to a computer and just "trusting it." Professional drivers from ride-share services to trucking companies were protesting as major retailers announced participation in the initiative. Five thousand autonomous trucks were on order.

"Technology is like a train," Kim was saying in an interview clip as Ava walked into the room. "Tech advancement creates an interconnected system, creating links to destinations previously unreachable." He smiled for the camera, but Ava thought he looked tired.

The news then showed Senator Hawkinson's response. "Unemployed parents are tired of being hit by Jeff Kim's technology train. My Better Futures for America bill is what we need to—"

The TV turned off.

Katz, thankfully, had heard enough. He stood and faced Ava. "The American economy is in trouble. The global economy will follow. The tech index loves this autonomous vehicle initiative and the jobs it's creating, but investors are nervous."

"They're expecting another riot in the District tonight," Ava said. "The mayor has a curfew in place for nine p.m."

Katz shook his head. "The dollar is devaluing further. People are quitting jobs they don't want to do, and companies are removing people from jobs that they can do cheaper. The innovation is moving very fast. I can't decide what's worse. On one side, you have the anti-technologists, the luddites who think we can regulate everything and keep things just the way they are. And on the other, you have this Trinity cult movement...worshiping some coming superintelligent AI that will solve all of their problems."

"I read that the riots are getting worse," Ava said.

Katz nodded. "People are going to get killed. We've seen this insanity before, throughout history. Conspiracy theories and propaganda. This Trinity nonsense is becoming a religion."

"Tel Aviv thinks that's a Russian disinformation campaign, no?" Ava offered.

"Maybe it is." Katz shrugged. "But we have some powerful reminders from our own history that these weeds take root in fertile soil. It doesn't take much for them to grow." He shook his head. "Speaking of Tel Aviv, they are very pleased with how close you've gotten to Hawkinson."

Ava bowed her head. "Thank you, sir. I should tell you that Guy Hawkinson has given me a job offer. I am to be his VP of Strategy."

"That's excellent news."

"My cover company, Hyperion Strategy Consulting Group, had a clause in their contract against clients poaching associates. But I was able to work out something with my superior there. It involved an introduction and an unofficial guarantee of business with the Israeli Ministry of Defense for Hyperion. I hope you will be able to make that happen and that I have not overstepped. But I wanted to move quickly on solidifying my new role at Hawk Technologies."

Katz raised his chin. "You did the right thing, Ava. I will handle this. We'll have it wrapped up tonight."

"Thank you."

"When do you start at Hawk?"

"Immediately. Tomorrow."

"Good. Now, you wanted to meet in person. What's going on?" Katz asked.

"Guy revealed their Caribbean research facility to company leaders. He said they'll take the top one percent of the company and invite them to work there. They have a new quantum computing facility there. He told us that this is where their AGI work will take place."

Katz nodded. "That's consistent with what we already knew. Take a look at this."

He handed Ava a tablet with photos and profiles of scientists, futurists, and billionaires. She recognized several prominent economists, environmental scientists, members of the British nobility, and political leaders, though interestingly only former ones. It was a curious collection and certainly not one she would have expected.

Katz spoke while she was examining the profiles. "This is the list of people who have disappeared from public view over the last six months. Mossad has a program to aggregate disparate bits of information and attempt to make correlations, pattern matching on a massive scale. We originally developed it to predict where suicide bombers might attack. Once we started watching the Hawkinsons, we reapplied the inputs to analyze his operation. Each of these people"—Katz tapped the tablet—"has met with Guy, Sheryl, or one of their key people. Did he mention any of these people to you? Have you seen anything during your time there that indicates how they are involved with him?"

Frowning, Ava shook her head. "No, but today he told us that this island facility would be a futurist's paradise. And that he's looking to bring together visionaries and scientists to, his words here, 'co-create the future.'"

"This can't be a coincidence."

"I agree," Ava said. "The machine picked this up? The connections?"

"That's right." Katz nodded. "We'd have never thought to correlate that data on our own, or been able to. We were able to chart where any Hawkinson-owned or chartered aircraft flew to and could correlate that with known agendas, social media posts, and other data for the subjects. Many of them have traveled recently to the US or British Virgin Islands, but the trail seems to stop there. We can't find evidence that any of them have left. Your job is to figure out how you can get on that list."

"I understand."

"We need to know what the Hawkinsons are doing there. If they have Jeff Kim's research and this massive quantum computing capability Guy talked about, they may not be far from a breakthrough. He's talking openly about developing artificial general intelligence. Our experts are skeptical. But there are other dangerous things he could be working on with the Pax AI technology. He has already proven capable of selling to our adversaries like the Russians. Tel Aviv has other concerns, however. Are you familiar with the work of Sir Alister Ravenscroft?"

Ava shook her head and said she had not.

"He's one of the world's leading scientists on computational genomics and genetics. Ravenscroft believes that we can use genomics to identify whether certain diseases are more common in one genetic base than others. He asks the question: does race or heritage play a role in disease prevalence?"

A sour feeling poured into Ava's stomach. She could already sense where this was going.

"Imagine if we could use race and genetics to target disease identification and then target bio-engineered medicines specifically tailored to that racial makeup. This is what Ravenscroft is postulating."

"Someone could weaponize genetic engineering."

"Imagine something like that in Iran's hands. Ravenscroft is based out of Cambridge. Or at least, he was."

Ava realized now that the danger wasn't that Hawkinson would develop a single weapon that could be used against her country if it fell into the wrong hands. The real danger was that Hawkinson now possessed the ability to devise infinite advanced concepts that could be weaponized. Weapons with no known defenses. He possessed the balance of Jeff Kim's research but none of his conscience.

Ava had to find a way to get onto that island and learn what Hawkinson's true purpose was.

Her phone buzzed. She looked down at the message to swipe it away, but froze when she saw the text.

It was from Colt.

28

Nadia was officially freaked out.

She knew that foreign governments sent intelligence officers to her country. She knew they ran whole networks of spies. But the fact that a team of foreign spies had followed *Colt* while he was on his way to meet with her...

Well, it scared the shit out of her.

All Nadia knew for sure was what she had received in Ford's encrypted message. She ran through the checklist Colt had taught her about how to spot surveillance. She wished she'd had more time to train. Trying to identify someone following you in the middle of evening rush hour was difficult for anyone. There were just too many variables. Too many cars, too many pedestrians. Her eyes darted from one to the other. She didn't *think* anyone was following her. But she couldn't be sure.

Am I black? she wondered. *More of a gray. Damn.*

After Ford's message, Nadia went back to work. *Your cover will save you.* She had to act normal.

The new plan was for her to meet Ford at her apartment tonight. He would access the building through a hidden entrance after the countersurveillance confirmed he was clean.

But Nadia's pattern of life would look normal.

When she entered the hallway, Ford was by the stairwell. He was in a good position to leave in a hurry. She went to her door, checked behind her, and opened it. Ford quickly left his position and followed her in.

"What the hell is going on?"

Ford gestured for her to keep her voice down. He walked into the living room and turned on the TV, then returned to the front door, pulled out his phone, and opened a white noise app. The sound of waves crashing emanated from the speakers. He set that on the stand next to her front door. Between the white noise and the TV, any casual listeners should be baffled.

"Okay, *now* what the hell is going on?" Nadia asked in a lower but still excited voice.

"The FBI countersurveillance team picked up someone following Colt when he went to meet with you this morning. That's what the wave-off signal was for. For the time being, we have to assume that there are eyes on him, so you'll be meeting with me."

"What about me? Are there eyes on me?"

"Not as far as we know, but we're posting an FBI team outside and they're going to stick with you. If someone *is* following you, we'll find them fast."

"Who is it?"

"We don't know for sure. But we do have a surveillance photo of a Mossad officer meeting with Guy Hawkinson."

"Ava Klein," Nadia said hurriedly.

"How'd you know?"

"I met her. She approached me in the bathroom."

"Did she say anything?"

"Small talk mostly. We were talking about the Island Research Initiative. That's what I needed to tell you. Klein said we should get lunch sometime."

A look passed over Ford's face, though Nadia couldn't read it. "What?" she asked.

"It's probably nothing. What's this Island Research Initiative?"

Nadia relayed everything Hawkinson said at the leadership forum with a particular emphasis on the technical capabilities. She also shared the digging she attempted when she returned to work, figuring everyone in that meeting was doing the same and her activity wouldn't be flagged. Unfortunately, she hadn't been able to come up with anything. IRI material was a closely guarded secret and no one below the VP level was read in.

"Only the top one percent will get considered," she said.

"And you just got hired," Ford said, still thinking. "Any ideas on if you can get selected?"

Nadia shrugged. "They aren't saying anything about what the qualifications are. Guy just said they were getting ready to choose the first class and would be making those decisions pretty soon."

"Where do you think you rank?"

"It's hard to say. I'm brand new. I'm just off my probationary period, but at least I'm a full employee. If I wasn't, I don't think I'd be eligible. There's a guy in my division who is very well regarded. He's been there for about two years, product lead. I imagine he's top gun."

Ford nodded, then stood up to leave. "I'm going to head back to HQ and talk this one out, but I think it's pretty obvious we need to get you on that island. I'll be in touch tomorrow with our op plan. In the meantime, you need to figure out how to get selected."

Nadia attempted to learn more about the Island Research Initiative, but her investigation on the second day confirmed that information was tightly controlled. If there was any information in the building, it would be on private drives or locked in the vault. There was a small research pod on the executive floor, walled off with keycard access and an actual security guard. She believed the top candidate for the IRI fellowship in her division was an engineer above her named Tony Singh. He was an early Hawk Technologies employee who had risen to product director for the Prometheus team.

Nadia sent a note to the VP, Doug Everton, on their chat app that she was interested in applying for an IRI fellowship and would like to speak to him about it. He replied and said he had time tomorrow afternoon. Not a great sign. If he was truly enthusiastic or supportive of her, he'd have asked to speak to her immediately. Nevertheless, Nadia thanked him for his time and asked what she could do to prepare for the interview. Everton said, "It's best if you come into this fresh. Don't prepare."

She had a message from Ford that they'd meet tomorrow night at her place to discuss progress.

The next day, Nadia approached Everton's office at the agreed-upon time. She carried her laptop, and was dressed in jeans and a hoodie.

Everton welcomed Nadia inside and offered her water, which she accepted. When he turned to the small fridge to get it, Nadia quickly scanned the room to see where she might be able to plant the bug. She had been observing him since the IRI was announced, looking for a way in. She learned a few things. Everton hated his laptop and preferred using his iPad with an attached keyboard that he carried everywhere.

Their conversation was mostly casual. He asked about Nadia's time in the Air Force, her deployments, and graduate school.

He asked why she wanted a fellowship on the island, and Nadia told him that it was a once-in-a-lifetime opportunity to play with the artificial intelligence technology that would define the future. Everton then asked some seemingly random personality questions: where she grew up, what her childhood was like, did she get along with her parents, was she seeing anyone, what did she think about the current state of things in the world? He wanted to know her opinion on the anti-tech rioting.

Everton concluded the meeting by saying that he thought he had what he needed. His eyes never left her. Nadia thanked him for his time and left, leaving her notebook resting beneath her chair.

Nadia went back to her workspace, which had a view of Everton's office, and waited. According to the daily meeting schedule, Everton was due to attend a two hour leadership team meeting at the top of the hour. As expected, five minutes before the meeting start time, Everton left his office to go to the restroom.

This was her chance.

She made a direct line for him as he crossed the office floor. "Hey, Doug," she said. Everton turned. "I think I left my notebook in your office. Mind if I go in and grab it?"

"Can you go now? I need to lock up early."

"Sure thing. Thanks. Sorry for the trouble."

"No problem."

Nadia rushed to the office, pulling out the quarter-sized button mic and removing the adhesive from the back. She entered Everton's office and grabbed her notebook, doing a fast scan. His vest was hanging on the back of his chair, but she discounted that. Too likely he'd discover the bug there. Nadia slid to the side of his desk and saw her target, a black backpack with the Hawk Technologies logo. She looked back at the door, which was three-quarters of the way open. The windows were set to their partially opaque mode, meaning someone outside could see in but not necessarily tell what she was doing. Nadia pulled the zipper down and placed the bug inside the backpack's media pocket, pressing it firmly against the material. She yanked the zipper back up and whipped her head around to make sure she was still clear.

As she walked out, she opened the notebook and began reviewing a page, nearly bumping into Everton as she did. Nadia apologized, wished him a good night, and went to her workstation. She put her headphones in, then called up the app to listen in. The app would automatically record anything the microphone picked up. She then pretended to work for the next two hours while she listened in on the Hawk Technologies senior leadership team discuss, among other topics, the selection process for the Island Research Initiative.

Ford arrived with dinner, and things seemed back to "normal," or at least as Nadia had come to understand it. He had the usual amount of too much food, this time pita, falafel, hummus, meat shaved off a spit, and every topping one could imagine. "If the Israelis are watching us, let's at least make them hungry," he always said.

When he stepped inside the apartment, Ford found her beaming, practically vibrating with excitement.

"You are not going to believe what I got," she said.

"Do tell."

Ford had also brought a black tactical-style backpack that

had become increasingly popular in the last several years. He set it on one of the chairs in her living room while Nadia grabbed plates and drinks, explaining how she'd gotten the IRI details from Everton's office. Ford sat on the other side of the couch, his expression uncharacteristically humorless.

"Okay, first things first. Good tradecraft. You observed your target, identified patterns, and figured out when he'd be outside the office. Using your meeting to do recon of his office was also smart. Textbook stuff. Planting the bug was dangerous. If you got caught, they'd have terminated you, at the very least, and we'd have lost all access to the company. You've got to be more careful than that."

"It worked, didn't it? At least I know what they're looking for."

"Remember, the intent here is for them not to be looking at *you*."

"I got it," Nadia said, irritated. She was going into this with barely any training and probably half of the background intelligence she needed to do the job they were demanding of her. They couldn't also get pissed when she went off-script and improvised.

"Hey—I'm serious, good work," Ford said. "I just want you to be careful. Langley is going to shit themselves when they listen to this. Give me the highlights."

"Everything starts with a psych eval. It's not unlike the ones we do as part of employment screening. An evaluation that's not supposed to feel like an evaluation. They want independent thinkers, people who push boundaries but aren't loose cannons. High IQ *and* EQ, which is rare to find. Religion is okay, but I noted they're not selecting any fundamentalists. They have a bias for agnostics and skeptics. They have a very strong bias for people who studied classic Greek and Roman philosophy."

"That's curious. Any idea why?"

"An offhand comment that Guy made in the meeting about America's founding fathers being steeped in it."

"Interesting. How does that affect your way in?"

"Well, I wish I'd had this before I met with Everton. I think Singh is still the leading candidate."

"They talk about disqualifiers at all?"

"There's the usual stuff: racism, violence, drugs. Anti-social behavior or anything that might suggest someone doesn't handle stress well. I heard someone in the meeting mention that the screening process is similar to the way they assess people for special forces."

"That would make sense given the makeup of most of the leadership team. That gives me some ideas. Now, let's talk about how we're going to communicate." Ford wiped his hands on a napkin and walked over to the backpack. He pulled out a small pouch in ballistic nylon, unzipping it and removing a black, rectangular brick that looked like a portable cellphone charger. "This is an encrypted, burst satcom transmitter."

"Cool," she said, eyes lighting up like a kid in a candy store.

"Ah. We're in *your* world now, aren't we, Miss Air Force?"

"Yup. This thing sends science beams into space so you can read my texts." She winked.

Ford kept a straight face, although she knew he was laughing on the inside. "This connects with your phone through a USB-C cord. Once you plug this into your phone, it automatically connects to the satellite." He removed a black metal flashlight, four inches long and the width of his thumb. He unscrewed the cap and removed the lens. "This is the transmitter. The whole thing is an antenna. The cable is in here; you just connect that to the brick."

"There's no dish?"

"Nope. Now this is designed to be used in the open if need be. All you do is connect the three pieces. If anyone asks, you're also charging your flashlight. You open up a text message and send it to this number." Ford pulled a small card out of the case and handed it to her. Printed on it was a regular seven-digit phone number. "Just enter a text message and send it to this address. The router will handle the rest."

"Okay," Nadia said.

Ford lowered his voice. "There is something else I need to tell you about. When you are looking around in Hawk Technologies' programs, keep an eye out for a deep-learning-based polygraph system."

Nadia took a drink of water from her cup. "What's so special about it?"

Ford said, "My understanding is that the program evaluates various biological metrics such as facial expressions, pulse, and eye dilation. For the visual stimuli, it uses a smartphone to track the person's face, then it transmits data using ultra-wideband communications. This is what I was told to tell you, anyway."

"Okay. Am I to assume that this would be from Pax AI's research."

Ford said, "We think this is one of the first advances to come out of that R&D, yes. But more importantly, we think the Hawkinsons gave this AI-based polygraph to the Russians."

Nadia narrowed her eyes. "Wait. How did you get this information if..."

Ford shook his head. "We can't discuss that."

"All right. Sorry."

"No worries."

Ford left around ten. He said he needed a couple days to

get a profile on Singh so they could figure out how to torpedo him.

A day later, the results for the Island Research Initiative Fellowship were posted.

Nadia's name wasn't on the list.

29

A day had passed, and Ava still hadn't replied. She again glanced at the text message Colt had left.

It's Colt. We need to talk.

She should have immediately informed Katz about the message. If Colt had her number, the US government made it available to him. Did that mean the FBI was monitoring her? She had expected them to, she reminded herself. But how closely? Had Colt simply used a routine lookup to find her number? Or was Ava included in an active investigation?

Every day here was a gift, so to speak.

Colt had a way of getting her off balance. Ava didn't like that. She wanted to be on top.

Colt must have expected her to respond immediately.

There must be a reason he was reaching out. He held some knowledge that she didn't. Let him stew. She would investigate what he was up to and go into their conversation prepared.

Working at Hawk Technologies as a full-time employee was interesting. Ava was officially hired and joined the leader- ship team, but she found herself isolated from the decision- making on the Island Research Initiative. She did, however, have access to the files once the selections were named. Ava surreptitiously reviewed each one, selects and non-selects, attempting to correlate datapoints and see if she could figure out a way in. Guy had a list of alternates in case one of the primaries dropped out or was unable to attend. Each candidate profile was attached to the company HR hiring file and the interview notes from their respective divisional vice president.

She paused at one name.

Nadia Blackmon. The girl Ava met in the ladies' room on the day of Guy's island announcement.

Ava scanned the woman's resume. US Air Force Academy, eight years active duty, master's degree in computer science from Cornell. She'd mentioned working for a startup called Cognitive that had since folded. Ava didn't recall hearing anything about that firm, even though they were based here in the metro area. A fast internet search retrieved articles on the fledgling company having emerged from "stealth mode." They made a big splash in the media—she counted numerous articles from *TechCrunch*, *The Verge*, and others—and then almost as quickly, folded. That was an incredibly short lifespan, even for a startup.

Her instincts twitched.

Ava scanned the bylines of the blogs and the articles covering Cognitive. She knew quite a few tech journalists from her time running Pax AI's marketing. Ava grabbed her phone and called the *TechCrunch* reporter who first broke the story on Cognitive.

"Hi, Kara, this is Ava Klein. I used to run marketing for Jeff Kim at Pax AI. We met at Disrupt a few years ago."

"Oh, hi, Ava. I totally remember." The woman gave a short laugh. "Well, I remember *meeting* you at Disrupt. The rest of that night was a little spotty. What's up? Where are you now?"

"I'm in D.C. with a consulting firm." She decided not to mention her new association with Hawk Technologies. The company's reputation in the tech community was not good, and many likened Guy's vampiric approach to sucking the top talent, products, and ideas into his company and discarding the rest as being a latter-day Gordon Gekko.

"Beltway bandit, huh?"

"Shoes are expensive," Ava quipped.

"Don't I know it," Kara said. "So, what can I do for you?"

"I'm looking into a company here in D.C. that you wrote a profile about a few months ago. They're called Cognitive. Apparently, they just folded, and I'm trying to get in touch with their C-Suite."

"Yeah, that one was weird. I got a tip from an old friend who used to work M&A for a consulting firm in New York. Said he'd hung up his own shingle and was advising now. Anyway, asked me to do a profile on them, so I did. I talked with their president for about a half hour. My friend is the one who told me they were closing down too."

"Mind if I ask who that was? Maybe I can talk to him?"

"You know I can't do that," Kara said in a playful tone. "Besides, he asked me not to, and I respect his wishes. Gotta protect my sources, you know?"

"I do. I do. Couldn't hurt to ask. Well, thanks, Kara, you've been a big help. Look me up next time you're in D.C., okay?"

"Will do."

Ava hung up.

A D.C.-based startup, backed by In-Q-Tel, appeared on scene. A former New York V.C. called a leading tech publication to do profiles on the company. Ava bet that if she were to call *The Verge* and others, she'd get the same story. An employee of that company gets hired by Hawk Technologies and then the company abruptly shuts down once she's in the door.

For nearly anyone else in the world, this would be a string of interesting but unrelated coincidences. But Ava had one data point that no one else did. Or at least, no one else on her side. She had a very good guess as to who the "New York consultant" was. Two years ago, Colt and Ava both found themselves at Pax AI, one as a consultant and one as an employee. They didn't know it at the time, but both were operatives of their country's respective intelligence agencies. They were reunited after their rocket-fire courtship and abrupt separation following a terrorist attack in Tel Aviv that killed her father. Old feelings came back immediately. Thankfully, or perhaps not, Ava was still undecided on that score, duty won out, and they didn't act on their rekindled feelings. Initially, Ava was hurt and confused as Colt rebuffed her. Then, once circumstances forced them to reveal their respective covers to each other, at least she understood why. The Colt McShane who was allegedly a top-tier consultant for a venture capitalist was a CIA officer.

Knowing *that*, she could easily deduce why Cognitive appeared out of thin air and then dissolved just as quickly.

Just as soon as Nadia Blackmon was hired.

Colt.

Was Nadia Blackmon a CIA officer? Or at least an agent?

If so, then the Americans were looking at Guy Hawkinson.

Ava pulled out her phone and texted Colt.

Colt chose the meeting place.

Mr. Smith's was a two-level brick restaurant and bar on the Georgetown waterfront, hidden beneath the elevated Whitehurst Freeway. Mr. Smith's was one of a line of red brick buildings in the Whitehurst's shadow.

Colt arrived twenty minutes before his scheduled time to meet with Ava. It was early evening and getting dark.

He'd detected the Mossad surveillance team on him just as he was coming across the Key Bridge into D.C. from Rosslyn.

Colt took the Whitehurst Freeway into the West End and then doubled back on Pennsylvania. He turned left onto 30th and took that downhill all the way to Water Street. Driving past Mr. Smith's, he pulled into a parking garage that looked like it had been shoehorned into that spot by a petulant god that wanted to wreak unnecessary havoc on motorists.

Colt emerged from the subterranean garage and made a series of turns, finally descending to Water Street in the alley between two buildings. He entered Mr. Smith's with the day's dying light crawling in from the front windows. Across the river, the Rosslyn skyline was backlit with vibrant orange and red.

He scanned the restaurant's first floor. It was busy with the happy hour crowd, but no one paid any attention to him. He found a seat near the back, ordered a beer for himself and a cabernet for Ava, and waited.

Ava arrived exactly on time and looked as stunning as he remembered. She wore dark jeans, a low-cut red blouse, and a black jacket. Colt noted she was in flats so she could move quickly if she needed to.

He stood when she approached the table. She took his hands and kissed him once on each cheek.

"It's nice to see you, Ava."

"It's so good to see you too, Colt."

"Please, sit down. I ordered you a cab."

Ava casually scanned the room. "If you don't mind my asking, who knows I'm here?"

"You mean, did I tell my employers?"

Ava nodded.

Colt shook his head. "This is off the books."

"I appreciate that," Ava said. "Not sure I believe it..."

"That hurts. After all we've been through?"

A sparkle in her eye and Colt was transported back twenty years to the beaches of Israel. A twenty-something Ava under the moonlight as waves crashed over them.

"In another life, maybe." Ava smiled.

"I suppose," Colt said. "So, you're working for Hawkinson now?"

To her credit, she didn't react. She took a sip of wine, shrugging.

"I don't buy the consultant thing," Colt said.

"You don't have to. I'm an employee now. Just got the job."

Colt said, "He doesn't seem like your type. What are you really doing here?" He lowered his voice. "Ava, if it is what I think it is, then I have an obligation to report you."

She leaned in close, their faces only a few inches apart. "Well you can relax. Mossad fired me. And the State Department cleared me to return to the country a year ago. They needed a favor from my government and"—she spread her hands—"poof. That's how deals are made."

Colt held up his pointer finger. "You wouldn't work for someone like Hawkinson. That story might get you past everyone else, but not me." He whispered, "And I find it hard to believe that you were fired by Mossad...you were such a good spy."

Ava shook her head, seemingly delighted with the conversation. She looked Colt in the eyes, exhaled, and took a sip of wine. "Well, hypothetically, if you were right, then you would know my secret, and I would know one of yours."

Colt straightened in his seat. "What does that mean?"

Ava ran her finger around the rim of her glass. "I know you have someone inside Hawkinson's company."

Colt felt the blood drain from his face.

"Oh?"

Ava nodded.

Colt desperately hoped she was referring to SLALOM.

"Talk's cheap, Ava...you might just..."

Ava leaned forward and whispered into Colt's ear, so softly that he could just barely make out the words "*Nadia Blackmon.*"

He tried to keep calm as Ava returned to her side of the table. They watched each other, waiting for the other to speak.

"What did we do wrong?" Colt asked.

Ava described how she put it together. It was good detective work. Her personal knowledge of Colt's background was the wild card. Almost no one else in the world could have connected those datapoints.

Ava said, "I'm not sure if you heard yet, but your girl wasn't selected. For the island, I mean."

Colt tapped his fingers on the table. "I need to get her in that group."

"There's a guy above her on the list. His name is Tony Singh. He's a prick, if you ask me. Get some dirt on him, and I'll make sure the right people see it. I'm on the senior team and in a position to influence."

"Ava, you know how dangerous this is. This isn't the kind of thing I can take to my bosses. If I keep her in place, no one else in your agency can know her name."

Ava's face was stern. "I promise." She winked. "Because I like you."

"I can't joke about this."

"We trade, Colt. I'll keep her identity a secret. I'll help get her where you want. But we trade. Fair?"

"What do you want in return?" Colt asked.

"I need to go too."

"All right. How?"

Ava said, "Guy is wary about sending his entire leadership team on the same trip. I'm on the bottom of that list. Same idea, different list."

"Do you have a list of names?"

Below the table, Ava handed him a slip of paper. Colt felt a schoolboy surge of excitement when their fingers touched, and then he pocketed her list.

"How long do I have?"

"Maybe a week," she said. "The top name there is my username for an encrypted messenger. Use that if you need to contact me again." She gave him the name of the app to use, followed by communications procedures.

"Okay. I'll get some dirt on Singh and contact you this way if needed."

"It's a deal. Now, is there anything else you might need me to do?" Ava asked, giving him playful bedroom eyes.

"If only."

"Maybe in another city..."

Colt took a gulp of beer, then set down the glass. "Actually, there is one thing. If you don't mind, I need you to call off your dogs."

Ava gave him a funny look.

"Is that all right?" Colt asked. "I mean, if we're dealing, you don't need to be tailing me."

She was about to take a sip of her wine, but stopped halfway, lowering the glass to the table. "Colt, what are you talking about?"

"Your street team. They've been on me for a week."

Ava dropped her voice low and hissed, "They aren't ours. Why would we? I don't want attention."

Colt felt his face redden. He felt duped. "When you said you came here alone..."

"I was telling the truth."

"Shit. I saw one of them on my way here. They were tailing me on the Key Bridge...I assumed it was you guys."

"Dammit, Colt," she said, her voice harsh. "I can't be seen with you. If someone is following *you* and they photograph me, I get burned."

"I know. I'm sorry. We don't know who they are, and it's not like I can ask."

"Well, why did you think they were ours?" Ava stood, hands on the table, her eyes now scanning the patrons inside and the crowd outside the windows.

"Because *we* knew you were going after the Hawkinsons..."

She muttered something in Hebrew under her breath. Judging from the tone, it was not a nice word.

"If it's not you guys, then who?" Colt stood.

She made a sound, shaking her head. No more questions.

Colt said, "Ava, the bathrooms are located down the hallway behind me. There's a door beside them that leads out to the back alley. You can..."

She grabbed his arm. "Do you really think you need to tell me what to do right now?" Ava made an angry noise, tugged on his arm, and kissed him on the cheek. "You owe me. Make sure you keep your promises."

She turned and disappeared down the hallway. Colt found himself watching her walk away, admiring the view. Then he cursed himself, threw some cash on the table, and headed toward the front door.

He needed to make himself a target.

30

Colt turned left onto Water Street from the parking garage.

The street was bathed in an eerie yellow glow from the lamps above. He accelerated down the street toward downtown, grateful that traffic was moving.

Cars were parked along either side of the street, but traffic was light. He moved fast and saw lights wink on at the end of the street.

Whoever was tailing him had followed him this far but likely hadn't figured out that he was in the bar. Colt raced the several blocks beneath the steel arches that supported the freeway above him, weaving around a car and blasting through the light at 30th to make them commit.

Bingo. He was sure one of them spotted him.

Now that he had a solid bead on his pursuers, Colt could take evasive action. He veered right and merged with the Rock Creek Parkway southbound and then immediately cut across to Virginia Avenue, heading into downtown. He stopped at a light on Virginia and was three deep in the traffic pattern, giving his pursuers time to catch up. Good. The closer they came to him, the less likely they were following Ava.

"Now who the hell are you bastards?" he said to himself.

Hawkinson's men? That didn't fit. Too reckless.

Guy had reached out to Petrov. Could they have made some type of pact? Would the SVR be running a defensive operation on Guy Hawkinson's behalf? Inside the US? If so, Colt almost admired the cojones on them.

Then he caught a glimpse of his tail and the admiration ceased.

The Russian president, a former KGB officer, encouraged his intelligence officers to be both aggressive and ruthless. The SVR was as capable as the KGB had been in its prime, but with none of the minimal restraint they'd shown during the height of the Cold War. Would the Russians kidnap an American intelligence officer from the streets of Washington?

Colt wouldn't put it past them.

Ford knew his location tonight, and an FBI countersurveillance was supposed to be following him. Colt texted Ford when he got in his car, sending him an emergency code to let him know that he was taking evasive action.

The light went green and Colt turned right around a curve and then took another right onto 20th, now heading south toward the National Mall. He needed to keep up the chase long enough for the FBI to zero in on them and intercept.

The problem was D.C. traffic. All of the outbound streets would be choked with vehicles, and standstills were common. Colt turned left on Constitution Avenue, joining the four lanes of traffic moving slowly along the National Mall. He pulled out his phone and dialed Ford. "I've got at least one car on me, probably two," he said as the phone connected.

"Okay. We've got you on GPS."

"How close are the G-men? I'm worried that I'm going to get stuck in traffic."

"We're close. I'm with Connell."

"You want me to stay in the car or try to handle this on foot?"

"Don't get out of the car."

"My friend said they're not hers."

"What?"

"She said they don't have surveillance up on me. Judging by the look on her face, I believed her. I'm trying to draw them away, but..."

Colt heard Ford relaying the information to Connell.

He gripped the wheel with both hands and balanced the phone between two fingers to swerve around a car that stopped suddenly in front of him. "I don't think these guys are following me just for the sake of it. If I get jammed up, they could make their move. I've got two guesses as to who's in that car, and neither of them follow the rules."

"Well, sucks to be you, then," said Ford. "You could take 'em to Irish Times. Nothing bad ever happens at that bar."

"What?"

"Sorry. I joke when I get nervous."

Colt didn't exactly lie to Ava when he said no one knew that he was meeting with her. Ford and Connell did, but they'd agreed to keep it quiet until after the meeting. Ford said the FBI counterintelligence team was operating under the impression that the surveillance on Colt was an aggressive but ultimately non-threatening Mossad detail trying to protect their undercover officer.

Colt accelerated as much as he could and turned right on 17th Street, heading toward the Tidal Basin. He flipped the phone to speaker and set it in the cup holder. "Going to hands-free," he said loudly. "I'm going to do a bunch of double-backs around the Tidal Basin. The streets down there are like a pile of spaghetti."

"Good thinking," Ford said.

The Washington Monument rose on Colt's left, a gleaming monolith in the night sky. The massive marble columns of the World War II Memorial towered over him to his right.

Colt looked in his rearview but couldn't make out the car that had been following him. It was dark enough now that he could only tell it was a car by the shape of its headlights.

The road split in a Y-shaped junction with the tree-shrouded John Paul Jones monument at the center. Colt took the right fork, which merged with Independence Avenue, and reversed direction, now heading toward the Lincoln Memorial on the southern edge of the National Mall. The Potomac Tidal Basin lay to his right and, beyond that, the river for which it was named. He could see the Pentagon's bright lights shining across the river.

Colt knew he needed his pursuers to think he was trying to lose them, so he pulled left as the traffic pattern split again and took the long, elliptical roundabout before pulling back onto the westbound side of Independence. His pursuers would think that he was either hopelessly lost or blatantly screwing with them. Either was fine. He spotted a dark sedan that completed the circle with him.

This next part would be dangerous.

If they were running multiple cars, Colt was at a place on the Mall where they could easily create a choke point. While this was a network of interconnected short streets, round-abouts, loops, and mind-bending traffic patterns, it also created numerous opportunities for an adversary to cut off escape routes.

"I'm going to double back onto Ohio," he said, "and then turn right on Independence by the MLK Memorial."

Traffic stopped.

Horns exploded from everywhere, and he couldn't tell if there was an accident or just an impatient driver.

Colt checked his rearview.

The sedan was three cars back.

The lighting was poor down here, making it impossible to tell if their door opened or not. Pedestrians filled the sidewalk, a large, dark mass moving through the night. Brake lights dropped in front of him and then they were moving.

Finally Colt found himself stuck at a red light at Independence. Too much cross traffic for him to attempt a right-hand turn.

A dark-colored car detached itself from the flow of traffic and raced into the crosswalk, horn blaring. People scattered.

Oh shit, this was happening.

Colt put the car in park. He'd need to lose them on foot.

He grabbed the phone and threw open the door.

Doors on the car in front of him opened, and passengers emptied onto the street.

The driver hit the lights.

Red and blue ones.

Then two more sets of red and blue lights erupted farther down Basin Drive, behind Colt's pursuer.

He froze as two men in FBI windbreakers rushed past him and Fred Ford sauntered up to his car, easy-as-you-please.

Colt disconnected the call and put the phone in his pocket. "Taking our time tonight?"

Ford smirked. "We didn't know if they were listening in on your car so we decided to play it safe. Smart move calling out your directions. That helped us cut them off."

The car following Colt was now surrounded by FBI agents.

He was just close enough to hear Special Agent Chris Connell say, "Welcome to Washington, asshole."

31

As far as Ava could tell, she'd gotten away clean.

She made her way out of the alley and entered the crowds on Georgetown's busy brick walkways, frequently crossing the street to cover her movements. She entered a hotel through a side entrance and approached the front desk, where she had the bell captain hail her a cab. Ava asked the driver to take her to the Farragut West Metro and took the Orange Line to Metro Center, merging with the throng of evening commuters making their way to the surface. She called an Uber, then watched the crowd as she waited for her car to arrive, making sure no one detached themselves from it to surveil her.

Nothing out of the ordinary.

When Ava returned to her D.C. penthouse, she flung her clothes on the floor, got in a hot shower, and leaned her head against the wall, letting the water hit her skin and steam fill the room.

Colt...only he could do this to her.

Ava was especially alert at work the next day. She was invited to join the Hawk Technologies leadership team as they sat behind closed doors in the executive conference room and made final plans for the island retreat.

Though she was new to the team, Ava was permitted to participate because she was part of the "Continuity of Operations" team, the key personnel who would remain behind and keep the company running. Guy was cagey about how long he and the other members of his senior staff would be gone. For the next few days they worked around the clock, with most of the decisions too sensitive to be made outside the security of the building.

Three days after their Georgetown meeting, Ava finally heard from Colt via the encrypted messenger. His communication was short, and the text automatically deleted a few seconds after she had read it.

The surveillance that night was Russian.

Ava cursed as she read the message.

She couldn't hold off any longer. Ava needed to confess her sins to Katz.

She set up a meet at the safe house in Bethesda that night, first informing Katz that she'd identified a CIA mole inside Hawk Technologies. Then she told him that an old CIA contact had reached out to her, and she used her discovery to gain the Agency's cooperation in getting her selected for the island.

Katz was furious that she took matters into her own hands and then waited to tell him the truth.

"That was you?" he said. "Do you know who was arrested that night? Russian operatives working for the GRU." Katz stood up and paced the room, waving his hands and cursing in Hebrew. When he calmed down, he said, "Tel Aviv will be angry. Involving the CIA changes things."

Ava said, "It will be handled at the lowest levels."

Katz shot her a skeptical look. "You will be very lucky if that is the case. But *you* don't get to decide that now. *They* do." He shook his head. "What choice do I have? Dammit, Ava. Keep me informed."

"I'm sorry."

"Wait..." Katz held up a hand. "If the Russians were watching this CIA officer you met, and he is working on an operation involving the Hawkinsons..."

"You think the Russians are working with the Hawkinsons?"

Katz said, "I will need to report this possibility to Tel Aviv immediately. Something doesn't make sense. Why would the Russians work with Hawkinson after all this time?"

Ava said, "Their relationship is transactional. The Hawkinsons must have given them something of value."

Katz froze at that. "If they are working that closely together, we may need to take active measures. It will hurt our probability of success if the Russians remain closely allied with the Hawkinsons. I will handle this."

Ava left the safe house, tail between her legs. If Colt failed to deliver, her mission would be over. Katz would string her up for exposing Mossad's involvement to CIA. Or worse, someone in the US government might decide they didn't like the deal and the FBI would arrest her for operating without official cover on US soil.

———

The next day was Saturday, but everyone at Hawk Technologies was working.

Guy arrived at ten, wearing a black leather bomber jacket and black tactical cap with an HSG patch in place of the typical American flag. A small squad of support staff swarmed into the executive conference room, set up coffee and breakfast, then disappeared just as quickly.

Guy said, "Team, before we begin, I just spoke with Doug Everton and he's unfortunately dropping out. He's got a personal matter that he needs to stay here and resolve."

"What's going on?" Guy's COO asked, but Guy just shook his head.

"It's personal and he asked me not to share. Ultimately, I think it's resolvable and he'll join the next class."

"Is this a security issue? Anything we need to be concerned about?" Dylan Haynes, the VP of security, asked.

"I don't think so," Guy said. "However, this means that we're missing a key leader from one of the AI research teams."

"What the hell," Haynes said gruffly. "That's two strikes on that department today."

"What are you talking about?" Guy asked.

"Background check. Just got flagged last night." Haynes sent a file from his tablet to the main screen in the conference room. Tony Singh's profile appeared. "Tony Singh, product director for Prometheus. One of the investigators said Tony is in the final stage of interviewing for a VP position at DeepMind."

Ava smiled.

She heard groans from around the table. Someone said, "Sellout..."

Colt had come through.

The private security and intelligence communities were incestuous. The competitor recruitment ploy was a smart play. Whether it was true or not, she didn't know. But no one would believe Tony Singh if he denied it.

Ava couldn't puzzle out yet how they'd managed to sideline Doug Everton.

Guy said, "He's out. We need loyalty. I sure as hell am not going to have someone with a foot out the door to one of our biggest competitors taking up a slot."

Voices around the table went quiet.

Guy looked over at Ava. "You were on Jeff Kim's senior staff at Pax AI."

"I was." Ava kept her tone even.

"You know what we're trying to build here, how important it is. We could use your longer-term vision as a counterbalance to some of the more *tactically*-minded people at the table."

There was some good-natured harrumphing from the other execs, all of whom were former soldiers or special operators. Some had tech backgrounds, but most had gotten MBAs or similar degrees after their military service.

Ava said, "I'd be honored. Thank you."

"Great. Your first job is to pick a replacement for Singh."

All eyes went to her.

She raised her eyebrows. "Um, now?"

Guy's head bobbed. "Yes, Ms. Klein."

Ava opened her laptop and spent a few uncomfortable moments navigating to the list of alternates. Her face grew hot as she felt all eyes on her. She was on dangerous ground now. If she chose Nadia and Nadia was exposed as a mole, Ava could be burned as well.

She also didn't have a choice. She owed Colt.

Ava decided to use an old marketing agency trick. Make them think it was their idea.

She tapped a few keystrokes and sent three profiles from the Prometheus group to the screen. "Of the candidates, I like these three. Wang, Heidel, and Blackmon. All three are very high performers. Wang and Heidel have the usual Silicon Valley internships and experience. Nadia Blackmon is an

interesting choice. She's a veteran, an AI engineer, and graduated from a Cornell master's program with top marks."

"I met her," Haynes said. He looked at Guy. "She worked
with special ops when she was in the Air Force. Cool chick."

Nods from the veterans around the table. "We could use
more tech wizards who speak our language."

"If it's a girl, would it be a tech witch?" one of them said,
which drew more laughter.

Ava offered a polite smile. "Nadia Blackmon is a smart,
capable young engineer. And the optics of selecting a woman
for a prestigious fellowship are very good." She saw a few of
the men around the table squirming.

Guy said, "Ava, no offense, but I don't give a shit about
optics. I only have one question. Is she top talent?"

"Absolutely."

"Then pull the trigger. Let her know we're wheels up in
twenty-four hours."

***

Ava raced back to her apartment in downtown D.C. By the
time she left the building, she'd received the standard electronic welcome packet for fellowship selectees. She was
instructed to pack lightly, but to be prepared for several weeks
away from home. She knew that people had been pre-
screened for health issues, and anyone with a chronic condition, illness, or serious allergy was quietly disqualified.

She needed to get word to Katz.

Ava opened her encrypted messaging app and sent him an
update.

He wrote back immediately.

Good luck.

Moshe drove her to the private terminal at Dulles

International the next morning. It was a Sunday and the main airport was all but deserted. The Hawkinson aircraft was the only one on the tarmac. Moshe planned to loiter in the parking lot until the aircraft departed.

"Try not to get caught," he said with a wink.

Ava gave him a thin smile. "See you on the other side."

She walked inside the private terminal. As soon as she entered, one of the general aviation employees walked over. "Ms. Klein?"

"Yes."

"Could you follow me, please?"

"I'm sorry, what's this about?"

"I was asked to bring you over here for some pre-departure screening. I guess it's because you were a last-minute add. You can leave your things here. They'll be brought on board."

Ava followed the woman through a side door and down a short hallway connected to a hangar. The day was dismal, wet, and gray, and the hangar was dimly lit and chilly.

"We can't do this inside?"

"This is where they asked me to bring you."

"Who?"

As if on command, two black Range Rovers pulled off the tarmac and rolled into the hangar. Behind them, Ava could see the Gulfstream aircraft. The last of the passengers, people she recognized from the office, were being escorted on board. Guy exited the rear of the Range Rover and buttoned his jacket. A thick man with an earpiece got out of the passenger seat. Sheryl Hawkinson was in the second vehicle. Guy had an odd expression on his face as he strode over to Ava.

"What's wrong?" Ava asked Guy.

"Dylan is probably jumping at shadows, but I need to humor him because he's usually right."

"I don't understand."

"Were you in Georgetown last Wednesday night?" Guy asked.

Ava felt dizzy at the question. It took everything in her power to behave normally.

"Guy, what's the meaning of this? Also, whatever the hell I do on my own time is my business."

"That's true, but we think we might have a mole in the company."

Ava's pulse raced. She tried to take covert calming breaths, like she'd been taught.

"Dylan's source says that the mole was meeting with their contact in Georgetown Wednesday night."

The Russians know, Ava thought. If the Russians were Hawkinson's source on this, that meant he was still working with them.

"Were you in Georgetown? Simple question," Guy asked again, frowning.

"Yes," Ava said, mustering ire and righteous indignation at the accusation. "I was shopping. And I had a spa appointment." She folded her arms. "If you'd like to check my credit card statement, I'd be happy to show you how much I tipped."

Guy studied her in silence for a long moment.

"No, that won't be necessary. I trust you. But I am going to have to ask you to hand over your phone. We can issue you a clean one when we get to the island. It's just a precaution. I'm sure you understand."

Guy gave her his most charming smile, the one she'd seen flashed across the board room and on countless media clips. But now, it looked predatory. He extended his hand, palm up.

Slowly, Ava reached into her jeans pocket and removed her phone, but didn't give it to Guy.

"We'll keep it in a locker in the executive suite." Guy

shrugged. "The alternative is you stay here. I'm sorry, those are the terms."

Ava handed over her phone.

Guy took it and lowered his hand to his side, then stepped out of her path and extended his hand toward the plane. "Please join us onboard. I think they've just opened the champagne."

As she began to walk, Guy said, "Ava, my security team is incredibly talented. If you're holding something back, now would be the time to let me know."

She turned to face him.

Guy said, "I know you didn't work for the Ministry of Defense. We both know who you really worked for. Don't worry, I'm not going to broadcast it. I know the Ministry was a cover." He lowered his voice. "Your being kicked out of Mossad has significant value to me. But I must know that I can trust you."

In her periphery, she could still make out Moshe's vehicle. She could be there in a sprint.

Ava forced a smile. "You can trust me, Guy."

She turned and walked past the Range Rovers and out of the hangar. She heard Guy and Sheryl talking but couldn't make out what they were saying.

She tried to convince herself that if the Hawkinsons had a problem with her past, they never would have hired her in the first place. As she ascended the steps to the Gulfstream, she could hear the passengers cheering inside, clanging champagne glasses and talking excitedly as they went on an adventure they knew little about. Ava felt like she was about to enter another world, one in which she had little control. And great vulnerability.

32

The NTCU common area had been turned into a de-facto war room. Additional monitors were mounted to the walls, with information feeds from multiple sources, including satellite. Thorpe requested high-altitude drone or U2 support from DoD, but so far, they'd been reluctant to approve it. He'd confided in Colt that he knew he didn't have many cards left to play with the deputy director and didn't want to burn his last few.

Arresting the four Russian SVR illegals who were pursuing Colt had served as a unifying event for the unit. Nothing like Russian spies running rampant in the nation's capital to bring the CIA and FBI together.

Ford and Thorpe, to their credit, kept their animosity at a low simmer. Thorpe was impressed with Nadia's intelligence reports from Hawk Technologies.

Some tension remained, though. Thorpe positively exploded when he learned that Colt disclosed CIA's involvement to a Mossad officer, even when Colt explained that Ava had already identified Nadia on her own.

Thorpe thought like a cop, for better or worse. Even

though he was a seasoned counterintelligence agent, he viewed the world through a particular lens. Trading with Ava got Nadia selected for the island. It was a risk, but one Colt felt he had to take.

Wilcox supported Colt's decision, praised the quick thinking, and admonished Thorpe not to burn Klein's cover. The FBI was getting sole credit for nabbing four Russian operatives on the streets of Washington. CIA's involvement was kept out of the papers.

Thorpe still believed that Ava's knowledge of the CIA mole in Hawk Technologies was dangerous and risked the operation. He raised the question of whether they should abort the mission. Colt and Ford held firm. They'd come too far to give up now.

Wilcox said he was going to call his counterpart at Mossad. They'd reached the point where they needed to coordinate efforts, and as long as Mossad cooperated, they wouldn't hold them accountable for using Ava as an illegal.

A day after Nadia traveled to the island, a small group at the NTCU stood around the table, looking up at the screen that would display the comms feed from YELLOWCARD. She was already overdue to communicate with them.

"Come on, kid," Ford said quietly.

One of the young FBI agents on Thorpe's team badged into the room and walked over to Thorpe, whispering something. Thorpe went back to his office, and Colt watched him log into his workstation before emerging a few minutes later.

"Everyone, listen up." He waited until all eyes were on him. "We just received word from one of our surveillance teams that Sheryl Hawkinson pulled her children out of Phillips-

Exeter. They boarded a chartered aircraft at Logan Airport thirty minutes ago. The Bureau, aided by some state and local law enforcement, are doing checks on senior staff at Hawk Ventures. Many of them appear to be leaving the country or have announced extended vacations from work. Company records indicate that a leadership retreat was planned for the upcoming week. Senator Preston Hawkinson has just departed on an 'overseas fact-finding mission.' But he's only taking his chief of staff and a top aide."

"What do you make of all this?" Ford asked.

"Not sure yet," Thorpe said.

"I don't know about you guys, but this feels a lot like a country recalling their ambassadors before a war," Colt said.

A few of them exchanged uneasy glances.

Thorpe said, "One last piece of intel. SLALOM is reporting that they've uncovered hundreds of transactions—funds transfers—from offshore accounts registered to dummy corporations. The money totals one hundred and fifty million dollars. At least one of the accounts has been tied to a Russian oligarch, Oleg Petrovich, who is an ally of the president. The president has used Petrovich to move money in the past."

"Do you think the Russians are funneling money to the Hawkinsons?" Ford asked.

Thorpe shrugged. "The manner is consistent with the methods uncovered by the Panama Papers, the disclosure of which did not seem to hamper Russian money laundering. By comparison, one hundred and fifty million is a pretty small payout."

"Let's hope it's not a down payment," Ford said.

"I've got YELLOWCARD traffic," a CIA officer from technical services called out.

"Put it on the screen," Thorpe said.

The text appeared on one of the monitors.

Safe arrival. Comms may be sporadic due to security. Expect more @1800L.

Colt could practically feel the collective exhale of relief around the room.

Colt left Langley shortly after Nadia's message. It was early on Sunday evening and a long day. The clouds broke earlier in the afternoon, while he was still in the Agency's basement, and Colt enjoyed a colorful drive home through the reds, golds, and oranges of autumn. If they heard anything else from Nadia that night, someone would call him. Right now, Colt wanted a sandwich and a beer and to turn his brain off for a while.

As he pulled into his driveway in Vienna, the sun cast long shadows across the tree-lined street. Multi-colored leaves blew across his yard as Colt approached his front door.

A car door slammed shut behind him.

Colt turned and saw the familiar bulky frame of a man who looked like he'd been carved from a gnarled block of wood. He wore a dark jacket and had thick, curly hair.

Moshe.

He last saw Moshe the day the fire nearly burned them alive at Pax AI's Mountain Research Facility. Now he walked across Colt's lawn, leaves crunching under his feet.

Colt nodded a silent greeting, and Moshe returned it. One professional to another.

Colt said, "I am surprised you weren't waiting for me in the dark in my living room."

Moshe said, "I thought that would be...how do you say...cliché."

They stepped into Colt's house and shut the door behind them.

"I'll be quick," Moshe said. "We've lost contact with Ava."

"When?"

Moshe said, "She was supposed to check in when she arrived on the island and she hasn't."

"Does she have a panic button?"

"Yes, but she hasn't activated it."

Colt studied him, wondering what they wanted and what he should say.

Moshe answered the question in his mind. "Ava told us about your friend." Meaning Nadia.

"All right."

"And I understand your people are now talking to mine about this."

Colt nodded. "Okay."

Moshe said, "But I wondered, since we know each other, perhaps I could come to you directly. People like us get things done faster, no?"

Colt said, "What do you need?"

"We need help getting Ava a message."

33

Guests arrived at the Hawk Technologies Caribbean Island Research Facility by way of the airstrip on the western end that could easily service the Gulfstream V and smaller prop aircraft. Except for Ava, everyone on her flight were IRI fellows. They were promptly taken by van to their welcome center.

Ava was surprised to be taken—alone—in a luxury coach to the VIP Welcome Center. She told the driver that she thought a mistake had been made—as a Hawk Technologies employee, she should have gone to the area known as "Research Village," but the driver demurred and said these were his orders.

On the trip, Ava saw that the island was divided into eastern and western sections. The predominant feature separating the two areas was a modest ridgeline, about twenty meters in elevation at its height and covered with tropical foliage. Research Village was on the western side of the ridgeline, near the airfield.

The VIP complex had all the makings of a luxury resort. The main building was three terraced levels of white, hurricane-resistant masonry and blue-green glass. Each level extended out farther than the one above it and wrapped gently around a hill, giving it the appearance of a spiral staircase. The main level opened to a sprawling outdoor pool area that connected the residences, restaurants, and recreation facilities. Clusters of palm trees dotted the landscape.

Ava was ushered into the welcome lobby, where young and attractive Hawkinson employees greeted the new arrivals. One of them handed her a champagne flute.

"Welcome, Ms. Klein. Your bags have already been taken to your suite." The woman handed her a small tablet device. "This contains all your welcome materials, and your room key is in the folio. Now, if you'll please come this way."

Before Ava could protest, she was gently guided into a large auditorium. It was designed similar to the one in the Hawk Technologies office, with several rows of concentric seating facing a central dais.

Sheryl Hawkinson currently stood on the stage.

The room was full when Ava took her seat. A quick count revealed about a hundred people. Most were dressed casually. She recognized a few, members of what Katz referred to as "the luminaries list."

Sheryl Hawkinson began speaking. "My friends, welcome to Hawk Technologies Island Research Institute. This is where we will co-create the future. On the other side of the island, at Research Village, Hawk Technologies researchers are making eye-opening breakthroughs in artificial intelligence and quantum computing." She paused for the anticipated applause. "Now, I don't think I'm understating the challenge before us when I say that society as we know it today is in dire peril. The dangers could not be more pressing, yet so many of our fellow humans choose anti-intellectualism over action. This is why our work here is so important. This is why you were chosen. The best and brightest minds from the sciences, the arts, philosophers, businessmen, and yes, a few politicians, were chosen to help us envision a bold new future that together with the technological advances being developed by our scientists, will be within our grasp!"

Sheryl paused, and images of the island appeared on the massive screens behind her.

"We wanted to create an intellectual paradise as much as a sensory one. I don't want you to think that our time together here will be all work and no play. When you're taking much-needed rests, you'll find world-class accommodation and recreation."

Sheryl paused again to study the crowd.

"Each of you was given a tablet computer with your personally designated amenities. The device supports visual recognition and has already been programmed with your face. Members of our staff will be available to answer questions. Thank you, and once again, welcome."

Ava had worked with the Hawk Technologies lead team on the preparations for this trip. She had just listened to Sheryl's speech. And she still didn't know what the hell they were doing here.

They hadn't said anything about AGI this time. She glanced around. No one else looked confused. No one else seemed to care how vague Sheryl had been. Had Ava missed something? Who the hell were these people and why were they invited here?

Ava marched into the lobby and found another resort representative, this one a young man in a Hawk Technologies polo and white Bermuda shorts.

"Excuse me, sir, I think I'm in the wrong spot. I'm an IRI fellow and somehow ended up here."

"Oh no," he said with feigned concern. "I'm sure we can

get you sorted out. What is your name?" She told him and he checked his list. "No, Ms. Klein, it looks like you're in the right spot. You are part of the *Visionary Team*." The kid put extra emphasis and mock importance on that. "I think your tablet has your schedule information, but you should be free until the welcome dinner to explore the VIP quarters if you like."

"Thanks," Ava said, confused. "Maybe I'll go stretch my legs."

She walked outside to the main entrance. A circular drive in front of the building wrapped around a fountain ringed with palm trees. The beach was available, and there was a dock with a few small watercraft. The road snaked north and was heavily lined with foliage on either side, obstructing views.

She went back inside and found the same staff person. "Excuse me, I saw that there is a marina? Is it possible to check out a boat?"

34

"You've got to be kidding me." Nadia read the message twice, just to make sure she wasn't hallucinating.

VERIFY GOLDCREST CONDITION ASAP. HIGHEST PRI. CONTACT APPROVED. CONFIRM.

GOLDCREST was the codename Colt assigned Ava Klein before Nadia departed. She wondered at the time why he'd name another agency's operative after a songbird, but decided not to press.

Nadia hadn't seen Ava since the plane ride here.

She had looked a little rattled when she first boarded, like someone had just given her some particularly bad news. They didn't sit near each other.

Nadia kept to herself during the flight, mentally noting what she observed—which seemed of little intelligence value thus far. It was mostly a bunch of computer geeks high-fiving and drinking champagne on a private plane. The aircraft cabin was small and difficult to maintain distance from others, but Nadia put her earbuds in and pretended to be distracted with a book. The buds had been modified by the Agency's tech ops wizards. They improved the reverse microphone feature, what Apple called "transparency mode," allowing her to covertly eavesdrop on conversations.

When they landed, Nadia and the rest of the passengers were ushered onto a van by the ground crew. Ava was directed to a different van. Nadia, feigning natural curiosity, asked one of the staffers why "that woman" wasn't traveling with them. The staffer just replied that she was going to a different location.

Research Village was a collection of one- and two-story buildings, precisely laid out in small clusters with central common areas. The roofs were solar panels surrounded by planters with turf and succulents. The dorms were clusters of four apartments in each building, and everyone had their own space.

The facility itself was divided into research bays and technical labs, each segregated based on an individual's ID card access. The cards were biometrically encoded with both a thumbprint and matching "DNA chit," which was an authenticated biological sample taken upon arrival. The two factors were authenticated each time someone attempted to use their card to open a particular door or workstation. Nadia was designated a "research lead" because she was filling Tony Singh's spot. While her access was not unrestricted, she was permitted to move between departments in order to properly coordinate efforts.

Nadia was not permitted to access a massive quantum computing farm, but she was able to discover some of its functions. She spoke with one of the division leads and learned that the "quantum factory," as it was known on the island, was about the size of a data center and largely submerged. Nadia imagined this was a functional decision as much as a security one. The facility would need an incredible amount of cooling, and building it at least partially beneath the island would allow them to easily pipe seawater into the heatsinks and cool the computers. This would also shield it from electromagnetic interference and reduce the radiation signal the computers gave off, further shielding the facility from detection by the US or others.

The research initiative's communicated goals were clear. The team on the island was supposed to create the world's first artificial general intelligence. The setup was impressive. The talent was top notch. But why all of the secrecy? Why the remote location? Surely there were many advanced technology firms around the world working on some type of AGI project.

Something wasn't right...

Nadia thought about this as she read Colt's encrypted message asking her to check on Ava. She thought about responding immediately that Ava was on the other side of the island, but decided against it. She had to be careful about repeated two-way communications. With the computing power available here on the island, a decryption program run out of the quantum farm could crack the encryption protocol on her CovCom device without breaking a virtual sweat. The more transmissions Nadia sent and received, the more likely Hawk cybersecurity was to detect it.

Nadia disconnected her device and stashed the components, already nervous she'd been online too long.

How in the hell was she going to get over to the resort side?

A chime on her Hawk Technologies computer announced an incoming message, which she promptly read.

Apparently Nadia no longer needed to figure out how to get to the other side of the island.

She'd been summoned there.

35

Wilcox called Thorpe, Ford, and Colt into his office and told them to sit.

"What you are about to read is the transcript of a secure message exchange between the Russian president and POTUS," Wilcox stated. "The Russian actually used the *hotline* for this."

Colt looked at Ford in confusion.

Ford said, "The hotline. The Washington–Moscow Direct Communications Link. The emergency channel established after the Cuban Missile Crisis so that the two heads of state could immediately communicate to avert potential disaster. Cold War. NORAD. ICBMs? The little red telephone that prevents World War Three?"

Thorpe said, "Actually, it's email now."

Ford looked at him. "No shit? Huh."

Colt nodded. "That hotline."

Wilcox thumbed the transcript. "Read, gents."

The Russian president was identified by his intelligence community codename, KOSCHEI. Koschei was a figure in Russian folklore known as "the immortal" or the "deathless one," a malevolent spirit that served as the chief antagonist in many Slavic folk tales. According to legend, Koschei could not be killed because his soul was hidden inside a needle, which was hidden inside an egg. The egg was inside a duck, the duck inside a hare, the hare inside a chest, and the chest buried on a faraway island. It was incredibly Russian. Koschei was something of a boogeyman in Russian mythology, the ever-present villain who could not be killed. American intelligence analysts on the Russia desk were divided on whether they thought the president would be flattered or offended by the moniker.

In the transcript, KOSCHEI claimed that Guy Hawkinson was developing dangerous cyber weapons and was already using them to threaten the "safety and sanctity" of the Russian people. He claimed that a blackout, which recently rendered half the city of St. Petersburg without electricity for two days, was the result of a cyberattack they could trace directly to Hawkinson. KOSCHEI demanded to know what the United States intended to do about it. He insinuated that perhaps Hawkinson, a favored mercenary of the US government, was acting as their proxy. POTUS suggested that KOSCHEI should be mindful of accusations of using military contractors as extensions of policy and vehemently denied that the US government had anything to do with a cyberattack on St. Petersburg.

POTUS asked about the money paid to Hawkinson, funneled through shell corporations registered in known tax havens throughout the world. KOSCHEI claimed he had, on the advice of his intelligence service, acquiesced to Hawkinson's demands and paid him the sum of one hundred and fifty million dollars. That proved to be a mistake, the Russian said, because Hawkinson was demanding more money.

KOSCHEI ended with a single line of text.

.   .   .

If the Americans will not act, the Russian Federation will.

Ford said, "Maybe they need to switch back to the telephone?"

"We think most of this is bullshit," Wilcox said. "The Russians are trying to cover their tracks. They got caught paying Hawkinson and are trying to play it off like he's blackmailing them."

"Do we think Hawkinson actually took down the power grid in St. Petersburg?" Thorpe asked. That had been the leading news story for days. Power had recently been restored to the city, but the nature of the blackout had yet to be uncovered or, more likely, disclosed. The Russian government claimed a cyberattack, and it was eerily similar to Russia's deactivation of Ukraine's grid in advance of their 2014 invasion of Crimea.

"NSA thinks it's a false flag. They can't find any evidence that someone hacked the Russian power grid," Wilcox said.

"Russia blacked out one of their largest cities for two days just so they could blame the West?" Ford asked.

"Hawkinson, specifically," Wilcox said, "but that's what the analysts think."

"What are the Russians planning?" Colt asked.

"Everyone is trying to figure that out," Wilcox said. "We think a military option is plausible. Hawkinson's island is considered part of the US Virgin Islands but is technically unclaimed by any nation. This falls under a pretty obscure part of maritime law." He shook his head. "I'm being serious. The lawyers are looking over hundred-year-old legal code to find out if the Russians attacked him, would that be considered an attack on American soil."

"The Russians wouldn't actually do that," Thorpe said. "Would they?"

Wilcox said, "The question is, *why* would they? What is important enough that you would risk war with the US to destroy it?"

Colt rubbed his chin. "If they're really considering this, we'll need to exfiltrate YELLOWCARD."

Ford huffed. "Not to mention a shit ton of civilians."

Wilcox rubbed his temples. His desk phone beeped and he depressed the intercom button.

"Director, your guests are here."

"Very well, thank you. We'll be right down." Wilcox looked at the group of men. "Time to go speak with Mossad."

It was common practice for high-ranking members of foreign militaries and intelligence services to visit Langley. Ariel Katz, Mossad's chief of Washington Station, was well known inside Langley and had worked with his American counterparts in this building and at the Pentagon many times throughout his long career at Mossad.

Katz traveled light and with minimal entourage, joining another officer from their Washington bureau and Moshe. Wilcox hosted the Mossad delegation in the small, wood-paneled conference room attached to his office.

When the doors closed, Katz began. "We would like to thank you for the discretion and assistance you've shown us recently."

Wilcox dipped his nose to look over his reading glasses. "I wish I felt that we had a choice in the matter. But you keep placing agents in our country illegally. Not even different agents at that. You could at least recycle them, Ariel." Wilcox offered him a tired smile.

Katz said, "American hospitality and grace knows no

bounds."

Wilcox said, "We both acknowledge that we have a significant interest in Hawk Technologies and their Island Research Initiative. We have reached out to our human intelligence source regarding your agent, Miss Klein. We have yet to hear anything back."

Katz bowed his head. "Thank you for the inquiry. We are most concerned."

Wilcox nodded toward Colt. "Go ahead."

Colt said, "Mr. Katz, here is what we know. Two years ago, our agencies worked together to thwart an SVR attempt at stealing R&D from an American company, Pax AI. At the time, we thought this theft was a failure. But we now believe Guy Hawkinson did steal a significant amount of Pax AI's most advanced research. Hawkinson's company has been developing that AI technology for at least the past year, hence the creation of their new company, Hawk Technologies. We also believe that about six months ago, Guy Hawkinson traded some of that valuable AI research to an SVR officer, Colonel Sergei Petrov. Petrov—"

"We know him," Katz said, his tone heavy. He said nothing further.

Colt continued, "We've also learned that the Russians have funneled money to the Hawkinsons, we believe for continued development of AI technology. We also believe that relationship has recently soured."

"Why?" Katz asked.

"There have been some recent developments." Wilcox informed Katz and his team of the recent message exchange between the US and Russian presidents, and how the latter was blaming Hawkinson for the cyberattack.

Katz exchanged a look with the two other Israelis at the table. "Thank you for sharing."

Colt noticed that Katz didn't look surprised by the information. Did he know something about the St. Petersburg incident that he wasn't saying?

Wilcox said, "Thanks to Pax AI's stolen technology, and a recent influx of investment money, Hawk Technologies has built one of the planet's most advanced AI research facilities on an island in the Caribbean. His access to Jeff Kim's research puts them years ahead of anyone else. We can also confirm that they have a massive quantum computing center, located below ground, shielded from EM interference and, we think, to take advantage of water cooling. Our early estimates are that they are likely a year away from a breakthrough."

"That puts them well ahead of the rest of us," Katz said. "We've been following a similar money trail."

Wilcox took off his glasses and rubbed them with his shirt. "Ariel, why are you guys so interested in the Hawkinsons? As far as we can tell, they're working on some pretty advanced AI. We understand that the capabilities are pretty strong, but I get the distinct feeling that you know more than we do. We sure would appreciate you sharing what you know about their work on that island."

Katz looked around the faces at the conference table. "I must stress that what I'm about to tell you must stay quiet."

"Of course," Wilcox said. The others nodded.

Katz said, "Over the past few years, we have been monitoring socioeconomic trends, political trends, and the development of information technology." He spoke with his hands. "Misinformation, disinformation. Information warfare. Propaganda. Different shades of gray, as you say. But a few groups stand out. One is Trinity."

Thorpe said, "We know all about this conspiracy theory, Mr. Katz. It supposedly started off with the Manhattan Project, and now they want to develop a superintelligent AGI to be their god, or some such nonsense. They hate tech companies and governments for slowing this process down. They protest because they want the development of AGI to happen quickly, without any safeties in place, because an AI god will supposedly solve all our problems, and the Trinity cult followers are the chosen ones." Thorpe waved his hand as if to say this was all garbage.

Katz said, "Correct. Trinity followers are the mindless technologists worshiping and racing toward a singular event they don't fully understand."

Colt watched as Katz sighed and shook his head as if he was fighting an unstoppable force.

Katz said, "The other group we are concerned about are the anti-technologists. Trinity's opposition. The anti-tech movement is motivated by fear of new technology, and fear of the pace of change. Like Trinity followers, they are also rioting in streets around the globe. They too are quick to believe in conspiracies, but unlike Trinity, they blame technology for their problems."

Ford was looking around. "I'm sorry, what does this have to do with the Hawkinsons?"

Katz held up his hand. "Our researchers have told us that both the Trinity movement and the anti-technologist movement are growing significantly. If current trends continue, within a few years, they will be large enough to have a serious voice in global politics."

Ford still looked frustrated. Colt understood. They were both worried about what they had just learned regarding the Russians. Ford started to speak, but Wilcox shushed him.

Katz said, "There is *another* group. One that remains in the shadows. Until recently, we have only heard rumors of its existence. It is a splinter group that was at one time associated with Trinity. They are calling themselves Archon."

"Archon?" Wilcox said.

Katz nodded. "Archon is well-organized and well-funded. They have the capability of a top-tier intelligence organization, with operatives embedded in governments and corporations around the world. Archon is recruiting. They are growing their membership with the elite. Likeminded global citizens who share their views. Archon is establishing themselves in places where they can monitor technological developments as we get closer to the dawn of AGI. Their goal, from what we have learned, is to be the first."

"The first to what?" Thorpe asked.

"The first to create an artificial general intelligence," Colt said, already connecting the dots.

Katz nodded.

Colt said, "How is Archon connected to the Hawkinsons?"

Katz said, "We believe the Hawkinsons stole the most advanced AI technology in the world when they raided Pax AI two years ago. We think the Hawkinsons were recruited by members of Archon to join their organization. They have been doing their best to develop AGI and other advanced technologies on their island. We think the Hawkinsons are going to use their technology to further Archon's cause." Katz took a deep breath. "These other groups. Trinity? The anti-technologists? Archon is actively growing them."

"Why would they do that?"

"Archon doesn't just want to win the race. They want to actively prevent anyone *else* from winning. Archon is engaged in a technological covert war on the rest of the world."

Wilcox said, "To what end?"

Katz raised his chin, his expression deadly serious. "We believe that the Archon organization intends to create an elite ruling class. A master race."

36

Nadia and about twenty-five others were loaded into vans at midday and driven to what they'd come to call "the resort." No one knew exactly why they'd been summoned to the other side.

This was Nadia's first trip over. She'd checked out an open water kayak the day before for some "exercise" to cover doing light recon. She didn't think she'd get anything valuable looking at the resort from the ocean, so instead she paddled around the western edge of the island and tried to get a sense of the place. The first thing she noticed were the squat metal pylons spaced approximately fifty yards apart that ringed the entire island, at least what she saw of it. They were not present at the beach that serviced Research Village. Nadia assumed they were sensors of some type. She recalled another of Colt's maxims—*Always assume someone is watching.*

Nadia hadn't discovered anything of real value on her scouting trip, but Ford once told her that ruling out the obvious was an important step in peeling back the layers. The vans took them on the only road that connected the two sides of the island, which ran along the northern edge. The road was heavily landscaped with palms, mango trees, and thick, ropey kapok trees. Sea grapes, tall grasses, and smaller palms filled the spaces between the trees. It wasn't entirely a green wall, but the foliage certainly obscured the view from the road.

The vans pulled up to a welcome center and the researchers filed out. Nadia carried her backpack, where she stored a hoodie because of how cold the labs were. She'd also brought her Hawk Technologies laptop and the tablet they issued her when she arrived. Nadia's phone, earbuds, and CovCom rig were inside a padded pouch beneath a false bottom in her pack. She also had a set of button mics. The pouch's lining would spoof any airport-grade metal detector or handheld scanning device.

As Nadia followed the others into the auditorium, she saw a group of VIPs being escorted to an adjacent auditorium.

Ava Klein was among them.

Guy and Sheryl Hawkinson came on stage and congratulated the group for their selection to the fellowship, reminding them that they were among the top one percent of the world's scientific talent.

"You will shape the future," Sheryl bellowed.

Nadia watched the reactions of her fellow participants. Most were eating it up.

Next, Guy began speaking. He told them how proud he was of what they'd accomplished at Hawk Technologies and how it was only the beginning.

He said, "While this fellowship is an extraordinary opportunity, and one you should all be immensely proud of, each person in this room is now a candidate for another special project."

This is it, Nadia thought.

Guy continued, "Each of you has shown tremendous

potential, commitment, and drive for our mission. You are all, in your own rights, brilliant minds, and I could see each of you leading a technology company into the next age. In a few moments, each of you will enter a separate interview process for potential selection into this special assignment."

He delivered more platitudes and then concluded his presentation. A set of doors opened to their left. Staffers were tapping people by row to follow them.

"Nadia Blackmon?"

"Yes."

"You're in about ten minutes. You can wait here."

"Okay, thanks."

Nadia went to sit down but then noticed the Hawkinsons walking to the adjacent auditorium where the VIPs were seated.

Would they get the same speech? Or new information?

Nadia wanted to find out. She reached into her bag and fumbled with the concealed pouch at the bottom. Finding the container holding the button mics, she fished one out and closed everything up. She maneuvered over to the door that connected the two auditoriums, checked that she was not being watched, and slipped over to the VIP section.

Ava was seated in the center of the auditorium.

Nadia began moving toward her but then caught a glimpse of a security guard on the far side of that row. Heading to the nearest empty seat instead, she used the chair in front of her for cover and pulled the adhesive cover off one of the buttons. She stuck it to the bottom of her chair in the shadows, where someone would have to genuinely search to find it.

Nadia then stood, casually walked back through the door, and sat down in her section. Then someone called her name, and she shouldered her backpack and filed out.

She was taken to a small waiting room with couches,

chairs, and three large windows overlooking the beach. Several of her fellow researchers wore headphones while they waited. Nadia set her bag down and opened it just enough that she could access her phone and AirPods. She put in the AirPods and activated the button mic.

Then she concentrated on the transmission coming in over the pods.

Sheryl Hawkinson was speaking. Nadia recognized her voice and delivery immediately.

"My friends, thank you for joining us on this historic occasion," she began. "We are finally ready to begin." Sheryl paused and the room broke into thunderous applause that sounded like waves crashing over the microphone. "By now, you have all received the assignments for your teams. The work of planning a new society will be difficult, it will be taxing, and we will want to quit. But we must not. This is a moment not unlike the birth of the Renaissance when humanity emerged from the Dark Ages. The Dark Ages bear striking similarities to the time we occupy today—people choose superstition over science, rhetoric over reason, and put blind faith in false idols."

There was more applause and the mic picked up scattered conversation in the audience. Sheryl must have held something up to represent a false idol or shown it onscreen, because Nadia was clearly missing context.

"With our new technological developments, and the recent partnerships we've made, Hawk Technologies is within a few years of developing a true artificial general intelligence. This AGI will be able to develop technological advances at a geometric rate. There will be no disease that can harm us. We shall live longer and more fulfilling lives. We will not worry about failed markets, because we will control the markets that drive the global economy."

As Sheryl paused again, Nadia tried not to react. *What was she talking about?*

Several of the researchers sitting next to Nadia were called and ushered out of the waiting area.

Sheryl continued, "Many of you have asked how will we make these advances? How will we feed the mouths of so many? How will we convince so many misled souls around the globe to follow our lead? The answer, we won't. Instead, we will *rule*."

Thunderous applause, and Nadia winced at the unexpected eruption.

Sheryl said, "Each one of you was chosen not just for your skill but for your vision. The same cannot be said for all mankind. Global governments and alliances are petri dishes for division and conflict. While we should strive to provide for our inferiors, we cannot let ourselves be dragged down by their ignorance! Political warfare would destroy this group, and the stakes are simply too high for us to risk it. Will there be death? Absolutely. We believe in radical truth and we shall not lie to you about that. But as all great tribes do, we must cull the herd, lest we be pulled down and drowned by the weakest among us."

Whoa. Nadia looked around. Someone was waving to her.

She realized she'd completely lost touch with her surroundings. The person sitting next to her tapped her on the arm.

"They're calling your name."

"Nadia Blackmon?" the staffer repeated.

The pieces all seemed to fall into place now. The Hawkinsons were going to build an AGI that would answer only to them. Control their markets. Cull the weak. Genetic engineering. They weren't just talking about creating a global oligarchy. They were talking about creating a master race.

But it could very well be a master race without an inferior one.

Nadia had to find a way to get outside so she could send a transmission. Soon.

"Ms. Blackmon," the staffer was saying, now standing right over her. "I need you to come with me, please. It's time for your interview."

Ava sat in the auditorium, feeling the blood drain from her face as Sheryl spoke. She kept thinking she was trapped in some nightmare. That this couldn't possibly be real. Katz had implied something bigger was going on here. But seeing Sheryl on the dais speaking so calmly, so resolutely about their creation of an... What was the word? An over-society? It was horrifying.

Eighty years ago, the Nazis attempted this and the world dismissed it as the ramblings of a madman. Then the madman murdered millions of Ava's people. Were the Hawkinsons the next iteration of that sickness?

"Now," Sheryl Hawkinson said, "we must take great measures to protect ourselves. We have so much work to do, and our enemies do not want us to succeed. Our work calls for the utmost secrecy and the highest levels of security. This way of life will seem intrusive and inconvenient, but let me assure you that this is for the best. Security must be our top priority during this critical phase."

The audience nodded in agreement.

"To that end, allow me to introduce to you a woman who is not only a world expert in security, and an expert in secrecy, but also someone I look to as a friend, a confidant, and a mentor."

An older woman walked slowly onto the stage.

"A woman who showed me what is *possible* if we just dream bigger..."

Ava rubbed her eyes, confused. She recognized the woman now stepping onto the dais. But...this wasn't right.

It wasn't possible. It...

The blood drained from Ava's face.

It was her aunt.

"Please join me in welcoming...Ms. Samantha Klein."

37

Ava watched Samantha scan the room until their eyes met.

Her aunt gave an almost imperceptible nod. Her expression betrayed little.

Samantha spoke in platitudes, emphasizing to the audience the importance of securing their future. She expressed how grateful she was for the opportunity to be among *like-minded* visionaries.

Ava couldn't believe what she was hearing. This didn't fit with what she knew to be true about her aunt. A woman who had impacted her adult life like no other. Her mentor and handler for over a decade. Either Ava had misjudged her own aunt, or this was fiction. Could this be a ruse? Was Samantha here at the behest of Mossad? Ava hadn't been able to communicate with Katz since Guy Hawkinson seized her phone. Perhaps Samantha was the answer? She seized onto that idea for her own sanity. But hadn't Sheryl said something about Samantha being a mentor? That suggested a longer relationship.

Samantha's speech ended and the attendees were dismissed.

The audience stood and was escorted to their respective assignments, working groups led by people who hadn't been introduced yet. Instructions on where to go were transmitted to their individual devices. One person after another looked at their personal message, eyes lighting up as they headed toward one of the staff holding up colored signs to designate their group.

Ava looked down at her tablet. She did not receive an instruction message.

She saw Samantha standing on the stage. She was speaking with Sheryl, but leaned over to catch Ava's eye, motioning her to join them. Ava took a breath and headed their way. Samantha stepped forward and embraced her niece.

"My, what a surprise." Ava did her best to act pleased.

"I'm sure this is something of a surprise to you, my dear. Of course, I couldn't pass up this opportunity." Samantha gave a practiced laugh and smiled at Sheryl. "It was a chance to be part of something *amazing*."

Ava's eyes were wide, her smile forced. "It's great to see you. When did this all happen?"

Samantha glanced at Sheryl. "Well, it was quite sudden, actually. The Hawkinsons reached out shortly after I last saw you in London. Sheryl said they were looking for someone with private-sector intelligence experience. We both know that I'm not getting hired to my old job anytime soon. Please do forgive me, dear, I'm sorry I had to keep it from you."

"I understand," Ava said, feeling queasy.

"She may have put in a good word for you as well," Sheryl said, smiling.

Ava looked at her aunt, who waved the comment away. *Now that was interesting.* Had Samantha pulled strings to get Ava selected? Was this how Guy learned that she had once worked for Mossad? Could *Samantha* be working for Mossad, and Katz had kept Ava in the dark? She wouldn't put it past him. But Ava suspected that to be unlikely.

There were so many questions, but her aunt's burning gaze clearly said that now was not the time for them.

Sheryl gently squeezed Samantha's shoulder. "We are scheduled to meet with Guy soon. For the *interviews*."

Samantha glanced at her watch. "We have a bit of time, no?" She then looked at Ava. "I'll be right there, Sheryl. I just need to speak with my niece for a few moments."

Ava and her aunt walked out of the building in silence, each recognizing that their conversation was not for prying ears. Ava opened a sliding glass door and they both stepped outside. The waves gently crashed on the beach. Wind rustled through palm fronds.

They kept walking along the stone path of the resort area and soon stepped on beach sand. The wind coming off the ocean was brisk and loud. It would eliminate any potential surveillance threat.

Samantha finally looked at Ava. "It's time we had a talk."

When they were far enough away from the buildings, Samantha sat in the sand and motioned for Ava to join her. They both looked out over the water as Samantha spoke.

"You are familiar with the Trinity organization from the news and reading your intelligence reports. Trinity dates back to the Second World War. To the Manhattan Project. It's named for the site in New Mexico where the Americans detonated the first atomic bomb."

"I know," Ava said. "I mean, I've heard that. Everyone has. But...it's not real. It's a made-up story. A conspiracy theory."

Her aunt gave her a sympathetic look. "I'm afraid that you've been misinformed."

Ava started to speak and then stopped.

Samantha said, "Did you know that during the Manhattan Project, many physicists believed the bomb would set off a chain reaction that would consume the world?"

"I didn't know that."

"It was a terrifying moment. And a unifying one. A core group of individuals involved in the Manhattan Project were so motivated by the experience that they formed Trinity, a secret society made up of scientists, military officers, and a few members of the US government. They selected their members with great care and swore each other to secrecy, but their goal was the same."

"They wanted to stop nuclear weapons?"

"What? No. No, Ava, that wasn't it at all. These were not pacifists. They were shaken by the power of their invention. The atomic bomb was not what frightened them into action." Samantha's tone conveyed the importance of her words. "The members of Trinity were adults in the 1940s. They had seen multiple world wars. With each decade, weapons became increasingly more advanced. These men were born before the automobile was invented, and with their scientific expertise they helped to split the atom and flatten entire cities. But do you know what terrified them more than anything else?"

"What?"

"That the rate of technological advancement was itself accelerating. The original Trinity membership included some of the most brilliant minds of their generation. And they were terrified of the curve."

"The curve?"

"The technological curve. The ones who understood it best were the most afraid. For eventually, machines would advance so fast and so far that it would surpass humanity's ability to react. Trinity's intent was to protect mankind, to ensure that our capacity to innovate was never eclipsed by our capacity to destroy ourselves. Trinity ensured that technological advancement continued at a sustainable pace so that the impacts could be modeled and safeguards ensured. As the group aged, they grew their membership through careful recruitment, choosing trustworthy and capable thinkers in the military, government, and private enterprise. Trinity's members sought out positions where they could keep tabs on mankind's technological progress, and positioned themselves to be able to guide both government and corporate policy."

"Trinity had agents around the world?"

"Present tense. Trinity *has* agents of influence around the world. But Trinity's numbers are shrinking, and it's now facing a new enemy." Samantha looked out to the water.

"Who?"

Samantha sighed. "Some years ago, the organization fractured. There were those within Trinity who believed that humanity could no longer save itself. Dangerous technological advances were like the Hydra from Greek mythology. A new threat replicates whenever an old one is defeated. This wayward group believed not only that mankind couldn't be saved, but that mankind *shouldn't* be saved. They believed that mankind was no longer worthy of saving. The faction instead wanted to use Trinity's influence and reach to build powerful technology corporations that they could control."

"That sounds exactly like the speech I just heard," Ava said.

"Yes, it does," Samantha said knowingly. "Yes it does indeed." She clasped her niece's shoulders.

"What happened?"

"There was a vote. Trinity has a leadership circle, sort of

like a board of directors. Its members voted and the faction lost. That is when things got bad. The faction broke off from Trinity and began calling itself Archon."

"Samantha, how do you know so much about this?"

Samantha looked at her niece. "This is what I need to tell you now. Ava, your father was a member of Trinity. He was recruited by one of the original members from the Manhattan Project."

Ava's mouth fell open. "My father was an intelligence officer."

"He was that, too. Trinity has agents in many places," Samantha said. "I know this for a fact."

"You are also..."

She nodded. "Your father recruited me, years ago."

Ava shook her head in disbelief.

Samantha clasped Ava's hand. "I am forever loyal to Israel. But there are tectonic shifts happening. Large, capable organizations pulling the strings, operating in secret. The further we travel up this technological curse, the greater the stakes grow. We must choose a side and fight for what is right."

Ava didn't know what to say.

Samantha stood up and brushed off the sand. "But we must be wary. We are in the lion's den."

Ava stood and they began to walk back toward the resort. "Wait. I have more questions," she began.

Samantha held up her finger. "Not now, I'm sorry. We don't have enough time." She reached into her pocket and drew out her phone.

"Excuse me," she said, and answered a call. "Yes. Okay...I understand. Thank you." Then she hung up, looking straight ahead as she announced, "The Americans have managed to smuggle a mole onto the island. Someone was trying to access certain bits of research that they didn't have the authority to see."

"What will happen?" Ava asked.

"They have a list. A handful of suspects based on cyber forensic evidence."

A handful, Ava thought. If Nadia was on that list, they would likely discover her.

Samantha said, "Hawkinson has asked me to witness the questioning. He plans to demonstrate a new polygraph system for me. Something he has developed with the Pax AI technology. It uses their deep learning algorithms to evaluate biometric data while the subject is answering questions. They say it's impossible to beat."

Ava's eyes widened. "Will I be questioned?"

Samantha took her niece's hand. "Have no fear. I won't let any harm come to you, Ava. But we cannot risk exposure. We must play along and protect ourselves, whatever the cost."

38

Moscow

Snow fell as Petrov returned to Russia. The operation, it appeared, was over. Petrov still didn't understand why he'd been recalled so abruptly. The SVR knew about the island and its quantum laboratory. They knew how Hawk Technologies was advancing Jeff Kim's earlier work. If a breakthrough was not imminent, it was at the very least on the horizon.

Petrov was driven directly from the airport to SVR headquarters. He had a headache from the plane, and his eyes were bloodshot.

Koskov shut the door as Petrov entered his office. "Have a seat."

"Why was my operation shut down?" Petrov protested. "It wasn't close to finished."

"Maybe not, but the president is finished with Hawkinson."

"Could we ask him for more time?"

Koskov actually laughed at that. "That would be hazardous for the messenger. It's over, Sergei."

"What changed?"

"There have been new developments that you were not privy to. The president no longer believes that Hawkinson will honor his agreement." Koskov paused to let that sink in.

Petrov blinked. Moscow would not cut ties with Hawkinson unless there was a good reason.

"Was the data cache that Hawkinson provided to us not sufficiently productive?"

Koskov shook his head. "Not at all. On the contrary, our scientists in St. Petersburg were thrilled with the progress they were making." There was a funny look in Koskov's eye.

Petrov made the connection. "St. Petersburg."

Koskov nodded. "Yes. Hit by a cyberattack a few days ago. The whole city went without power. Certain security systems were down for over three hours. Just enough time, I'm told..."

"Someone wiped out our research."

"All destroyed. Everything Hawkinson gave us. Everything we have discovered since. Nothing is left."

Petrov shuddered. "I am afraid to ask. But will I be..."

"Blamed? Officers in the GRU's Unit 74455 were able to examine cyber forensic evidence. The attackers did their best to hide it, but we know who was responsible. The attack originated from an island in the Caribbean."

Petrov reddened.

Koskov raised his eyebrows. "The president only blames one person. Guy Hawkinson."

Petrov said, "What will happen to him?"

Koskov smiled. "I have never seen the president this angry. My understanding is that a very special type of revenge is in the works."

39

Langley, Virginia

Fred Ford appeared to be at a loss for words.

He handed Colt a just-released transcript of POTUS and KOSCHEI communicating via the hotline. Colt quickly read it.

Then he read it again.

"This can't be true," he muttered. "A Russian commercial satellite malfunction? *Atmospheric reentry imminent*? What the hell are they *really* doing?"

"Whatever it is, it's going to hit the Hawkinsons' island," Ford said. "And by the sound of those hazardous area dimensions, it's going to *wreck* some shit."

"How long do we have?"

"Hours, maybe a day." Ford was already marching out of the NTCU room. "Come on, follow me."

They arrived at Wilcox's office moments later. Thorpe was already there.

Wilcox looked up as they entered. "Did you two hear?"

"Yes, sir, we just read the hotline transcript," Ford said.

Colt's pulse was racing. They needed to get Nadia off the island.

Wilcox said, "The National Security Council just approved a ConOps."

Thorpe said, "DoD has the lead on evacuating civilians from the island. They're sending a pair of C-130s to take people to safety."

Ford looked confused. "And take down Hawkinson?"

Wilcox shook his head. "No one's taking down Hawkinson just yet."

Thorpe said, "Air Force Special Operations Command at Hurlburt Field in Florida's panhandle launched six CV-22 Ospreys with pararescue airmen and a combat control element. They'll be standing by, but..." Thorpe looked at Wilcox.

Wilcox said, "I brought up the risks involved in sending teams of special operators to raid an island with dozens of Hawkinson's security personnel, former special operators themselves. The alarm bells began ringing. Hell, Senator Hawkinson is scheduled to fly to the island in a few hours, bringing Sheryl's daughters with him. Think of the optics if we send a team in there, they resist, and this thing goes south."

Ford shook his head. "What a shit show."

Colt understood. No one wanted Americans shooting Americans.

"Well how the hell do we get intel from the island before the Russians destroy it?" Ford asked.

Wilcox sighed. "Right now the US government is focused on preventing civilian casualties. We can't conclusively prove Hawkinson's collusion with the Russians. Nor do we have sufficient evidence to prove he stole Pax AI trade secrets. Before the government can arrest Guy Hawkinson, we need to collect the evidence required. Given Senator Hawkinson's position as a ranking member on the Senate Intelligence Committee and the Hawkinsons' political action committee funding a third of Congress's reelection campaigns, the NSC is not willing to take the risk."

"How do we get our agent out?" Colt asked.

"We're working on that now."

Colt looked at Ford, and then back at Wilcox. "You need to send us down there now. We know our agent's identity. If her cover is intact, we can leave her there. If it's blown, we can..."

Thorpe looked skeptical. "You can what? *Rescue* her? No offense, Colt, but come on..."

"We have to try."

"How would you do it, if I gave you the green light?" Wilcox asked.

Colt bit his lip, thinking for a moment. "You said the senator was headed to the island?"

Wilcox nodded. "That's what we think."

"Then I may have a plan. Something I heard the DGSI do on an operation in Tunisia once." Colt ran them through his idea.

When he was finished, Ford laughed. "I would like to be on record as saying that this will be a clusterfuck of Biblical proportions." Then he grinned at them. "I'm in."

Wilcox tilted his head. "This would get us in a lot of hot water..."

"You said the president doesn't want any bloodshed. Does that include his American CIA officers operating undercover? If YELLOWCARD is burned, we need to extract her."

Wilcox huffed.

Colt narrowed his eyes. "What is it?"

"Well, just before you came in, I received a communication

from our Israeli friends. They have asked to send an...*evacuation specialist*...to assist in a joint rescue operation for our agents. If one was to be attempted."

Colt grinned at the description. *Moshe.* He turned to Ford. "Trust me, we want their evacuation specialist with us."

40

Samantha had joined the Hawkinsons soon after they returned from the beach, telling Ava that she would summon her at the right time. Ava didn't know if that meant minutes or hours.

At first, Ava couldn't decide what to do next. Should she warn Nadia? *Could* she warn her? What would her aunt say if Ava told her about Nadia's CIA connection? Did Samantha know that Guy Hawkinson already suspected Ava herself of being a spy?

All these questions swirling in her head were nothing compared to those she had about her father's participation in Trinity.

But Ava could only do one thing right now. And she had to act fast.

Ava took the VIP center's elevator up to the third floor and peered inside a waiting room where the "interviews" of suspected spies would likely soon be taking place.

She turned as a stairwell door opened behind her. A column of Hawkinson R&D employees began marching through the hallway, heading toward the waiting room. As she stood off to the side, nodding and smiling, she counted five of them in all. *A handful of suspects.* Nadia was among them, confirming Ava's fears.

Ava made sure no one was watching and then caught Nadia's eye, gesturing toward the women's room across the hallway and mouthing, "*Now.*"

Nadia saw her but gave no indication of understanding or compliance. She just kept walking. A Hawkinson staff member held the door open as they entered the waiting room.

Ava turned and headed into the women's room. Inside, she turned the faucet on the nearest sink up all the way, providing ambient noise and a reason for her being there.

Then she waited, hoping...

Nadia came in a few seconds later. She walked to the sink next to Ava and began washing her hands. They didn't make eye contact.

Ava whispered, "They'll be giving each of you a polygraph. Some type of AI-based technology. It's new, and from what I understand, it can't be beat. I suggest you get out of here."

Before Nadia could respond, Ava turned off her faucet and walked out of the bathroom.

Nadia watched the door close as Ava left. Pulse pounding, she headed into one of the bathroom stalls and shut the door, then sat down and opened her tablet.

Think.

Ava had just informed her that she would be interrogated using this new AI-based polygraph system. Nadia had enough trouble with interrogations without having to defeat a near-perfect lie detector. She had to escape.

But then what?

Hawkinson's security team would know she fled, which would only raise more suspicions. She had no clear way off the island. That meant she needed to beat the polygraph.

Shit.

Nadia felt her body temperature rising. The Hawkinson staff member had told her to hurry up in the bathroom. They would probably send someone to look for her soon. She needed to act fast. *Think about the problem. What do you know? What was the report Ford showed you. Hawk gave the Russians a deep-learning-based polygraph system. It evaluates various biological metrics such as facial expressions, pulse, and eye dilation. For the visual stimuli, it uses a smartphone to...*

The phone...

Their program uses a phone. Communicates the data using UWB. Ultra-wideband technology.

Nadia opened her tablet and began typing as fast as she could. She first made sure to hide her network movements. Then she accessed the dark web marketplace account she used to download the malware that helped her defeat the FBI agents' tracking devices several weeks earlier.

There.

Her purchase was still available for download. Click. Thirty seconds and the tool would be on her tablet, hidden and password-protected in case anyone tried to check.

She heard the restroom door opening.

If the tech companies had patched their software and Hawkinson kept their phone software up to date, this might not work. But it was her only chance.

Footsteps on the restroom floor.

"Hello? Ms. Blackmon? We're waiting..."

She looked at her tablet. A few more keystrokes to automate her program so it would seek out and infect any Bluetooth-enabled phones within range.

"Ms. Blackmon, is that you? Apologies, but they asked me to come get you. It's time."

Ava looked down at her tablet. She had just received an invite to meet on the third floor of the VIP center's main building. Very near where she had just met Nadia.

A room around the corner had been reserved for Hawkinson's executive team. Ava headed back that way. When she arrived, Samantha was looking down at her tablet, swiping furiously with her index finger.

"What are we doing here?" Ava asked.

Samantha said, "I told you that the Americans placed a mole on the island. Now, we're going to unmask the mole."

Ava felt her insides grow cold.

She was afraid of this. If Samantha was trying to prove her loyalty to the Hawkinsons, the quickest way for her to do that was to offer an enemy spy's head on a platter.

But that would require Ava to do two things she desperately did not want to do. Burn Nadia. And likely expose herself.

Ava's mind raced for a way to spare Nadia without risking her own position. Did Samantha think Ava knew the US agent's identity? If so, was Samantha trying to reinforce Ava's cover as well? In past operations, the two women would have discussed this. Ava didn't know what to think of her aunt right now.

Samantha badged them through the door, and they walked down a short hallway to another door blocked by a guard. He nodded when he recognized Samantha, who badged them through again. The Hawkinsons were taking no chances with security.

Ava followed her aunt into a room with panoramic windows overlooking the ocean. Guy and Sheryl were both seated at a conference table on their individual phones.

Sheryl was speaking when they entered.

"—the flight is delayed, *again*. My *children* are on that plane. I want someone's head on a—"

Sheryl stopped speaking when she saw Samantha and Ava.

"What's *she* doing here?" she said, looking at Ava.

"She's going to help us find your traitor," Samantha announced.

Ava turned, her eyes piercing her aunt, who seemed to be ignoring her. *What the hell was she thinking?*

"Guy!" Samantha called out. "We're ready."

Guy sat at the head of the long conference table. Two security men flanked him. They stood along the wall like statues, a submachine gun suspended at each man's chest from tactical slings. Guy looked up from his phone and said, "I'll call you back." He rose and walked over to a podium, then picked up a tablet and tapped the screen. "Are we ready for our first contestant?"

"Yes, we are." Samantha looked at the computer. "Is this the new toy you've been telling me about?"

Guy looked at the computer fondly. "It is. Wait till you see what she can do."

Samantha said, "I've been disappointed by men's promises before..."

Sheryl snorted with pleasure.

Guy shrugged. "Give me some time, I'll make a believer out of you."

Ava scanned the room. At the far end of the table, a laptop was set up next to a tripod-mounted phone.

The camera lenses on the back of the phone faced an empty chair.

Then the doors opened, and a security guard escorted Nadia into the room.

The Hawk Technologies staff member guided Nadia to the chair opposite the phone's camera lenses.

Guy smiled warmly as she entered. "Ms. Blackmon, good afternoon. Please, have a seat." He pointed at the chair. "I apologize in advance for the awkwardness here. This is simply a formality."

Nadia examined the setup. "I don't understand." She looked around at the faces in the room. Ava detected a micro expression of horror when their eyes met. But Nadia regained her composure and asked, "Is this the interview for the special project? That's what I've been waiting for."

"Something like that. Please, sit," Guy said, still pointing toward the chair.

Nadia sat.

"Ms. Klein." Guy turned in his seat to look at Ava. "Good of you to join us. You recommended Ms. Blackmon for the fellowship. Is that correct?"

"Yes, it is," Ava said.

Guy's voice was soft. "Why'd you choose her, Ava?"

"She was the top candidate on the alternates list after we determined that Singh was ineligible."

"Okay." Guy nodded, seeming to accept her response.

Why didn't Nadia listen to me? Ava thought. *I told her not to take this interview. She should be trying to find a way off this island.*

Guy turned back to Nadia.

"Ms. Blackmon, as you're aware, the work Hawk Technologies is leading is extremely advanced. Any number of our competitors would love to find out what we're up to here on this island."

Guy walked over to the table and began typing on the laptop. Ava had an indirect view of the screen. The staff member who had brought Nadia began fixing a clip onto her finger and thumb, then walked over to the phone and tapped on the screen, giving Guy a nod.

Guy said, "Ms. Nadia Blackmon. You are one of five people we'll be interviewing this afternoon. We'll question you by using this special tool we've developed. It uses deep learning to evaluate your face and compare it to similar faces that have been under similar stimuli. The program is based on years of research conducted by the FBI's Behavioral Analysis Unit, as well as other organizations from around the world. The designers of this tool have identified thousands of individual characteristics to measure. Body posture, micro expressions, eye movement, changes in breath and pulse, you name it..." Guy looked at the screen. "Did you ever take a polygraph examination when you were in the military?"

"I had a CI poly, yes."

"A good polygrapher is like an old-world fortune teller," Guy said with a smile. "They're almost mystical. But unfortunately, those machines could be beat. A polygrapher uses the machine to determine whether someone is being deceptive. But there are many variables. Operator ability. The machine's calibration and type...which determines how well it can pick up on physiological responses related to deception. It tends not to work on sociopaths, who generally aren't concerned with the consequences of their actions."

Guy busied himself for a few moments of typing and what Ava assumed were calibrations. The anticipation must have been agonizing for Nadia, and Ava suspected that was part of the interrogation process. Build tension to erode her confidence.

Guy looked back at the staff member. "Why is it doing this?"

The staff member hurried over. "Hmm. Not sure." He walked over to the phone. "Connectivity issues. It's related to the ultra-wideband connection...says it's unable to sync."

Sheryl said, "Problem with your tool, Guy?"

Guy shot her a look, then turned back to the technician. "What's the solution?"

"You can still use some of the polygraph functionality, but it won't be nearly as robust. Eighty-five percent of the output is face and eyes."

Guy shook his head, then looked up at Samantha. "Well, Samantha, another disappointment, I'm afraid. We'll have to do it the old-fashioned way."

Guy turned back to Nadia. "Don't worry, this device is still able to measure your heart rate. That, plus a bit of experience, should give us what we need. If you're lying, we will know."

Nadia's chest moved up and down slowly as she breathed.

Guy continued, "Now, despite Ms. Klein vouching for you, there are a few irregularities in your background. We need to get to the bottom of it."

"What are you talking about?" Nadia asked.

"You worked for a company called Cognitive, is that correct?"

"That's right," Nadia said.

"Cognitive appears not to exist. Normally, I might chalk that up to an eager grad student padding their resume with a made-up employer. However, my security team found that there *was* a company called Cognitive, but they were only around for a few months before disbanding. *Weird*. Right?"

"I started talking with Cognitive when I was finishing up grad school. They had a connection with one of my professors. Cognitive offered me a job. Said they were in 'stealth mode.' I couldn't talk about it with anyone. They didn't want people to know what the company was working on. I was only with them for a few months when they lost funding and the owners decided to shut it down."

"All right." Guy proceeded to ask questions about her identity and background, presumably to establish a baseline. He began with easy questions. What was her cadet squadron at the Air Force Academy? What color car did her father drive? Where was her first deployment? He tried to trick her into disclosing classified information regarding a program she was part of while in the Air Force, but to her credit, Nadia said she couldn't discuss that.

Then, Guy began asking more invasive questions. He unapologetically probed her sexual orientation and romantic history, intentionally trying to make her uncomfortable. He told her to describe a time when she'd stolen something, not even asking whether she had, just assuming it was true. Nadia denied ever doing so.

The questions continued for fifteen minutes in agonizing and increasingly personal detail.

Ava tried to read the screen from her indirect vantage point, but without proper orientation, she couldn't tell whether Nadia was succeeding. For her part, Nadia remained largely calm, though she flushed at certain questions and once told Guy that she wasn't going to answer him when he'd gotten too personal. She said if he wanted to fire her on the spot, he could. When he challenged her, Nadia said he could go to hell. Ava fought to suppress her smile.

Finally, the moment of truth.

Guy said, "Ms. Blackmon, our security system caught you

repeatedly trying to access restricted files and research efforts that you were not cleared for. Care to explain why?"

Nadia hesitated for an instant, and then said, "I was military, Mr. Hawkinson."

"I'm sorry? What does that have to do with—"

Nadia said, "I come from a world where it's better to ask forgiveness than beg for permission. I needed to get something done for a program I was working on. But due to the intensive security on the island, I wasn't given access to the same information I could get back in our Virginia headquarters. In the interest of time, I decided to go around it."

Guy glanced down at the screen to see her polygraph data. Ava couldn't tell whether he was satisfied with her answer. When he looked up, he said, "Who do you work for, Nadia?"

She paused to exhale. "I work for Hawk Technologies on the Prometheus team. At least I did. I'm strongly reconsidering that now."

"Have you now or ever been engaged in espionage against my company, Ms. Blackmon?"

Nadia looked insulted. A longer pause. "No."

Guy looked at the computer monitor again.

The room was silent.

Ava willed herself not to look at her aunt. Nadia didn't flinch.

Then Guy's and Sheryl's phones both chimed loudly.

"*Guy.*" Sheryl snapped her fingers as she read the message.

Guy turned to his sister. Seeing her expression, he rose and walked over to his phone, swiped, and read for a few seconds.

Their faces transformed to a mix of anger and fear.

Guy looked up and scanned the room, then walked over to the laptop next to Nadia and closed it. "I think I have what I need."

He disconnected the Velcro strap from Nadia's wrist. "Thank you for indulging this little experiment, Ms. Blackmon. I'm sorry for having to be so intrusive. I hope you understand." Guy stood. "Arturo will see you out." The security guard hovered near her.

"So I'm free to go?"

"You are, yes. Thank you."

Two questions ran through Ava's head.

How the hell had Nadia just beat the lie detector?

And what had the Hawkinsons just read on their phones?

Nadia looked straight at Ava. She looked very upset, and for a moment Ava feared she was going to expose her.

Then Nadia shouted, "You're a real bastion of integrity, *Guy*."

"Excuse me?" Guy said, frowning. "What did you say?"

Nadia locked eyes with Ava for a moment and then looked to Guy. "I said, you're a real bastion of integrity. Treating people like this. I want to work here. But this was a ridiculous violation of trust."

Sheryl pulled her brother by the elbow. "Give her a break. She's not who you're looking for. You just read that message, right? We have to go."

"Sorry, Blackmon." Guy shrugged. "Sometimes you have to break a few eggs. No hard feelings."

Bastion of integrity.

That was meant for Ava.

Before she departed for the island, Mossad had provided her with three mission options, each with its own code word. The mission brief called for her to collect, evaluate, and then make a recommendation to Katz on which of the three mission options she would execute.

The code words were *ivory*, *juniper*, and *bastion*. Ava's communications capability had been taken from her. Katz must have reached out to the CIA. Nadia must still be communicating with her handlers. And Katz just sent Ava a message.

Bastion.

Mossad was going to execute a strike on Guy Hawkinson's island.

Nadia was escorted out of the room. When she was gone, Sheryl said, "Guy, we need to go. Now." She left in a hurry, grabbing her purse and phone from the podium.

Ava noticed a clip-on ID card where Sheryl's phone had been. In her haste, she'd left it.

Guy held up a hand. "Samantha, what's your read on Blackmon?"

"I don't trust her."

"The machine does."

"Your AI polygraph?"

Guy shrugged. "The AI program wasn't working. This only used legacy capability. But she beat that clean." He left the room.

Nadia felt like she was about to have a heart attack as she walked outside the building with one of Guy's security guards escorting her.

She was pretty sure that her ultra-wideband disruption malware had worked, allowing her to escape the AI-based polygraph. But she couldn't believe that she passed the legacy polygraph. She just followed her training. Repeating her cover story over and over in her mind until she believed it. Doing her best to answer every question calmly. And digging her fingernail into her palm to feel the pain and place her vitals out of sync.

Guy seemed to indicate that she passed, but that old lady sure as hell didn't look like she believed her.

"So, where to now?" Nadia asked the guard escorting her.

"You can catch a shuttle back to Research Village if you like," he said.

"Blackmon?"

Nadia's blood froze. Guy Hawkinson, who had been walking to a vehicle behind her, spotted her.

Now he was walking toward her.

"Ms. Blackmon, I'm glad I caught you."

Interesting choice of words.

"It's not like I can go anywhere," she said, still feigning righteous indignation over being questioned.

"Yes, well. Look, we've got a security leak and we're trying to plug it."

"Want some free advice? Don't treat your people like suspects and they'll trust you."

"I'll remember that. Listen, I'm having a reception on my yacht this afternoon and I want you to join us. I insist."

"First you interrogate me and now you want me to go to a cocktail party?"

Guy flashed a smile. "Trust me, you'll want to be there. Top members of my team and some of the research cadre. It's partially a celebration of what we've accomplished and partially to plan the next phase. You showed me something in there. I appreciate that you didn't back down. I'm sure that was scary for you. Anyway, we board in an hour."

He turned and left.

Nadia studied Hawkinson as he walked away. From a mission standpoint, it could be a great collection opportunity.

It could also be a way for them to dump her into the sea.

41

Ava needed to find out what the hell was going on.

Her aunt had been watching her during Nadia's questioning. She seemed to be waiting for Ava to speak up and challenge Nadia. Then, after the interrogation ended, the Hawkinsons and her aunt practically disappeared into thin air, leaving her alone in the room.

Ava knew there were likely cameras on her, and this could very well be a test. But it was also the *only* bit of luck she'd had in days. She walked toward the podium, snatched up Sheryl's ID card, and walked casually out the door toward her room.

The alert appeared on her tablet shortly after.

At first, Ava was sure it had something to do with the stolen ID card. But it didn't.

All personnel were to prepare to evacuate the island.

Immediately.

Ava wondered if it had something to do with the message Nadia had conveyed. *Bastion.* Had Guy received a warning? Or perhaps Nadia's polygraph results were worse than Guy let on? If Guy felt Nadia had provided the US government with certain incriminating information, he might be activating risk mitigation plans. Nadia could be face down in the sand right now for all Ava knew.

She heard turboprop aircraft flying overhead. The planes landed and took off again as quickly as space was made available on the runway. The VIP resort was soon emptied out. Ava heard some of the elite guests talking about departing by yacht. But everyone else was being driven to the airfield.

Ava had other plans.

Whatever Guy Hawkinson was up to, she wasn't buying it. The evacuation would be the perfect opportunity for her to slip into the research facility and gather as much evidence as possible.

Ava hid in her quarters while her building was evacuated. Two boats remained, including a black-and-silver yacht anchored about half a mile offshore. She thought it belonged to the Hawkinsons. It was early evening now and the island was almost empty, save for some critical support staff and most of the security team. She'd evacuate with them. But first, she had to complete her mission.

Ava ran across the beach to the main resort and up to the pool deck, now empty, then entered the quiet building. Heading to the reception area, Ava found several unattended staff vehicles: three golf carts and an all-terrain buggy, all with Hawk Technologies livery. Ava took the buggy and guided it to the small path that led to Research Village, bypassing the main road.

As she raced along the path, she saw the island's mountain on the right. To the left, the island fell sharply into the ocean. Seeing another cart approaching her from the opposite direction, she accelerated, pulling into the grass to allow it to pass. Then she guided the buggy back onto the path, not bothering to look behind her.

Ava arrived at Research Village for the first time since landing on the island. The buggy crested a small hill and descended into a parking lot. The architecture was like the resort, white stucco and blue-green glass, fountains, and palm trees, though this area was more utilitarian. She saw several clusters of two-story buildings that looked like dormitories on the left and a long, low building across the parking lot. A covered walkway led into the mountain. Ava saw several researchers moving about in the parking lot and a few small groups being escorted out from the mountain. HSG security personnel directed them onto vans—they'd likely be driven to the marina to board the final boat.

Ava parked the buggy and walked over to one of the researchers, a director by the insignia on her badge.

"Excuse me," she said, and touched the woman gently on the arm. "My name is Ava Klein, I'm the Hawk Technologies Vice President of Strategy. Are you in charge of access to the building?"

"Yes, ma'am. We've just finished locking down the research facility. Some security personnel are inside doing a last check for people."

"I see," Ava said. "Look, this is awkward, but I need your help. There's a classified project that we need to lock down before we leave the island. I haven't been given a tour of this area yet, and I haven't been able to communicate with my research team since they shut everything down. I don't suppose you could help me make my way in so I can check?"

The woman looked over to the van, about fifty yards away. "Uh, I don't think I'm supposed to do that. I think we're supposed to head out any minute now..."

"I have a vehicle. I will drive you to the marina as soon as we're done. We can leave together. This is very important. It's a prototype that Guy is going to present to the, well, the folks who were staying on the *other* side of the island." *Those people.*

"Well," the woman said, feeling more important, "I suppose."

"Thank you," Ava said, and before the woman had time to reconsider, she ushered her toward the covered pathway and subterranean door. The woman swiped her ID card and pressed her thumb on a scanner until the light beside the door glowed green. Ava then followed her in through the unlocked door.

As they walked in, the researcher explained how the three-level facility was laid out so that Ava could orient herself. Most people worked on the main floor, which housed all the research labs. They were primarily dedicated to AI, though there were two robotics bays. The second level was power, environmental control, and utilities. The third level was the quantum computing bay. Only the techs were allowed down there, but none of the researchers needed to physically go there because they were all tied in.

Once they were inside, the woman led Ava to a small room off the main hallway. The lights illuminated as soon as she badged them in. Several computer terminals were inside, monitors on snaking arms and keyboards. The woman explained that everything was hooked into a central computer. "Makes things easier to navigate." She inserted her card into a slot on the monitor and the device unlocked. "This terminal will show you the status of all the projects. Just enter yours and you can see if it's been secured or not."

Ava had just sat down when the door opened behind them.

"I've got it from here," Guy Hawkinson said.

Ava looked up from the terminal. Guy was flanked by two guards armed with HK UMP submachine guns.

"Please leave us," one of the security men said to the woman who had let Ava in the building. "Get to your evacuation spot, now."

The woman, realizing she was in trouble, left in a rush.

"Get up," Guy said to Ava.

They closed the door and set the windows to opaque. One guard held her at gunpoint while the other frisked her, making no allowances for modesty. Once they were certain she didn't have any weapons or signaling devices, they zip-tied her hands and ankles. One of the guards gave her a hard shove and Ava fell to the ground.

The second guard turned his head and put a hand beside his earpiece. Then, he turned to his boss. "Mr. Hawkinson, your sister is asking for you. The senator's plane will be touching down shortly."

Guy said, "Let's go."

The guard said, "Also, they say that the aircraft is having some comms failure on board."

Guy frowned at Ava. "Interesting."

"Yes, sir."

Guy stepped back to the door. "I'm sorry, Ava, this is where our relationship ends. I had high hopes for you. I had hoped that you would see the value in what we're trying to do here. I suppose vision doesn't run in the family."

"My aunt is going to know about this..."

Guy shot her a skeptical look and walked away, saying, "Who the hell do you think gave you up?"

———

The Cessna Citation X descended on its final approach to the island. The aircraft, registered to a general aviation firm based out of North Carolina, was one of the many jets in the CIA's fleet used to transport personnel for Agency missions.

Earlier, this aircraft had launched from Reagan National Airport and landed at Fort Lauderdale-Hollywood International Airport, where it waited for the arrival of an aircraft leased by Hawk Technologies to transport Senator Preston Hawkinson to the island. It was diverted by air traffic control to Fort Lauderdale due to an unspecified security issue.

Once on deck, Senator Hawkinson received a phone call from the National Security Advisor, informing him that he was to remain on the ground and in his aircraft for the next few hours due to a Homeland Security Threat. With apologies, the NSA told the senator that he was unable to provide more information at this time. But a car was waiting to take him to Miami's DHS field office where he would be briefed on the situation.

"I'm afraid this is mandatory, Senator," the NSA said. The senator departed with his chief of staff, leaving Sheryl's daughters and a few of his entourage in the plane.

Once he was gone, two Customs and Border Protection officers entered the plane and confiscated all mobile phones and devices.

"What? How am I supposed to call my mom?" asked Sheryl's oldest daughter, who had just turned eighteen.

Her sixteen-year-old sister said, "Or check my Snap account?"

Fred Ford, snug in his new ICE uniform, said, "Sorry, ladies. We'll give your phones back momentarily. Just follow Agent Schmuckitelli here."

Colt and Ford got a few funny looks from one of Senator Hawkinson's staff members as they marched the girls out of the aircraft, but he must have figured hey, they were US government officials, so whatever they were doing must be okay.

Sheryl Hawkinson's two daughters were funneled into a Cessna Citation X waiting in the next hangar, out of sight of the senator's aircraft. The girls were quite upset when Ford broke the news that they wouldn't be getting their phones back until landing. He handed them the latest issue of *The Economist* instead, and told them, "We've got orders to take you to your mother. The senator won't be coming until later."

"Who's he?" one of the daughters asked, pointing at a curly-haired man in a button-down shirt and cargo pants, his black pistol visible in its shoulder holster.

Colt searched for the right words. "Um, he's our international security representative."

Moshe stared back at the girls, stone-faced and silent.

The girls sat down in their cabin seats and avoided eye contact.

Soon the CIA's Cessna Citation X, using the flight plan and aircraft callsign of the Hawk Technologies aircraft, took off from Fort Lauderdale. An FAA representative, briefed by the CIA, made sure that no one in the tower argued when the tail number didn't match.

The flight lasted a little over two hours and contained little conversation. Colt hoped that the stateside team was able to keep the senator's communications blackout running until they were able to achieve their mission.

As the Citation touched down on the island's runway, the three men peered out the windows, trying to catch their bearings.

"I see one aircraft on the runway. Looks like the evacuation. Lines look pretty short. They must be nearly done," Colt said.

Their aircraft came to a halt and powered down.

One of the CIA pilots said, "They have men outside waiting. All armed."

Another pilot leaned over to Ford and whispered, "Remember, once we get the signal, we have twenty minutes to take off. Whether you're with us or not. So check your comms, and don't be late."

Ford nodded. "Got it."

Colt glanced at the two teenage girls. They looked alert.

Ford said, "Okay, let's get the girls to their mother."

Moshe and the pilots remained in the aircraft.

One of the pilots opened the cabin door, and Colt, Ford, and the girls began walking down the stairs. Three HSG men waited on the flight line, a pair of black SUVs behind them.

"Where's the senator?" one of the Hawk security men shouted.

Ford said, "He couldn't come. Some type of emergency. We've got orders to escort these young women to their mother, or to fly them back stateside if she's already evacuated."

The lead HSG man said, "It's all right. We'll take 'em from here."

"Afraid I can't do that. Legally, I mean." Ford held up a US Customs and Border Protection badge.

The HSG men exchanged glances. One began to pick up a radio, but another waved him off. "All right, but you'll have to drive one of these vehicles back here yourself. We're headed out to sea with the last boat."

Colt glanced at his handheld CovCom device. YELLOW-CARD had just dropped a GPS pin near the marina. He gave Ford a knowing look.

Colt said, "Is it all right if both of us come? Safety and all, with this evacuation. You know?"

The lead HSG man said, "Sure, whatever, man."

Ford nodded to the girls. "Go on in the lead car. Time to go see your mom."

42

The guard directed Ava to stand in the far corner and face the wall. She was bracing herself for what might come next when she heard the guard say, "Roger," in response to something communicated over his headset.

Then silence for another two minutes, until someone knocked on the door.

Ava turned to look as the guard opened the door. It was Samantha. Ava looked at her aunt's face, feeling a mixture of betrayal and disbelief.

Then, in one quick movement, Samantha raised a small pistol from her side, placing its barrel near the guard's temple, and fired. The sound was loud enough that Ava jumped. The guard's head cracked open into a dark red and gray mass as he slumped to the floor.

Samantha wiped away flecks of blood from her face and hands, swearing in Hebrew and shaking her head. "Yuck. I detest the wet work." She looked up at her niece. "You see what I am willing to do for my family?"

Ava stared at her aunt in shock.

Samantha bent low and searched the dead guard. She found his knife, unfolded it, and moved to cut Ava's bonds.

"First you sell me out to Hawkinson and now you free me?"

"Dear, we don't have a lot of time." A swiping motion, followed by a *snick*, and Ava's hands were free. Samantha handed her the knife so she could free her ankles. "I had to tell Guy about you because you wouldn't give up the American. We needed to feed him someone so he would trust us. Well, we fed him you so he would trust me. Now we have fewer options, I think."

"You're still working for the Institute, then?"

"No. Not yet," Samantha said. "But I will. I never stopped being loyal to Israel. You must believe that. Mossad needs someone on the inside. You were burned, Ava, I saw it in their eyes. They didn't trust you. Too many mistakes. You were right in London. They never should have used you. But now something good has come of this. Giving you up has convinced Hawkinson of my loyalty. You must tell Katz everything that's happened here. Tell him that I'm inside. I will be Mossad's agent."

"Didn't you tell me not to trust him?"

"Maybe not with your career, but you can trust him to do the right thing for Israel. He's a careerist, but he's loyal to our country. Now listen, there isn't very much time. An airplane has landed. It was supposed to be Preston Hawkinson's, but I believe it might actually belong to the CIA. That is your way out. The senator was diverted and detained, but someone on his staff got word to Guy. Listen, Ava. We have to leave this island now. I know why they are evacuating. The Russians are going to destroy this place. They have already notified the Americans. They are conducting some type of strike."

Ava held up her hands. "*What*? Are they crazy?" This was too much to process at once.

"The Russians have some kind of orbital weapon. They're going to strike the research center and maybe the whole island because they think Guy betrayed them."

Her aunt snorted.

"What's so funny?"

"The idiot Russian president is so easy to manipulate. His hubris is his downfall. My sources told me that Mossad conducted a cyberattack on St. Petersburg. Then the Russians do this. I know exactly how this game is played. Mossad must have made it look like the Hawkinsons did it so they would drive a wedge between their two adversaries. It was skillfully done, but the Russians were stupid not to see through it." Her aunt handed her the pistol. "Here, take this."

Ava grabbed the pistol and stuffed it into her jeans pocket. She placed the knife in another pocket and then grabbed the HK, which she slung over her shoulder.

"Samantha, what are you going to do?"

"I'm going with Guy. I told you about my past with Trinity. I need to figure out what is going on with this Trinity splinter group, Archon. I think they have recruited the Hawkinsons to join them. We need to know how far this thing has spread."

Ava walked up to her aunt and embraced her.

"Tell Katz that I will do this for Israel. But Ava, please don't tell him what I told you about me working with Trinity." Her aunt's face hardened. "Most people would not understand that."

Ava slowly nodded. "I will do as you say."

Her aunt said, "Thank you. Now you must head for the runway. The Americans have sent aircraft to evacuate the civilians. The Hawkinsons are sending some of their people there. Others are leaving by yacht. If you can make it to the runway without being spotted by HSG guards, you'll be fine. Don't go to the marina. And don't stay here. I've disabled the cameras nearby for the next few minutes, but soon they'll try to raise this one." She pointed to the dead guard. "When he doesn't respond, they'll know you've escaped. I'll say you were gone when I arrived. Now run, Ava."

They began heading toward opposite exits, then her aunt stopped and turned.

"*Ava*. One more question. That American girl, Nadia Blackmon. I can look out for her if you want. Tell me, is she with the CIA?"

Ava shook her head. "No, Aunt Samantha. Not her. If she was, I would know."

Then Ava walked away, wondering why she had just lied.

Approximately thirty seconds after the SUVs were gone from sight, Moshe placed an earpiece in his right ear and raced down the aircraft stairs. A black duffel bag was slung across his shoulder. It held, among other goodies, an Israeli-made X95-S Flattop SMG submachine gun. The weapon had an integral suppressor and could fire at a rate of over 750 rounds per minute.

Moshe spotted an unattended tactical buggy parked fifty feet away, near one of the hangars, and headed toward it. He looked up at the CIA pilot at the top of the Citation stairway. He tapped his watch and Moshe nodded. Then he stepped on the gas pedal and accelerated along a jungle path toward Research Village.

Ava ran out of the research facility. She climbed into one of the three ATVs left near the front entrance, turned it on, and started driving south along the path toward the airfield. She had traveled no more than a few hundred meters when she heard the gunfire.

Gravel pellets exploded up in front of her.

Warning shots.

She slammed on her brakes, skidding to a halt.

Breathing heavily, Ava placed her hands up as the shooters made themselves visible.

Two HSG men, walking out of the brush to her right. She hadn't even seen them. The first man had a SCAR aimed at her midsection. The second man had a radio.

It was the second man who scared her more.

He had been with her only moments ago. Guy Hawkinson's other guard. One of the men who took her prisoner.

Colt and Ford jostled in the middle row of seats as the SUVs arrived at the marina. Colt angled his CovCom device so that Ford could get a glance. The map showed a GPS pin near their location. That meant YELLOWCARD had signaled them from right here. The timestamp indicated that it had happened only an hour ago.

About a half-mile offshore, Colt saw a magnificent multi-level yacht the size of a small cruise liner. Nearby in the marina, a powerboat large enough to fit a dozen people waited to take the last load aboard.

"We need confirmation that their mother is aboard," Ford said.

The HSG man radioed the ship. He walked over to the small powerboat and retrieved a pair of binoculars, handing them to Ford. He then radioed the ship and asked to get Ms. Hawkinson on comms.

Ford looked through the binoculars at the ship. He could see Sheryl Hawkinson standing on the fantail, looking back at them with her own set of binoculars. An armed HSG man with a radio was standing next to her.

"Get my goddammed daughters on that boat and over here now!" came a call from the radio.

Colt said to Ford, "You mind if I take a look?"

Ford handed him the binoculars. Then he said over the radio, "Sure thing, ma'am. Sorry about this. We're just following orders. Would you happen to have a ship's manifest? We'll need that for our paperwork."

Ford saw the HSG men ashore walking the daughters onto the boat. Its diesel engines started up with a rumble.

"Go to hell, asshole," replied Sheryl over the radio. That got a few chuckles from the security guards.

Colt continued to scan the ship. He could see a handful of passengers on the bow abovedeck. But he still didn't see...

There.

Nadia was standing on the fantail next to a few men who were dressed in casual clothes. She was probably no more than fifteen feet from Sheryl. Close enough to hear their conversation. Colt adjusted the focus of the binoculars. She looked fine.

And she had her right hand in a distinct shape as it rested on the outer rim of the ship's hull. Nadia was making a thumbs-up sign.

The small powerboat departed the dock, taking the daughters to the yacht. A few of the guards were left behind. Colt heard one of them say, "They'll do one more. Still waiting for the guys at the R&D site to check in."

Colt said to Ford, "We should probably get going. Plane to

catch." He brought the binoculars down and handed them to the nearby HSG man.

Ford glanced at Colt, and then to the guard. "Well thank you for your time, gentlemen."

Colt and Ford were given the keys to one of the SUVs and told to leave it at the airfield.

As they were driving away, Colt said, "She's all right."

Ford said, "Okay. Well, one down, one to go."

"What the hell are you doing here?" the HSG man with the radio asked Ava. He looked concerned as he began making a radio call for someone to respond. Ava assumed he was trying to reach the guard her aunt had killed moments ago.

His companion still had the SCAR trained on her.

"He let me go. Mr. Hawkinson called and said there had been a misunderstanding. He told me to head to the evacuation at the runway. I..."

"That's finished. The last plane just left," the man with the rifle said. "You'll have to come with us."

Ava tried not to look scared.

"Call Hawkinson. Or Kirby," the man with the rifle said. He was watching Ava intently.

The sound of an ATV running at full speed caught their attention. Both men looked at the buggy racing toward them on the path.

"Who's that?" asked the man with the radio.

"Dunno," replied the man with the rifle.

They spread out slightly on either side of the path. The buggy slowed to a stop. A man with a button-down shirt and curly hair stepped out of the vehicle. He was waving for them to come with him.

"They have been trying to reach you. Come. Come." His accent was thick.

"Who?" one of the guards said.

Moshe kept waving for them to come closer, pointing at something in his vehicle. "Come. See. They need you to come so you don't get hurt. Evacuation is almost done."

The HSG men were starting to get the feeling that this guy might have a screw loose.

Moshe lifted the duffle bag so that it sat on the ATV's dashboard. "Here. Look." In one quick movement, he slid his hands into the unzipped bag, raised the X-95 just inches higher, and began firing.

Short, controlled bursts into the center mass of each man. Both wore body armor. They collapsed back into the gravel, suffering various injuries.

Moshe then ran forward and fired two shots into each of their heads.

Ava was simultaneously sickened, saddened, and grateful.

Colt and Ford arrived at the airfield just as Ava and Moshe were pulling up in their ATV. Both Ford's SUV and Moshe's ATV parked right next to the CIA's Citation jet. The CIA pilots were running through their checklist when the ground rumbled beneath Colt's feet.

Moshe's head snapped toward the direction of the explosion, his X-95 aimed at the runway. A few towers of runway concrete and dirt were now falling back to earth.

"Those bastards just destroyed the runway," said Ford.

43

Guy Hawkinson had watched the violence on the island from the office onboard his yacht. He had a monitor on his desk that was tied into the security feed throughout the island. He could see angles from each camera, which covered almost every square inch and switched between night vision, thermal, and regular as the conditions dictated.

Firefight wasn't the right term. More like an execution.

Ava had somehow escaped. And just as she was being recaptured, a lone rider came in to save her. It made him sick to witness.

Two of his men were confirmed killed. Another in the research center hadn't responded to radio comms. Guy knew what that meant.

How had this happened? He sighed. In the end, it would matter little.

If the Russians were going to launch missiles at the island, as his father's staff member had warned him, Ava would likely die with the others.

He had just remotely detonated charges that left the runway unusable. So whoever came in on that jet—whether they were CIA or Mossad or something else—wouldn't be leaving this island.

Guy would now issue orders for his remaining men to evacuate using the last speedboat left at the marina.

"Strike lead, this is Hawk Actual."

"Go Actual."

"Evac now."

"Roger that."

"You will be on a comms blackout in approximately thirty seconds."

"Copy."

The government operatives would be trapped on the island and then obliterated by the Russians. Any evidence of Hawk Technologies' nefarious activities would be eliminated. The United States government would then seek retribution against Russia for the murder of their personnel, and his uncle would ensure there was sufficient furor at the atrocity.

Guy opened a terminal window and typed a series of commands.

As he thought about all he and Sheryl had planned, Guy realized his mistake with Hawk Technologies. They'd moved too fast. That was sloppy. Archon had been too confident in their ability to direct events. And they had underestimated Israeli and western intelligence agencies.

But Hawk Technologies, if it could be salvaged, still had the benefit of the research conducted on this island, and the company would likely be able to preserve most of the talent. Guy tried not to think of how far this mess would set him back. He'd sunk hundreds of millions of dollars into this facility and was about to watch that go up in a literal ball of fire.

He typed in the execute command and the island went dark.

The hard drives had already been wiped. Now, controlled detonations of plastic explosives destroyed the servers and collapsed the roof of the subterranean facility. The legacy computers and the quantum computing array were both crushed under the weight, leaving no evidence of wrongdoing.

The security feed went black.

Guy was grateful for the assistance of the airlift and boat lift support. Most of his employees would be transported to St. Croix and Puerto Rico, where they would be sent back to the mainland at Hawk Technologies' expense. All any of those people knew was that Guy Hawkinson built a technological paradise to conduct the world's most advanced research on artificial intelligence.

Guy pushed himself back from the desk, walked over to the bar in his office, and poured a thirty-year-old Macallan into a tumbler. Watching the Russians destroy his life's work seemed like the appropriate moment to have a glass of two-thousand-dollar scotch.

This was a setback. A significant one, to be sure, but it was neither final nor total.

He had plans, and he would see them fulfilled. This was a hard lesson, however. Guy knew he needed to rethink his operation. They'd moved too quickly, and it cost them. He would not make that mistake again.

Guy walked out to the deck. The Russians were likely to strike soon. They would need to make best speed away from the island as soon as the last of his men came aboard.

"Ospreys are on final," the CIA pilot called out.

After the runway had been detonated, Colt and the others

had set in motion their secondary extraction plan: Air Force Special Operations Ospreys flying in out of Puerto Rico.

Shortly after the runway had been destroyed, Colt felt a shudder and then the island went dark except for the buggies' headlights.

"What was that rumbling noise?" he asked.

"Was it the Russians?" Ford shrugged.

"I don't think so," Colt said. "Felt like an earthquake. Think Hawkinson rigged his stuff underground?"

Ford said, "What is he, Dr. Evil?"

Colt heard the thunderous twin rotors of the Air Force Ospreys approaching. They would soon be landing on the runway, the Combat Control Team deploying to secure the airfield.

"We should get moving," Ford said. "We need to get to the LZ."

They took off at a run down the asphalt path. The Ospreys weren't lit, but they could hear them and barely make out their murky shapes against the night sky. The green glow of night vision goggles was just barely visible in the cockpit.

Colt was in the lead and dropped his weapons at the airfield gate so they weren't mistaken for hostiles.

They walked to the airfield with hands in the air. Combat Controllers were already fanning out to secure the field. The CIA pilots had verified them already, so their identities were quickly confirmed. Colt found their team lead, a captain, and gave him the rundown.

"I think we've got two hours to get to minimum safe distance," Colt said.

The captain nodded. "I understand, but we've still got to check the island for civilians. I've got two birds with PJs on them. The other two are holding back for my signal."

As if on cue, a pair of Ospreys roared overhead in helicopter configuration.

"How long will that take?"

"We'll be fast. It sounds like we can't access most of the facilities anyway."

Colt, Ava, Moshe, and Ford joined the two CIA pilots onboard the Osprey.

As the Combat Controllers ran up the ramp and found seats, the captain boarded last, announcing that they didn't find anyone on the island.

As the Ospreys headed to Muñiz Air National Guard Base in northeastern Puerto Rico, Colt and Ford thanked the Air Force special operations team for their efforts. They didn't have an explanation as to how or why the island was evacuated.

Ava sat across the Osprey cabin, watching Colt, a slight smile on her face. They locked eyes for a long while, both knowing what the other was wishing. It would be nice to have a few days off in Washington before she traveled back to Israel.

Just then, one of the aircrew tapped Colt on the shoulder, gesturing for him to look out the open rear bay door.

As Colt watched, fiery streaks began raining down from the heavens, heading toward the island.

44

Arkhangel-1 was one of the most closely guarded Soviet secrets of the Cold War.

While the Americans knew the Russians were pursuing space-based weaponry to counter the so-called "Strategic Defense Initiative," their intelligence suggested that the Soviets were far behind. While the US did pursue space weapons at the end of the Cold War, SDI was actually an amazingly successful deception campaign that played expertly on Soviet paranoia and their massive inferiority complex with the West.

The Soviets pumped billions of rubles into their space program, which netted laughably poor results relative to their investment. Their shuttle flew only twice, and the most advanced rocket type launched by Baikonur Cosmodrome, the Energia Polyrus, failed to achieve orbit.

It was a miracle that Arkhangel even flew, let alone achieved operational deployment.

Officially termed a "weather satellite," Arkhangel was launched in 1990. The Soviets had originally intended to reveal its existence to the Americans the following year. Unfortunately, the Soviet Union collapsed and the Russian government found itself with more pressing issues.

In 1998, the satellite's orbit degraded and it crashed harmlessly to the earth.

But the Russians were inspired by the idea, reviving the Arkhangel concept in 2003 after the US Air Force announced they were developing a similar satellite-based weapon.

Arkhangel-2 launched in 2019.

As a prototype, Arkhangel-2 did not carry the full-sized projectiles of the American concept. The Russian scientists who designed Arkhangel-2 didn't believe they had a power source capable of launching twenty-five-foot-long projectiles, but were terrified of informing their president that they could not deliver. Instead, the Russian weapons developers created a scaled-down "tactical version" that could be used on a modern battlefield.

Arkhangel-2 was equipped with five-foot-long tungsten projectiles that could generate an explosive force orders of a magnitude larger than the most destructive conventional weapons in use today.

Arkhangel-2 carried forty-eight of these projectiles onboard.

And on the order of an embarrassed and vengeful Russian president, all forty-eight were launched at the Hawkinsons' island.

The satellite was a crude-looking fat tube of metal thirty feet in length with a large bulge in the center and a solar array on the upper end. The satellite's central "bulge" was the two projectile launchers in their stowed configuration. They opened on command (several engineers breathing relieved sighs that they actually did), revealing two honeycomb structures holding twenty-four launch tubes each.

The Russian president gave the order from a small military command and control center within the Kremlin. Launch panels swiveled open and the propellant engaged, firing the five-foot projectiles toward the earth.

Eighteen actually fired.

Four struck the island.

They were more than enough.

Glowing white hot as they entered the atmosphere, the tungsten rods looked like shooting stars, streaking toward their target at over ten times the speed of sound.

On impact, the resulting fireball was large enough to be seen clearly from the nearby Virgin Islands.

Damage from debris was contained to the island itself, and a ten-mile radius surrounding the intended strike zone.

Observers would report brilliant streaks of orange lancing down from the sky in what was initially believed to be one of the brightest meteor showers ever recorded. Adroit sky watchers immediately dismissed this as unlikely, and rumors began to surface that it was either a secret government satellite crashing or a space weapons test.

Spokesmen from the White House, Defense Department, the joint US Space Command, and the military branch US Space Force each issued immediate statements denying that the United States had just tested a space weapon. The denial only boosted online speculation furthering the opposite. The anti-technology crowd latched onto the narrative, and within hours, it became the new rallying cry for their cause.

US Air Force RQ-4 Global Hawk surveillance footage following the strike showed that the island was a blasted moonscape. In fact, there was little island to speak of. It was completely obliterated, now just jagged rocks above the ocean.

The US Navy destroyer, USS *Jason Dunham*, was now holding station only a few nautical miles from impact site, sending back plenty of high-res pictures that were added to countless intelligence briefing slides and social media memes.

The damage was absolute.

45

"Good evening. Thank you for joining us on World News Tonight, I'm Randall James. 'Reckless and irresponsible' are the words White House and Defense Department officials are using to describe the destruction of a Russian weather satellite that broke apart in the upper atmosphere yesterday evening. Debris from the object crushed in the Caribbean Sea approximately two hundred nautical miles from Puerto Rico, apparently with minimal warning. While most of the debris fell into the ocean, several pieces struck a private island in the US Virgin Island chain that was owned by Guy Hawkinson of the prominent Hawkinson family. The Hawkinsons used the island as a corporate retreat and as a research facility for their newly formed advanced technology company. The damage is described as total. The White House said the Russian government failed to give sufficient warning so that US officials could ensure the area was evacuated.

Amazingly, there was no loss of life. The United States Air Force mounted a daring helicopter rescue effort, augmented by the Hawkinson family's own hastily executed evacuation facilitated by private air and watercraft—"

. . .

Colt turned off the television.

"Weather satellite?"

The Agency had sent another aircraft down to retrieve Colt, Ford, Moshe, and Ava from Puerto Rico. They were back in Washington shortly before dawn. Ava and Moshe were transported immediately and quietly to the Israeli embassy and would be flown out on a chartered aircraft later that day. Colt didn't even have an opportunity to say goodbye.

He and Ford barely had enough time to get a few hours of sleep before they were back at Langley to sort out the damage.

"Here's what I know, gents," Thorpe said. "KOSCHEI told POTUS that he was launching the attack, which you know, and gave us a very short window to respond. We think the Russians didn't believe there were any civilians on the island, just Hawkinson employees, whom they have termed 'collaborators.'"

"I can't believe we're letting them walk on this," Colt said. He equally couldn't believe the *realpolitik* rationalizations that he was hearing since they'd arrived. He was *there* and had barely escaped with his life.

Thorpe, for his part, did his best to mollify Colt. "I don't like it either and I said as much to Wilcox and the FBI director, for whatever that may be worth to you. Cold comfort, I know. The White House knew they didn't have a good response for Senator Hawkinson after we turned up with no evidence."

"So we just let the Russians solve it for us?" Ford said. "Why send us in at all?"

Thorpe gave them a tired smile and nodded slowly. "The White House considers this a draw. The Russians took care of a problem for us and we get to excoriate them in the press. We're going to sanction the hell out of them and there's talk that they're going to try to impose restrictions on the Russian space program. UN monitors at all of their launch facilities to certify that the cargo is what they say it is."

Ford cursed under his breath.

"Have we gotten anything more from YELLOWCARD?" Thorpe asked.

Colt said, "Just one message. She said she's safe. She managed to get onto Hawkinson's boat and evacuated with him and some of the top scientists. Her cover is intact and she wants to stay in. There were a few other interesting notes, but we're still working to confirm those." Colt wasn't sure whether to be relieved that she was okay or terrified for what might lay ahead.

When they'd finished their briefing with Thorpe, Colt and Ford went home to get some rest. They were needed back early the next morning. Thorpe told them Wilcox wanted to thank them in person for their bravery and for expertly handling such a dangerous mission, but he was at the White House with the National Security Council.

In the weeks that followed, FBI counterintelligence attempted to interview the Hawk Technologies employees who evacuated the island, as well as any American citizen who'd been at the resort—the few that could be identified. Most declined to be interviewed, and those who agreed had Hawk Technologies attorneys present. The interviewers got very little information, and all the employees interviewed stuck to the same story: they were selected for an advanced AI research fellowship. Hawk Technologies was reportedly giving each of those individuals substantial bonuses. No one flipped.

Senator Preston Hawkinson launched his own assault as soon as he returned to Washington and had been unrelenting ever since. He claimed that the White House administration, part of the opposition party, attempted to sideline him as a political ploy and used "America's vast and unaccountable intelligence apparatus" to do so. The senator used his position on the Senate Select Committee on Intelligence to launch an investigation into the CIA and FBI's handling of the situation and the "gross and pervasive intelligence failures" resulting in their inability to discover "Russian space weapons." The senator refused to use the White House's talking points that it was a weather satellite. He was also demanding to know what the Space Command, Space Force, and NORAD were doing to protect the American people.

It was an incredibly effective smokescreen.

Within a few weeks, there was so much furor over the Russians and whether they possessed orbital weapons that no one was talking about Guy Hawkinson or his island. Polling showed he'd even become a sympathetic figure. Public opinion was split on the "satellite theory," as it became known, with the belief that it was space debris just barely edging out the theory that it was a deliberate attack from a weaponized satellite. Rumors were circulating online that Guy Hawkinson may have been attacked directly because the Russians attempted to blackmail him for his research but he valiantly stood his ground and refused.

Few things played better in the court of public opinion than a decorated former soldier standing firm against the Russians.

STONEBIDGE was deactivated, but the NTCU continued running YELLOWCARD. There were fears in the Agency that Senator Hawkinson was coming for them. He couldn't attack them directly because he couldn't be too blatant about protecting his nephew's businesses, but there was growing clamor that the senator's investigation would turn into calls for reform. After all, the Agency failed to identify a secret Russian weapon in orbit over Americans' very heads. The old guard feared it would be like the seventies all over again.

Colt kept his head down, continuing to run his agent with Ford's guidance. Nadia stayed in place. Hawkinson's yacht sailed to Venezuela, where his entourage flew from Caracas to Switzerland, where Nadia and most of the inner circle remained. She provided reports that Guy took frequent trips to unknown locations, and she suspected that his Archon work continued.

Colt remained steadfast in his commitment to the cause. Even if Preston Hawkinson tried to bring the Agency down around his ears, Colt was going to find a way to expose what the Hawkinsons were doing. He needed to learn more about their connection to Archon. Was this conspiracy really as vast as Katz believed? Was this next leap in technological development really the game-changer Guy Hawkinson thought it was? And if adversarial nations like Russia were willing to risk a war to put a stop to it at this early stage, what would happen next?

Colt kept thinking about one line from Nadia's most recent transmission.

They have more than just the island.

A Future Spy
Book 3 of The Firewall Spies

As superpowers race to control the world's most powerful technology, Chinese and American intelligence officers play a daring game of spy versus spy.

Genius tech CEO Jeff Kim has just discovered that the ultra-wealthy Hawkinson family stole his advanced AI prediction technology. This technology was his secret possession. A cornerstone in which he would rebuild his life's work. But now he has serious competition. To solve his problem, Kim decides to reach out to a man he never thought he would speak to again. A Chinese intelligence officer named Liu.

Liu, a seasoned and capable MSS officer stationed in the US, is in charge of many of China's most important economic espionage operations. And pressure from Beijing has been intense of late.

Chinese tech industry advancements in AI are not progressing fast enough to stop an unprecedented economic collapse. As fears of an angry citizen revolt grow, Chinese leadership has ordered the MSS to gain the code to the new American AI prediction technology by any means necessary.

When Liu investigates the Hawkinson's operation, he discovers some shocking revelations. The Americans have placed a spy in the Hawkinson's inner circle. As a series of seemingly unrelated incidents come together in Liu's mind, he develops one of the most ambitious espionage operations the MSS has ever undertaken.

For it to work, he will have to activate China's own mole. The crown jewel of Chinese intelligence. A sleeper-agent placed so high up in the US government, they will have access to all of America's most classified information.

But CIA officers Colt McShane and Fred Ford have caught wind of China's plan. And now they must find the sleeper agent before their own is identified and killed.

Which spy will be caught first?

Get your copy today at
severnriverbooks.com/series/the-firewall-spies

ALSO BY THE AUTHORS

The Firewall Spies

Firewall

Agent of Influence

A Future Spy

Tournament of Shadows

BY ANDREW WATTS

The War Planners Series

The War Planners

The War Stage

Pawns of the Pacific

The Elephant Game

Overwhelming Force

Global Strike

Max Fend Series

Glidepath

The Oshkosh Connection

Air Race

BY DALE M. NELSON

The Gentleman Jack Burdette Series

A Legitimate Businessman

The School of Turin

Once a Thief

Proper Villains

The Bad Shepherd

To join the reader list and find out more, visit

severnriverbooks.com/series/the-firewall-spies

ABOUT THE AUTHORS

Andrew Watts graduated from the US Naval Academy in 2003 and served as a naval officer and helicopter pilot until 2013. During that time, he flew counter-narcotic missions in the Eastern Pacific and counter-piracy missions off the Horn of Africa. He was a flight instructor in Pensacola, FL, and helped to run ship and flight operations while embarked on a nuclear aircraft carrier deployed in the Middle East. Today, he lives with his family in Virginia.

Dale M. Nelson grew up outside of Tampa, Florida. He graduated from the University of Florida's College of Journalism and Communications and went on to serve as an officer in the United States Air Force. Following his military service, Dale worked in the defense, technology and telecommunications sectors before starting his writing career. He currently lives in Washington D.C. with his wife and daughters.

Sign up for the reader list at
severnriverbooks.com/series/the-firewall-spies